Man
IN THE
Meadow

ROGER GROENING

 FriesenPress

One Printers Way
Altona, MB R0G 0B0
Canada

www.friesenpress.com

ISBN
978-1-03-916634-9 (Hardcover)
978-1-03-916633-2 (Paperback)
978-1-03-916635-6 (eBook)

1. FICTION, MYSTERY & DETECTIVE

Distributed to the trade by The Ingram Book Company

To Laura, Tom, Amy

CHAPTER 1

DAN MAKES AN ANNOUNCEMENT

It was an unseasonably hot, humid, Saskatchewan Saturday at the end of September. The cottonwoods on both sides of the Northford community ball-field were motionless, their sweating leaves hanging listlessly in the thick, still air. Sergeant Arnold Powell, an avid baseball fan, sat uncomfortably on the aluminum bench grandstand seating, watching the game beneath the brim of his Stetson. His body oozed perspiration as Annie Russell, the mayor's enchanting but unavailable wife, sat close, her thigh snuggled up against his. Annie had promised him a bacon cheeseburger in the shade of the Dickey Dee patio after the game. He was looking forward to it, but frustration was setting in. The game had dragged, as baseball games tend to do, and now—with the end of the ball game in sight—Hank Goertzen appeared reluctant to step into the batter's box.

There were two out in the bottom of the ninth, with Northford down three to two against Lloydminster in the championship game of the 1975 Northford Invitation Baseball Tournament. But Northford had a great chance to win. They had speedy runners on second and third, and Hank Goertzen—Northford's best hitter and bench-press champion—was nominally at the plate. But something seemed to be holding him back.

Generally, Hank approached the plate as he did a set of barbells, quickly and with an aura of overconfidence. He was a strong young man who loved to demonstrate his prowess at lifting heavy objects or hitting a baseball deep into the outer recesses of a ball-field. But not today. Hank approached the hitting area tentatively, as if getting to the plate was the last thing he wanted to do. He looked like he had a bungee cord tied around his waist. Parts of him moved towards the plate, but other parts resisted. Overall, he gave the impression of a man who was at odds with himself.

"Any chance Hank gets a hit and ends this ball game before I sweat to death?" Arnold whispered to Annie, taking a sip of water from his canteen.

"Probably not." She smiled. "But I hear sweating to death is a good way to lose weight."

"Never joke with a fat man who hasn't had lunch," Arnold said. "I'm moving into desperation mode. We need a hero to end this game. Hank is a good hitter, but he looks like he doesn't want to be. He looks like he wants to be somewhere else."

"I wonder where he wants to be," Annie said. "For a ballplayer, this situation is perfect. He has a chance to be a hero. What could be better?"

"For a muscle-bound hunk like Hank, nothing could be better. Usually, he's eager to demonstrate his heroics, but not today."

"Must have something on his mind," Annie said softly. "Doesn't work for me. Before Ken and I perform on any stage, I try to block out any fancy ideas—not that I have that many—or else I'd forget the lyrics."

"Thinking can definitely hold a person back," Arnold agreed. "When Madeline left me, she complained that I was 'overthinking.' It was bothering her. Perhaps I was." He shrugged. "But this is not a thinking situation. This is a hitting situation."

"Madeline was just unhappy, Arnold," Annie said casually. "She told me once that she was just looking to improve her joy factor. She said it had nothing to do with you."

"That's what she told me too. And fair enough. But all my wives have left me 'looking for a joy factor.' A common theme, evidently. All of them did seem happier after they left. Especially Madeline, and *she* left me for the religious fervour of Pastor Gerald Schultz! I confess it bothers me that I got beat out on the joy factor by a dour, religious zealot."

"Four-Square Gospel does pay well," Annie pointed out. "Or at least, I presume they do. That church is brimming with money."

"Well, Madeline does like free rein on quality gardening products," Arnold muttered grumpily. "I was a bit of a downer in that department. But it's not like I prevented her from buying whatever she wanted. I just wasn't enthusiastic about it. I was under the false impression that gardening was a simple lifestyle habit. Apparently not. Still, moving in with Gerald Schultz? It was definitely a blow to my self esteem. I'm actually beginning to think that high self esteem is overrated. Anyway, I still don't get what she sees in Schultz. The man is in his early fifties, just like me. I don't get the upside for her. Can't just be about gardening products and a bigger kitchen, looking out over the river."

"It could be about that. But then, Schultz is also more spiritual than you," Annie whispered. "At least, he says he is. Lots of people believe him, including Madeline. She does seem happier now."

"No question. She is. Happiness is a gift I give to my departing wives." Arnold sighed. "What is troubling Hank? Is the sun bothering him? He knows he can hit Leonard Heinrichs. He could end this game with one swing."

"Why is Leonard pitching for Lloydminster?" Annie asked. "He plays for Northford."

"Lloydminster was short a pitcher today."

"Does Northford think that's to their advantage?"

"Possibly. Leonard's knuckleball has been hit into the fair-ground's grandstand."

"That's a long way."

Hank finally stepped into the box, smoothed out the sandy soil, dug a hole for his back foot, and readied himself to strike out.

■ ■ ■

It had been six months since anyone had agreed to have sex with Hank, but that was about to change. The night before, at McKnight's Disco, an incident had occurred to give Hank some hope. He'd been hanging out with some fellow grader operators at McKnight's when a young woman from Lloydminster had made him an offer. His recollection, tinged as it was with the effects of copious Extra Old Stock beer, was that the woman offered to have sex with him if Northford lost the ball game.

"It is my wish that Lloydminster win tomorrow," she had whispered into his ear, "which means, Hankie boy, that Northford needs to lose.

You're their star player, and I know that you can make it happen. You have the power to grant me my wish, and I have the power to grant yours. If Northford loses, I will meet you at the Lake McCaskill beach after the game. I might bring my swimsuit, or I might not. But I will definitely make it worth your while. Do I need to spell it out any more for you, Hank?"

Hank had never been good at spelling, but he had assured the excessively attractive young woman from Lloydminster that this would not be necessary. He understood.

Leonard fluttered his first pitch, a knuckleball, towards the plate, and Hank took it for a called strike. Hank had a sense that the next pitch would be a fastball, on the low-outside corner, and it was. Hank ignored it, and Ken Russell, the mayor and home-plate umpire, called another strike.

"Might be an idea to swing at a pitch, Hank," Ken muttered under his mask. "Hard to hit a ball without swinging."

Hank frowned and mumbled something about the sun being in his eyes, but then dug in for the next delivery. Hank saw the ball leave Leonard's hand, but then almost magically (although not really), it vanished into the Bermuda Triangle of the sun's glare. That was fortunate for Hank, as it allowed him to swing wildly, without knowing where the pitch was going. Hank swung high, successfully missing the ball and ensuring the Northford defeat and (presumably) hot sex at the Lake McCaskill beach.

But in life, joys are often mixed with sorrows. While Hank missed the ball, the ball did not miss Hank. It struck him in the upper-rib area, sending his body to the ground like a sack of Russet potatoes. As Hank lay in the batter's box, he experienced a range of discomforts. The pitched ball hurt, but it was not the only matter that troubled Hank. Lying there, he realized that he had made an error in judgement. He had not asked for the woman's name. It occurred to him then that knowing her name would likely make their beach engagement more personal.

■ ■ ■

Arnold was only mildly disappointed at the Northford loss. "Time for a cheeseburger, Annie," he muttered to Annie with a half smile. "Let's head out of here."

But it was not to be. Just as Arnold stood up to leave, a distant scream erupted from the right-field area. It was high pitched and urgent. Arnold looked to the west, his half smile giving way to sober concern, as he noted the flakey Dan McCroskey—artistic director of the Northford Arts Centre—running towards the ball-field from the nearby trail head, his arms waving about in wide arching circles, as though he were a windmill.

"Man in the meadow!" Dan screeched—among other panicked syllables they couldn't quite make out.

It was not a message that Arnold wanted to hear. But he heard it none the less.

Dan McCroskey wasn't a runner, but he was running. It struck Arnold as peculiar. Dan had firm views on running. He was against it. He had once been a runner, but a few years back, an Achilles injury had forced him to give up the habit. He'd gone from being a runner, and judgemental of walkers, to a walker, judgemental of runners. The fact that Dan was running onto the ball-field was all wrong.

He also noted that Dan didn't seem to be looking over his shoulder, his entire focus apparently fixated instead on reporting what he had seen. He concluded that Dan wasn't being followed by the man in question or in any immediate danger. Frowning, he turned to Annie. "Unless Dan has been popping magic mushrooms, the bacon cheeseburger will have to wait. Looks like I probably have some police work to do."

There are times when a man simply lies down to rest in a meadow and the police do not need to be involved, but Arnold suspected that this was not one of those times, given the frantic state of Dan's message. The clues were overwhelming that something was amiss. Not only was Dan running but he was also shirtless.

Dan belonged to a subset of humans who consistently erred on the side of upper-body garments. Arnold had noted Dan's devotion to upper-body wear that summer at Lake McCaskill. It had been a day of extreme July heat, yet Dan had worn a fleece jacket while sitting in the shade. Dan wasn't even forty yet and already he had established idiosyncrasies that generally took years to cultivate. It had baffled Arnold and made him wonder whether there was something fundamentally wrong with Dan McCroskey.

Dan had a thick mop of long, light-brown hair with curls bending around his well-worn, green and white Saskatchewan Roughrider ball cap. A similarly coloured Roughrider backpack hung loosely over his naked upper torso. In his right hand, he held a crumbled green and white t-shirt. It was not clear why he was holding the t-shirt, instead of wearing it, but there was no doubt that he was. His lightly muscled upper body—designed for theatre directing, not weightlifting—looked puny under the wide straps of his backpack. His baggy, beige hiking pants and white Adidas, heavily smeared with grass stains, added to the look of a man who had just encountered a man in a meadow. Likely a dead man.

■ ■ ■

Mayor Ken Russell vigorously jammed his face mask under his armpit. The metal frame of the mask pressed deep into the soft flesh of his upper arms. "Goddam you, Hank," he muttered vaguely, looking down at the fallen Hank. "You let two perfect strikes go by, and then, you swung at a pitch that hit you."

Hank lay in the box, looking up at Ken with a pained expression. "Sun was in my eyes."

"Then don't swing at the goddam thing," Ken muttered. "I would have called it a ball."

Ken's expanding body was carried well on a big frame. He had a tall, athletic build, wide shoulders, and a muscular chest, so there was ample room to hide his love of pasta. But age and diet had encroached on his ability to convey fitness. His midsection had been the first part of his physique to give his fitness story away. He had been athletic in his youth, and even now he took to the net for the local senior men's hockey team (albeit with mixed reviews). He had confidence, polished goaltending technique, and an instinctive hockey sense, but his glove hand was slow, and his lower-body movement slower.

Still, slow glove hand or not, he was a major player in Northford. Not only was he the mayor but he was a prosperous businessman too, owning numerous rental houses, the Capri Hotel, and an historic apartment building just west of the Northford Arts Centre. Ken was also married to Annie, a mid-forties former prom queen of Northford High, and a still highly desired and admired woman in town. Annie had an abundance of charm and style that added to her beauty, as well as to Ken's career path. Ken fully recognized that it was Annie who deftly managed his political career, his business interests, his wardrobe, and the logistics of the "Annie and Ken" musical duo—although he forgot it on occasion.

Music was how Ken and Annie had met. They had been classmates in school when Ken had been the lead vocalist for a band that played mostly Buddy Holly tunes. Annie had been the lead alto singer in the school choir, but when she heard Ken sing "True Love Ways," she'd been mesmerized. She discovered that not only did Ken have a fine singing voice but he was also amenable to her suggestion that they form a musical duo. By graduation, they had established themselves as a popular duo around town, and twenty-five years later, they still were. They were in reasonable demand, putting on shows occasionally as far away as Regina. They wrote many of their own tunes, and played cover tunes of Bob Dylan, Sonny and Cher, and Ian and Sylvia, among others. In the meantime, they had two children who were now independent enough that Annie could take on the duties of owning and managing the Dickey Dee burger joint while trusted sitters kept an eye on them.

As Ken walked over to Arnold, he turned his head towards the on-coming Dan McCroskey. Ken did not enjoy Dan's company. In fact, Dan grated on him. Dan talked (endlessly it seemed) about the myths of antiquity, and his plans to dramatize these myths on stage. Ken did not care about antiquity or its myths. For that matter, he did not care for theatre in general, and Dan McCroskey's version of theatre in particular.

Ken also did not care to be drawn into a matter that sounded like police business. He took a deep breath, calming himself by imagining a perfect golf swing. It took some effort. In real life, his swing was far from perfect. His drives erred towards hooks and when he adjusted, he sliced. This morning he had given ample air-time to both problems, slicing and hooking on alternating drives, all of which had resulted in a losing golf match with the Lloydminster mayor.

As Ken arrived at the grandstands, he noted that Arnold was once again sitting beside Annie, and rather too closely.

"I suppose it's nothing of consequence, Arnold," Ken announced as he grabbed his face mask from under his arm and fidgeted with it. "You best hear the little wiener out. You could also sit a little further from my wife. It isn't a good look."

"Neither is your golf game, Ken," Arnold said, smiling and leaning back against the hard edge of the aluminum bench behind him as fans departed the bleacher seating. "I hear you were in triple digits this morning, and against the Lloydminster mayor too. That must have been embarrassing."

"Low blow, Arnold," Ken muttered quietly. "Just had an off day. It happens." He glanced over at the still oncoming Dan McCroskey, and then slowly but deliberately rearranged some dirt with the toe of his left shoe. "But it *is* hard to lose to a man with no economic-development plan. Lloydminster is dying, and the mayor has conceded defeat, convincing himself that Lloydminster is just a victim of global forces." He shook his head in frustration at the man. "But still, he made some shots today. Have to give him that. Made me think I might give up the game. Waste of my time, really."

Arnold sat up straight and stretched his upper body as a new bead of sweat formed on his forehead. "Damn, it's hot," he muttered. "Smart of you to golf in the morning." He paused, taking out a handkerchief from his back pocket and dabbing his face. "The other day you told me you loved golf. That you wanted to spend your retirement golfing."

"I used to love Jesus too," Ken replied, stretching his neck to one side and then the other in a show of agitation. "We change, Arnold. We grow."

"Or regress," Arnold countered, putting his damp handkerchief away.

"Speak for yourself."

"I was," Arnold conceded, standing and turning towards the still approaching Dan. "Stick around and hear what Dan has to say. If he's correct in his concern about this man in the meadow, and I assume he is, there might be an issue that involves you, as mayor. If it's a body in the woods that he's yelling about, it could have implications for the town. What with you wanting to attract investment and all."

"You're making fun of me, Arnold. I don't like it. Attracting investment makes Northford better for everyone. Young people need to see that they can have a future here. Not like Lloydminster. All the young people there go to Saskatoon. Do we want that?" he asked rhetorically, waving his face mask around in the air for no evident purpose. "I don't think so. Still, I am not in the mood to listen to Dan McCroskey this afternoon. Maybe tomorrow. If it's a local person, let me know. If it isn't, I don't need to know about it. Strictly a police matter, Arnold."

Ken looked back to Hank, who for some unclear reason remained in a fetal position on the sandy soil of the batter's box. "Hank looks more comfortable at the plate now than he did before," he observed, shaking his head. "He's an enigma. The strongest grader operator in town but with the weakest work ethic. The man devotes himself to finding out-of-the-way service roads so that he can sleep in the grader. Quite successful at it too."

"Apart from hitting home runs, Hank's post-high-school career has been underwhelming," Arnold said. "I heard he was going to apply to the police force but then decided against it. A good decision for both of us. He wouldn't have fit in."

Ken laughed, glancing over at Dan McCroskey, who after his initial exit from the nature trail had apparently encountered some physical setbacks delaying his bleacher arrival. "If there's a dead man in the meadow, it's probably just a wayward hiker who refused to pay the hostel fee, took some drugs, and died of exposure in the woods. Don't know why these backpackers refuse to take a bus."

"I guess, technically, that would make them 'not a backpacker.' Some folks want to experience life without supports. It's a thing," Arnold answered, looking over at Hank, who was just now slowly getting up from the batter's box, and dusting himself off. "By the way, Ken, why did Hank swing at that pitch? It was high and inside."

"Who knows? I have no idea how Hank thinks. Sometimes I wonder whether he does," Ken responded in a sober, mayoral tone. "I had a hundred bucks on Northford winning. That's good money down the drain. All he needed was a measly single ... off Leonard Heinrichs!"

"He is quite hittable. It was a ball, right?" Arnold asked.

"It hit him, so yes, it was," Ken said with a grimace. "He swung that bat like a man who wanted to strike out! Of course, what do I know? I'm just the umpire." He shrugged. "Okay, got to go. Catch you later, Annie. Let me know what's going on, Arnold. You know, town reputation and all."

9

"You aren't just the umpire, Ken," Annie said, smiling sweetly and giving him a sustained kiss on the cheek. "You're also the mayor and a great singing partner. Now, I'm off to the Dickey Dee." She sighed and shook her head. "Tragic. We lose the ballgame and find a body. Not much of a way to end a fine afternoon. Maybe you guys could stop by the Dickey Dee later. Let me know what's going on. My customers expect me to be in the know."

■ ■ ■

Dan had stopped for a moment to survey the ball-field and the emptying stands, then (seemingly finding things satisfactory) had burst into action again, running towards the bleachers before encountering obstacles.

The green John Deere garden tractor sitting idly beside the drainage ditch demanded that Dan alter his path. But as so often happens, avoiding one problem leads to another. Dan's detour around the tractor caused him to run into the rusty wheelbarrow that Oscar White—an American draft dodger turned school custodian, and reportedly, a Buddhist—had hidden from view. The collision was head on, with no glancing angle to diminish the impact. Dan knocked the wheelbarrow over, which was fine, as it was metal and could easily handle the impact. But Dan's body did not fare as well. He bounced off the wheelbarrow and into the ditch, submerging himself in a foot of murky rainwater. It was a dramatic entry for sure, but then Dan knew a thing or two about drama.

In due course, he managed to extricate himself from the drainage ditch and resume his quest to deliver his message regarding a man in the meadow. He finally made his way to the bleachers and deposited his soaking-wet body beside Arnold just as Ken and Annie were leaving the scene.

"This better be good, Dan," Arnold said, moving slightly away from the sweating, somewhat boggy, informant. "You have intruded on our sports drama, while admittedly adding some of your own. The mighty Hank Goertzen, Northford's Babe Ruth, has struck out, leaving some disappointed fans, especially Mayor Russell. He lost money, and that makes him sad. So, what is this about a man in a meadow? I presume this is a dead man, and not just a random birdwatcher having a nap. Local man?" Arnold asked, grabbing his canteen from where he'd left it on the bleacher seat and taking another sip of his water.

"Very dead," McCroskey said, wiping his chest with his sopping wet t-shirt. "Also, very local. I work with him. Or I did."

"You work with Clayton Dalrymple," Arnold noted in a matter-of-fact tone.

"Exactly, Clayton Dalrymple. He's the man lying dead in the meadow, not too far from here. It's a colourful aster meadow, all purple and yellow. They're in full bloom this time of year. Never expected to meet Clayton in the woods. But there he was, lying all quiet and passive. He didn't sneer or condescend at all. Quite a surprise."

"I suppose that would be a surprise," Arnold said, shaking his head and looking quizzically at Dan. "I talked to him yesterday. He was doing a lot of seriously sinister eye squinting. He seemed painfully uncomfortable. Like a man who'd just sat on a broom handle."

"He isn't squinting now. His face is actually somewhat relaxed," Dan said, removing his backpack and tossing it on the hot aluminum bench beside him, along with the wrinkled ball of the t-shirt he'd been gripping in his hand.

"I didn't realise there was an aster meadow nearby."

"That's just what I call it," Dan said quickly. "It's just a meadow that's full of asters in the fall, maybe a twenty-minute walk in along the trail. Anyway, that's where Clayton's body is. Hiding behind a hawthorn bush at the edge of the meadow."

"Dead men don't hide, Dan," Arnold said skeptically, making a few notes in his small index-card writing pad. "They just tend to remain in the place where they died. Unless someone moves them. Did you touch anything?" He hoped not.

"I'm scared to touch a dead person, so I didn't," Dan said quickly. "I did make some footprints near him though. I didn't know I was going to find a dead man."

"I don't suppose that you did," Arnold said firmly. "Describe how you found him."

"I was birding and saw a dark object behind the hawthorn bush," Dan said, gesturing enthusiastically with his hands, as if Clayton's body was nearby. "I was curious and walked over to check it out. I was surprised it was Clayton. He was not a nature enthusiast."

"No, he certainly wasn't," Arnold offered. "In fact, he was quite opposed to the nature trail. Wonder what he was doing there?"

"He wasn't really doing anything, Arnold. Just lying there," Dan said. "You're right though. He voted against the walking trail in town council. Said it was a waste of money. I guess he learned his lesson."

"What lesson is that?"

"Don't vote against a nature trail that you're planning to use. Makes you look silly. Not that he cares about that now, I guess. Killing himself and all."

"You think he killed himself?"

"He has a bullet wound in his head and there's a handgun beside him," Dan said. "Pretty obvious suicide."

"We'll see about that," Arnold cautioned. "What did you do after you found Clayton?"

"Not much, really," Dan said, furrowing his brow as he tried to remember. "Inspected the body for a minute. Then panicked for a minute. Started towards Natasha's house to tell her, but then I stopped, turned around, and went south to the trail head. I figured you would be at the ballgame. You can't be any more dead than Clayton was, so there didn't seem much point in talking to Natasha. More of a police matter."

"There are no gradations of dead," Arnold said. "Either he is or he isn't."

"Well, he is, as I've already told you. This will be a major disappointment for Clayton."

"If he killed himself, presumably, death is what he was after," Arnold said. "How would that be disappointing?"

"He once promised to tap dance on my grave," Dan said. "Now, he can't do that. Unless he comes back as a zombie. Which, of course, he can't because zombies don't exist."

"Never mind the zombie humour," Arnold said. "The town just lost a citizen, and a town council member. A little respect for the dead perhaps?"

"Sure thing, Arnold," Dan said contritely, looking up at the sky as a small aircraft flew over. "That's my cousin, Marty. Does aerial photographs and crop dusting. Makes a lot more money than me, and he lets me know it too. Sheila tells me that I'm not half the man that he is."

Arnold laughed lightly, smoothing out some errant sand in front of the bleachers with his foot. A small ant appeared, carrying a leaf twice its size, moving in a halting style but relatively straight line towards a location somewhere underneath the grandstand. "You are not half a man, Dan. You can rest assured that Sheila is right about that. Do you think Sheila will grieve Clayton's death?"

Dan grimaced, following his cousin's airplane as it turned and made a return flight over the ball-field. "I guess you know about her thing with Clayton then," Dan mumbled. "They were having sex, but I don't think she really liked him. No one did, as far as I can tell. Let's face it. It might be rude to say, but no one will grieve Clayton's death. That's simply a fact. Still, I admit to being a little traumatized. I've never seen a dead body before, outside of a funeral home anyway. Quite unpleasant."

"Death tends to be unpleasant, especially for those who are still alive."

"Weird. Yesterday, Clayton was in perfect health, being a rude jerk. Today, he's dead, lying in the meadow, and not being anything at all, really. Quite the change."

"Death is a sudden change. An end to personality, regardless of the type. I take it, Dan, that you did not like the man? Perhaps *you* shot him?"

"Seriously, Arnold? Do I look like the kind of person who would do that?"

"Not sure what that kind of person looks like," Arnold said. "He *was* having an affair with your wife."

Dan became agitated then, jumping off his seat beside Arnold and onto the dirt leading to the ballfield. For a moment, he looked like he was going making a run for it. But he didn't. "My ex-wife. Or soon to be, anyway. Sheila thought her affair was a secret, but then ... facing reality has never been one of her strengths. She's been slipping over to Clayton's house a few times a week for over a year. She goes before her morning nursing shift. It's like her morning workout. The whole business takes her less than an hour. Anyway, I'm over being disappointed. Clayton was not the only thing preventing marital bliss. We had broader issues. The fact is that Sheila was in the mood to kick me out long before Clayton arrived. Her affair with him just precipitated our marriage's inevitable conclusion. I should thank him, except that I can't do that. He is dead. But to be honest, I would never have gotten around to leaving on my own. My life is about to take a turn for the better though. I'll be moving out and into one of the Russells' apartments next week. I'm going to love being on my own," he said hope-fully, looking far into the distance, past the fairgrounds, towards his new apartment residence.

"Aren't you being a tad premature?" Arnold cautioned. "You haven't moved yet. Being on your own might be hell."

"Nothing could be worse than being married to Sheila," Dan said, still standing by the bleachers, bringing his visual focus back to the emptying ballfield and a limping Hank Goertzen, who was still dragging his body towards the parking lot.

"Sheila was that bad?" Arnold asked. "Clayton didn't seem to think so."

"Clayton was not a normal person, Arnold," Dan said knowingly. "He lost his soul in the Soviet Union. If he thought he could find it with Sheila, he was quite deluded. But then, according to Natasha, he *was* deluded. I guess now he's a member of the deluded dead. Might never get over the image of Clayton lying there with a bullet hole in his head. Mind you, it could have been worse."

"How?" Arnold asked, as he noticed a mass of ants gathering around his right boot. He ducked down, looked under his bench seat, and noted an ant hill not more than six feet away.

"Well, he doesn't seem to have been tortured. Looks like a sudden death," Dan answered. "Not like Fausta, who was thrown into an overheated bath. That would have been a painful death."

"And who is Fausta?

"Roman Emperor Constantine's wife."

"Presumably ex-wife?"

"I guess so. She died."

"Who killed her?"

"Probably Constantine. Or at least, he had his people do it."

"He was upset with her; was he?" Arnold wondered where this conver-sation was going. It seemed highly peculiar to him that he was discussing the demise of Constantine's wife, as a dead body awaited his attention in the woods. But Dan persisted.

"That is the impression we get," Dan said, with deep, histori-cal earnestness.

"What did she do to deserve this?" Arnold asked casually, noting that his interest in the answer was extremely superficial.

"Constantine did not approve of her love life."

"That can be upsetting," Arnold said, knowingly. "Like you didn't approve of Sheila's love life. Still, you didn't throw her in a hot bath. Good for you, Dan. That kind of discipline needs to be recognized. But Constantine was clearly a man prone to overreaction. I take it that Fausta was not in a position to resist."

"Constantine did tend to overreact. He was also not broad-minded or flexible. I am guessing that he wanted out of his marriage."

"An end of marriage success story," Arnold sighed. The already questionable relevance of the conversation with Dan was beginning to waver. He needed to get to his police cruiser and radio the office to get Doc and Dr. Morley out to the scene. Blithering with Dan about Constantine and his ex-wife was mildly interesting but not helpful.

"Death does tend to end a marriage, Arnold," Dan answered.

"I suppose it does." Arnold shook his head. "Constantine was hopefully brought to justice?"

"He eventually died," Dan said.

"Death is an equal opportunity form of justice, I suppose," Arnold said, and then finally extricating himself from the conversation with Dan, walking over to his car, and radioing Constable Billy Stafford. "Get Doc Rubenstein and Dr. Morley out to the ball-field, ASAP. We have a dead man in the aster meadow, off the Woodlands Nature Trail. Clayton Dalrymple. Also, we need the GIS team out, and a few constables to secure the area. I'll wait at the ball-field for the medical people. The others can go ahead to the scene. Got it?"

"Vera predicted that Clayton wouldn't die in bed," Billy said.

"As usual, Billy, your wife was right," Arnold said and then signed off, smiling wearily.

When Arnold returned to the bleachers, he approached Dan but stayed standing, thinking that further conversation would be minimized if he didn't sit. Dan had perched himself on the first row of bleachers and was busily unwrapping a tuna-salad sandwich that looked like someone had been sitting on it for a few days.

15

"Called in the troops," Arnold said. "I'll wait for Doc and Dr. Morley. You can take off, Dan. I presume our discussion of Constantine and Fausta has been exhausted? By the way, what happened to your sandwich? Did you sit on it?"

"Sort of. They were in my backpack, taking on the weight of the day. But the tuna taste is still there." He took a big bite.

"That's unfortunate, Dan," Arnold mused. "Tuna is an acquired taste, I gather. I haven't acquired it."

"You're missing out. You can have one of mine," Dan said, digging another sandwich from his backpack and offering Arnold a thin waxed-paper package with white goo visible inside, spewing outwards from the edges of the bread. *Probably mayonnaise,* Arnold thought, a condiment he did not like.

"No thanks, Dan. I hope to never be that hungry," Arnold said, continuing to stand, looking around the ball-field in anticipation of medical help arriving.

"Was Clayton having difficulties?" Dan asked, taking off his sweat-stained Saskatchewan Roughrider ballcap.

"If he killed himself, I suppose he was having some sort of struggle. Why do you ask?"

"His wife said that he was under investigation by the RCMP. Big legal trouble. Is that true?"

"It is," Arnold said. "Did Natasha tell you anything about his state of mind?"

"Just that he was in crisis mode, and she wasn't sympathetic. Apparently, he was at the end of his rope, and she was okay with him being there."

"Not exactly a supportive position," Arnold observed. "The tensions in that household must have been high."

"You have no idea, Arnold," Dan said, shaking his head. "Clayton dragged Natasha through hell."

"Not a good place to spend a lot of time," Arnold said, taking a deep breath, and looking at the descending but still blazing sun. "Too hot ... like hell here in Northford today. Tell me more Dan. Natasha obviously shared more with you than with others in town."

"Perhaps she did. She didn't trust easily. She only told me a few things. Not much really. Why should she share details about her life? Her business is her business, not mine."

"No one is saying that she should. Just wondering what details she did share."

"Natasha hated her husband. Okay, Arnold? That much I can tell you. They had history, and it wasn't pleasant. But really, Natasha knows more about my life than I do about hers. She even offered to help me move."

"Very nice. I hear you're moving next door to Emily 'shorts' Little," Arnold said. "Are you interested in her, Dan? You should be. Our little writer is a bright light in this town and we're lucky to have her. Left her boyfriend on his own in Saskatoon. Can't imagine what he was thinking not joining her. The guy is missing out on a special person."

"I agree, Arnold," Dan said quickly. "Emily's awesome. Although I hear she isn't crazy about being called 'shorts.' Still, it suits her. But then everything suits Emily Little."

Arnold nodded. "She's the best young reporter the *Northford Sentinel* has ever had. Lucky for us that she came to Northford, instead of staying in Saskatoon."

Emily Little had been offered a journalist job with the Saskatoon paper but hadn't been happy with the latitude of stories she'd get to work on. She needed breadth and range. She wanted to write books on local historical topics and had decided that Northford would be a good place to live. Arnold couldn't help but admire her spunk. Publisher O'Brien over at the *Sentinel* had told her that she could have free range and encouraged her to dig into the town's past, stir up some debris, and exhume a few skeletons, and so she had.

She'd already written some great stories, including one historical piece about the time Happy Felsch had come to town with the Virden team. Felsch had been banned from major league baseball in 1919 for gambling and so was playing for Virden in a tournament in Northford. While in town, he'd gotten drunk and thrown darts against the wall of the Capri Hotel bar. She'd also written one on Oscar White's father, who'd travelled through Northford in the early 1930s, together with a barnstorming team called the Texas Colored Giants. The Giants were owned by a Saskatchewan man, Rod Whitman. Came into town with a midway, jazz band, and a magic act. It was Arnold that told Emily about the game. As a twelve-year-old boy, Arnold had watched the game with his uncle. Emily did some research and discovered that Oscar's father had liked the town so much that he'd mentioned it to his son, Oscar. So, when Oscar had been looking for a place to live after dodging the Vietnam draft, he'd chosen Northford.

"I have to tell you, Dan, Emily is also an astute crime journalist. She's helped our department problem-solve cases a number of times. She pays attention. I might also add that Emily is impressed with you, Dan."

"I noticed," Dan observed, blushing slightly. "Though with that kind of build up, I'm thinking my chances with her aren't high. Like you said, she already left a boyfriend behind in Saskatoon. It's not like she's really looking for a partner."

"Just saying, Emily's a catch," Arnold said definitively. "Living in the same building with Emily is bound to be an improvement for you. Why not just move in with her?" Arnold asked, taking out his notebook, and making an entry. "My notes indicate that Emily is open to that."

Dan appeared startled. "You make police notes about Emily's romantic desires, Arnold?"

"I like to be in the know," Arnold said as he smiled mischievously and picked up Dan's sweaty t-shirt, which he felt was a bit too close to his canteen, and examined it for a minute. "No wonder you took your shirt off, Dan. It stinks rather strongly. Looks and smells like you haven't washed it for a while either. Stained too. I'm no clean freak, Dan, but no self-respecting person would wear that shirt."

"That's why I took it off."

"Point taken," Arnold observed. "Your t-shirt was disgusting. Hope you know how to do your own laundry. Doubt that Emily will be interested in helping you with that."

"I can do my own laundry, Arnold. Prefer to, actually. Emily did actually offer to let me move in with her," Dan said, sounding pleased, then stuffed the last half of his tuna sandwich into his mouth.

"But you're hesitant?" Arnold asked, raising his eyebrows and pushing his damp, greying brown hair back off his forehead.

"I am," Dan said quickly, through the enormous lump of tuna sandwich still lodged in his mouth. "I figure that moving in with Emily could upset my prospects of ending up with her. I'm very good at disappointing people. Sheila says that I'm a major disappointment to her."

Arnold sighed. He couldn't help it. He felt sorry for the man. "You're a good father for your two boys. Hard to find better pre-teenagers."

"Even Sheila would agree with that. Nathan and Evan are good kids."

"I understand that you were a disappointment to Clayton, though," Arnold said. "I hear that he was trying to get you fired?"

"He was. He said that it was bad for the Arts Centre to have a gay artistic director and that he would see to it that I was dismissed."

"I know about that," Arnold replied. "But you weren't fired."

"Not for lack of Clayton trying. I got lucky I guess."

"Are you gay?"

"Of course not. Whatever gave you that idea?"

"You said that Clayton was trying to get you fired for being gay."

"That's true; he was. But I'm not gay. I'm interested in theatre, and maybe I could be more masculine, but what's wrong with being the way I am?"

"Nothing at all. But Clayton still had an issue with you. He was homophobic?"

"Absolutely. The man was insufferably homophobic," Dan said quite loudly and angrily. Having finally managed to empty his mouth of tuna sandwich, he grabbed his water bottle from his backpack and drank deeply. "Sheila's father was homophobic too. So is Sheila, for that matter. Quite the dysfunctional family, I tell you, Arnold."

"As a man who's been divorced three times, I try to avoid judging other families," Arnold murmured. "Of course, sometimes it's too obvious to ignore. I am aware of Sheila's father. He was a troubled soul. Sheila didn't have an easy childhood. I get that."

"She didn't. True enough," Dan said, grabbing a bag of carrots from his backpack, placing the end of a large one in his mouth, and taking a loud bite. "Neither did Clayton. But my level of sympathy for either of them is thin. Very thin, Arnold. Clayton heard about me getting fired in Saskatoon for putting on a play with a gay sex scene and used that against me. Then he started fucking Sheila. Well, that was fine, I suppose, but then they started acting like my judge and jury and tried to destroy my career. That's where my sympathy for both of them ended. I'm angry about it. I don't handle anger well. Anyway, it was Natasha who hired me, and so she was able to prevent me from getting fired. But it was no thanks to Clayton. He was determined to mess with my life."

"That must have been upsetting," Arnold said sympathetically, picking up a dirt-smeared baseball that had been left to lie by itself under the bleacher seating.

"It was. I hated the man," Dan said angrily, stuffing another chunk of carrot in his mouth, giving his voice a rather desperate, garbled sound. "There was no let up with Clayton. If he was a character in one of our plays, he would be the villain. In fact, he *was* a villain, wasn't he? A criminal."

"That is not public knowledge as of yet," Arnold said cautiously. "But yes, he was under investigation. I confirmed as much with you a few minutes ago."

"Why did he come to Northford anyway? He was some big shot KGB agent in the Soviet Union, so why didn't he stay there? That's what I'd like to know," Dan asked, not really expecting an answer.

"He came here to be with family. Doc Rubenstein is Natasha's brother-in-law. He married her twin sister, and they have a son together. Clayton's nephew."

Dan nodded. "I realise that. Natasha told me as much, but it still makes no sense to me. Clayton couldn't stand Doc, and vice versa. Then Doc sent Fyodor away to Singapore anyway. Obviously, he didn't want Clayton involved with the boy's life. Hard to believe that family actually wanted to be together."

"Perhaps there were other issues," Arnold said, shrugging. "Natasha wanted to come to Northford anyway, in part because of Doc. But Clayton's motivations weren't as clear. Perhaps he made some sort of compromise with Natasha. Did Natasha ever talk about the death slogans painted on her garage?"

"She did. It was very upsetting for her. She caught Muscle John in the act."

"Yes, but William and Adele Sawatzky put him up to it. Seems a coincidence that a man who has death slogans painted on his garage and is under legal pressure is suddenly found dead. Might look like suicide, but it makes a person wonder."

"It is suicide, Arnold. You'll see," Dan said firmly in a low voice, pulling out the last of the carrots and flipping the empty plastic bag into his backpack. "No doubt about it."

"Doubt lingers in wait for cracks to appear."

"Doubt all you want, Arnold. When you see Clayton, you'll agree with me. Definitely suicide. But I have work to do. Can't chat with the police all day. Just follow the Woodlands Nature Trail, a quarter mile or so north of the fairground entrance. You can't miss the meadow. It has purple asters growing in it."

"And a lonely dead body," Arnold added.

"Not that lonely," Dan said. "Chickadees were keeping him company."

"I'll need a written statement, Dan," Arnold offered, glancing up at the sun that was sliding behind a cascade of clouds, briefly offering some relief from the heat. The ballfield was now empty of fans, and a calm quiet filled the space. Arnold noted the distant sound of a window air conditioner, a car with a faulty muffler, and the calling of pigeons rummaging through the remnants of hotdogs under the bleachers. "Come by the station tomorrow, Dan. I'll be around, and if not, you can give a statement to Constable Billy Stafford."

As Dan wandered off towards his Falcon, parked in the Arts Centre parking lot, Arnold thought about Dan. He thought about Clayton's affair with Dan's wife, Sheila, and then the public efforts at getting Dan fired from the Arts Centre. Natasha and Doc had been Dan's strongest supporters. The Arts Centre Board was mostly afraid of Clayton and hesitant to stand up to him. *Dan had a lot to gain from Clayton's death,* Arnold thought. But Dan was not the only one who would.

It had been a difficult year. The RCMP had been investigating Clayton's art-fraud scheme, among other matters like tax fraud. The pressure on the man had been mounting. And Clayton had been clearly stressed by the whole business lately. Arnold suspected that Clayton was likely aware of the dealings between RCMP, External Affairs, and the Soviet Embassy officials in Ottawa. Clayton was about to be sacrificed. Arnold was well aware of what happens when a man like Clayton is put in an impossible position.

Then there's the matter of Natasha, Arnold thought. The police had initially thought that she was involved with Clayton's criminal activity. But they had changed their mind. There was no evidence suggesting that she was involved, and so the police had determined not to charge her with anything. Arnold wondered whether Natasha was even aware that she had been suspected. Innocent or not, he sensed that Natasha had more skeletons than the average Northford resident. The woman was deeply suspicious, especially of the police. She may or may not have been involved with Clayton's criminal activity, but he was convinced that she had some of her own dealings that she wanted to keep hidden.

Of course, Arnold thought, *that makes her fit in rather well in Northford.* Still, he imagined that with Clayton dead, Natasha was not likely to stick around. Dan was clearly infatuated with her, but it was unlikely that was reciprocated. *Dan has no chance with her,* he thought. Natasha may well have appreciated Dan's devotion and admiration, but that was all that was going to come of that. But he knew that Doc and Natasha had a past with Clayton. Clayton had been an obstacle to them both he was sure but no longer. Clayton's death was convenient for Natasha, for certain, and Doc too stood to gain by it. But Natasha and Doc were not alone in benefitting from his death. There were others who stood to gain and no one who stood to lose, it seemed, other than Clayton himself.

CHAPTER 2

THE BODY

It was five-fifteen when Doc Alexei Rubenstein's silver Volvo pulled into the Northford ball-field parking area. The crowd was gone, and Arnold was alone, sitting in the muted shade of the backstop, waiting for Doc. The sun continued to shine, although with diminished focus. An increasing range of distended shade was engulfing the infield along with the empty bleachers.

Doc slowly emerged from the inner sanctum of his Volvo. He cautiously reached his arm upwards to grab the top of the car door and raised himself out of the vehicle. He paused over his wire-rimmed glasses to stare at the empty ball-field, and then, settling his eyes on Arnold, he began to walk, unsteadily, to where Arnold sat. Doc's white Fedora with brown trim was tilted low on his face. His blue satin shirt was buttoned to the top, and his sleeves were rolled up to his thinly muscled biceps. His grey dress pants had ridden up on his legs as he straightened himself up from what appeared to have been a demanding driving experience.

As soon as Doc left his Volvo, it became apparent to Arnold that he had been drinking. The man wavered slightly, as if there were a stiff breeze, which there wasn't, his body moving in a zig-zag pattern towards Arnold, saved from falling only by the shortness of his steps.

Doc was in his late forties, but he looked older. He moved slowly, especially when he drank, which is mostly what he did on Saturdays. When he drank, he walked exceptionally slowly, partly because his balance was quickly impacted by alcohol. He was a slight man with a sedentary life-style, and it easily showed. *"Sometimes, it's hard to tell if Doc is actually moving,"* people joked. Today, however, it appeared that his car had been moving at some speed. His usually spotless Volvo was slathered in mud along both sides.

"No need to rush, Doc," Arnold said sarcastically, moving towards the approaching man and gesturing him towards the bleachers. "You got through the mudslide all right?"

"Very funny, Arnold," Doc said, having meandered rather indirectly to Arnold and following him to the metal seats. "I ran into a little problem on Municipal Road 344. The water was deeper than I expected. Muddy bottom too! Who knew a ditch could be a swamp? I am quite sure my car was still sinking in mud when I bailed ship."

"Who knew an intelligent man would choose to drive on 344 after a rain? In a municipality of bad roads, 344 wins the lottery. Why were you even on it?"

"I was picking blueberries at Lake McCaskill."

"There's a paved road from Lake McCaskill. I imagine you know that."

"Of course, I know that. But I wanted to see the countryside," Doc responded. "It was lovely until I hit the ditch."

"I imagine it was still lovely after you hit the ditch. You just stopped noticing. What happened?"

"Shit happened."

"Driving on 344 after a rain can invite that."

Doc sighed impatiently. "I concede that my judgement was flawed. That has happened before. Will again. Nevertheless, time moves on, and good comes with the bad. I hear that Clayton is dead?" Doc said, rubbing his chin as if trying to remove some unpleasantness. "I will maintain a pro-fessional bearing, Arnold, but I confess that this news has brightened an otherwise cheerless day. The blueberries were badly picked over."

"How is it that Clayton's death brightens your day? He's your brother-in-law. Family."

"Sadly, true," Doc responded abruptly. "We are not close. But let us check him out, shall we? Make certain and all that. Imagine Morley's coming?"

"He is," Arnold answered, pointing to the parking area where a flash of red Camaro was just arriving. "There's his car. I presume he's in it, though it looks like it doesn't have a driver."

"Morley *is* shorter than the average driver," Doc acknowledged. "But he follows the traffic rules better than the average Camaro driver. One of the few people in town that drives a muscle car without speeding."

"Good point. Were you speeding when you hit the ditch? Drinking?"

"I might have been driving faster than the road conditions allowed, but I was unfortunately sober."

"But you've had a few since then?"

"Yes, Arnold, since going home, I have had a few vodkas," Doc said, dropping his body onto the bleacher seat beside where Arnold stood. "The clinic is closed on Saturday. What else am I to do?"

"You could take up macramé."

"I prefer to drink," Doc said, lighting a cigarette and pulling his white Fedora down even lower over his eyes.

"Smoking isn't exactly a recommended health practice," Arnold observed, still standing, but seriously considering sitting down. "Especially for a doctor."

"I am not recommending it, Arnold. I simply do it," Doc said casually. "I don't recommend drinking either. But I also do that. I am Russian, fully endowed with an attraction to all manner of unhealthy habits, including an attitude of fatalism."

"We all die," Arnold mused. "But do we have to invite death?"

"Death does not require an invitation. It comes when it feels like it. Bad habits or not."

"Fair enough, Doc. When did this ditch incident happen?"

"Around ten this morning," Doc said, somewhat regretfully, as he waved faintly at a fly that was buzzing about his head. "After my car hit the ditch, I walked a half mile to the Schoendienst farm. Exceptionally long and muddy driveway. I was exhausted by the time I got to the front door, and then their dog—a German Shepherd named Rex—growled at me and bit my pant leg. I cursed at the dog. It was quite pathetic really. My lack of courage with dogs did not surprise me, but still, I was unimpressed. I have held up better against KGB agents. But that is what I did. Perhaps Canadian life has made me soft."

"Me too, Doc. We don't seem to have enough enemies. Did old man Schoendienst come to the rescue?" Arnold asked, finally settling his body down beside Doc.

"Eventually, he called Rex off of me. But other than that, Schoendienst was of little help. Didn't even offer me a drink."

"But I imagine he pulled you out. Farmers have tractors for that sort of thing."

"They do, but Schoendienst's tractor was in the machine shed."

"He couldn't take it out?"

"No. His wife made that quite clear. That woman is someone you don't want to encounter without headgear. Schoendienst initially offered to take the tractor out, but his wife put a quick stop to it. She told Schoendienst that the tractor was cleaned and tucked away for the winter, and that is where it would stay until spring. I had no choice but to call Muscle John Friesen for a tow. Took his sweet time, too. Caught him in the middle of a romp with his new girlfriend, or so he said."

"Good for Muscle John," Arnold said.

"How do you mean?" Doc asked, puzzled. "He didn't pull me out until much later in the morning. He wasn't exactly responsive."

"He doesn't tend to be," Arnold responded carefully. "But a girlfriend will be good for him. Might bring him back to what he does best: shooting pool and driving a tow truck. He's developed some troublesome hate-mon-gering habits lately. Some people aren't well suited to Christian teachings. Muscle John is one of them."

There was some truth to Arnold's assertion. The story of Muscle John Friesen need not be told in full here, but some introduction is appropriate. Muscle John had been running Friesen's Pool Hall on Mackenzie Avenue for twelve years, ever since his high school graduation. Though he did (technically) graduate, John had spent the better part of the six years it took him to do so—the years between grade ten and twelve specifically— dividing his time between the school weight room and the local pool hall. John had never chosen to develop reading habits; however, he was literate enough to be influenced by magazines. His father, Jake Friesen—a man who'd spent most of his parenting life in the North Sea oilfields—had given John his collection of Sport Magazines when John was (marginally) in grade nine. John had noted an advertisement of a muscle-bound man—who had taken a Joe Weider supplement—kicking sand in the face of a frail, weakling of a boy who evidently had not.

Across the page from the advertisement had been a full-page picture of Willie Mosconi, who'd won the World Straight Pool Championship nineteen times. Mosconi didn't look muscle-bound, but when it came to pictures, John could extrapolate, and he did. He may or may not have read the article. Sometimes he claimed that he had, sometimes he bragged that he hadn't. Either way, the article and advertisement had convinced John to take on the challenge of playing Mosconi-level pool and building a Mr. America level physique. He accomplished both with impressive discipline. By the time his father showed up for John's high school graduation, John was referred to (with reverence) as Muscle John, who was not only built like Mr. America but also played pool like Willie Mosconi.

When the principal had handed out the diplomas, he'd called for "Muscle John," not John Friesen. As Muscle John accepted the dainty Saskatchewan High School diploma, the student body had called out "Pool Shark, Muscle John! Pool Shark, Muscle John!" in a resounding pattern that so impressed Jake Friesen that he'd gone out and bought the Northford Pool Hall for his son. Jake had also bought Muscle John a tow truck, so that he could operate a side gig in case the pool-hall business slowed down.

Muscle John prospered. He won every tournament he played, and became something of a legend in Northford. Aspiring players would come to town thinking that they could defeat Muscle John, but they couldn't.

The towing business did well too. Muscle John was the first pick for most Northford folks needing a tow. Overall, it could be said that Muscle John was a Northford success story. Except for one thing: He was dissatisfied. In good measure, his problem was centred around his struggle in keeping a girlfriend. He fell in love regularly, generally with any of the young women he hired at the pool hall, but reciprocation was a problem. Recently, he'd hired Janet Sawatzky and had initially felt confident that she might be interested in him. He had shown her his Tinker-car collection, and she had smiled, in a loving supportive style, which he viewed as promising. But it wasn't.

Janet, it turned out, didn't like Tinker cars, or for that matter, Muscle John. But she needed the job and thought that showing an interest in her boss's Tinker-car collection might be helpful. When Muscle John had gradually become aware of Janet's lack of interest in him, he'd felt like the world had basically come to an end. Turning to religion in his time of need, he'd begun attending Four-Square Gospel church. When Pastor Gerald Schultz had suggested that the end times were around the corner, Muscle John had agreed. He felt the same way.

The desire to prepare Northford for the return of Jesus resonated with Muscle John. When he'd met William and Adele Sawatzky, Janet's parents, he'd recognized that the path they were on was the correct one and got quite excited. As such, when William and Adele had told him to paint death slogans on Clayton and Natasha Dalrymple's garage, he'd felt that this was a great idea.

Natasha and Clayton were Russians, and as William and Adele had pointed out, they were also atheists and Jews. Muscle John was vaguely opposed to all of these designations, so he'd rallied to the death-slogan idea. It had also helped that Muscle John loved graffiti art, and the opportunity to practice on the Russians' garage wall had appealed to him.

■ ■ ■

"I thought getting dirty was what a tractor lived for," Arnold said, imagining old man Schoendienst, a farmer who did not want to get his tractor dirty. It seemed odd.

"I thought so too," Doc mused, taking a deep drag on his cigarette and blowing a perfectly formed trio of smoke rings into the air. "But I appeared to be wrong. I tried to convince them. Even offered to give them blueberries. They scoffed at that. They said no one in their right mind would pick blueberries when you can buy them packaged from a store. Getting a bit old and tired those two."

"They do make a point, though. Why *do* you pick blueberries?"

"It's an activity, Arnold. Gets me out of the house in the morning," Doc said. "If I didn't get out into the countryside, I might drink all day."

"You could stay home and read."

"I tried that," Doc said slowly, rolling his eyes. "Doesn't do much for me. Have you ever read a Russian novel? Suffering and death over the course of eight hundred pages. It is rather overwhelming. Even for a Russian."

"If you insist on reading Russian literature, Doc, no one can help you with that. So, why are you and Clayton not close?"

"Where do I start?" Doc asked rhetorically, momentarily taking off his glasses and squinting at Arnold. "I have known Clayton much of my life. Some people grow on you over time. Not Clayton. How did he die?"

"That is what we need you to help us with," Arnold said, impatiently glancing at the now parked Camaro. The daylight was not endless. "Dan thinks it's suicide. His description makes it sound that way. Handgun left beside him. Bullet to the head."

"Did he leave a note?" Doc asked indifferently, shuffling his feet as if he were anxious to get somewhere.

"No mention of that," Arnold said. "Maybe he left one at his house? I'll stop in on Natasha after we've attended to the body."

"She can be cool and overly formal," Doc mused gently. "She is not a fan of the human species and is frankly annoyed about being one of us. But you are not delivering bad news, so she may offer you a drink and smile slightly. Clayton's death will not disappoint her, and she will not pretend that it does."

"It disappoints me," Dr. Robert Morley grunted, his squinting face giving the impression of an impending bowel movement as he approached them at the bleachers. Morley had pulled his newly waxed red Camaro alongside Doc's disturbingly filthy Volvo and walked his fast-paced penguin walk to where Doc and Arnold sat. "It might seem crude, but I wanted to be there when he died."

"You'll have to settle for the pleasures of an autopsy," Arnold quipped, standing up to meet Morley, shaking his hand firmly, and looking towards the entrance to the Woodlands Nature Trail.

"There will be some admittedly perverted pleasure in that," Morley said. "Good to see you, Doc. I imagine that sympathies are not in order. I knew the man."

"So, did I," Doc answered glumly.

"A bit premature," Arnold said. "All we have is Dan's pronouncement. It's not that I am doubting him, but we should see the body before we start the grieving process. For all we know, Dan is imagining things, and Clayton is at home cooking up some devious plot to overthrow the mayor's next election."

■ ■ ■

Late-afternoon colours gave the Northford Woodland Forest a surreal look as Arnold, Dr. Robert Morley, and a still mildly intoxicated Doc Alexei Rubenstein headed out along the nature trail to the body of Clayton Dalrymple. About a quarter mile from the trailhead, the walking path entered a meadow brimming with still blooming purple and yellow aster flowers. The meadow was bordered by encroaching trembling aspen and bur oak. Shade was covering much of the meadow, but not in the northwest corner, where a ray of late-afternoon sun shone on the body of Clayton Dalrymple, lying peacefully behind a hawthorn bush.

Constable Billy Stafford and a few junior constables were already on the scene, securing the area. The sound of twirling aspen leaves, the crunch of dry pinecones on the path, the chorus of chickadees, and the deep breathing of the men filled the outdoor space as Dr. Morley approached Clayton's body, crouched down on his haunches and stared intently at him. Doc opted to stand behind Morley, looking over his shoulder, while subtly leaning against a bur-oak stump, evidently to help his body steady itself. Dr. Morley quickly confirmed that the body was indeed dead, and Doc chipped in to say that the body was, indeed, Clayton Dalrymple.

Clayton was lying much as Dan had described. The body was partially hidden from the nature trail by the hawthorn bush, which was full of purple blackberries. Clayton's head was to the west. His grey, flat hat—a foot or so from his head—sat among a patch of purple asters. His legs, ending in brown cowboy boots, were splayed apart, pointing to the east. His right arm was directed to the south, as if he were pointing to someone or something. His left arm was resting on his chest, much of which was bare, given that the top six buttons of his paisley satin shirt were not done up, exposing his muscular but hairless chest to the elements. He also wore a tweed sports jacket, also open, the back partially folded and creased beneath him. A few dry trembling-aspen leaves had fallen onto his chest and drifted into the inner confines of his shirt. There, the trembling of the leaves had stopped.

The bent hands of the Rolex watch on Clayton's left wrist had stopped at nine-thirty. The crystal casing was smashed, with shards of glass pressing inwards. The interior of the watch showed signs of an odd yellow powder. A handgun lay an inch or so from Clayton's outstretched right hand, and a small but gaping bullet wound with a light smattering of blood was visible on his right temple. Arnold noted that no exit bullet wound was evident. To the west of the body, Clayton's black pea coat was neatly folded on a cottonwood stump, together with a blue plastic mug with a light trace of green-liquid residue.

"That's a Russian M1895," Doc said, noting the gun. "With a silencer."

"Interesting choice," Arnold mused. "Clayton didn't want to disrupt the sounds of nature? Or someone else didn't maybe. He was right-handed?"

"He functioned as a right-handed person, but he was a natural lefty," Doc said. "Being left-handed was not allowed. He adapted."

"That happens," Arnold said. "You might think, though, that if he were going to shoot himself, he might revert to his natural hand."

"Maybe," Doc said. "But he was a dyslexic migraine sufferer. He sometimes confused left and right, especially when he had a headache."

"I imagine a M1895 could give a person a headache," Arnold said, scratching his chin. "My first wife had migraines. Terrible things. Death becomes attractive. Clayton is also wearing his watch on his left wrist," observed Arnold. "Usually, you wear a watch on the non-dominant arm."

"True enough," Doc said. "Although Clayton was quirky. Did things his own way from the moment he got up in the morning to the time he went to sleep. For all I know, he slept in some unique way peculiar only to him. You could ask Natasha. Not that they slept together anymore. Actually, I'm not sure that they ever did."

"Not a sign of a good marriage. Especially at their age," Arnold said.

"Their marriage was full to the brim with bad signs, Arnold," Doc murmured. "Hardly relevant now."

"Might be relevant. We'll see. What do you guys make of the bullet wound?" Arnold asked.

"He was shot at close quarters. That is certain," Dr. Morley said. "Must have done it himself. No one with a gun could get that close to a living Clayton."

There was blood on the grass to the south of the dead man's head. Smatterings of blood stood out in a bold pattern of abstract art on his open shirt. His brown, tweed sports jacket held spots of blood around the neckline, along with another batch of the yellow powder that was in the broken Rolex. *It looks the same, anyway.* Similar yellow powder was in his hair, around an abrasion on his skull, and along the edge of his receding hairline.

"Clayton loved the western-cowboy look," Doc said. "But he sadly added the sport jacket and satin shirt," Doc said, still balancing himself against the oak stump. "I always thought that Clayton would have benefited from fashion guidance. But Clayton gave advice. He did not accept it."

"I propose that his fashion decisions, however suspect, were not the cause of death," Arnold opined. "It does look like a self-inflicted gunshot, but on the other hand, it doesn't. He didn't break his own watch. Or hit himself on the head. Someone else was here. Someone with ... yellow powder?"

There was a trail of single footprints coming from the west but no tracks leaving. These prints were similar in size and heel formation to the cowboy boots that were on Clayton's feet. Arnold noted the clear definition and depth of the prints. He thought to himself that the rain from last night had created a perfect setting for footprints, still ... Clayton was not that large of a man. Clayton was six feet, and well muscled, but not a heavy man. Another set of footprints, considerably larger than the cowboy boots, were evident to the south of the body, coming from the nature trail. The ground was still soft from the early morning rain, so the prints were easily visible. Arnold noted that another set of smaller footprints, fainter and fresher, was east of the body. They seemed to come from the trail, and then move back to it.

Those must be Dan's running-shoe prints from this afternoon. Some of those tracks seemed deeper than the others, particularly one indentation coming towards the nature trail. Dan had mentioned that, upon leaving the body, he had briefly started going north to Natasha's house, and had then changed his mind, going south towards the ball-field. The prints seemed to generally support Dan's self-reporting.

"Looks like Clayton walked here on his own, probably from the forest-service road to the west," Arnold said out loud. "One path to the scene, no path leaving. But he met someone. The set of larger prints did not come from Clayton. Not only are they larger than his cowboy boots but the tread is different too. Looks like a work-boot tread. It seems Clayton met someone with big feet and a yearning to smash his Rolex and hit him on the head. Yearnings that appear to have been satisfied. If it was an arranged meeting, it was not a friendly one. Still, there is no sign of struggle. They didn't roll around in the grass, fighting over who was going to die. Clayton simply put his jacket away neatly, finished his drink, sat down, and put a gun to his head. Or so it appears. What do you think about time of death, Dr. Morley? Is the watch time accurate?"

"In the ballpark," Dr. Morley answered, with a puzzled look. "But I'm guessing he died somewhat earlier than nine-thirty. Based on rigor mortis, my thinking is that he died perhaps an hour earlier. But time of death can be imprecise."

Clayton's skin-tight, blue, bellbottom jeans had ridden up his legs, revealing the top edge of his freshly waxed boots. His clothes seemed clean, with no loose dirt or grass stains that might indicate a struggle.

"Why did he walk around with his shirt unbuttoned at the top like that?" Dr. Morley asked. "Made him look like a hoodlum."

"He *was* a hoodlum," Doc replied. "He also liked to show off his muscles. He was a good-looking man. Had a James Bond look."

"Now he has a dead James Bond look, with a trail of black flies coming and going from his open mouth. Death is undignified, even for the good-looking man," Arnold observed. "He always had the look of an unhappy person. Still does."

"He was chronically unhappy," Doc said grumpily. "Clayton gave no indication that he even desired happiness for himself or approved of it in others. Tried to wipe it out wherever he found it. He delivered pain and suffering. It was, in a sense, part of his belief system. Of course, he could not escape pain and suffering himself. But he was well aware of this. He was Russian."

"He certainly didn't escape it this morning," Arnold said, looking carefully at Clayton.

"What's this gross stuff?" Dr. Morley asked, looking into the blue travel mug with its traces of green liquid."

"That would be his breakfast drink," Doc said. "Surprising that it is here. His pattern would be to drink it in his workshop."

"He was committed to patterns?" Arnold asked.

"Natasha and Clayton were devoted to daily ritual," Doc said. "They drank an herbal concoction every morning. Clayton drank his in his workshop. Natasha after her run. That was their routine."

"But he broke the routine this morning and took his drink to the woods. Why?" Arnold asked, not expecting an answer. "He dressed the same as he usually did. Even wore that dumb flat hat of his." He gestured towards where it was lying amongst the flowers.

"Oh yes, he would never leave home without his flat hat," Doc said. "Very attached to it. It made him look like a gangster."

"Gangster or not, I don't like how it's positioned," Arnold said, mostly to himself.

"Why?" Doc asked.

"His hat is too close to his head," Arnold said. "Anyway, I don't think a man would wear his hat if he was about to shoot himself in the head. Wouldn't he have put that on the stump as well? Did he have any suicidal tendencies, Doc?"

Doc had been standing by the dead man with a puzzled look. "Clayton did threaten suicide once. When he first arrived in Northford, he mentioned it. I am not sure that I believed him. I don't think Natasha did either. He was manipulative in his conversation. But I do accept that he had a period where he was second guessing his decision to defect."

"What prompted the defection anyway?" Arnold asked Doc.

"Living in the Soviet Union isn't easy, even for a man like Clayton," Doc said. "He took down a lot of important people. But he also was well aware that, in the Soviet Union, the tables can turn quickly. The accuser can easily become the accused. He wanted to get out before that could happen."

"He was KGB," Arnold mused, "but left a prestigious position in the Russian Embassy in Ottawa to come to Northford. Why here? He didn't come to Northford to hang out with you."

"He didn't come here for me," Doc answered slowly. "He came here for Fyodor. My son. Clayton was intensely devoted to Fyodor, and he wanted to be close to him."

"But you sent Fyodor to Singapore to study," Arnold said.

"Precisely," Doc answered, standing up straight for the first time. "I had no intention of allowing Clayton close to the boy."

"You sent Fyodor away to prevent his contact with Clayton?"

"Partly."

"Clayton must have been upset by that."

"He was."

Arnold considered this as he continued taking in the scene. "Where are his glasses?"

"Clayton never went anywhere without his glasses," Doc said. "He would occasionally take them off in meetings, but he was nearsighted. He needed them. Though I guess if you are going to shoot yourself, you don't need to see clearly."

Dr. Morley went through Clayton's pockets and pulled out a pair of silver-handled glasses. "Here they are. It is typical of suicide to take your glasses off. Like you are going to bed. Isn't that the case, Arnold?"

"It is," he replied, snooping around the cottonwood stump and looking deeply into its crevices. "What's this?" He reached into a wide crack and carefully pulled out a cigarette butt. "Clayton smoked Rothmans?"

"He did," Doc answered. "Smoked six cigarettes a day. Never more, and as far as I know, never less. Each one marked a moment in the day."

"This butt appears to have marked his death," Arnold said, slipping the butt into a plastic evidence bag. "I guess he had a smoke before he died. Then he picked up his butt and hid it away. Very considerate. He probably also pulled his car off the forest-service road properly before walking here."

Once the work at the meadows was sufficiently done, Clayton's body was moved to the service road and loaded onto the ambulance to be taken to the hospital mortuary. Dr. Morley joined the body, and as they drove along the tree-lined service road to the Northford hospital, he reflected on his own relationship with the deceased man. He had not liked Clayton and his death was a victory of a sort, as well as a considerable relief for Dr. Morley.

As the ambulance pulled away from the forest-service road, it was able to easily get past Clayton's 1967 blue Mustang Fastback, which had been pulled neatly off to the side.

CHAPTER 3

ARNOLD INTERVIEWS DOC ON THE NATURE TRAIL

If Arnold had been hungry earlier (and he had been), he was hungrier now. Cheeseburgers were on his mind as he walked with Doc back along the nature trail towards the trailhead and its parking area. He took comfort knowing that the Dickey Dee would be open late. The evening temperature was still warm, certainly enough to warrant outdoor patio burgers. He told himself that after advising Natasha of the death of her husband, he would drive to the Dickey Dee. *Something to look forward to, at least.*

Doc and Arnold walked along the nature path, each man taking one of the ATV tracks—ATVs were not allowed on the walking path, but the rule was actively disobeyed.

"Love the dreamlike look of the woods at this time of day," Arnold said pensively. "I should walk this path when there isn't a dead body on the trail."

"A dead body does not invite peaceful thoughts," Doc said, sounding even more Russian than usual. "It does seem dreamlike though. Almost as if it is not real. Still, it seems like an unexpectedly reflective word for a police officer."

"Perhaps I am an unexpectedly reflective police officer," Arnold joked. "Although I am never sure that reflection gets me closer to any form of wisdom. Perhaps that's asking too much. I'm drawn to reading books that encourage introspection."

"You mentioned you aren't big on Russian novels."

"I have read quite a lot of Russian novels actually. Maxim Gorky was a favourite writer of mine in my university years. He was exposed to the brutal realities of life. It encouraged his desire for change. Sadly, he was betrayed at the end of his life. It was tragic, I felt, how Stalin used him. But then, Stalin was responsible for many tragedies. Russian literature is not light and cheerful. It is devoted to harsh realities. As I got older, and started my life as a police officer, I realised that I had more than enough exposure to the dark side. Now, I read books that are less despairing and more hopeful. Life is difficult, but the human spirit is impressively resilient."

"Was it hard for you when Madeline left?" Doc asked.

"Yes, it was. I'm not saying that we were a great match, but I miss her."

"At least you had no children with this wife, to be dragged into Gerald Schultz's nonsense." He shook his head. "Madeline moving in with the Big-Four Gospel pastor surprised me. I did not think that Schultz was much of a catch."

"Pretty sure that he isn't," Arnold said, thinking briefly of his two kids from his first marriage and reminding himself that he needed to give them a call sooner rather than later. "But Madeline seems to think that he is a 'highly evolved human,' and her view on the matter is the one that counts."

"That is obviously true. Madeline risked a lot for love."

"I'm not sure she risked that much. Just life with me. Madeline has grander expectations though. She's not sure of the details, but she is quite certain that she wants more. She's easily dissatisfied. Being a policeman's wife was not a good fit for her. Schultz nurtures her high expectations and gives those expectations some institutional credibility, even if the content remains deliberately obscure. She thinks of herself as a spiritual person, and I did not give that view sufficient respect. I admit that. It would be hard to be less spiritual than me, I suppose."

"Well, Schultz *is* a minister. Claiming access to the spirit world is a professional requirement."

"I suppose."

"You don't think he believes what he is preaching? That he is putting on a show?"

"He may well have some unformed beliefs, but mostly, my sense from Schultz is that his primary skill is entertaining. He's good at selling hope, and folks are eager to hear that message. He has a growing audience. Perhaps I'm just jealous. In high school, I was into entertaining as well. Was even in the drama club. Quite liked it."

"I had no idea. What plays were you in?"

"In grade twelve, we did *The Cherry Orchard*. I don't remember the plot, but I remember that it drew me closer to the merits of Chekhov. He has a gentle touch for the human dilemma."

"It surprises me that a police officer would decide to join a drama club, never mind read Chekhov."

"I wasn't always a police officer, Doc."

"Of course. I don't think I've ever asked what drew you into the police service."

The men paused on the path to watch a scampering red fox dart behind a trio of red pine before continuing on their way.

"My father was with the RCMP. He enjoyed his career, and apart from moving around the country every five years, our family had a good life. It was hard on my mother, the moving, but my parents made the best of it. My father was a good model for us, career wise. Family wise, perhaps not. All of my siblings went into some form of police work, but none of them have had marriages that lasted. Me included, as you know," Arnold said, pausing again to watch a woodpecker hammer away at the trunk of a pine tree. The sound reverberated through the woods, adding to the rustling of dried acorns on the path and the breeze spinning the trembling aspen leaves still clinging to the tree tops. "My father was also a big reader of crime novels. Dashiell Hammett and Raymond Chandler were his favourites," Arnold said wistfully, reflecting on his reading pleasures. "They became mine too. They still are."

Arnold noted the same red fox, darting now through the trees in a section of forest that led to the ravine to their right, and momentarily wondered where it would spend the night. *Perhaps a den along the ravine cliffs,* he thought. Then he returned to the conversation with Doc. "Working in the police service never seemed a big stretch for me. Adult life is constant drama, with people playing roles. Reality is consistently deceiving. A smoke and mirror show. Police work involves scratching the surface and trying to uncover the truth."

"How successfully?" Doc asked skeptically, as he picked up a piece of rotting deadwood, examining its surface. "Any idea how many insects live in this deadwood, Arnold?"

"I'm guessing more than one and less than a million," Arnold said. "Of course, I could be off by one or two. As for success in police work, well, that depends on expectations. About fifty percent of murder cases go unsolved. The numbers will vary with other crimes. Given how people lie and deceive, the case success numbers aren't that bad actually. Solving crimes is hard work. Basically, police work involves talking with people who pretend to tell the truth while we pretend to believe them. Humans are skilled at creating a fake story and vigorously defending it. Whether they have committed a crime or not."

"True enough, Arnold. Since Sophia died, I pretend that my life is fine. But it is marginally pathetic. I am just barely holding it together."

"I have rather suspected that, Doc," Arnold said softly, touching Doc lightly on the shoulder in sympathy. "I have noticed you have been drinking more. Stressed, I imagine. The answers to how Sophia died were not easily come by?"

"No. They were not. All I know for sure is that Sophia went to the Soviet Union to attend her mother's funeral. Clayton, Natasha, and Sophia were drinking at a Lake Baikal restaurant. Natasha left early, leaving Sophia and Clayton alone together. Sophia did not return, but Clayton did. The Soviets claim she fell into the largely frozen Lake Baikal and drowned."

Arnold was already familiar with the story. Nothing stayed quiet in a small town for long. "It's hard to believe. I take it you have views on the matter?"

"She might have drowned in Lake Baikal, but she didn't fall without someone's help. I suspect it was Clayton. He claims that Sophia left the restaurant on her own. He said that they argued, and that Sophia stomped out into the night, angry and drunk. There is no way that this is true. Sophia drank a little but never to excess. And she would never have allowed herself to become drunk when alone with Clayton. But I have no proof. The whole business is very upsetting. It doesn't help that we were having problems at the time."

"We all have problems, Doc. You and Sophia were on better terms than many in this town. Still, I heard a rumour about you and Natasha having an affair back in the Soviet Union. Was that true?" Arnold wouldn't normally have asked, but with Clayton's death, being nosey was somewhat mandatory. He was beginning to wonder what other mysteries lay in the history of Clayton and Natasha. He listened intently to Doc's slow, drawling answer, thinking that he should take notes but feeling it would disrupt the sharing.

"It was true. It lasted for a number of years. It was after we were both married. Sophia knew about it. She did not approve, but she did not leave me. Maybe she didn't care. Frankly, I was never sure. Does that make me a suspect?"

"You appear to have an alibi, Doc," Arnold said. "Can't be berry picking at Lake McCaskill and killing your brother-in-law at the same time. Are you still having a thing with Natasha?"

They came to a bend in the trail where it descended slightly into a valley, with a steep ravine on the right and spruce trees forming a canopy over a dry creek bed. They slowly descended, the tree roots making the ground uneven but giving the men firm footing.

"Unfortunately, not. I have some trust issues with Natasha," Doc continued, carefully stepping down the path. Doc had grabbed a slender but still firm stick from the forest floor to help with his balance. His state of inebriation had improved, but his confidence had not. "I keep thinking that she knows something about Sophia's death that she is not saying."

"Have you talked to her about it?" Arnold asked, as they got to the bottom of the descent and walked over the wooden foot bridge, which had tall reed grasses growing on each side. Next, they would begin their ascent back up out of the valley, following the path that continued quite steeply upwards and then to the right, along a grove of trembling aspen along the ravine's edge.

"In a veiled fashion. Natasha feels that she should have stayed at the restaurant and supported Sophia. But she didn't. The next day, they claim that Sophia's body was discovered in Lake Baikal."

"But you don't believe that she fell in."

"Like I said, she wouldn't drink so much that she would fall off a walking trail," Doc said. "I have been on that trail. It is narrow, and there is a steep cliff, but Sophia was not like me. She was disciplined and knew her alcohol limits. She would not have fallen off the edge. She was pushed. I assume by Clayton."

"Is it possible that Sophia challenged Clayton? Maybe he needed to silence her."

"That is precisely what I suspect. Sophia was somewhat like my father. She felt morally obligated to challenge authority. She constantly challenged Clayton, even though he had the power to hurt her. It is quite suspicious that, a year after her death, Clayton was assigned to the Soviet Embassy in Ottawa. I think he had a long-term plan to defect. He needed the Ottawa assignment to do that, and she likely was a threat to that."

"I have wondered about that," Arnold said. "About whether Natasha knew about his plan to defect. I assume that she knew. It was certainly to her benefit. What do you think?"

"Natasha has not talked to me about that. But I agree with you, Arnold. I would think that she knew of Clayton's defection plan, or at least suspected. She certainly wanted to defect herself."

Arnold nodded thoughtfully. "It was in Natasha's interest for Clayton to get the Ottawa assignment, positioning them for defection. If Sophia was a threat to Clayton's plan, and I am guessing that she was, Clayton had both the ability and inclination to take action. In this way, potentially both Clayton and Natasha benefited from Sophia's death.

"From what I know of Natasha's past," Arnold continued, reflecting on Natasha and Clayton's police file, "she was a young woman, in her late teens, living in Irkutsk when she met Clayton. As a dancer from Irkutsk, she couldn't get into the Bolshoi without a sponsor, and Clayton had been willing to help. He offered her a chance to study at the Bolshoi, and she took it." He glanced at Doc for confirmation, waiting for his nod before continuing. "I can easily imagine that his help was conditional. Sometimes people make decisions well aware that the cost will be heavy. But they still do it. I guess that's what Natasha did."

"Absolutely," Doc said. "One of the conditions for Natasha was that she marry Clayton. Clayton was five years older, and already established as a man who could be helpful to know, but also dangerous to know. She knew that the cost could be high. It was."

Arnold thought of his own life. He had just been out of high school a few years when he met Lillian in a downtown bar in Saskatoon. They'd known each other from school, but not well. They'd ended up having sex in the storage room off the beer vendor—not exactly a romantic setting, but still effective, in a sense. A few months later, Lillian had showed up at Arnold's apartment saying that she was pregnant and they needed to get married. Arnold had not wanted to marry Lillian, but he did. He had also not wanted to be a father, but he was. His son Jackson was born, and then a year later, perhaps in a desperate attempt to be a planned family of a kind, he and his wife had a daughter. His daughter Kathy turned out not to need parenting, or at least, she did well without support, while Jackson didn't. By the time Arnold and Lillian divorced, Jackson was established as a boy who spent most of his school experience in the student services counselling office. Jackson managed to get through school, but shortly after graduating, promptly married a young woman in an effort to save her from an abusive family. The decision had taken Jackson on a path he couldn't handle, and now, ten years later, his son was divorced, and struggling with drug and alcohol addiction.

"I imagine Natasha came to regret that decision?" Arnold asked, still thinking about his own regrets.

"Yes and no," Doc said. "If she hadn't married Clayton, Sophia, Fyodor, and I would never have been able to leave the Soviet Union. Clayton facilitated the emigration process for our family to reward Natasha for marrying him. You can potentially follow your romantic desires in the Soviet Union, but there can be costs."

Dusk was settling in, a slight haze blanketing their forest walk. The leaves on the path were softened by the wet ground, making it comfortable on their feet. For a few minutes, it was quiet again. Arnold wondered whether they were close to the trail head. He still had business to attend to with Natasha.

"I'm sorry for your loss, Doc," Arnold said finally. "Although I might add that I have found the cost of romantic desire to be high in Canada as well. But I do understand that the Soviet experience is another level of cost. The business with Natasha and Clayton must have been hard for you. But we will get to the bottom of what happened to Clayton at least. Maybe those answers will be helpful to you. I hope so."

"Thanks, Arnold," Doc said. "I doubt that Clayton's death will resolve anything that matters to me. But I admit that *his* death, at least, will not be difficult to get over. The grieving period will be short."

"Isn't that often the case? I am quite sure that grieving over my death will be exceedingly short-lived."

"I am quite sure that is the case for me as well, Arnold."

"Back to Clayton—he had excellent English skills. He had no accent at all. How did he manage that?"

"He was a KGB linguist specialist," Doc said. "Clayton easily passed himself off as a Canadian. He was brilliant with languages. He could adopt whatever patterns of speech and behaviour were necessary to achieve an objective."

"And what was his objective?" *Clearly, Clayton was a talented man,* Arnold thought to himself, reflecting for a moment on how skilled gifts can be used for a wide range of purposes, some contributing to the common good, some taking from it. Clayton, Arnold considered, had been committed to taking.

"He was a fan of money and power," Doc said. "Both were of relatively equal importance to him, but he made certain that one did not go without the other. Not exactly a unique fascination. But he pursued objectives vigorously and strategically. Not that it made him happy, but happiness was not his goal. A bourgeois sentiment, in Clayton's view."

"I suppose it is. Still, a nice feeling to have from time to time," Arnold said. "I know that he hung out at the Community Partners drop-in centre. Apparently, he went there to talk to Leonard, the summer director. It always struck me as odd that he would go to a drop-in program for marginalized folks. Do you know what prompted him to go there?"

"Remarkably, over the years, Clayton had convinced himself that he was a marginalized victim. At the drop-in centre, he felt like he was in his element. He liked Leonard. Leonard listened to his lamentations. So did Oscar White, who frequented the drop-in often."

Interesting, Arnold thought. Oscar was the custodian for both the school and the arts centre. Arnold had a small but important connection with Oscar, having watched his father play barnstorming baseball in the thirties. It allowed them to have an easy rapport. They sometimes talked about Oscar's family and what it had been like for his father to play ball in Canada and to be prevented from playing Major League Baseball because of the racist boycott of black players.

"Anyway," Doc continued, "baseball was a big part of what drew Clayton to the drop-in. It was a western sport that caught Clayton's fancy. He became an active student of the game. He found out that Leonard knew things about baseball, and they became friends of a kind."

Arnold nodded. "Annie says that Emily Little from the *Sentinel* would join them sometimes. She loves baseball. Emily and Leonard are friends of hers. I know that they both found Clayton's background interesting."

"More interesting than I did," Doc said quickly. "His past was sordid, not interesting."

"For some, sordid is interesting," Arnold said. "His Soviet background might have been a template for treachery, but certainly, at many levels, interesting as well."

"When you are young, like Emily and Leonard, and haven't experienced a police state, perhaps you find it more interesting than you should. Personally, I don't find the Soviet Union that interesting. To me, it was a gruesome reality I wanted to escape."

"What about for Clayton and Natasha?"

"They both wanted to escape the Soviet Union as well, and they did. Obviously. But defection did not work that well for Clayton. He was essentially a criminal. He was involved in crime in the Soviet Union, and he continued his activity in Canada. There is no doubt in my mind that much of his activity was outside of the law in both countries. As for Natasha, well ... she simply wanted to carry on the work her sister had started in Northford with the Arts Centre. Natasha wanted to dance and live a life in aesthetic pleasantry. She cares nothing for politics. She cares about the arts. About culture. Mostly, I think, for their own sake. Not because they are a bridge to some better world."

"You mentioned before that Clayton was very attached to Fyodor, your son. Why was that?"

"I am not sure. Maybe he wanted a son."

"But you sent Fyodor away."

"Clayton's influence was not in Fyodor's interest."

"What did you make of Clayton's affair with Sheila McCroskey?"

Doc shrugged. "Clayton had control over Sheila. He liked control. Just like I imagine he had with young Janet Sawatzky."

"Speaking of sordid," Arnold said with a grimace. He could see the descending sun at the trail head and breathed a quiet sigh of relief. "Janet Sawatzky and Clayton. A huge power imbalance there. I spoke with Janet about it and why she was driving around the countryside with him. She basically told me to mind my own business. She was nice about it but clear. She insisted that there wasn't a problem. She was just tired of high school boys with nothing to offer."

They finally entered the trail head and emerged into the full light of early evening, stopping for a moment at Oscar White's green John Deere garden tractor. Doc sat down on it for a moment, his blue dress shirt wet with perspiration at the armpits, extending along his chest. "Janet is my patient," he said. "We talked about it. I warned her about Clayton, but she also told me that she had the matter in hand. She was getting as much as she was giving, or so she said. At some level, perhaps that was true, but still, she is a young woman, vulnerable, disowned by her parents ... hardly in a position to ensure her rights and safety. I also raised the matter with Clayton. You can imagine what he told me."

"I imagine the same thing he told me. I talked to him as well. He said he wasn't breaking the law. Technically, I suppose that he wasn't. I wonder what it was that Clayton had to offer."

"Sponsorship. He promised to sponsor her through medical school."

Arnold's eyes widened a bit. He hadn't heard that particular rumour. "Was he planning on following through on that promise?"

"Who knows? Maybe. Clayton did actually have a few soft spots. He might have actually liked Janet. She *is* a good listener."

"She's also beautiful."

"That she is. Clayton destroyed people, but he also liked to save some. He'd thought that he was saving Natasha from a life of backwater dancing in Irkutsk. Maybe he thought he was saving Janet. But there was a cost."

"There always is."

"On another matter, Arnold, Clayton told me that he was under investigation, but can you tell me what he was being investigated for?"

"Tax fraud and art theft mostly. He was involved with a black-market, art-theft network."

"Including some KGB agents at embassies?"

"Yes. You know about that?"

"It was one of his hobbies in the Soviet Union. He was involved in a network of corrupt agents who sold confiscated art on the black market. Sophia knew about it. Natasha probably did as well."

"We have been investigating Clayton for a while and became aware of his past. Initially, when he moved here, the file they gave us was thin. It isn't anymore. But did Natasha know about his dealings? We have wondered about that but haven't found any evidence to support it."

"She will have been careful. It is hard to believe that she didn't know, but it is common practice in that kind of marriage to look the other way."

"I suppose. Do you think that there's any chance the KGB are involved in Clayton's death?"

Doc shook his head. "If the KGB wanted to kill Clayton, they wouldn't mess around with yellow powder. But it is odd, Arnold. The Arts Centre is preparing a play where the lead character is killed with a slingshot and hard yellow cheese. Is that a coincidence?"

"No such thing as coincidence."

Doc picked himself off the tractor, tripping on the clutch as he did and falling heavily into a muddy dip along the drainage ditch that directed water away from the ball-field. The dirt on his grey dress pants turned slimy with the previous night's rain as they walked together to the parking lot. Arnold looked at his watch. Early evening dusk was now embracing the parking area. Arnold wanted to get in his cruiser and head to the Dickey Dee, but he couldn't. Not yet. He had work to do. He needed to advise Natasha Dalrymple that her husband would not be home for supper.

As Arnold drove north along McKenzie Avenue towards Saskatchewan Street, he thought about Clayton's dead body, the footprints, and the parked car on the forest road. The suicide idea did not hold up. His growing sense was that murder and some form of international intrigue had arrived in Northford. It would be interesting to hear Natasha's thoughts.

"Probably over my head, if this is an international incident," Arnold muttered to himself. He had already been told by Constable Billy Stafford that the Saskatoon office was sending Inspector Dick Sanders to help with the case. Arnold speculated that Sanders would come with instruction from Ottawa to minimize public exposure and close the file. "File closures are a Sanders specialty. That means leaving some stones unturned, but which stones?"

Arnold pulled his black Chevy police cruiser up to the Darlymple house, perched at the west end of Saskatchewan Street, and parked. He was in no rush to chat with Natasha.

CHAPTER 4

MAYOR KEN RUSSELL PAYS MUSCLE JOHN A VISIT

Ken Russell wanted to join Arnold at the scene to see Clayton's dead body, but he hadn't said so. Instead, he'd tried to convey an impression of respectful silence. As mayor, Ken generally spoke his mind, but on this occasion, he'd thought better of it, considering that expressing an interest in Clayton's death could be misconstrued. He was right. It would have been. Still, despite his silence on the matter, respectful or not, he had walked away from Arnold and Dan feeling that he was under suspicion. It was only a matter of time before the talk around town would go to seed, then grow intrusively like the grapevines on the west side of his house. Clayton's death might seem like a gift—in fact, he was quite certain that it was—but he had a feeling that there could be a heavy cost. Public opinion could be harsh and disinterested in the truth.

Ken ambled to his restored 1959 Chevrolet Impala, resting in the shade of the giant cottonwoods along the third-base line. He was proud of his authentic restoration work, the orange paint finish, and the gleaming chrome. The car was a beauty. But apparently, he was giving the car away. It was a good cause and all, but it hurt to give it up. He would miss it. Annie had advised him that morning that it would be nice if he gave the car to Leonard Heinrichs, the Community Partners director. *"Think of it as a deserved bonus for Leonard's excellent work this summer,"* Annie had said. Ken conceded that Leonard had been underpaid and deserved the bonus, but he was unclear why it was his problem to solve. Then again, he did know why: Annie was his wife, and the board chair of Community Partners. It was what Annie wanted. So, Ken understood that it was best, all around, if he offered the gift of his car with a gracious spirit.

Annie had suggested that he needed another restoration project anyway. *"The Impala is restored, but my grandfather's 1952 Hillman Minx isn't. The vehicle has spent ten years rusting away all by itself. It's time it received the same loving and skilled attention the Impala received."* Ken had agreed. But he was still working on being enthusiastic about it.

Ken slowly lowered himself into the Impala. He started to drive off, rather faster than he intended. Kids were playing in the area, he reminded himself. He slowed down, gently easing the vehicle towards the Main Street exit. He felt a momentary sense of sadness that Annie enjoyed Arnold's company so much. He wondered what that was about. He also wondered for a moment whether Annie no longer found him interesting. It was certainly possible. He didn't find himself that interesting. He used to have a sense of humour, but he had lost it and had no idea where it had gone.

As Ken arrived at the exit leading onto Main Street, he rolled his window down and spoke for a minute with William and Adele Sawatzky. William and Adele had been standing at the ball-field entrance since early that morning, announcing the coming of the "end times" to fans and players arriving for the tournament. William and Adele were committed activists, promoting the second coming of Jesus, and the joyous prospect of God crushing all oppressors. While the list of oppressors was a moving target, Ken felt that, as the mayor, he was in a good position to be regarded as an oppressor. It felt good, in a perverse way. It almost made him forget that Annie might not find him interesting.

"Hot day for end-times promotion," Ken said to them, rather too casually.

"Not promoting, Ken. Just announcing," Adele answered sternly. "And it's not as hot as hell. What is our small discomfort compared to an eternity in hell? By the way, Ken, is it true that there's a body in the woods? Heard that fancy pants Dan McCroskey, yelling about it. Hopefully not one of the faithful. Why is it so often the undeserving who are taken?"

"I'll take it up with town council, Adele," Ken said sarcastically. "Always good to ask the big questions. By the way, does Dan wear fancy pants?"

Ken thought it was a clever question. Adele didn't.

"You know perfectly well what I mean, Mr. Mayor," Adele muttered, waving around her placard. "Dan loves to dramatize stories about false Gods from the past, pretending he knows about the world of the divine, even as he parades around like a married man when everyone knows that he is fornicating with his own sex. It is too disgusting to even think about."

Ken took a deep breath, thinking for a moment that Adele was obsessively drawn to thinking about matters she regarded as disgusting. Ken wondered what had happened in her life. There was a story there, although he was fairly certain that he didn't want to probe into the details of it. He took another deep breath and felt a sense of calm as he focussed on the sensations in his body. As he pulled away from the fairgrounds, turning left in the direction of Friesen's Pool Hall, he made a mental note that he would call Pastor Gerald Schultz and ask him to postpone the ministerial mega-service planned for the next night. Public worship and celebration needed to wait for a time when there were fewer dead people lying about in the woods.

Ken parked the Impala in the no-parking zone just in front of Friesen's Pool Hall and walked in. The hall was dark, and the low-ceiling space was thick with cigarette smoke. A row of eight occupied pinball machines lined the south wall, while the north side of the hall held a twenty-foot-long oak counter. A massive cash register held court on the counter close to the entrance, along with a glass display case with chocolate bars, packs of chewing gum with sports cards, and cigarettes. A soft-drink machine, filled with ice water, hummed loudly on the east end of the counter, from which customers could grab their own bottles of Coke, Pepsi, Sprite, or 7up. Payment was on an honour system. The rear of the hall had a plywood door with a handle the size of a baseball bat. This was the entrance to Muscle John's private quarters, where he tried his best to entice his female staff (most recently, Janet Sawatzky, who worked the till and counter purchases on Saturday afternoons). Muscle John's efforts had dropped off recently as Janet had continually rebuffed him, and more importantly, he had gotten himself a girlfriend.

Ken paused for a moment to allow his eyes to adjust to the low-hanging lighting in the hall, watching for a few minutes as Muscle John Friesen—proprietor and Northford pool champion for the last twelve years—leaned his considerable bulk over the pool table and side-banked the five-ball into the corner pocket.

"Nice shot, John."

Muscle John straightened up, looked at Ken briefly, and muttered, "I've done better, but it was pretty good. Care for a game, Mayor? Play you for twenty dollars. I'll use my left hand."

"You're a left-hander, John," Ken said, smiling.

"Right. Okay, I'll shoot with my right," John countered. "Either way, the money is mine."

Muscle John had a face that always seemed to send a message of indifferent disdain. It was a message further supported by his larger-than-life physical frame. He looked like Bluto, Popeye's fiendish bully.

Despite John's size, his actual physical prowess was not what it used to be. The muscles he'd had in high school had largely given way to softened tissue. But he still looked fierce, and he weighed a lot. His muscles might have grown soft, but if he sat on you, it would still hurt. No one wanted that to happen. As a result, the customers at Friesen's gave him a wide berth.

But Ken Russell was not afraid of Muscle John. After all, Ken was the mayor and the owner of multiple buildings. Ken had seen guys like John before. They never amounted to anything in a small town like Northford, never advancing their influence in any significant way. Ken conceded that Muscle John was a legitimate pool shark, though, the best in Northford. Perhaps even the best in the broader region. Occasionally, a stranger in Northford walked in and mistook John's confidence for empty bravado. They always left humbled and poorer. The word around town was that John had never lost a game he didn't want to lose.

As dominant as his pool reputation was, no one in Northford knew for certain how Muscle John would match up with the best in Saskatoon, or in Regina. He would drive his used, 1965 Pontiac GTO from one end of town to another, but as far as anyone knew, Muscle John never left regional limits. In Ken's view, this sharply diminished Muscle John's standing. To

Ken, John looked like a supersized goof, from his bloated head to his enormous feet, almost sliding into a caricature of himself.

Muscle John acknowledged the mayor's refusal with a grunt, and a tip of his ball cap, and then, turning his back to him, started shooting again. A small gaggle of fans stood around the table, silently nodding approval, first at his shot selection and then his flawless delivery. One after another, the balls dropped. When he had finished running the table, he clicked his cue stick into the side mount, looked at his fans, and smiled slightly. Then he looked back at Ken and the smile evaporated. "Seriously, Mr. Mayor, let's play. I would love to have some Ken Russell cash in my pocket."

"I have cash for you, John," Ken said, "if you replace a toilet in my apartment building. Number four seems to have a problem."

"Of course, it does," John responded, hitching up his jeans. John's expanding girth made suspenders necessary, but he was unaware of this. "Pretty sure it isn't the only apartment of yours that has a problem. Janet says that it stinks in the hallways. You have no idea how to manage an apartment building."

"We had a sewage issue last month. It's been fixed. Janet is happy now. You talk to her?"

"Of course, I talk to her. We have a thing. On and off. Suits my style."

"I've heard it's mostly off. Been to her place?"

"Back off, man. None of your business."

"Fine," Ken said. "It's just that I heard you came on to her, and she didn't like it. She doesn't want you coming around. I'm just looking out for her. Anyway, will you take the job?"

"I'll do it for cash. Forty dollars for my time. You supply the new toilet. Make sure it's in the apartment. But pay now. I'm a busy guy. No time to run around collecting accounts."

"Of course, you are, John," Ken said, handing him forty dollars' worth of fives and then casually adding, "I won some tournaments back in the day, even thought of doing some hustling. No time to play anymore. Sad, really, when you think about it."

"Then don't think about it," John said.

As Ken left the building, he fingered the remaining fives in his pocket. He had been expecting John to ask for eighty dollars.

Ken stepped outside and took a deep breath, feeling the late-afternoon air in his lungs. He slid back into the orange fabric of the driver's seat. The toilet assignment concluded; his mind returned to Clayton. With Clayton dead, quitting politics no longer seemed necessary. He had seriously considered it. Clayton had done a good job of sucking the joy out of politics. Clayton had run against him in the mayoral election that had just wrapped up, and had almost won, nearly stealing Ken's chance at a third term. Of course, it helped that Clayton had spread lies about him, but politics could be dirty. With Clayton, it certainly was.

One of Clayton's lies had involved a winter business conference that Ken had attended in Barbados. Drunken behaviour had ensued, and someone in Ken's hotel suite had thrown a television off the sixth-floor balcony. No one had been injured, but someone could have been. The story might have died a natural death, if not for Clayton Dalrymple's powers of fabrication.

During the election campaign, Clayton had claimed to have reams of evidence, none of which he ever revealed, that Ken had actually thrown the television himself, and that in fact, a resort staff member had been killed in the incident. Clayton further claimed that Ken had covered up the matter by bribing the Barbados police. The story was not true, but Ken's efforts to defend himself had fallen on deaf ears. It was an effective story. Even though most people felt that Clayton was probably exaggerating, the story still caused folks to doubt Ken's integrity.

Ken continued down Main Street, planning to take a brief detour to his municipal office to check on phone messages, and then on to the Dickey Dee. As he drove, he thought about yesterday morning, wondering whether he should say anything to Arnold about it. Bringing a plate of Medovik, a Russian dessert cake, to Clayton had been Annie's idea. It was a popular honey cake in Russia, and Annie suggested that it would be a kind gesture and a peace offering that would be appreciated. *"Even though you won the election, you still have to work with Clayton on council,"* Annie had said. So, Ken had delivered the cake. Granted, the visit had been a failure, but that wasn't Ken's fault. Clayton had been silently enigmatic, giving Ken a clear message, that peace was not imminent. Clayton had accepted the cake but with the coldness of a prairie winter night.

There were no messages for Ken at his office, and he briefly wondered whether his secretary had slipped out for the afternoon. Generally, there were messages, even on a Saturday. He was briefly relieved but not for long. He felt mildly irrelevant as he left the office and slipped back into his Impala. There was a dead body of a council member in the Northford woods, and yet no one had called him to inquire, complain, or whatever it is that people like to do when they call the mayor. Something seemed amiss.

In due course, Ken drove down Main Street to the Dickey Dee, parked off to the side (safely away from other vehicles), and turned off the motor. The purring sound of the V8 engine quieted and then stopped. He smiled. He had put the engine in himself. It had been the final task of the restoration project. The powerful rumble of the engine stayed with him for a moment as he reflected on the silence. Then his mind returned to his morning visit with Clayton yesterday. It worried him. If Arnold learned about it, it could give the wrong impression. Clayton was the only witness though, and he wasn't talking. Annie knew about it, of course, but he thought it unlikely that she would mention it to Arnold. Why would she? Annie had a keen political sense. Ken decided to take a chance and withhold the detail. If, by chance, Annie mentioned it, he would simply acknowledge the event for what it was: an innocent peace offering. In politics, and in life, it was always better, Ken thought, to limit information to a need-to-know basis.

CHAPTER 5

ARNOLD INFORMS NATASHA OF HER HUSBAND'S DEATH

It was well into the evening when Arnold pulled into Natasha Dalrymple's driveway. It had been a long day. Missing lunch, sweating at the ballpark for longer than desired, delaying a cheeseburger, viewing a dead body and the suspicious scene surrounding it, having an inordinately long conversation with Dan McCroskey, and an even longer one with Doc.... Of course, the conversations with Dan and Doc had been mostly business, which was fine, and both conversations had been informative. But still, he longed for the work details of the day to end and for cheeseburger eating at the Dickey Dee to begin.

Mick Jagger was singing on the radio, complaining about his lack of satisfaction. Generally, Arnold loved the Jagger lament, but it seemed too close to home for the day's events. He punched in his other pre-set radio station. Arnold only listened to two stations. The sounds of the Brandenburg Concerto filled the vehicle. Arnold loved classical music. Especially the stringed instruments. At home, in the evening, he played a steady diet of Beethoven and Brahms cello sonata recordings. In his police cruiser, it depended on how the day was going. On difficult days, he often preferred the world of classic rock: Jefferson Airplane, Eric Burdon and the Animals, and Queen, and on a really dark day, Led Zeppelin. The Rolling Stones were always good to hear, and the Beatles, but he generally preferred the vocals of Gracie Slick and Jefferson Airplane, when navigating difficult police work.

Arnold reluctantly turned the radio off, turned off the engine, and stepped out of his vehicle, noting that William Sawatzky was raking leaves into a massive pile in his front yard. Arnold wondered whether William was planning on having a fire or burying a body. He wasn't burying Clayton, as much as he probably wanted to. Clayton's body was safely in the hands of Dr. Robert Morley, now likely deep in the bowels of the Northford General Hospital. William and Adele Sawatzky lived a few houses to the east, at the corner of Saskatchewan and McKenzie. Arnold felt a moment of empathy for Natasha. It must be difficult to live so close to an archenemy.

It must be unsettling, he thought to himself, *to have neighbours who paint death slogans on your garage.*

Arnold walked slowly and deliberately toward Natasha's front door, trying to envision the outcome of his conversation with her. He thought about the tone of voice he wanted to use. He reminded himself that he needed to be cautious with his tone. He was aware that he should feel some measure of sympathy, but at the same time, he noted that he felt none. He would have to pretend. He had a difficult message he had to deliver. Whether or not Natasha was close to her husband was beside the point. Regardless of their relationship, the news that her husband was not coming home for supper needed to be delivered sensitively. Arnold remembered the last conversation he'd had with Natasha. She had been cynical, caustic, and critical, giving the local police department failing grades. Given the news he now had to deliver, Arnold reflected that his standing with Natasha was not likely to improve.

That spring, Natasha had shown up at his office to register a formal complaint regarding the Sawatzkys. It was a legitimate complaint. She had caught Muscle John Friesen spray painting "death to the atheists," on her workshop/garage. She had challenged him, and he had confessed that (while he was in agreement with the slogan) he could not in good conscience take credit for the idea. That had come from William and Adele Sawatzky.

Arnold had tried to reassure Natasha that justice would be done, but she did not believe him. Her confidence in police impotence was deeply felt. *"Nothing will be done, Arnold,"* she had said. *"Nothing at all. You know it. I know it. You will talk to them, you will warn them, and then the matter will be considered dealt with. But it won't be."*

Natasha was not wrong. Charges in the matter were laid but with no significant penalty. Muscle John was sentenced to do community service work at the Northford Four-Square Gospel Church—work that he was already doing as a volunteer. William and Adele were ordered to cease and desist with the harassment. But that had proved ineffective. They'd stopped the death slogans but still left homemade eviction orders in the Dalrymples' mailbox: *"Leave Northford or burn in hell."*

The Dalrymple home was a modern, split-level affair at the end of Saskatchewan Street, with a rear door leading to the Northford Woodlands Forest. A deep gully separated the backyard from the forest, although an arched, wooden foot bridge allowed for pedestrians or cyclists to cross over. The gully had minimal water during the summer, just enough to invite birds and willow growth, but in the spring, heavy flows filled the gully. By fall, it was almost always dry, as it was now.

A two-car cedar garage was attached to the east of the house. A person could walk directly into the garage from the side door of the house. Arnold glanced into the window of the garage, noting the workshop area, and Natasha's black BMW. There was an empty space where Arnold supposed Clayton had parked his Mustang Fastback, which by now was at the police compound.

Natasha opened the front door slightly. Pausing for a moment, and then recognizing Arnold, she stepped back just as the overhead light in the red and white portico came on. Arnold opened the door fully and walked in.

Natasha presented herself with an erect posture and a half smile, mildly warm but not fully embracing the idea of staying that way. She wore a tie-dyed blouse of many colours, and a yellow skirt, hemmed slightly above the knee. A pair of dressy teal sandals, the kind one might wear for a formal event, adorned her feet. Arnold thought to himself that the rainbow was fully represented in her clothing.

"You look like a dancer," Arnold said awkwardly, removing his Stetson as he cautiously stepped into the foyer.

"I am a dancer," Natasha said coldly, flipping a strand of her straight brassy blonde hair over her ears. "You know that, Sergeant. You have seen me dance at the Arts Centre. Of course, I am not as agile as I was, when as a young prodigy, I left Irkutsk to study at the Bolshoi. But that is the past. Time brings loss. I may be past my dancing prime; forty-two is not young for a dancer, but the posture and balance of my training has not left me. Can I assume that you did not come here to tell me that I look like a dancer?"

"I did not," he said. "Stupid thing to say, really. My apologies. I am somewhat anxious. We should perhaps, have a seat, if you don't mind."

Arnold entered into the open space of the family room and sat down on a brilliantly white sofa that looked like it had, until recently, been wrapped in plastic. *Perhaps, it was,* he thought to himself. *Either that, or it's a recent purchase.* "Lovely sofa," Arnold said quietly. "Hope my clothes are clean." He carefully balanced his hat on the sofa's closest arm.

"I hope so too," Natasha retorted, sitting down opposite Arnold in a wood, press-back chair. She continued in a tone more imperious than Arnold thought was warranted. "A recent purchase from Eaton's. It wasn't free. I imagine you have come to inform me of Clayton's death? Dan phoned."

Arnold was surprised, and it showed. "He should have waited for me to tell you," Arnold said rather brusquely. "Informing family is not a pleasant task, but it is my job. Not Dan's. Still, I concede that Dan is correct. Clayton's body was found this afternoon in the Northford woods."

"Dan said that he found the body. Apparently, Clayton was shot?"

"He was shot, yes. But the scene is somewhat confusing. We have some work to do."

"Clayton—or Ivan Kalik, I suppose, his real name—was never destined for a long life. When you live on the edge, it is easy to fall off."

"I suppose that's true. Why did Dan call you?"

"Dan and I work together, Arnold. We are friends. He gets excited. Can't help himself. He did not intend on offending you."

"Still, it wasn't his place." He sighed and then got down to business.

Arnold explained that the scene around Clayton's body was being investigated as a possible suicide, although homicide was being considered.

Natasha took the news with stoic calm. Having been informed of the basic facts around her husband's death, she rose from her chair, seemingly considering the visit to be concluded. But Arnold did not get up. He had further business. He wanted to get some sense of her relationship with Clayton. It also seemed fitting that he find out about her activity that morning. So, despite Natasha's body language telling him that he was free to leave, he didn't.

Arnold noted a framed poster on the wall, advertising an Arts Centre play, a Dashiell Hammett murder mystery with a squinting Inspector Sam Spade blowing a cloud of cigarette smoke into space. It reminded Arnold that having a smoke might help relax the mood of the visit.

"Would you mind if I smoked?"

"If you are not leaving, we might as well," Natasha said. Arnold slowly rose, offering her a cigarette from his Du Maurier package. He lit hers, and she smiled ever so slightly but said nothing. Arnold lit his cigarette, and as he tucked his lighter away, he noted that there were no ashtrays on the coffee table, or for that matter, anywhere in the room. Natasha made no move to retrieve one.

To the left of the poster, directly over the fireplace, hung a certificate with a dancing figure and Natasha's name. The certificate had the Saskatchewan Provincial logo on it.

"Was that award for dance?" Arnold asked. "Congratulations. Your skills have been a great gift to Northford."

"I won a dance competition in Saskatoon a few years ago. It is always pleasant to have your work appreciated and recognized. Would you not agree, Sergeant?"

"I am sure that it is, Natasha," he said, finding himself slipping into her more formal speech patterns. "I have never won anything, but I agree that there is pleasure in being appreciated." Arnold took a light draw on his cigarette. The smoke enveloped and then curled away from his face. He left the cigarette in his mouth for a moment, trying to emphasize the notion that procuring an ashtray might be a good idea. But Natasha made no move to produce one. He started to seriously wonder where he would put his ashes. For that matter, he was curious where Natasha would put hers.

Natasha continued to sit with her hands clasped together in her lap, looking quite regal in spite of the cigarette poking out from between two of her fingers. A small table on her left held a few neatly stacked *Chatelaine* magazines. On her right, a glass-top display table featured a small, bronze dancing figure. A long wooden coffee table held a dance figure at each end. The room had a minimalist look, except for the dominating dance theme. Still, Arnold considered, an ashtray would be a fitting addition.

"I should thank you for informing me, Sergeant Powell. You have done your duty. Is there anything else you need to say to me? Or ask me?"

There was. "Do you have an ashtray?" he asked rather more urgently than he wanted.

"Will you be staying long enough to require one?"

"Probably."

"In that case, you might want to reach under the sofa and pull one out. I do not like to have them visibly lounging about," Natasha said, coolly.

Arnold pulled out the smallest ash tray he had ever seen. It was glass, with three miniature legs and a single indent for cigarette placement, clearly not designed for group smoking. "A very small but attractive ashtray," Arnold observed, placing it gently on the coffee table that sat between them.

"An ashtray's beauty is diminished by its function, which is to hold ash, and ultimately, cigarette butts. A small ashtray limits use and retains some measure of dignity. At least that is my limited thinking on the matter," Natasha pronounced in a monotone voice. "Ashtray size is one of the few things that Clayton and I agreed on."

"You talked with Clayton about the size of ashtrays?"

"Not directly. But we did smoke together every day. Recently, he mentioned that he liked this one. I said that I preferred small ashtrays. He nodded and did not disagree. That is as close to agreement as one could get with Clayton."

"You and Doc—I mean Alexei—are close?" Arnold asked, feeling that the ashtray conversation had exhausted itself.

"We are. Or were, at least. We are not as close as we used to be. We were lovers, back in the Soviet Union. I might as well tell you. It is bound to come out." Her voice had quieted to a near whisper. "Perhaps, with Clayton gone, we can return to such intimacies. That would be nice."

"I do have a few more questions, Ms. Dalrymple. May I call you that?"

"I would rather you not. You can call me Natasha. If you want my full name, it is Natasha Gulko. Gulko was my father's name. I took on Ivan's last name, Kalik, when we married, but frankly, I never liked Ivan *or* his last name. I liked him even less when he changed his first name to Clayton, and his last to Dalrymple. Ridiculous name as far as I am concerned. Some baseball player, apparently," she said indifferently.

Arnold Powell leaned forward, sitting on the edge of the sofa, not wanting to make himself too comfortable or drop an ash in the wrong place. The perch felt precarious, as though he would disappear into the fabric if he sat back. He also noted that he was sitting lower than Natasha. The seating dynamic did not make for intimate conversation, but then, Arnold realized, the arrangement likely suited her.

"I do have work to do," Natasha said. "Proceed quickly, if you can manage it."

"There was a Russian M1895 handgun lying beside Clayton. We are checking prints. Did he have a gun like that?

"Yes, he did. I am not knowledgeable about guns, but I am aware that Clayton was a collector."

"Do you have any reason to think that he would commit suicide?" Arnold asked then.

Natasha laughed lightly, blowing an impressively defined smoke ring gently but firmly into the air. "For a tough guy, Clayton had a high degree of sensitivity. He threatened suicide shortly after he defected. He was disappointed with Canada. He had thought he would have influence here. That did not happen. All he had here was a life of petty crime without the power of the KGB uniform. It did not satisfy."

"What kind of petty crime?"

"You will know more about that than I, Sergeant. He was under investigation by the RCMP. He liked to dabble on the edge of the law. The details of his involvements were not my concern or interest. But as you know, he was under legal stress. His options were diminishing."

"Are you aware of anyone who would harm him?"

Natasha laughed, a bit more loudly this time, and looked around the living-room space as though she were trying to find something comforting. *"Everyone* wanted to harm him. Clayton had that kind of attractive personality. But most of the people *capable* of hurting him were in the Soviet Union. He made enemies wherever he went, but in Northford, most folks aren't prepared to kill. They may paint death slogans on your garage, or speak ill of you behind your back, but killing others is less of a practical option here. Good thing, I suppose. In the Soviet Union, killing others for various purposes has become quite commonplace, almost to the point of being accepted as a natural part of the human experience."

Natasha paused then, and Arnold noted that she seemed surprised by the length of her own speech. Finally, Natasha's eyes settled on a dimly lit lamp, sitting on a bookshelf along the east wall, and walked over to turn it off. As she returned to her press-back chair and resumed her regal posture, she smiled at Arnold.

"Is the evidence not clear?" she asked gently. "Suicide or murder would look quite different, would they not?"

"Generally, but sometimes there are complications. Given Clayton's background, an inspector from Saskatoon will be joining the investigation on Monday," Arnold said. "We will unfortunately be troubling you again."

"Given that Clayton was a Soviet defector, I can imagine that there might be complications. His death will be of interest to Canadian authorities, perhaps even the Soviets. But it is not of particular interest to me," Natasha said firmly. "Anything else?"

"Do you know anything about his plans this morning? He was wearing a sports jacket and had a pea coat with him as well. It looked like he was meeting with someone. Is that possible?"

"Life is jam full of possibilities. He did mention having a meeting with someone. I do not know who or where. Clayton did not tell me about his business activities. We kept our conversation to a bare minimum. Strange for a married couple or perhaps not so strange. Clayton did as he pleased. Sometimes he was around; sometimes he wasn't. I preferred it when he wasn't. I imagine that he did as well."

"But he did say he had a meeting?"

"Yes, he did. I assumed it was in Saskatoon. He has business associates there. He certainly did not mention going to the Northford woods. Mind you, maybe he was feeling nostalgic for the Soviet Union. People die in the woods quite a lot there."

"What do you know about his legal troubles?" Arnold asked, watching as her posture stiffened slightly. He was surprised. It was not easy to be even more rigid than she had already been.

"I know that he was about to be charged," she said. "Not sure with what. Selling stolen art on the black market, I imagine. That was one of his special hobbies. He had a well-established network. I can tell you that he was concerned about his legal situation. I imagine he was looking at some dire consequences. You would think a man like Clayton would get used to legal troubles. But apparently not. He had been quite distraught recently."

"Well," Arnold said, "he likely would have been deported and handed over to the Soviets. He had cause for concern." He noted that Natasha did not show any emotion at the thought.

"Returning to the Soviet Union would have been a death sentence." She inhaled deeply and blew a cloud of smoke around her attractive but indifferent face.

"Did you have information on him? Information that could be damaging to him?" Arnold asked.

"I did," Natasha said with a matter-of-fact tone. "I could have gotten him into trouble in the Soviet Union. But I didn't. I could have gotten him into trouble in Canada as well, but I didn't. I didn't have to. He did that all by himself. It was only a matter of time before he and his corrupt network of KGB agents would be caught. He loved the profit margin of taking stolen art and selling it on the black market."

"Why didn't you inform on him?"

"I benefited from remaining silent," Natasha said, raising her voice slightly, as well as her eyebrows, which were now higher than Arnold would have thought was possible. It was like her admission was causing her bodily upset, as if she had sat on something long and hard and was noting a measure of its discomfort. "Exposing him would have cost me more than I was prepared to pay."

"What would it have cost you?"

"Probably my life," Natasha said, with a resigned smile.

"Did he threaten you?"

"Of course. Almost every day." Natasha again stood up, moving back to the lamp she had turned off and turning it back on. The dim bulb did little to improve either the lighting in the room or the mood.

"Given that, surely Clayton's death is good for you."

"Yes, it is," she said in a brisk tone. "I admit that I wanted him dead. *Everyone* who met Clayton wanted him dead but wanting a man dead is quite different than killing him. You probably wanted him dead. But you didn't do it. Right?"

"I try to avoid killing anyone. In my line of work, killing members of the public impedes a police officer's promotional options," Arnold said, looking directly at Natasha as she stared blankly into the abyss of the room. "Do you know of any direct threats that Clayton received?"

"No direct threats," Natasha said dismissively.

"Indirect threats?"

"Maybe. There was a man who came by the house recently to meet with Clayton. I don't know who he was, but Clayton was agitated."

"Was this a man from Northford?" Arnold asked, skeptically. Something in her expression wasn't sitting right with him.

"Never saw him before."

"Appearance?"

"Quite large. Somewhat menacing."

"Can you describe him in more detail? What was he wearing?" Arnold asked, squinting his eyes slightly and flicking a drooping stretch of cigarette ash into the ashtray.

For the first time in the conversation, Natasha laughed somewhat warmly. "I could try. I am not very good at remembering details. But I believe that he wore a grey coat."

"What time of day?"

"Late afternoon," Natasha said hesitantly. "Just before supper."

"It has been quite warm lately. Not much cause for coat wearing."

"It has been," Natasha added tentatively. "But some people like to live dangerously."

"Did Clayton say anything about this stranger?"

65

Natasha emitted a surface chuckle, somewhat derisive in tone. "No, he did not. But then Clayton was habitually secretive. I might be mistaken. I occasionally am. I admit to being paranoid about the KGB. I have good reason to be. They murdered my father, though probably Clayton did the honours. Still, I did wonder whether this man was one of the corrupt KGB agents Clayton did business with. Maybe the man was blackmailing Clayton. Maybe Clayton wasn't sufficiently cooperative. He was addictively uncooperative, you know. But I could be wrong. For all I know, the man was a life-insurance agent. Clayton was a good candidate for life insurance."

Arnold thought about that for a moment, shifting his position on the soft sofa. He felt incredibly awkward. The sofa did not allow him to sit upright enough to present a firm, serious presence in the room. He was also baffled by Natasha's near complete absence of emotion. The news of her husband's death didn't reveal even a momentary look of upset or tenderness. *Perhaps,* Arnold thought, *there really wasn't any to reveal.*

"You seem to know more than you initially suggested," Arnold said. "Why didn't you tell me this before?

"Tell you what before?"

"About your suspicion of blackmail. About the KGB killing your father. Or Clayton killing your father."

"I have no evidence that he was being blackmailed. I also have no evidence that he killed my father. I just think he did. Simply cynical speculation based on my experience of how he operated. I really know very little about Clayton's life, and frankly, what I do know, I wish I didn't."

"Clayton defected, with you, about five years ago. If the KGB wanted to blackmail him, or kill him, they would have done it sooner; wouldn't they?"

"If you are a person of interest to the KGB, they will get around to you. Sometimes they like to make you wait. They enjoy that. But what do I know?"

"You didn't inform our office of any suspicious activity at your home. If you thought he was being blackmailed, or that the KGB were in contact, you should have been in touch with us."

"Maybe I should have. But I didn't. It is possible that I didn't care if he was in trouble. Why go to the police? All I know is that a strange man visited Clayton. If Clayton was in trouble, that wasn't necessarily a problem for me. Maybe it was good for me. I suppose this is all very suspicious and makes me a look like a suspect?" Natasha took a final draw on her cigarette and then crushed the remainder into the tiny ashtray. She needed to lean over to perform this action, and it meant bending her back rather more than she wanted. She groaned slightly. "I have not done my stretches today," she explained. "I am not as young as I once was. But then, that has already been noted."

"I never do stretches," Arnold said. "But then, I suppose that my conditioning has also been noted. As for a being a suspect, at this point, I am merely trying to understand what happened in the woods today. It would be helpful if you could tell me where you were this morning, between seven and nine-thirty."

She nodded, thinking for a moment before speaking. "I left the house just before seven. I ran for an hour ... to the river-park loop. Then I met with Emily Little at the *Sentinel* a little after eight o'clock. She was running a piece for the paper on the upcoming Medb play. Then I picked up some items at the pharmacy, chatted with Bernie Lieberman, and jogged home. I got home around nine this morning."

"Anyone see you on the run before your meeting with Emily?"

"People were out. A scantily dressed woman came out of Dr. Morley's house around seven-thirty. She got into a cab. Morley and Clayton are different in most respects, but they both like sex in the morning. There was also Janet Sawatzky, who waved at me just before eight. She was walking into the school library. Janet is a nice girl, quite downtrodden, but has recently become another of Clayton's women. She is rather young to be described as a woman, but given what she was doing for Clayton, we might as well promote her to that standing. She was living within the dregs of the adult world."

"I am aware of that relationship."

"It wasn't a relationship, Arnold. Janet was simply doing what a desperate young woman sometimes needs to do to get what she wants. It was nothing more than that."

"I suppose that you're right about that, Natasha," Arnold said quietly. "I prefer to hold off on commenting on Janet's relations with Clayton. Back to your situation. Was Clayton gone when you came home?"

"Yes, he was. I looked into the workshop. His car was gone. So was the breakfast mug and the cake. The empty plate was still sitting on the workshop table, which was strange."

"What cake?" Arnold asked, trying desperately to make some eye contact with Natasha, but to no avail. "And what was strange?"

"Ken Russell delivered the cake to us Friday morning. Yesterday. A peace offering that Clayton rudely accepted, I might add. As to what was weird, well ... that is likely a minor matter."

"Let me decide what is minor, if you don't mind, Natasha," Arnold said, thinking that anything Natasha was willing to share was likely worth paying attention to.

"The breakfast mug not being there, beside the plate. Clayton always drank his breakfast drink in the workshop. And he would leave it there. He was not a big believer in picking up after himself. But it wasn't in the kitchen either. Where was the mug? I don't know. I found its absence rather unusual."

Arnold conceded that it was both odd and probably minor after all, though he made note of it. Leaning back in the sofa, he sank deeper and deeper into its seemingly limitless contours. He felt that he might be disappearing entirely into the sofa. Talking with Natasha did make the notion of disappearance attractive, of course. She was a beautiful woman, but the personality she presented was decidedly unattractive.

"The mug was in the woods with him. Do you have any idea why Clayton would have taken his mug to the woods?"

"I did not know that he had," she said, frowning slightly. "Dan didn't mention that. Or at least, I don't think he did. I have been a bit flustered. But I can say with certainty that bringing a mug to the woods was not typical for Clayton. I cannot explain that. Of course, he was under legal stress. Hopefully his last round of chess with Sheila was satisfying."

"Chess?"

"I am joking. Bad taste. I apologize. Sheila didn't come to our house for chess. Although if she had, she would have learned a lot. Clayton was an expert player. But Sheila came for sex, and presumably, Clayton provided that."

"You are sure that they met this morning?"

68

"I am. I was still at home, a few minutes before seven this morning, when Sheila poked her head in the front door. She saw me in the kitchen and took off. Usually, she waits for me to leave. Not today. I suspect that she just wanted to annoy me. When I left the house, I saw her lighting up a smoke in the alley. It was obvious to me that she was going to return to our house. I presume that she did."

"What time was this?"

"Seven o'clock."

"Where was Clayton when you left for your run?"

"In his bedroom. He likes Sheila to come to him. It's a thing."

"Doc said that Clayton makes the breakfast drink."

"He does. He makes a batch once a week and puts it in the refrigerator. I poured a mug for both of us and left them on the kitchen counter. I was going to drink mine after my run."

"Anything else on the counter?" Arnold asked. He tried, with some success, to emerge from the sofa, raising his upper body towards the coffee table, so that his knees actually touched the white shag carpet.

"Just the piece of Medovik cake," Natasha said calmly, picking up a *Chatelaine* and flipping through the pages as though she were looking for something. "Clayton is obsessed with health, but Medovik is a guilty pleasure for him. Personally, I don't eat Medovik. Sweet foods are not 'my thing.'"

"So, when you left, both mugs were on the counter, full of juice, and a piece of Medovik cake. What was the arrangement of the mugs?"

"They were arranged like a trophy. Close to each other, with Clayton's handle to the left, and mine to the right."

"And what did the counter look like when you returned from your run?"

"It was bare. I always drink my juice when I get back from the run, but this morning, my mug was gone. It should have been on the counter, but it wasn't. I don't know what happened. Clayton or Sheila must have drunk it, or dumped it out, and then cleaned the mug. Very rude if you ask me."

"You are sure that Clayton was by himself when you left?"

"Yes. Other than seeing Sheila for a moment before I left, no one else was around."

"Did you say anything to Sheila when she poked her head in?"

"I prefer not to speak to Sheila. Not a fan. I didn't mind her affair with Clayton, but I do not approve of her treatment of Dan."

"You and Dan are close?

"Not in the way you make that sound. But we work well together. I have come to sympathize with his personal situation, as he has come to sympathize with mine."

"Doc told me about Clayton's morning routine. Sounds like a tight schedule?"

"It is tight, but Clayton is efficient. Especially with sex. He does not believe in foreplay."

"Tell me more about this breakfast drink."

"Clayton makes a large pitcher of it every weekend and puts it in the refrigerator. It lasts us the week. The taste is awful because of the mixture of local plants he puts in. It consists of carrot and cucumber juice, together with a dried herbal plant mix. The combination of flavours is unbelievably pungent. Drinking it requires commitment."

"Which both of you shared?"

"We shared a commitment to health."

Arnold asked Natasha to show him into the kitchen and demonstrate the mug placement for him on the counter. He looked inside the refrigerator and noted a glass container about three quarters full of a green liquid with a distinctive smell and unappealing appearance. "I suppose commitment to health *would* be required to drink that," Arnold observed, as he closed the refrigerator door. "Not that it helped Clayton today."

"If a person is going to shoot themselves, even a vitamin supplement like a breakfast drink can't prevent it," Natasha said briskly, standing by the kitchen counter and looking out the large window that faced the Northford woods. "If you limit a person's choices sufficiently, suicide becomes a reasonable option."

Arnold decided to ignore the comment. *Clearly*, he thought to himself, *she's criticizing the pressure the police had placed on Clayton.* Still, she also appeared to be in favour of it. He was curious what her broader point had been. Natasha didn't seem like the kind of person who said anything without a purpose.

"How did you get to the office this morning?" Arnold asked.

"I drove my BMW. I showered, got dressed for work, and grabbed a yogurt, and then got there a little before nine-thirty."

"Anyone see you?" Arnold asked, more skeptically than he'd intended.

"Oscar was mucking around in the drainage ditch. He saw me. William and Adele saw me as well. I had a smoke with Dan shortly after I got to work. Probably a little after nine-thirty. Oscar gave me a slight wave. The kind he does."

"Anyone else in the office?"

"Madeline was in her office when I got there. Also Dan."

"Do you always work on Saturday?"

"No, but we have a show coming up in the fall. Lots to do."

Arnold was quiet for a moment as he jotted down some notes. "Do you think you could you identify the handgun?"

"I think so. We could look at his workshop and see if any handguns are missing. He had them on a wall display. I could show you."

They went through the interior door into the workshop, and Arnold took a careful look around. Natasha eyed her surroundings carefully as well, seemingly as interested in the setting as Arnold.

The workshop was pristinely clean and organized. There was no doubt that Clayton was a man of order. It was also apparent that he had skill with metal sculpture. Arnold noticed a number of specialized tools, carefully arranged, near a six-foot-high bronze statue of a human figure kneeling and leaning forward, with its head down in a prayerful posture and pressing up against the chest of a smaller figure, like a child. The two figures were clearly in an embrace. It was a touching piece of work.

"His work looks very professional," Arnold said. "Not that I know anything about metal sculpture. But it looks like he was serious about the art form."

"Clayton was serious about everything. Not a light-hearted bone in his body. As for his handgun collection, looks to me like the M1895 is missing," Natasha said, surveying the wall of guns on display.

"You're sure?" Arnold asked. "You said that you don't know anything about guns."

"I don't. But I can read," she said derisively. "The name tag above the empty slot on the wall says, 'M1895.' Each item in his collection is identified with a tag. His guns were collectables. Worth putting a tag on, I guess. Probably have value to the right person."

"Have you had a break-in?"

"No break-in. But if Clayton planned to shoot himself, he will have needed a gun. Looks like he took one."

"True enough. It might have been required for his 'meeting' as well."

"For certain. In Clayton's world, a gun is often required for a meeting. But was there actually a meeting? I could not say."

"Someone else was in the woods with him."

"How do you know this?"

"Large footprints. And someone hit Clayton with something, leaving behind a broken watch, bruising, and a scattering of yellow powder. Do you know anything about that?"

Natasha took a long pause and sat down in the workshop chair Clayton used for sculpture. She took a deep breath, and sounding more genuinely reflective now, said, "Dan mentioned the large footprints and yellow powder to me on the phone. He was quite perplexed by that. So am I."

"Why?"

"For the same reason it perplexes you, I suppose. It is strange. I'm confused by it." After another pause, she continued. "I don't understand what the connection can be, but it is curious that the production we are working on for this fall is about a character who is killed with hard cheese. This yellow powder might not even be hard cheese, but what if it is? That would be odd."

"More than odd, Natasha. Does the character in your play have large feet?"

"Foot size is not mentioned in the ancient Irish myth of Medb. None of the actors in the play have large feet, or at least, not as far as I have noticed. Of course, it is possible that someone with large feet has been watching our rehearsals."

"Using hard cheese as a weapon of death seems a bit ridiculous."

"It is, for certain, but that is the way the legend of Medb has been passed down. We are simply honouring it. Our play is a dramatic reproduction of myth. The story is not claiming to be true."

"But it is true that Clayton is dead, and yellow powder was found at the scene."

"I am not disputing that, Sergeant. But if the powder *does* turn out to be cheese, someone would almost certainly have gotten the idea from our play, and I don't understand who or why. Of course, it is probably *not* cheese. And if not for the timing with the play, I doubt anyone would have thought of cheese at all upon seeing it."

He had to admit that she had a point but didn't let himself become distracted by it.

"You have absolutely no idea who might have misunderstood the play? I notice you didn't bring up the yellow powder until I did, though you just admitted that Dan had already told you about it. That confuses me. Why did you wait for me to mention it? Assuming that it *is* cheese, it would obviously be connected in some way with your play."

"I suppose that is why," Natasha said earnestly. "It could incriminate the Arts Centre, one of our actors perhaps, or perhaps someone who watched a rehearsal. I don't want the Arts Centre to be connected to Clayton's death. No one at the centre has any cause to be involved in it. He was not popular, but no one benefits from his death."

"Other than you."

"Fine. Other than me. I do benefit. I concede to having a motive, but I did not kill him."

"Then why are you withholding?"

"Am I withholding?"

"I believe that you are."

"Really? Alright, Sergeant, I admit to a slight measure of withholding. I am sorry. But there is a reason. When Dan mentioned the yellow powder and the large footprints, I kept thinking about yesterday afternoon and the missing gun. I was withholding because it involved Dan. But Dan didn't do anything. He did not kill Clayton."

"Then what *did* involve Dan? What missing gun? What happened yesterday afternoon, Natasha? Talk to me."

She sighed heavily and closed her eyes for a minute before speaking again. "Now that Clayton is dead, it all sounds so serious. To be honest, I guess it was serious. But not the way it seems. I did not think that Clayton

73

would be dead today. In fact, it was just the opposite. I thought I would be. Clayton promised to kill me this morning. But obviously he didn't."

"You thought you would be dead today?" He shook his head, baffled. "And yet you went for a run this morning, did business with Emily at the *Sentinel*, and went to the pharmacy and then to work, all of which seems rather unnecessary on a day when you are expecting to die. You even drank that horrible health drink, which hardly seems worthwhile if you expected to die. Please, Natasha. Maybe I'm just a bit daft, but I don't understand."

"I am a person of strong habits, Arnold," Natasha said with a firm, even tone. She got up from her chair then, and with her posture still stiff and formal, she walked over to the west window of the family room. The evening sun was really low now, and the moon was nearly full. Natasha studied the scene for a moment, and then (taking a deep, slow breath) she did a deep knee bend, with her feet close together and turned outwards, spreading her arms gracefully outwards before letting them drop slowly back to her sides and straightening herself back to a standing position.

She still moves like a dancer, he thought appreciatively, noting that the exercise seemed to have improved her disposition slightly, as she then walked towards the sofa where Arnold sat, turned on a standing lamp, smiling briefly, and then returned to her chair, regaining her previous seated position almost precisely.

"You may not understand my morning activities in light of what I have told you, Arnold, and that is fine. I concede that it looks suspicious. But the fact remains that that is what I did. I am not sure that I understand it myself, except that I am a person who doesn't concede defeat. This morning, I did think that my life was over, but I was wrong, wasn't I? You never know what can happen. Anyway, even if I had died today, carrying on with my business would have been a better choice that sitting in my house waiting for Clayton to 'do me in.' No advantage in that for me. Turns out that I was right. I got a break. I have not had many in my life, so I will gladly take it."

"I am sure that you will," Arnold said softly, making a note in his writing pad. Arnold was quite relieved. He had been wondering whether Natasha might turn on a real light. The room was not well lit, and among his various physical troubles on the sofa, he'd been having difficulty seeing his notepad clearly. The standing lamp helped a great deal. He placed a series of question marks on his pad, adding a note that Natasha had many witnesses who would likely corroborate her morning activities.

Is she lying about the prospect of being killed this morning? Why would she lie about that? If she'd had some plan in place to prevent getting shot, like ensuring that Clayton died instead, she didn't need to come up with this story about Clayton killing her.

"Alright. Please explain how you 'knew' that you were going to die today," Arnold said. "I'm not questioning the truth of your statement, simply trying to understand it."

"Fair enough," Natasha said coolly. "I will explain as best I can."

"Thank you. And I still want to know what you were talking about when you mentioned Dan and the missing gun. I didn't get the sense that you were referring to the gun we found in the woods."

"Yes. I will get to that." She frowned slightly and then began. "Yesterday afternoon, Clayton was at the Arts Centre and very upset. He was angry and drunk. Never a good combination for anyone, especially Clayton. I know why he was upset. As I was as well. We'd had a frank discussion on Thursday evening that involved our unsavory past and diminishing future. It was not a promising picture, or discussion. It all began with me digging through Clayton's personal things, finding secrets that he did not want me to find, and then me sharing those secrets with him. The whole business was unpleasant."

"What secrets?" Arnold asked.

"Those," Natasha said calmly, "are personal matters and have nothing to do with what happened to Clayton, or at least, I don't see how they could."

"Alright. So, you fought on Thursday evening. What happened on Friday afternoon?" Arnold asked, raising himself up by grabbing onto the edge of the coffee table. It was thankfully firm, heavy, and able to take his weight. He managed to escape for a moment from the confines of the sofa but remained perched on the very edge of returning to its fabric oblivion.

She nodded. "Alright. On Friday afternoon, perhaps early evening, Clayton stormed past my office door in a state of intoxicated anger, muttering nasty things about Janet. He had just finished talking with her, and I gather that she'd rebuffed him. Clayton doesn't like that. Never has.

Then, not more than ten minutes later, Dan came to my office. He was in a panic. He said that Clayton had been rummaging through the trunk of his Mustang and dropped something. After Clayton drove away, Dan had gone to look at whatever it was and discovered that it was a handgun. When I asked, he told me that he'd just left it lying there.

"We went out to the parking lot to look, but by the time we got there, the gun was gone. Dan said that he saw a big guy lurking about at the parking entrance. Maybe it is the same man that was at our house. I don't know. This man could have taken the gun. I don't know that either. It is also possible that Clayton came back to get it. Clayton wasn't in the habit of leaving handguns lying about in parking lots."

"That's very interesting, Natasha. And what about your impending death?"

"That is interesting. As a climax to our discussion on Thursday evening, Clayton had announced that, together, we would be going to the woods on Saturday morning—this morning—to perform a double suicide. He was not giving me a choice. He is not a big believer in democracy. The problem, however, was that I knew that he had an airline ticket for Singapore, booked under one of his assumed names. I had found it among his belongings. So, I knew immediately that I was the only person who would die. He was going to shoot me and then grab an afternoon flight to the bounties of Singapore. It was very upsetting to me, but there seemed to be nothing I could do. I could have called the police, I suppose, but I had no evidence of anything. Clayton would have denied it. I could have run, but with his skillset, he would certainly find me with little effort. I felt that I had no choice but to resign myself to death. So, that is what I did. But I was damned if I was going to let Clayton escape. So, the next morning, I called the authorities in Saskatoon to warn them of Clayton's plans and give them the name on his false passport."

"But Clayton didn't escape. He didn't even try."

"That is true, but I don't know why. Perhaps he overheard my phone call? He was in the other room, and in hindsight, I might have heard someone on the other line."

"But that would still not explain why he didn't take you to the woods. When you got home from your run this morning, he was just gone?"

She nodded. "I have no idea why he left without me. When I came home, I was expecting to die. I was surprised—pleasantly mind you—to find out that Clayton was gone. Finding out later that he was lying dead in the aster meadow was a significant relief."

"What about the cheese and large footprints?"

"I have no idea. And do not forget, it may not be cheese at all." She shrugged, and he had to admit she had a point. "As people here have a habit of mentioning, Arnold, 'Shit happens.' This time it happened to the right person. Still, I hope you find the answers to all of your questions."

"And I hope you find the answer to all of yours, Natasha," he said quietly.

She sighed, and for a brief moment, smiled ever so slightly, nonchalantly replacing the *Chatelaine* on the table. "That is unlikely, Arnold. But I suppose there is no harm in hoping."

As Arnold walked back to his cruiser a few minutes later, he wondered why Natasha was holding back information. He was sure that she was. She claimed ignorance of how Clayton died, and yet, Arnold felt strongly that she knew more about it than she was letting on. And her conversation with Dan in advance of Arnold's visit was highly suspicious. The whole visit was confusing. At times, Natasha had seemed exceptionally forthright, and her story was consistent with his limited knowledge of both her background and her life with Clayton. But there were things said that did not fit. The visit of a 'large stranger' did not sit well with Arnold. He was quite sure that Natasha would have told the police about a large stranger with unknown intent. Why wouldn't she? She had complained about the death slogans on her garage quickly enough.

It felt like Dan had given her information about the scene, and now Natasha was presenting that story to distract him, or perhaps explain away the large footprints at the crime scene. But why? She had a perfect alibi for that morning.

CHAPTER 6

ARNOLD MEETS DAN AT THE DICKEY DEE

It was nearly nine in the evening as Arnold pulled his cruiser away from Natasha's house. He drove south on McKenzie Avenue, slowing down as he passed the fairgrounds and baseball field on his right. The traffic on McKenzie Avenue was light. Muscle John Friesen's dark blue GTO muscle car passed him, travelling slightly over the speed limit. Arnold had glanced sideways at the vehicle as it passed, expecting to see Muscle John, but it wasn't him at the wheel. Instead, it was a young woman with a tattoo on her slender neck and a cigarette dangling from her lower lip. She'd given Arnold a condescending wave as she passed.

Arnold stopped at the red light at the Main Street intersection and momentarily felt pleased for Muscle John. Arnold felt that the man was often unfairly maligned by the elites in town. He was unsophisticated, for sure, and had sadly got caught up in William and Adele's hate mongering, but he ran two businesses competently and deserved more respect than he received. He was the first person anyone would call if they had any sort of problem with their vehicle and needed a tow or had left their keys in their car. Earlier in summer, he had called Muscle John himself to open his car door. The man hadn't even lectured him about leaving his keys in the ignition. Arnold had been impressed by his professionalism. Still, Muscle John was easily swayed by the Four-Square Gospel crowd, whose hatred for foreign elements in town (especially atheists and Jews) was building. It was concerning. *Could Muscle John be involved in Clayton's death?* It seemed unlikely. Anyway, he had been in his tow truck this morning, bailing Doc's Volvo out of a ditch.

Arnold considered that traffic would have been heavier when Clayton had driven the forest road on Saturday morning. Looking west, with the sun already set and well into its final performance for the day, Arnold noted that the horizon was dazzling with pink and yellow quilt patterns. He turned west on Main Street, and then right again onto the fairground-entrance driveway. He drove past the baseball field to the entrance to the Northford Woodlands Nature Trail, from which Dan had emerged earlier that afternoon, and turned onto the forest service road. The service road's only access point was on the north edge of the fairgrounds, slightly west of the nature trail. Moments later, Arnold arrived at the spot where Clayton's Mustang had been found and checked his watch again. Eight minutes had elapsed. Clayton's vehicle would have been seen enroute by any number of people that morning. *Verifying the time of Clayton's arrival at the aster meadow shouldn't be difficult, at least.*

Having timed Clayton's driving route, Arnold returned to his office. A skeleton crew of evening staff lounged about. Constable Billy Stafford was out doing traffic duty at the exit of McKnight's Disco. McKnight's patrons provided easy cash flow for the Northford detachment. It never ceased to amaze Arnold that, despite patrons' knowledge that McKnight's was monitored by law enforcement, intoxicated drivers continued to pour out of the club and get in their vehicles. It was really too easy.

Sitting down at his desk, Arnold surveyed the various file stacks. He more or less knew where everything was, but he conceded that his system looked disorganized. And perhaps it was. Billy told him that it was not a system at all. But there was a system ... of a sort. Each pile reflected a relative level of work demand. The closer the pile was to the center of his desk, the greater attention it demanded. Arnold noted that the Clayton Dalrymple file was the closest one and probably would be for a while.

As Arnold pulled out his notebook to summarize his meeting with Natasha, he saw a handwritten note stuck to the handset of his telephone. It was from Emily Little, the *Northford Sentinel* all-star reporter. Arnold had developed a deep respect and admiration for Emily's investigative journalism skills. She was astute and a detailed observer, and while she might be prone to embellishment, her knowledge of human behaviour was unencumbered by censorship. Emily Little was committed to genuine inquiry, pursuing a topic and taking her articles to wherever her inquiry took her, never sanitizing things for her own comfort or that of her readers. Still, Emily was quirky. She sometimes took inordinate amounts of time drawing maps for her stories, attaching series of graphic drawings to the text.

Sometimes Arnold wondered whether to Emily the newspaper story was mostly a vehicle for her graphic art. But then, he considered, perhaps that was okay. He loved her drawings. They were beautifully crafted and gave flavour and tone to stories that many pages of words couldn't do as well. Her drawing skills were evident as well in her handwritten notes, examples Arnold thought, of artistic calligraphy. Arnold's grandfather had been an amateur calligrapher, and he had been amazed as a child at the beauty and precision of his penmanship. It was a far cry from his own awkward scrawl.

Emily's note indicated she had seen Clayton's Mustang leave the Arts Centre parking lot in a hurry on Friday afternoon. The Mustang had turned left on McKenzie Avenue, driving north. Dan had emerged from the Arts Centre front doors to the spot where Clayton's car had been. Dan had stopped to look at an object on the gravel, picked it up, and then walked back into the Arts Centre building. To Emily, the object had looked a lot like a handgun.

Arnold drew his own map of what Emily described in her note. The Arts Centre parking lot was east of the building, just west along McKenzie Avenue. If Dan had been standing at the east front doors of the building, he would have seen Clayton's car leave. He would have seen Clayton drop the gun. Emily's story matched Natasha's information, except for the observation that Dan had picked up the gun. Natasha had clearly said that Dan had left the gun alone. The discrepancy was worth inquiring about.

Arnold also drew a map of the aster-meadow scene, the position of Clayton's body, the gun, the footprints, the cottonwood stump—which had held the pea coat, mug, and cigarette butt—the location of the bullet wound, and where the Mustang was parked on the forest road. He also made a few notes about his earlier conversation with Doc (Alexei Rubenstein). Feeling that he had exhausted his memory of the day's events, he closed his notebook, shut off the light to his office, and sat in the dark for a while. Sitting in the dark calmed his mind. He imagined possible scenarios that might have occurred in the woods that morning. But he needed more information. Imagination is fine as far as it goes, but an investigation requires the accumulation of puzzle pieces. Facts. Without the necessary pieces, trying to put a puzzle together was frustrating and futile. So far, his accumulated pieces formed a confusing picture of Clayton Dalrymple's death.

Stepping outside the detachment building, he took his jacket off. The evening air was still quite warm, but instead of taking the cruiser, he decided to walk to the Dickey Dee. It would give him time to think. He walked north on McKenzie Avenue and passing Friesen's Pool Hall he noted that although a closed sign was on the front door, the lights were on. Through the window, he could see Muscle John and the tattooed young woman passing out drinks to a small bevy of casually dressed folks at the bar. It looked like a private party. Arnold told himself that interviewing Muscle John could wait. Muscle John didn't leave town.

Arnold turned right onto Main Street. The Dickey Dee was about a kilometre east, and open till eleven on warm-weather weekend evenings. There was no panic to get there. His hunger pangs had backed off, but he sensed they were coming back. The anticipation of a double-bacon cheeseburger was building.

Arnold reviewed his plan for the next day. He would start by properly interviewing Dan McCroskey. The matter of the gun in the parking lot was curious. It was also curious that Dan had called Natasha with the news of Clayton's death, giving her information about the large footprints and the yellow powder.

Arnold ambled along Main Street, his left knee sending him warning messages. Doc had told Arnold that he had early arthritis in his knee, but that walking was good for it. So was losing weight. Arnold felt that he was doing fairly well on the walking remedy, but not so well with losing weight. It was hard to shed pounds, especially with the Dickey Dee being so convenient. As he got closer to the burger shop, he began to consider adding a vanilla milkshake to the evening's program.

The Dicky Dee was situated on the southeastern edge of Northford. It was the second building that travellers coming from Saskatoon would see after McKnight's Disco. The building itself wasn't much to look at. But the look (and certainly the food) had improved since the previous owners had been running the place. Annie Russell had renovated the building shortly after taking over from William and Adele Sawatzky. She had upgraded the kitchen so that it met health-code requirements and solved the rodent problem.

William and Adele had struggled to make a go of the place. Consistently violating public health guidelines did not help their cause. The drive-in season in Northford was not long, so a food-services venue needed to be open for business during the summer. But under William and Adele's regime, much of every summer had been spent in closures, enforced by the health department. The fact that the place was overrun with mice also diminished public enthusiasm, so that even when the drive-in was open, the place was generally empty. Eating a cheeseburger while fending off scampering rodents did not appeal to most customers. Then there was the issue of food-poisoning complaints, a phenomenon that kept the Northford Hospital busy most summers. But all of this changed when Annie Russell had bought the place.

The Dickey Dee was now clean, with a modern, commercial kitchen, new patio tables and chairs, and a menu that satisfied the tastes of a broad range of Northford citizens. School and church groups held committee meetings at the Dickey Dee. That had never happened before. Annie had replaced its fading-blue outdoor paint with a red-barn look, accented nicely by white trim corners. The curling grey roof shingles had been replaced with cedar shakes and the broken rafters replaced with fir beams. The rickety metal picnic tables, with sagging bench seating, had been replaced with circular tables of treated spruce. The only downside of Annie Russell's Dickey Dee was that the lineups were too long.

As Arnold approached the drive-in, he saw Dan's beat-up Falcon in the parking lot. He decided to slip onto the patio from the rear. He wanted to arrive at his favourite table (number six) without walking through the main eating area and encountering Dan. But it was not to be. As soon as he approached the patio area, he saw that Dan was already firmly entrenched at table six and looked like he planned on staying awhile. He had even taken his Saskatchewan Roughrider ballcap off.

Arnold stopped for a moment, considering his options. He did not feel up to interviewing Dan, but the smell of cheeseburgers enticed him to sit. Dan was munching on a gorgeous-looking cheeseburger, precisely the kind Arnold had been anticipating since that afternoon. So, even though he had already spent more time with Dan than he preferred, he walked up to table six and sat down. "Care if I join you, Dan? Two bachelors on a night out?"

"Please do, Arnold. Living the bachelor dream."

"Yes, indeed. Eating by yourself on a Saturday night. Doesn't get any better than that. Or does it?" Arnold asked. "Was Sheila a good cook?"

"Not really. But Sheila's limited cooking skills were not the problem."

"What was?"

"Her attraction to Clayton and her lack of attraction to me."

"That *could* become a problem. Do you cook?"

"I'm easily lost in the kitchen," Dan said. "I suppose I'll need to get a map."

"Or just come to the Dickey Dee," Arnold said. "That was my response to Madeline leaving."

"With all due respect Arnold, that's obvious. You're growing out of your uniform."

"Saskatoon Tent and Awning is on it."

"I imagine that you have had enough of me today." Dan smiled sadly.

"To be honest, I *was* hoping for quiet. But it's also an opportunity, Dan. I have a few questions for you." Arnold thought to himself that sometimes people will say things over a burger that are interesting. Of course, sometimes they don't.

"You weren't able to eat at home tonight?" Arnold asked.

"Not really," Dan said, rather despondently. "Sheila is working the evening shift and said that it would be better all around if I was gone when she came home. Turns out I'll be going to Emily's tonight instead of next week."

"Emily is aware?" Arnold asked, hopefully. He really wanted Emily and Dan to form a partnership of a kind, though he wasn't really sure why. His stake in their relationship struck him as removed, at best. Still, he seemed to care. Perhaps he just felt protective of Emily, wanting her to be happy in Northford, and felt that Dan was the best prospect for aiding her in that process.

"She is. Emily said that I was more than welcome to crash with her. I don't even know what 'more than welcome' means, but I'm not in a position to question the details. I would happily crash with Emily for the rest of time, if you ask me, although you didn't. Anyway, I shouldn't make too much of her offer. Her apartment is across the hall from the one I'll be renting, so she's probably just being nice."

"She is that." Arnold smiled. "But she also likes you, Dan. You might want to bear that in mind."

"But she just broke up with her boyfriend from Saskatoon," Dan said, adding more salt to his fries. "What are you eating, Arnold?"

"Double bacon cheeseburger with fries. Will probably add a vanilla shake. By the way, I have it on good authority that Emily canned her boyfriend because he was reluctant to come to Northford. I don't think that he's a factor at this point. I believe you could have a path to her heart, should you choose to take the right steps."

"That is way too much pressure, Arnold," Dan muttered. "I can't believe that the Northford sergeant is giving me relationship advice. You've been a married quite a few times, Arnold. I mean, really, I probably shouldn't take advice from you."

"Actually, Dan, you probably should," said Annie Russell as she approached the table and took Arnold's order. Once she had it down, she added, "Arnold may not be gifted at marriage, but he's attracted three wives. That's a skill in itself. On another topic, what's the verdict? Suicide or murder? What's it going to be?"

"Can't say as yet, Annie," Arnold answered. "Looking for a man with at least size-twelve boots. Don't believe there are any women around here with feet like that. But sadly, there are a lot of men."

"True enough. There's no lack of large feet in this town," Annie observed. "Assuming it is a local set of big feet you're after."

"It would be a good place to start," Arnold said.

"What about the smashed watch and yellow powder?" Annie asked.

"Who did you hear that from?" Arnold asked, surprised.

84

"You know me, Arnold. People talk. I listen. In this case, Dan has been quite talkative."

"Too much so," Arnold muttered. "What are you doing Dan? Calling Natasha about Clayton? Talking to Annie about the scene? This is a police investigation."

"Natasha is my work friend. I have the right to talk to her. Annie too. She likes to know things. I just mentioned the large footprints and the yellow powder. Quite peculiar. Maybe Annie can help. She knows everyone, Arnold."

"Maybe she can." He sighed. "The large footprints should be easy enough to track down if they belong to someone from here. By the way, Dan, when I got back to the station this evening, Emily Little left me a note. Any idea what she said?"

"I am sure that I don't. Why would I?"

"She saw something on Friday afternoon that involved you. What do you think she saw?"

"I saw lots of things on Friday. Doesn't everyone?" Dan smirked.

"Not everyone saw Clayton leave the Arts Centre parking lot in a hurry. Apparently, he dropped something. You did not, however, mention this to me."

"Sorry about that," Dan conceded. "Clayton was tearing out of the Arts Centre parking lot on Friday. Around six or so. I was having a smoke at the front doors. I saw him, and yes, something dropped from his duffel bag. But I didn't see Emily."

"She saw you. She saw you pick something up. Any idea what that was?"

"A handgun?"

"Why are you asking that as a question? You were the person who picked it up. You tell me."

"I'm sorry, Arnold. I should have told you right away," Dan said, contritely. "I was going to tell you tomorrow. It's true that Clayton dropped a handgun from his duffel bag. He was tossing the bag in his trunk, and it fell out. After he left, I took a look."

"What did you do with it?"

"I picked it up and headed for the office with it. I was going to bring it to Natasha. But then I changed my mind. I put it back. Didn't want to get involved."

"Involved in what?"

"I wasn't sure, but I felt certain that Clayton was up to something. He was drunk and angry. He rushed out of the building with his bag, bumping into me as he passed. Didn't apologize. Of course, that was normal for him. Just grunted some curse words at me like I was in the way. Which I guess I was. Then he went to his car and threw his bag into the trunk. But the gun dropped out of it. He didn't notice. He sped away, and I walked over to look. Saw the gun, and my first thought was that Natasha was in danger. So, I picked the gun up. But then I saw a large man standing at the city-park entrance. I'm pretty sure he noticed me. I decided to put the gun down. Whatever was going on was none of my business. I didn't want to get involved."

"Given that the next day you found Clayton dead in the woods, you are involved. Like it or not. You are also withholding information. That's a poor choice, Dan. Did you tell anyone what you had seen?"

Dan paused, studying Arnold for a moment and taking a bite from his burger. The Dickey Dee was nearly empty. Only Arnold and Dan were on the patio. Inside, a table of four teenagers were throwing back Cokes, belching and finding the phenomenon hilarious. Dan leaned in close to Arnold, and whispered, "To be honest, I went to Natasha's office and told her about it. We went to where the gun dropped, but it was gone. I was scared."

"Scared of what?"

"The large man for one thing. Mostly though, I was scared for Natasha. I thought that she was in danger."

"If the gun you picked up is the same as the one at the scene, I guess we'll find your prints on it?

"Oh no. I used my shirt sleeve to pick it up. No way I wanted my prints on a gun."

"This doesn't look good, Dan. You picked up a gun that belongs to a man who has just been shot. Then you withheld it from me. If Emily hadn't witnessed it, you would have kept the matter to yourself."

"Oh no, I was going tell you. Honest."

"I guess we'll never know for sure, will we? What did this large man look like?"

"Huge. Like a sumo wrestler. He was standing by the entry arbour. Never saw him before. Not from town; I'm pretty sure." Arnold wondered how big this stranger was going to get. He had gone from being a large, menacing man, according to Natasha, to a sumo wrestler, according to Dan.

"And then you went to Natasha's office? Did you tell her about this man? How did she respond?"

"Natasha told me that she had seen a large man around her home. Thought he might be blackmailing Clayton. She said the man was probably KGB. She wasn't sure though. Anyway, by the time we returned to the parking lot, the gun and the man were both gone."

"You're sure about that?" Arnold asked, picking up the tin ashtray on the table and examining it. He thought to himself that the tin would melt down very easily. He'd been thinking of getting into metal sculpture ever since seeing what Clayton had been doing in his workshop. He'd been impressed. Arnold had been thinking for a while now that he needed a hands-on artistic hobby and loved the idea of working with a backyard smelter.

"Of course, I'm sure," Dan said, looking around as if for someone to help him out with the conversation. But he was on his own. "I should know what I saw."

"You should. You should also know that your involvement looks suspicious," Arnold said softly, putting the ashtray down and moving it over towards Dan.

"Suspicious?" Dan said, with a defensive tone. "Arnold, I am the least likely person to become involved in anything to do with guns. Guns scare me. I like to imagine guns, use them as props, but real-life guns freak me out. I'm a drama director. What do I know about handguns?"

"You knew enough to avoid putting your prints on one," Arnold said, making a note in his writing pad.

This clearly unnerved Dan. "I'm a theatre director," Dan said again. "What do I know about crime? Sure, I watch crime shows, plays.... I know the importance of wiping a weapon clean. But everything I know is from the theatre or television. I'm not comfortable dealing with the real world. Never have been. I deal with a world of stories generated for the stage."

"But somehow you have become involved in a real-life drama, with a dead body lying in the woods," Arnold said, looking directly at Dan and then making a notation in his pad.

"I'm only involved by bad luck, Arnold. I have no idea what's going on. I find a gun, and then I find Clayton. I don't know what to make of it. Was Clayton killed by a Soviet agent? They killed Trotsky. Why not Clayton?"

"Why not, indeed?" Arnold mused, straightening his back. "But the death scene in the meadow looks like a staged theatrical event to me. The yellow powder is an added touch that an artistic director might think of. Especially an artistic director who is putting on a play about someone who gets killed with hard cheese."

"That's true enough. I've been wondering about that. I guess Natasha told you about the play we're putting on," Dan said, relaxing his posture and slouching low into his chair, pushing the table body away towards Arnold. The added distance from Arnold seemed to relax him.

"She did. You have an explanation?"

"Well, in our play, 'Medb,' the lead character, is killed with a slingshot and hard cheese," Dan said, sitting abruptly upright again. "It's just an old Irish myth. Not real at all. Not even a little bit."

"You seem to have lost your appetite, Dan," Arnold said, picking up Dan's ball cap and examining the sweat band. "I always wanted to wear a Roughrider hat, but Madeline said that a Stetson was a better match for a man my age. Perhaps she was right. You certainly have used yours. Quite worn." Dan's burger was half eaten, looking forlorn and neglected on the plate. Then Arnold smiled broadly, spotting Annie bringing out a heaping plate of crispy brown French fries and a double-bacon cheeseburger, loaded with tomatoes, pickles, and a healthy dose of mustard and ketchup. "And I'm just about to start satisfying mine."

Arnold dug in. He was seriously ravenous, even if the look was not pre-cisely as professional as he preferred.

"Eat away, Arnold," Dan said, pushing his plate away to the centre of the table. "Don't let me hold you back. But I believe that I'm done. All this talk of death and bodies is too much for me."

"It *is* a rather dreary subject, isn't it?" Arnold asked rhetorically, looking out into the parking lot, reflecting on Northford folks choosing to spend a Saturday fall evening dining at a burger joint. Were they like him? With no one at home to spend the evening with. Or like Dan? In a state of transition. Everyone had stuff to deal with; that was one thing he knew for sure. He had been in Northford long enough to know the drama in people's lives. Sometimes he had to get involved in it. Like it or not. Like now. He had been well aware that Natasha and Clayton were having problems. The police had amplified those problems with the pressure of the investigation into Clayton's dealings, but they hadn't created the problems. Those were long standing, having emigrated along with the couple. But clearly, they had come to a point of crisis and action.

But who all was involved in this crisis? Dan McCroskey? Arnold struggled to imagine Dan being involved. Dan *was* a bit of a "fancy pants," whatever that meant, and a romantic dramatist. He had problems at home, but his standing in Northford was excellent. Granted, Clayton had been messing with that standing. Trying to take him down. Had Dan taken action to defend himself? It seemed unlikely. Dan was not a man of action. He was a man who preferred a life of fantasy. And yet, Dan was being cagey, not fully transparent, or at least, so Arnold felt. Then there was the question of the footprints at the scene. Why only one set of prints moving towards the trail going north?

"Tell me more about this Medb play, Dan," Arnold said, returning to his burger, taking a massive bite, and wiping his mouth with his serviette. The burger was exceptional, as always, but messy. Arnold felt slightly sheepish and unprofessional, taking such a big bite and having a smear of ketchup around his mouth. "Why is the main character shot with cheese?"

"Medb is killed by her nephew as an act of revenge for his mother's death. Medb had shot his mother while she was pregnant. The nephew survived, but the mother didn't. The choice of hard cheese is part of the story. Odd perhaps, but the nephew happened to have hard cheese available. So, he used it."

"Interesting. So, it's a play about a revenge killing?"

"It is. But I can't see the connection to Clayton's death."

89

"The makes two of us, but I have a feeling that there is one. Tell me about Natasha," Arnold said, switching his focus.

"She is beautiful, self-possessed, and very big on dancing."

"I imagine everyone in Northford knows that. You said you were concerned about her safety. Why?"

"Natasha is a very troubled person. Beaten down by her life. She puts on a good show but is deeply unhappy. Sad and trapped. She lives in fear."

"What is she afraid of?"

"Clayton, mostly. He had something over her. Don't know what, but I do know she was scared of him. She admitted that much. But what does that matter now? Clayton killed himself, right?"

"Maybe he did. But Natasha said that Clayton was going to kill her today. Did she tell you that?"

After a long pause, Dan reluctantly nodded. "She did. At least, she said that's what Clayton told her would happen."

"Did she have any reason to doubt that?"

"No, I think she believed him. Clayton kept those kinds of promises."

"When did Natasha tell you that Clayton was going to kill her?"

"Friday, late afternoon or early evening. She told me after I saw the gun drop."

"But you didn't inform the police. You did nothing. Why?"

"It wasn't my business. It was up to Natasha. She insisted that I not interfere. She said that Saturday was her judgement day."

"Judgement day?"

"Yes. Natasha said that Clayton was not the only one who had sinned. She said she had sinned also and deserved to die."

"We all sin; we all die, Dan. But I'm not sure that anyone deserves to die. They just do. Anyway, she didn't die."

"She didn't, obviously. But I'm just saying that she expected to and was resigned to it. Clearly, things did not go as she expected on Saturday morning. She got a reprieve. But Natasha didn't do anything to intervene. I'm sure of that. Neither did I. Must have been the large-footed yellow-powder person with a dislike for Rolexes."

"Well, I guess we'll see about that," Arnold said wistfully, chewing a forkful of fries that he'd covered in a blanket of ketchup and a layer of salt and pepper. The salt and pepper hung to the ketchup in beautiful harmony. As for the double-bacon cheeseburger, it was going down fine. Arnold had attacked it with vigour at the early stages, but he now left it temporarily half eaten as he began to focus more seriously on the fries. His hunger was quieted, almost satisfied, but there was still much work to do. Arnold began to question whether he would be able to finish his food, let alone the thick vanilla shake that was sitting beside his water glass.

Arnold took a deep breath, picked up the salt and pepper shakers, and studied them. He wondered what kind of smelter he would need to melt glass. Then he looked around the room to see if anyone was watching before taking another massive bite of his double-bacon cheeseburger and then moving his plate slightly towards the centre of the table. He felt that he had eaten enough.

He was appropriately satiated by the food and was beginning to gain some perspective on the difficulty of the day. Still, his other feelings were far from satisfied. Having finally eaten, other details crept into his sensory world, like how uncomfortable the Dickey Dee chairs were. They always had been, but usually, he didn't notice this until after he had eaten. Now, having had enough, he noticed how his chair cut into his lower back. He wondered sometimes whether Annie had chosen these chairs so that customers wouldn't overstay their welcome. Annie was strategic that way. She was a gracious and charming host, but she knew how to take care of herself.

When Arnold had first taken on this job in Northford, some ten years earlier, he had thought that perhaps he'd had a chance of a romantic escapade with Annie. She had shut that down rather quickly, telling him that he had a good thing with Madeline, and that he shouldn't mess it up. She'd also assured Arnold that she had a good thing with Ken and had no interest in other men. She liked men generally, and men in positions of authority in particular, but that was all. Annie's position on such matters never deviated, and Arnold had come to respect it. Of course, Madeline had ended up leaving him anyway, but still ... at least Annie had saved him from making a mistake he would have regretted. It would have damaged his reputation in Northford too and probably prevented him from retiring there, which is what he hoped to do.

"Tell me your whereabouts this morning, Dan," Arnold asked then, looking intently at him, watching as he nervously played with his soiled serviette.

"I was out birding with my boys quite early," Dan said eagerly. "Left the house around seven. We got home at eight-thirty. Sheila was just leaving for her shift. We had breakfast, and I took the boys to soccer practice just before nine. Got to the Arts Centre a little after nine."

"Did you drive?"

"Yes, took my Falcon."

"Anyone see you?"

"Oscar waved at me as I drove in. William and Adele saw me and Natasha at nine-thirty, having a smoke. Other than that, I'm not sure. Lots of people saw me at the boy's soccer practice when I dropped them off."

"Do you think that Natasha is involved? It would be understandable if she proactively defended herself."

"Natasha would never hurt anyone. She's an artist. She might have been tempted to defend herself, but she didn't. What she *should* have done is call the police to protect her. I told her that. But she wouldn't."

"What was her response when you suggested it?"

"She was skeptical that the police would believe her. Anyway, she didn't want to be saved by the police. She didn't want to be saved by anyone. She wanted to accept her fate. Her demise. Even if it came from Clayton."

"So, Clayton insisted on a double suicide. Natasha knew that he had an airline ticket and was going to escape, so the double suicide was not going to happen. She was the only one who would die. Natasha calls the authorities in Saskatchewan to warn them about Clayton's escape plans, but she does not bother to tell the police here that she is going to be killed?" His scepticism showed on his face.

"As it turned out, she didn't need to. She's alive, and Clayton is not."

"Exactly. So, how did that happen?" Arnold asked rhetorically, thinking that Natasha hadn't called the police because she had the matter in hand. She must have had a plan—a plan that made it unnecessary to call the police. He guessed that Natasha knew that she wasn't going to die. Of course, he reasoned, he could be wrong about that.

"Natasha has a pretty good alibi, Arnold," Dan said emphatically.

"She does." Arnold nodded. "And a good alibi is a good friend. You have a good alibi yourself."

"Exactly, and I don't even need one," Dan said enthusiastically. "I don't believe in killing anyone, even objectionable people like Clayton."

"It's good to have beliefs, I suppose, Dan. Got to believe in something. Changing the subject, why did Sheila not find you desirable?"

Dan looked out the far-west window into the darkness of the late evening. A few light standards cast shadows on the parking area, where Dan had left his Falcon. A young couple sat at one of the picnic tables now, holding hands and smoking. Dan took a deep breath and reflected on his marriage. "For starters, she thinks that I'm gay. I joined the volunteer fire brigade to try to impress her. She said that meant nothing. It was just a volunteer brigade. I even took a firearms course and got my license, so that I could go hunting with her dad. But her dad scoffed at the idea. Said I would probably shoot my foot off." He shrugged. "Which I probably would have."

Arnold nodded but didn't respond, even as he took silent note of an apparent contradiction in Dan's story.

"Anyway," Dan continued, "I failed to convince Sheila that I was manly. She only desires manly men."

"Why did she marry you then?"

"She wanted to have a child. I happened to be good-looking and available. Maybe she thought we would have nice-looking children. Of course, she was right. We do."

"Your boys are nice-looking, sure. So, she needed you to have children?"

"Partly."

"She could have picked a more masculine partner if that was her preference."

"She could have. But her father hated me."

Arnold thought he understood. "Her father was a nasty bastard, no doubt of that. I had to arrest him once for disturbing the peace at a hockey game. There were a lot of people he didn't like. I guess you were one of them. But what does that have to do with Sheila marrying you?"

"Sheila married me to aggravate him."

"She hated her father that much?"

"Absolutely. Her father was homophobic. You know her younger brother, Henry?"

"Yes, indeed. In a group home for the mentally handicapped last I heard. What does he have to do with anything?"

"When he was little, Henry used to prance around like a girl, dress up in Sheila's clothes, and pretend to be female. This enraged their father, of course, and so as soon as Henry was old enough, he had him put into the group home. Henry had already outgrown that phase, of course, but their father didn't care. And once Henry was out, his father refused to let him back into the house. Anyway, the man's dead now, and Henry likes it in the group home, so I guess it's fine. He even plays with the boys sometimes when they go traipsing about like Robin Hood in the woods."

"Right." Arnold had never heard anything bad about the boy. *Young man now, I guess.* "Back to Sheila. So, your theory is that she married you to annoy her father?"

"Absolutely," Dan said. "As soon as her father died, her interest in me faded. Mind you, it was never all that active. I'm just not the kind of man she's attracted to. But Clayton is. Or was. I was always a huge disappointment to her."

"Because of the Saskatoon incident?"

"For sure. Her dissatisfaction came to a head when I was fired, and then shortly after, her father died. My decision to depict Phillip in *Of Human Bondage* as a gay man in an explicitly gay scene was a real problem for her."

"Sounds like it was for the school too."

"For sure. It was a Mennonite school, very touchy on the topic of homosexuality. But I have no regrets. You need to show the audience, not tell them. I think the Phillip character was struggling with his sexuality, just like Somerset Maugham. I got fired over it. Ended up being a good thing though. Led me to Northford. The Arts Centre and the school here are great. Northford is regressive and progressive at the same time. A healthy tension is alive and well here. Overall, this is a good place for artists. Good things are happening. And working with Natasha has been inspiring."

"The Arts Centre has been a good thing, for sure." Arnold nodded. "So has the Community Partners drop-in centre." Annie was the board chair of the drop-in, which they had set up in a renovated a space that had once been a Chinese restaurant. "I hear that Clayton went to the drop-in a lot. And so did you."

"I did. Lots of folks hung out there. Leonard was a director who attracted folks to the centre. It was definitely a place to meet. Oscar White, Clayton, Emily, and Leonard were in a fantasy baseball league together, which met at the centre. You should talk to Leonard. When he isn't pitching, he's actually quite impressive."

"Fantasy baseball? Interesting choice of a hobby for a former KGB agent."

"Clayton liked numbers. Baseball has that quality. You like baseball too, Arnold. Is it because of the numbers?"

"The numbers are part of the draw. But also, the drama of a single hitter against a single pitcher. The beauty of a fielding play, a ball hit into the gap, a home run. Intellectually, it has an appeal too. The action is built on mathematical precision, physics, and never mind the possibilities it offers for colourful metaphors."

"I think for Clayton it was all about the numbers. He wasn't into the romance of the game."

"I guess he wasn't a romantic in general. Is Natasha? I wonder why she didn't leave Clayton if she was so unhappy."

"She couldn't. She said they were bound to each other by darkness. It was complicated for her."

"What kind of darkness?"

"Some dirt that they had on each other. It wasn't a normal marriage."

"No such thing as a normal marriage, Dan."

"Maybe, but Clayton and Natasha's life in the Soviet Union had some unique features."

"No doubt. Still, they've been here for five years. You would think that whatever past issues they had could be left in the old country," Arnold said, finishing his milkshake and getting up to leave. "Good chat, Dan. Come by the detachment tomorrow morning, and we'll do a formal statement. Have a good night."

Leaving his payment and a tip on the table, tucked under his plate, Arnold left the Dickey Dee, walked past the parking area—where Dan had parked his Falcon—and looked around. It was dark, except for the parking-lot lights, but the scene caused Arnold to reflect on how easy it is to make assumptions. He was beginning to accumulate information, some new and some old, but he wondered how much of it was trustworthy. He heard a dog bark nearby and the sound of a truck horn blowing on the highway, but otherwise, the evening was quiet. Everything in Northford seemed the same as always, except that the way things seemed and the way they truly were never matched perfectly. Not in Northford. Not anywhere that Arnold had ever been.

With his hunger issues resolved, Arnold headed back to the Northford RCMP station. The streets were empty except for a group of young people loafing outside of Friesen's Pool Hall. It was past ten when he stepped through the front doors of the detachment. The lights were on in his office, and Constable Billy Stafford was sitting with his feet up on Arnold's desk, his face looking mildly lost.

"You're on traffic duty tonight, Billy," Arnold said. "And this is not your office. One of us is confused, and I think it's you."

"We're both confused, Arnold," Billy said. "Otherwise, we would have solved the case by now. But we haven't. I know it's my turn to do traffic duty. One of my favourite parts of the job. But dealing with a murder is more important, right?"

"We've decided that Clayton was murdered?"

"That's what Vera says. But you tell me. What have you learned so far?"

Over the next few minutes—leaning against the doorframe with crossed arms and wondering when Billy was going to give up his chair—Arnold filled him in on the basic facts as told to him by Natasha and Dan.

"Interesting. So, we know Clayton wasn't alone. We also know that he had an airplane ticket to Singapore and a chance to escape to a country with no extradition treaty. A person from Northford, with winter around the corner and an airline ticket to Singapore, doesn't shoot himself. Maybe he changes his mind about killing Natasha. Fine. There is no advantage for Clayton to kill Natasha. But there is an advantage for him to get out of town. He could save himself, but he doesn't. Why? I will tell you why. Because someone killed him first. Vera would say that it's obvious. She watches *Mannix*. She knows a thing or two about crime."

Arnold smiled briefly at Billy's ode to his wife's wisdom. "Maybe Clayton knew that the police would be waiting for him at the airport and changed his mind?"

"How would he know that?" Billy asked, sitting up in Arnold's squeaky chair.

"Maybe he overheard Natasha's call? Or maybe, like Vera would undoubtedly say, someone killed him before he had a chance to leave. Someone with big feet and a stash of yellow powder. Can I have my chair back?"

"No worries, Arnold. Your chair is good for thinking. In fact, I just had a brain wave. I figure I have the case solved, Arnold!" Billy gushed. "Natasha shot him!"

"How did you determine that?"

"It's obvious, Arnold," Billy exclaimed, vacating Arnold's chair. "Clayton threatened to kill Natasha. She knew she was going to die, and that Clayton would try to escape. So, she shot him before he killed her. Proactive thinking on her part. I would have done the same thing. If you have a stone in your shoe, you take it out. Makes perfect sense. Nothing much lost on that woman. It's really quite simple. I don't know why I didn't think of it earlier."

"Perhaps because Natasha was not in the woods when Clayton died. She wasn't at home either. She was out running. She has a gaggle of witnesses," Arnold said, settling himself down in his chair. "Anyway, if she was planning to kill him, why would she call the police about his escape plans? She would have known that Clayton wasn't going anywhere."

"Good point. Maybe she called them to confuse us? But even I can see through that ruse. Trying to throw us off her real plans. It won't work, I tell you. I'm on to her."

"If you're on to her, Billy, how did she manage to shoot him while out running?"

"I don't have all the details worked out, okay? But I will. Just a matter of time. One thing I know for sure though: Natasha did it. You can waste my talents, having me aimlessly ticketing customers coming out of McKnight's, but that is not going to solve this crime. Vera says that ticketing intoxicated drivers is no way to run a police department. Either you are into crime detection and prevention, or you aren't. Focus on what is truly important or get out of the way. Ticketing drivers holds us back from what we really need to be doing. That's what Vera says."

"I feel properly chastised. So, in what direction would you and Vera take this case?" Arnold asked, jokingly.

"Towards Natasha," Billy said. "Vera would tell you the same thing. There's no doubt that she did it. All we have to do is determine how. It's a clear-cut case."

"No offense to Vera. Great person. Love her dearly. But seriously, Billy, there are other problems with your suggestion that Natasha shot him. For one, Natasha does not have large feet. The other person in the woods did."

"She could have an accomplice with large feet," Billy said confidently.

"That's possible but highly speculative. We have no evidence to suggest that."

"Natasha has motive. She wanted to save herself."

"True, she has a motive. But we're back to why she would call in a warning about Clayton's attempted escape. If she knew he was going to be killed, she had no need to make the call. And I'm not big on your idea that she was trying to confuse us."

"To be honest, I cannot rebut what you've just said. I'll have to ask Vera. She'll know. She always knows."

Arnold took off his Stetson, placing it on top of a leaning stack of files. "Clearly, Natasha was in danger. Both Dan and Natasha acknowledge that."

"Mannix would say that Natasha is hiding something. She found a way to beat Clayton to the punch. Can't explain the phone call to the airport police yet, except that maybe she made the call before she had time to figure out a plan to kill him."

"Okay, that's a possibility, Billy. I'll give you that. Can't rule out the accomplice theory either, I suppose. But teaming up with an accomplice who specializes in shooting yellow powder seems an odd choice. Natasha may well be hiding something; in fact, I do think she's withholding information, but she'd be smart enough to come up with a higher quality accomplice. If an accomplice killed him, intending to make it look like a simple suicide, their efforts were somewhat pathetic. Fooling around with yellow powder? The yellow powder didn't kill him. The gunshot to the head did.

So ... was it some kind of point they were trying to make? About revenge maybe, like in the play? But if so ... to what end?"

"I don't know, but if Natasha isn't involved, I don't know who is," Billy said, sitting down in the visitor's chair, looking very disappointed. "I try my best, and apparently, it's not enough. It's never enough. Makes a person want to retire."

"Trying our best is our job, Billy. Quitting is not really an option. Unless you really want to retire, in which case, you should. In the meantime, maybe we can do a bit more police work and find the answer to our questions?"

"Now you're thinking, Arnold. That's exactly what Mannix would do. Police work. Speaking of which, I did a bit of police work today. I made a few calls. Found out something that will be of interest to you. Looks like the yellow powder actually *is* hard cheese."

"How do you know that?" Arnold said, surprised. "The lab hasn't reported back yet."

"I understand it's not standard procedure, but I called my friend Fred Beckham, the chemistry teacher at the high school. Fred and I curl together. Great guy, though not much of curler. He plays third, even though he's not a real third. Can't hit the broom if his life depended on it. Thankfully it doesn't. Just a recreation league, really, when you get down to it."

"Speaking of getting down to it," Arnold said impatiently, "how 'bout telling me what Fred had to say about the yellow powder?" He got up to close the small west window that was regularly left open just enough to blow documents around the office.

"Of course. It's just that Fred and I go way back. Wouldn't have asked him for a favour if we didn't. Anyway, he did a preliminary examination of the powder. I know it's not official, but he knows his chemistry. He should by now. My goodness, the man has been teaching since the dinosaurs left town. I gave him a small sample of the powder, and sure enough, he calls me at home and tells me that the yellow powder is hard cheese. Dried Parmigiana Reggiano to be exact. Of course, this will need to be confirmed by forensics. Interesting, eh? Vera says this cheese goes well with pasta. I used to love pasta. Not now. I'll have to switch to Italian food."

"Good idea, Billy. Italian food is great." He shook his head and suppressed the urge to roll his eyes. "You definitely did not follow procedure, regardless of how long Fred has been teaching." Arnold scrunched up a ball of used foolscap and tossed it into the waste basket a good twelve feet away. "But it *is* good to know. And fits with what Dan told me about the Medb play the Arts Centre is putting on. The main character, Medb, is killed by hard cheese that was shot from a slingshot. Revenge killing. But of course, Clayton wasn't killed by hard cheese. It looks like that was thrown in for some special effect. But who beside a theatre director would be interested in special effects?"

Before Billy could make any suggestions, Arnold's phone rang. He picked it up and spoke for a few minutes to whoever was on the other end.

"It's confirmed," Arnold said, as he replaced the receiver in its cradle. "That was forensics. Your friend is right. Hard cheese is the answer to the yellow-powder question. Also, the bullet in Clayton's skull matches the M1895 that was lying beside him, and his prints are on the gun. Makes sense, of course, considering it's his gun. Residue on Clayton's right hand and his head wound came from the gun too. Maybe Clayton just changed his mind. Instead of killing Natasha, he appears to have shot himself. Still ... he didn't shoot himself with the cheese. That pleasure had to have come from someone else."

"Maybe the cheese is a signature of some kind?" Billy said. "Some sort of message?"

"Could be, but if it is, it certainly isn't a clear one. Maybe that's on purpose. Meant to confuse us? Distract us?"

"If it was, it worked," Billy reminded Arnold.

"Whoever it was, why leave such obvious footprints and smash the Rolex and his skull like that, leaving a residue of hard cheese?"

"Why indeed?" Billy said, tucking his shirt in.

Billy had the kind of body that refused to accept that a shirt should be tucked in. Minutes after tucking, Billy's shirt would always magically untuck. Billy did not concede to experience though. He spent the better part of each day tucking his shirt in, consistently unsuccessfully. Despite his committed practice, his shirt never looked entirely settled inside his pants.

"Both Dan and Natasha mentioned a large stranger," Arnold reflected. "I'd like to have some other witness supporting the existence of such a person. At this point, my feeling is that the large-stranger story is about as real as Santa Claus."

"Are you saying that the large stranger is Santa Claus?"

"No. I'm suggesting that someone is misdirecting us."

"For what purpose?" Billy asked, tucking his shirt in again. His physical excitement seemed to be pushing it up.

"If we knew that, we would know more than we do now," Arnold mused. "Dan says that the character in the play used a slingshot. Maybe this killer did too. Who owns a slingshot around here?" he asked rhetorically. "Dan's boys do," he said, answering his own question. "I've seen them practising with one, taking shots at trees and such. But they were at soccer practise this morning. Before that, they were with Dan in the woods."

He paused for a moment, seemingly considering something. "I wonder who's missing some hard Parmesan Reggiano?"

Billy didn't appear to be listening. "A slingshot couldn't break a watch. It's just a kid's toy."

Arnold shook his head. "It's not only a kid's toy. Not all of them anyway. A quality slingshot can do damage. But what would be the point of shooting Clayton with cheese at all? In the play, it's about revenge. Is it the same here?"

"Almost everyone wanted revenge on Clayton," Billy said. "Especially the KGB. Clayton did not leave the Soviet Union on good terms. Even Mannix would be upset if one of his informants defected to the other side."

"Maybe the cheese shooter wanted to confuse us about the time of death?" Arnold suggested. "He did specifically break the watch."

"Another misdirection?"

"Maybe, although not very well done. The ID team says that the watch hands were not tampered with," Arnold said. "Clayton's watch was shot at nine-thirty in the morning, but Dr. Morley thinks that Clayton died earlier than that. More like eight-thirty or so. If that's true, Clayton was dead when the cheese hit him."

"Why shoot cheese at a dead man?" Billy asked. "That's ridiculous. With all due respect."

"Ridiculous indeed, but I do believe that's what happened. Makes more sense than shooting cheese at a living Clayton. If a living Clayton got hit with cheese, he would have defended himself. There's no indication that he did."

"So, where does that leave us?"

"It leaves us not knowing precisely what happened, with Inspector Sanders arriving tomorrow." Arnold leaned back in his chair, taking aim but missing the waste basket with another ball of scrunched paper.

"What happens then?"

"Based on Dick's track record, not much. You'll go back to traffic duty, and I'll make the coffee, while we watch as Sanders plays fast and loose with the truth and focusses on file closure."

"Nothing wrong with file closure, is there?"

Arnold shook his head, thoughtfully. "Sometimes it's for the best. Especially if the truth is inconvenient ... which it so often is."

CHAPTER 7

CLAYTON DALRYMPLE (IVAN KALIK)

In the spring of 1969, Ivan Kalik had been assigned to the Soviet Embassy in Ottawa. His duties were to direct the new Soviet Embassy Research and Counter Propaganda Group. It had been a major promotion for Ivan. He was a rising star in the KGB, and he was being rewarded. Any time an agent was assigned a department directorship in an overseas Soviet Embassy, it was a crowning achievement. So, it was surprising that, on the first-year anniversary of achieving this sought-after promotion, Ivan had failed to show up for work.

It was a Wednesday morning in mid-April 1970. A spring rain fell lightly but persistently, washing away the salt from the roadways. Charlotte Street was nearly empty of pedestrians, and vehicular traffic was busy sending waves of water onto the sidewalk. The sidewalk planters were still bare from a long winter, but they were being watered. It would have been a good day to sleep in, read the morning paper, and hang out in the high-end Ottawa apartment he shared with Natasha. But Ivan was not the sleeping-in type. He had come to Ottawa with a purpose. It was time to act on it.

Instead of walking east to the embassy, as he usually did, he walked west to the *Ottawa Citizen* building, armed with Soviet code and ciphering books, including the names of Soviet double agents working in Canada. He'd left two half cups of coffee and a sink of unwashed breakfast dishes at the apartment.

After breakfast, Ivan had disappeared into his office, emerging shortly after with an attaché case and an expressionless face already in game-day mode. Natasha wondered if this was the day it would happen. She suspected that he had a plan to defect but was not certain. Ivan had said nothing to Natasha about any plans. Still, as he left the apartment, instructing Natasha to hide at the neighbour's place across the hall, she felt certain that their defection was precisely what was going to happen.

A few hours later, Natasha watched through her neighbour's keyhole as men she recognized as KGB agents entered their apartment. Within an hour, they left, leaving the apartment-door open and furniture strewn about as if a tornado had blasted through. But they did not knock on the neighbour's door, and Natasha was left unharmed.

■ ■ ■

Ivan walked along various side streets until he arrived at the front doors of the *Ottawa Citizen* newspaper building. Upon entering, he asked for a reporter—a man he had met through embassy functions—and announced his desire to defect. The reporter was skeptical and discussed the matter with his boss, who was also skeptical. Ivan was known to communicate with a measure of implied agenda. The agenda might not always be clear, but it was clear that there always was one. The newspaper backed off. They didn't want the responsibility of being set up in some way, so they advised Ivan to attend the offices of External Affairs.

An hour later, Ivan showed up at External Affairs. Initially, he was rejected there as well, but he persisted. By the afternoon, he finally met with an upper-level civil servant who took a chance that Ivan's defection request was serious. The official looked over Ivan's materials and became convinced that Ivan had valuable information that he was genuine about sharing.

Ivan was sent to a military camp near Ottawa and debriefed. He was forthright with information, and it all checked out. Within a month, a deal was made. For ongoing services as required, his Canadian entry and protection would be accommodated, as would his wife's. He was given a stipend and a new name: Clayton Dalrymple. Together with Natasha, a former Soviet ballerina, the couple moved to Northford, Saskatchewan, where Natasha's brother-in-law, Alexei Rubenstein, and his son, Fyodor, lived. (Sadly, Fyodor's mother, Natasha's twin sister Sophia, had died not too long before his posting in Ottawa.)

The local RCMP detachment—Sergeant Arnold Powell and staff—were given the bare facts of Ivan's background, his defection, and potential usefulness in Canada. The police were told that the Dalrymple couple should be given complete privacy regarding their past life in the Soviet Union. The public story would simply be one of standard immigration for purposes of family unification.

Initially, Clayton was true to his word and supplied valuable information to Canadian authorities. Within a few years, however, his connections and knowledge became out of date, and his services were rarely demanded. This meant that he received only minimal payments. The role of financial administrator at the Arts Centre, and later the Four-Square Gospel expansion project, was not full-time, or even half-time, so he had plenty of free time to engage in hobbies or take on other work. That is what he did. He became an agent for visual artists and did well. His clients, on the other hand, did not. They discovered that doing business with Clayton was expensive.

Within a few years, complaints emerged. It came to the attention of the RCMP that Clayton was selling art without the knowledge of his artists. He was also failing to advise Revenue Canada of income from those sales. As the matter went under investigation, the RCMP also discovered that Clayton was involved with a network of dealers who were selling stolen art. This network included Soviet Embassy officials in Ottawa, Singapore, and Istanbul.

The Ottawa RCMP office pursued the tax-fraud investigations, feeling it to be sufficiently within Canadian jurisdiction, but care was taken. A separate department, operating together with External Affairs, handled the investigation of Soviet Embassy involvement in the stolen-art network. The week before Clayton died, the RCMP had made an arrangement with Soviet officials. Criminal charges in Canada would be set aside, and Clayton would be handed over to Soviet officials. The Soviets wanted to hush up the matter of corruption within the embassies. Despite this arrangement, Inspector Dick Sanders from Saskatoon had informed Clayton that he was about to be charged and advised him that he could help his case if he exposed his embassy network. Apparently, Clayton did not agree. Or care. He had remained unreceptive to cooperating with authorities right to the end.

CHAPTER 8

DR. ROBERT MORLEY

As a highly touted young forensic pathologist at the University of Calgary Hospital, Dr. Robert Morley had sacrificed diligence for speed, or at least, so the lawsuit claimed. Morley had not helped his case by being stridently overconfident and pompous during the civil trial. The judge had not taken kindly to this. A mutually unpleasant give and take occurred between them, with Morley calling the judge a colossal fool, not competent to wash the floors of a judge's chamber. This did not endear the judge to Morley. It also did not endear him to the University of Calgary Hospital. Morley not only lost the case but his job as well. The hospital promptly fired him, calling his dismissal a win for everyone—though especially for them.

Morley had been married at the time of his dismissal but not after. His wife, Betty, who had been having an affair with the trial judge—a fact that did not come up in the news articles at the time—let Morley know that she would not be joining him in Northford, where he had found a new job. "My leaving you is good for both of us," Betty had said. "I get the judge, a man who very well may be a colossal fool, as you describe, but an old and rich one. And you get to move to a city where the cost of prostitutes is cheaper than in Calgary."

Morley moved to Northford as a single man and stayed that way. He bought an aging bungalow on Reed Avenue, just a few houses south of Arnold Powell's home. Twenty years later, both he and the bungalow were still together, although the bungalow remained older than Morley. Despite his relatively satisfying relationship with his house, he did not remarry, holding the view that his intimate needs could be satisfied quite economically, and with less fuss, by hiring an array of scantily attired women who arrived by cab early in the morning and left shortly after. Betty had been right. The cost of prostitutes was cheaper in Northford.

Despite his personal idiosyncrasies, Morley was an intellectually rigorous citizen. If there had been a referendum on intellectual prowess—and thankfully, to date, there had not been—Dr. Morley would have won. He was broadly read, something that became evident during any interaction with the man. He had an ability, and an inclination, to discourse at length on a wide range of topics, many of which failed to grip the typical Northford citizen. Despite his developing reputation as a pontificator to avoid at a formal social event, it was broadly conceded that he knew things.

Dr. Morley was also a formidable chess player. He joined the chess club in his first year at Northford and easily defeated the previous champion, Mayor Ken Russell. Russell had conceded gracefully, acknowledging Dr. Morley's chess mastery, even to the point of thanking him for bringing new rigour to the chess club. "Your skills are a gift to the club. Our standards have been raised, thanks to you, Robert," Mayor Russell had graciously said, still hoping to defeat Morley in the next tournament. But it had not happened. Morley easily won the annual tournament every year, generally with a quick drubbing of Russell in the final match. The nature of these defeats prompted Mayor Russell to discontinue offering gracious concession speeches.

History shows, however, that kingship is a fragile position. Kings come and go, and when they leave, it is often unpleasant for them. This is what happened to Dr. Robert Morley. When Clayton Dalrymple arrived in town, Dr. Morley's reign as chess king promptly ended. Clayton defeated Dr. Morley in one of the shortest final matches recorded in Northford history. Subsequently, the beatings persisted. It was difficult for Dr. Morley to accept that Clayton was a superior chess player, but in due course, he had no choice. It was becoming obvious to everyone in the club that Clayton was a vastly superior player.

A similar setback occurred in the field of antiquity scholarship. Dr. Morley was an amateur antiquity historian, and fluent (or so he claimed) in Greek and Latin. He confirmed this at a community theatrical event that Dan McCroskey put on, where Dr. Morley read Hesiod's "Theogony," an ancient Greek origin story, entirely in the original Greek. Everyone at the event had been impressed, if not also rather bored by the reading, except for Clayton Dalrymple. Clayton took specific issue with Dr. Morley's performance, questioning whether he even knew what it was that he was reading. "You seem to have memorized the poem, which is fine, but you are not fluent in Greek," Clayton had said. "It's almost as if you don't know any Greek at all."

Dr. Morley did not take kindly to the suffering Clayton imposed. But there seemed little he could do about it. He imagined various acts of revenge, but these mostly remained imagined, at least until he determined that he was a better dresser than Clayton. *Much better.* Or so he thought. Clayton may well have made questionable fashion choices, but Morley was truly not much better. When it came to dressing, Morley consistently made unfortunate fashion decisions. The general consensus was that he was choosing the wrong playing field on which to compete with Clayton.

Unlike Clayton Dalrymple, Morley was not gifted with a comforting physical appearance. Morley needed to wear clothes that would take the eye away from his short legs, lengthy upper body, long arms, no specific neck to speak of, and an exceptionally expansionist rear end. But he didn't. Instead of a wardrobe that softened the visual impact of his physical appearance, he wore striped shirts of dazzling colours, with broad white collars and cuffs. These shirts drew the eye to his upper body, and this was not to his advantage. It was unfortunate, because in his competition with Clayton, Dr. Morley was not helping himself.

■ ■ ■

As Dr. Morley examined the body of Clayton Dalrymple, he wondered whether anyone would be grieving. As he cut into Clayton, he recalled the man's unsettling flat, affected style and cutting commentary. Dr. Morley smiled slightly, knowing that his life in Northford had just improved.

Dr. Morley found himself whistling "Ain't Misbehaving," a rhythmic, cheerful tune. He didn't usually whistle. It just didn't seem right to whistle while doing an autopsy, but he couldn't stop himself. In fact, as he worked, he found himself tapping his foot to the beat of the tune.

Dr. Morley studied the bullet wound. There were gunpowder traces around the entry wound that matched the M1895 handgun. It was evident that the handgun had been fired at close range but distant enough that there was no exit wound. The bullet should be inside Clayton's skull, and sure enough, that's where Dr. Morley found it, comfortably lodged in the tissue of the paranasal sinuses. The bullet also matched the handgun found beside Clayton.

In taking routine test samples, Dr. Morley confirmed that, in addition to being shot in the temple, Clayton had incurred a blow (from hard cheese) to the front of the forehead and right arm, with some abrasions. Abrasions were also evident on Clayton's left arm and wrist.

Dr. Morley noted that the lab results on the breakfast-drink residue found no trace of poison, and he thought that was curious. He'd had a feeling that the body had been poisoned, as well as shot. It wasn't a strong feeling, but something about the body reminded him of a past autopsy he'd done where poison had been the cause of death. He did not pursue the matter further, however, as there seemed no need for it. Death by gunshot, self imposed or not, seemed an appropriate way for Clayton Dalrymple to have died.

Of course, the question of the yellow powder on Clayton's scalp and watch was curious. The powder being confirmed as hard, dry Parmigiana Reggiano didn't help that. It was evident to Dr. Morley that the speed of the cheese impact had been significant but not fatal. *Cheese is not generally a cause of death,* Dr. Morley considered, *although an overdose of blue cheese, in particular, could result in the desire for death.*

Desire aside, it was evident that Clayton had been dead when the cheese attack had occurred. How much before, Dr. Morley could not precisely say.

Dr. Morley smiled as he contemplated the image of Clayton, dead or alive, being blasted by his own gun, followed by a shot of hard cheese. He briefly considered that, perhaps, there was a God.

CHAPTER 9

ARNOLD AND CONSTABLE BILLY STAFFORD CONSULT

It was nine on Sunday morning when Constable Billy Stafford walked into Arnold's office, sipping a coffee from the staff kitchen. He knew that Arnold had made the coffee that morning, so he tried his best to calibrate his expectations, but his taste buds told him that the stuff was undrinkable slop.

Billy looked at Arnold, who was sipping his coffee with a smile. He seemed pleased with the taste. Arnold even released a satisfied sigh after each sip. "How do you manage it?" Stafford inquired curiously, marvelling at what he was seeing.

"Manage what?" Arnold asked, puzzled.

"Drinking this coffee. You seem to enjoy it. This is not real coffee, Arnold. This is a hot Saskatchewan River sediment beverage. A prairie pig would turn it down."

"Of course, they would. Pigs hate coffee. But don't be knocking the Saskatchewan River. Looks dirty, but it's a clean dirt. Just a muddy bottom. Catfish grow big and healthy."

"Do you eat them?"

"No, but some people do."

"Some people shouldn't. Anyway, we need to make a deal. If you're making coffee, let me know. I'll stop off at the Capri for a takeout."

"Doesn't Vera make coffee?"

"Not anymore. She has become a firm believer in the merits of green tea. Drinks copious amounts of the stuff and spends much of the night in the bathroom. She likes being in the bathroom. It's a lifestyle of a sort, I suppose. But she stays away from the coffee. Says that coffee is a death drink. Sounds a bit extreme to me, but Vera knows about health. She's exceptionally healthy. Always has been. Has never taken a sick day in her life, although she generally does not feel well. She has problems with the gas. Still, personally, I prefer the coffee. Who wants to live a long life without coffee? Not me."

"I'm with you, Billy. Full-bodied coffee, the kind that can hold up to the ravages of time. Day-old is great. Warm it up and enjoy."

Arnold was sitting back in his reclining chair, his glasses down on his nose, his RCMP issue jacket open and his Stetson jauntily angled on his greying head. He started yet another oral recounting of the scene surrounding the body of Clayton Dalrymple.

When he was done, he shook his head, deep in thought. "Quite interesting, the large footprints and the hard cheese."

"What's interesting about it?" Billy asked.

"I have never heard of a case where a dead body was hit by hard cheese. Have you? Unique, and yes, interesting. Emily will be pleased. She's always looking for a good story."

"It's a story, all right. Vera says it's never happened on *Mannix*, and if it hasn't happened on *Mannix*, it hasn't happened. Vera says you can take that to the bank."

"I'm not sure we want to take anything to the bank just yet, Billy," Arnold muttered. "I may pop by the pharmacy though. Acid reflex. Need to cut back on the cheeseburgers." Arnold stood up to reach for a glass of water on his desk. After a few sips, he took a deep breath and sat back down, feeling the growing discomfort of heartburn. He had been struggling with the issue for years.

"Kind of good to know that Northford has achieved something that Mannix hasn't," Billy said. "Mannix doesn't have heartburn either. At least, I don't think so. But Vera would know."

Arnold winced a bit, telling himself that he would stop by the pharmacy as soon as he was done interviewing Doc Rubenstein, who he noticed had just come through the entrance to the station and was waiting in the front lobby.

"Quick review, Billy, before I talk with Doc," Arnold said, sitting up straight in his chair for once. "Morley says that Clayton was dead when the cheese hit him. Somewhere between eight-thirty and nine-thirty this morning. There are three sets of prints at the scene. The cowboy boots from the car, which match Clayton's boots. Then we have the larger work-boot tread footprints to the south of the body. The third prints belong to Dan's running shoes. Of course, we know that he was at the scene, as he discovered the body. Those prints are also lighter, as they were made yesterday afternoon, rather than the morning when everything was still very damp."

"If you ask me, Arnold," Billy said quickly, "the killer is the person wearing the work boots. No question about it. Clayton didn't shoot himself with the cheese."

"On that point, we are agreed, but that doesn't mean that the person with the large-boots killed Clayton," Arnold said, trying to imagine for a moment the scene in the clearing yesterday morning. It seemed evident that the person with the large boots had shot hard cheese at Clayton. But why? Arnold figured that this same person was probably also connected in some way to the Medb play. *Maybe they hung out at rehearsals?*

"If he didn't kill Clayton, that rules out the KGB," Billy said, as he stood up from his chair, shoved his hands far too deeply into his loose-fitting dress pants, and then pulled them out again to work at tucking in his blue Sunday shirt. "I don't claim to be that smart, Arnold, as you well know, but I'm thinking that the KGB would not shoot cheese at a dead body. Further, if they did, they would only shoot to kill. From everything I've read about the KGB, which granted, is hardly anything, they don't mess around shooting cheese at dead people or going to theatrical rehearsals. But guess what? I might be smarter than I look. I found out that Muscle John has been going to Medb rehearsals, and his feet are massive. Suspicious or what? Mannix would call that kind of information a game changer."

"Or misleading," Arnold said. "Muscle John has big feet; that's true. But so do at least another hundred or so Northford men. We seem to have an exceptional number of men with big feet here. Not sure why. Still, a visit with Muscle John is in order." Arnold almost inhaled a gulp of coffee.

"What are you going to ask him? Where he was on Saturday morning?"

"That would be a good question," Arnold said, trying to keep the amusement from his tone. "I suppose I should ask him that."

"You definitely should. My goodness, his answer could solve the case."

"Not sure about that. We know he has an alibi for most of Saturday morning. He was pulling Doc out of the ditch. Of course, we don't know what he was up to earlier. I guess we'll have to find out," Arnold said, closing his eyes as if some insight might come along in the darkness there.

"Coming back to the KGB idea," Billy said confidently, "Vera says that the KGB connection is out of the question. They don't bother with a city our size. Trotsky was killed in Mexico City. Way bigger than Northford."

"That it is, Billy. A fair bit bigger. What else does Vera say?" Arnold asked, already reviewing his notes for his Doc interview.

"Now this is what I call a barn-storming session, Arnold! Love it! Just kicking some ideas around. Mannix does that all the time. It works."

"You mean brainstorming or the pencil sharpener?" Arnold asked, adding a question to his notepad.

"Brainstorming, of course, although thankfully, the pencil sharpener also works," Billy said with a determined tone, as he inserted his pencil into Arnold's desktop pencil sharpener.

Billy sharpened his pencil down to about half of its original length, put it into in his shirt pocket—where it now fit perfectly—and then sat back down. "That, Arnold, is what I call problem solving. That pencil has been sticking out of my pocket all day. Drove me crazy. Anyway, you should talk to Vera. She'll tell you straight out how Clayton died. Vera is not like me. She knows things."

The phone rang, and Arnold picked it up. After a brief exchange, he replaced the handset on its cradle. "Dr. Morley said that the breakfast-drink residue found at the scene tested clean." He shook his head. "That's baffling. The drink was apparently a concoction of apple, bell peppers, carrots, celery, cucumber, ginger root, kale, lemon, Swiss chard, and sundry other greens. Certainly, sounds toxic to me." He chuckled.

"You should order a retest," Billy said. "Mannix would."

"I was joking, Billy, but still, I actually don't trust the test results either. Neither does Dr. Morley. He has a feeling that poison is somehow involved.

Dr. Morley can be sloppy in his work, but his instincts are good. If he thinks Clayton was poisoned, he probably was."

"The KGB are famous for poison!" Billy said, his eyes widening at his next epiphany: "Maybe Vera is wrong! Maybe Northford *is* big enough for the KGB! Maybe Dan and Natasha really *did* see a large stranger!"

"I doubt it," Arnold replied casually. "You go to the same gym as Clayton, right?"

"I do," Billy said, tucking his shirt back in. "I wonder if Clayton's estate gets his membership fee back. I guess it doesn't matter. He won't need the membership or the cash. Dead men don't work out, and they don't spend."

"But their estate remains interested in what they leave behind," Arnold murmured.

"True enough. I suppose Natasha would want the fitness club refund. Good point, Arnold. Love the way you stay focussed in a conversation. Not like me. I drift," Billy said, noticing that Doc was growing agitated in the lobby. "Clayton told me that I didn't have an attention span. None at all. He told me that I should just give up trying. That there was no hope for me."

"No hope at all? Give up everything?"

"Everything." Billy nodded. "Like basically, my life. He said that I had the body and mind of a dough boy, and that I should do myself a favour and shoot myself. That my life was useless, and I was just taking up space."

Arnold frowned, standing up from his chair and readying himself to get Doc. "What prompted that?" Turning to look at Billy, he saw that Billy's finely creased dress shirt was almost completely untucked yet again.

"He just didn't like me," Billy said, tucking his shirt back in. "I can annoy people with my friendly nature. It made it look like Clayton was my friend, and he didn't like that. Found it embarrassing, so he needed to be rude to me. It was, in a sense, my own fault. I told Vera about it. She said I shouldn't worry and that she loves me just the way I am. Still, I have to admit, I would kill to have a body as ripped as Clayton's. My goodness, even in the meadow, Clayton looked great."

"But he was still dead," Arnold responded. "His fitness level failed to be of much value in the end. Did he interact with others at the gym?"

"In his way. He insulted people. In that sense, he was actually quite sociable. But he generally didn't talk to me, except to tell me that I was a loser. Generally, he did not give anyone the time of day. For me, that was fine. I always know the time. My watch is quite reliable. Vera gave it to me for my birthday."

"Which one?"

"The one I'm wearing. Wear it every day. Just what I do," Billy said nonchalantly, looking down at his pants to see if his shirt was still tucked in. It wasn't.

"I meant which birthday, Billy," Arnold said softly, shaking his head slightly.

"A few years ago. Whatever age I was then."

"Sorry I asked." Arnold sighed. "Do we have anything on the Mustang, Billy?"

"Still looking into it," he said. "We're checking the trunk and interior. Prints, hair, anything we can find. Vera says we should check for semen. She says that sex is probably involved. We know that Clayton liked sex. He had a lot of it. I don't know how he had the energy for it. I'm a once-a-week man myself—if I'm lucky, which I sometimes am." Billy got up from his visitor's chair. Sighing deeply and not bothering with his shirt this time, he walked over to the window that overlooked Mackenzie Avenue.

Arnold shrugged. "Clayton did have sex yesterday morning but not likely inside the car. What about Clayton's cowboy-boot prints? Are they a match with the prints coming from the service road?"

"Perfect match. Those prints belong to Clayton."

"But still no match for the large footprints?" Arnold asked, feeling an overwhelming sense of fatigue. He reminded himself that he needed to go back to meditation to help him fall asleep. He'd felt fine the previous day, even somewhat energized by the complexity of the case, but then, when the night had descended and his house had filled with quiet, his thoughts had rambled at some length and with some depth on the various avenues his life could have taken had he stayed in the arts and left police work to the less sensitive in spirit.

"I was just thinking, Arnold—I do that sometimes when I get tired— that I have a great alibi. I was in the gym that morning. But Clayton wasn't there. Should have been. If he'd gone for his workout, he would be alive today."

"There's a lesson there."

"The problem in this case, Arnold, is the weapons. Vera says that between slingshots and handguns, there's a steady diet of weaponry. She says that, without weapons, Clayton would be alive. She says that, without weapons, violence would plummet. She's against both. Mind you, she does love the pork, and I suppose that would be hard to harvest without some sort of weaponry. She gets quite excited about a plate of ribs. Speaking of which, should we ask Doc to come in? He has been waiting for a while."

"Yes, indeed. Ask him to come in. Kind of nice to keep a doctor waiting. Doesn't happen often," Arnold said, as Billy Stafford left the room.

"Have a seat, Doc. Let's get this statement done," Arnold soon said, taking his tape recorder from the top drawer of his metal desk.

"Busy desk," Doc said as he sat down, viewing the stacks of files.

"Piles of unsolved crime, Doc," Arnold murmured. "We specialize in leaving cases in various states of limbo. It reminds us of our limitations and relative incompetence."

Arnold cleared enough surface area to set the tape recorder down, merging several smaller file-folder stacks into one, creating a precarious tower just next to his telephone. He positioned the recorder between the file tower and the phone, turned on the record button.

CHAPTER 10

ARNOLD INTERVIEWS DOC RUBENSTEIN

Doc Alexei Rubenstein was a slight man, well under average height, with a sober but pleasant face. His short brown hair was neatly trimmed, accompanied by a retro ball cap with a New York Yankees logo. He wore an orange long-sleeved shirt with a white t-shirt underneath. His loose-fitting jeans hung low on his hips, looking around for a belt, and partially covered a pair of black dress shoes, smartly polished and clean in sharp contrast to the casualness of his jeans and his day-old beard growth.

Doc's rear end slid on the brown vinyl visitor chair, preventing him from maintaining a formal posture, but he looked relaxed and sober. He was even smiling, resting his left arm on his lap to hide the coffee stain that coloured his sleeve, as he waited for the interview to start.

"Sunday, September 28, 1975. Interviewing Doc Alexei Rubenstein at 9:42 a.m.," Arnold said into the recorder and then looked up at Doc. "It was you who identified the deceased as Clayton Dalrymple, originally known as Ivan Kalik?"

"Of course, Arnold," Doc said. "He is, or was, my brother-in-law. But you know that."

"You were also his family doctor?"

"I was, but you also know that."

"There are other doctors in Northford," Arnold said.

"I did mention that to Clayton, but he insisted on seeing me. It gave him pleasure to show off his muscular good health for me. I said yes. He was family, even though I didn't like the man. To be honest, if it was legal to kill a man in Canada, I might have done it. But it isn't, and so I didn't." Doc was still smiling.

"I guess that limited your prescription options?" Arnold joked.

"It did." Doc's smile now seemed a bit more tentative.

"Any health issues?"

"I'm okay. I drink too much. But then, I guess you're not asking about my health?"

"I wasn't," Arnold said.

"Clayton was generally in good condition. He worked out regularly and ate a healthy diet. He drank, but not as much as me. He smoked with restraint, six cigarettes a day. But he carried a lot of anger. His blood pressure was through the roof. He was taking medication for that. More recently, he was under immense stress, but then, you are well aware of that as well. Your department was the cause of much of it. But he didn't die from stress or heart failure."

"The bullet wound kind of gives that away, doesn't it?"

"It does." Doc's smile had faded, and he was now sitting upright, looking directly at Arnold and giving away no particular emotion. For a moment, Arnold was reminded of Natasha.

"What was your relationship with Clayton's wife, Natasha?"

"She is my sister-in-law. My deceased wife's twin sister. I suppose you are aware of our affair back in the Soviet Union. But we are not presently sleeping together. Perhaps with Clayton gone, we will again. I will give it a day or so, but I intend on inquiring with Natasha about that. I am quite lonely these days. Does any of this have anything to do with Clayton's death?" Doc asked calmly, looking around the room curiously. "You have no artwork in your office, Arnold. Why?"

Arnold leaned forward in his chair and whispered, into the tape recorder, that a suggestion from the public had been made to decorate the office with artwork. Then he leaned back and casually mentioned the obvious. "The department does not have a budget for art. Wish they did, but they don't. Back to you, Doc. You do have reason to want Clayton gone."

"No question," Doc said. "I hated him. He was my nemesis. I also feared him. I admit to having motivation to kill him, but I did not. As I said before, it is illegal in this country. It would also damage my medical practice. Can we move on to Clayton?"

"We can. Give me some background, Doc. How far back do you and Clayton go?"

"I suspect that you know much of it, but perhaps I can fill in a few details. I knew Ivan as a young boy. We used to joke that he would either join the KGB or a take up a life of crime. We thought it was funny. As it turned out, it wasn't. He did both. He joined the KGB *and* took up a life of crime. Sometimes within his job description, sometimes not. We stopped being friends after he joined the KGB. Being friends with a KGB agent is never a good idea. I tried to keep my distance, but he made that difficult, given that he managed to wind his way into our broader family. And there wasn't a thing I could do about it."

"How did he do that?" Arnold asked, noting his heartburn acting up and taking another sip of water.

"He became my brother-in-law. I had married Sophia during university, at Irkutsk, which is where we are all from. Clayton met Natasha, and offered to take her to Moscow, where she would be accepted at the Bolshoi. All she had to do in return was marry him. After some insistence on his part, she accepted the arrangement. Natasha was ambitious, talented, and naïve. That was the end of Natasha's naivety, but the beginning of her career as a ballerina."

"If she was living in Moscow, how did the two of you carry on an affair?"

"We had a few breaks in our affair, but we also had patience. When Clayton and Natasha moved back to Irkutsk, the affair picked up again. Later on, after he and Natasha returned from Moscow, he was in charge of Mongolian operations for the KGB. He wasn't around much. That helped us to carry on."

"What about Sophia, your wife?" Arnold asked, raising his eyebrows and taking another sip of water.

"That was a sensitive situation. It coloured our marriage, for certain. But Sophia was a practical woman. She knew about our affair. She was not pleased, but she coped with it. Mostly, she coped because she was devoted to Natasha, and anyway, we all had a greater enemy to deal with: Clayton. That helped to smooth the edges of our personal issues."

"Did Clayton find out?"

"I was never sure. The KGB tends to know everything. He probably knew. But he did not say a thing about it to us. When Sophia and I applied for permission to emigrate, Clayton offered to facilitate. He had influence and used it. It was a period in the early sixties when the Soviets were interested in getting rid of some Jews. I suspect that Clayton wanted to get rid of me, without killing me. Nice of him, I suppose."

"How did Natasha feel about that?"

"She was unhappy. I was in Canada with her sister, enjoying a medical practice, while she was in Irkutsk, with a dance career, yes, but always at the bidding of a man who held her fate in his hands."

"When did you and Sophia emigrate?"

"Fall of 1961."

"How was it for you when Clayton and Natasha defected and moved to Northford?"

"It was ... mixed. It was great to have Natasha here. But it was hard to live so close to Clayton. He had no power over me, but his presence created tension. He'd had the two people closest to me killed. My father, firstly, and then, I believe that he had Sophia, my wife, killed. I have no proof of either, but reasonable grounds for suspicion. His presence was why I sent Fyodor to school in Singapore. Or at least part of the reason. Fyodor is a superb student. He needs a quality school that can nurture his foreign-service career goals. But I also did not want Fyodor exposed to Clayton. I minimized that as best I could," Doc said quietly, and then, stretching his neck to one side and then the other, he asked, "Will any of these questions help with determining the cause of Clayton's death?"

"Probably not, Doc. But I don't know. Maybe more background will give me a clue. But my apologies for probing into matters that may not be relevant. I am proceeding as I feel it is necessary, but I will move on. For the formal record, please state your activities on Saturday morning?"

"I left for berry picking around seven in the morning, as Lake McCaskill is a good hour away. I got stuck on the way back though, not too far from

Northford, in the ditch beside Municipal Road 344. That would have been around ten in the morning. Muscle John pulled me out a little while later."

"Can anyone confirm when you left town?"

"The streets were quiet. The only person I recall seeing, as I headed west on Main Street towards Lake McCaskill, was a solo backpacker, trudging across the fairgrounds. I imagine the hiker is long gone by now, so I suppose that might not be helpful in terms of finding a witness."

"Probably not. Weird there was a hiker though. The hostel closed on Labour Day."

"Maybe the hiker camped out?"

"Maybe." He shrugged it off. "What did you do with the blueberries?" Arnold asked. "I could use some."

"I have a bucket for you actually. I froze four ice-cream pails. Gave some away. Muscle John took an ice-cream container. So did Dr. Morley."

"Do you have any information that can add to our understanding of Clayton's death?" Arnold asked, clearing his throat and speaking clearly into the tape recorder.

"I doubt it," Doc said. "I will say, however, that Natasha and Clayton had secrets between them, and secrets together. I am not privy to all of them—as I mentioned, they are secrets—but I can surmise some of them, and there is nothing that would strike me as relevant to his death. Natasha would not have killed him. I am quite confident of that, even though she had cause. She has seen enough death and has no desire to be party to it. But I don't have any specific information that can assist you. Not at this point, anyway. But if I encounter anything in my travels, I will advise you."

"Thank you, Doc," Arnold said. "If you could also write me a prescription for heartburn, I would be forever indebted."

Doc wrote Arnold a prescription, and after he left, Arnold sat for a few minutes, writing some notes. He liked Doc. He was not so sure that he liked Natasha, but that was another matter all together. He felt that Doc deserved to be happy, and if Natasha had been a friend to him in the past, perhaps she could be again. But first, Arnold needed to understand what (if any) involvement she'd had in the sordid mess that it was his responsibility to solve—or at least until Inspector Sanders showed up and took over.

A pang of heartburn swept over him then, and he swore to himself that, later that day, he would eat a salad ... or, perhaps, nothing at all.

■ ■ ■

Doc left the police station, feeling tired out from Arnold's questioning. He asked himself whether Clayton's death changed anything for him. It certainly changed things for Natasha. He wondered if she was involved in any way. Apparently, she had an alibi. That was good. He decided that he would stop in on her after lunch. He wasn't sure why, but he just felt he needed to feel out how she was doing.

He decided to stop at the Capri Hotel's café for lunch, and to have a few drinks, before visiting Natasha. He wasn't sure what he would say to her. He had not talked with her since the news of Clayton's death had broken. He wondered if she might even share an intimacy. He truly had no idea. Despite their affair, Natasha had always been a mystery to him but one well worth coming back to. In Doc's mind, she still was.

The Capri Hotel was a special place for Doc, both the bar and the cafe. He had been unfairly barred for most of the summer, but he'd dutifully paid his dues and been allowed back at the beginning of September. The barring had been a misjudgement on Mayor Ken Russell's part. As the owner of the Capri, he was understandably annoyed at the damage to the bar. Still, the primary fault lay with Clayton, not Doc.

Doc had been sitting in the Capri bar on a mild spring night, alone and moving gently into an intoxicated state, when Clayton had walked in and sat next to him. It had been a surprise. Clayton did not generally frequent the Capri or hang out with Doc. But that night, they'd sat together nursing a few vodkas. No words had been exchanged. It had been awkward for sure. At least until the fight had broken out.

The fight had started when Clayton stood up to make a few toasts. The first ones were benign, but then, he'd begun toasting to the beauty of women in general and then to the beauty of Janet Sawatzky in particular. Janet was at the bar that night with a few friends and appeared to accept the accolades with a positive spirit. Subjective statements, however, tend to invite opposing views, and that is precisely what happened. Muscle John had objected not to the content of Clayton's toasts but to his right to make them, saying that Janet was one of his staff, and as such, he had a civic duty to protect her from unwanted toasts to her beauty, whether she agreed with the proposition or not.

There was no question that Muscle John had thrown the first punch. Not that it mattered. The first had been quickly followed by others and then by the throwing of bar furniture. Chairs, tables, beer glasses, and a few lightweight patrons were tossed indiscriminately around the room. Destruction ensued. The property damage was extensive. The furniture, along with the beer glasses, had been unable to withstand the wear and tear of the event.

Emily had written a detailed story on the event for the *Northford Sentinel*, describing that over fifty beer glasses, many still containing beer, had been lost in the battle. Injuries had not been as plentiful as the scene would suggest, Emily had explained, but she wondered how many patrons would later claim traumatic injuries. She'd detailed how Muscle John had reinjured his rotator cuff while breaking a metal chair over Clayton's head, and Bernie Lieberman, of Lieberman's Pharmacy, had suffered a nosebleed that would not stop until well into his stay at Northford Hospital, despite having spent the entire melee in the bar's bathroom.

Emily had also told how Clayton, whom she described simply as one of the involved parties, had slipped out of the Capri with his brother-in-law, Doc, Northford's favourite family doctor—by way of the backdoor behind the bar—just as the fight had been reaching its apex.

The last part of the *Sentinel* article had told the story of how all four tires of Muscle John's red and blue tow truck, parked innocently enough beside the Capri, had been slashed that night. The article had seemed to suggest that Doc and Clayton were likely responsible, but that no charges as yet had been laid. Emily had interviewed Arnold about the matter, and he had said only that tires could thankfully be replaced but joked about the difficulty in replacing fifty glasses of beer. Emily had understood the levity of Arnold's remark and tried as best she could to turn the article into a lighter piece, pointing out that Sergeant Arnold Powell was prone to making light of crime, especially where loss of beer was involved.

All humour and news articles aside, Clayton, Doc, and Muscle John had all been barred from the Capri for the summer, and that had been difficult for Doc and Muscle John, both of whom loved to spend idle summer hours there. Thankfully, the ban did not apply to off-sale purchases, or for that matter, the summer patio. As the Capri owner and mayor, Ken had wanted to make a point but with only minimal damage to his profits. By the end of August, all the participants were invited back, although the practice of public toasting was strictly forbidden.

Chapter 11

Arnold Powell and Billy Stafford discuss the Medb play

Arnold Powell sat alone in his office, reflecting on the interview with Doc. He leaned back in his chair, looking out the window of his office to the deserted expanse of McKenzie Avenue. Northford streets were always empty on Sunday morning. Northford took church attendance seriously. It was not considered in good taste to walk about in public until after services were over. So, Arnold waited. He would fill his prescription at noon.

Constable Billy Stafford walked into Arnold's office and dropped himself into the visitor's chair. "I got to thinking last night, Arnold—amazing what can happen when you do that. It rained on Friday night, right? That's why the ground was so ideal for footprints."

"I think you're right, Billy."

"Then I got to thinking that drunks are often up to no good, right? What if a random drunk with large feet was loitering in the woods on Saturday morning. He comes across Clayton's dead body. Clayton has already shot himself. But being up to no good, the drunk takes out a slingshot, and some hard cheese, and shoots Clayton."

"Why?" Arnold often wondered what had prompted Billy to enter the police force. The man tried, there was no doubt of that, but his relationship with reality was consistently strained.

"We need to do more police work to answer that question, Arnold. But it helps to start with a theory. Maybe the drunk had seen a rehearsal of the play and wanted to try a re-enactment. The person obviously had some ill will towards Clayton. Most people did."

"That is true."

"I'm just trying to help," Billy responded, adjusting himself in the interview chair. It was an uncomfortable chair without a cushion or lumbar support, perfect for limiting the time anyone spent on it. "Vera says that we're overthinking," Billy stated emphatically then. "She says that can happen to the best of police forces, and we aren't even in that group."

"Madeline told me that once," Arnold said quietly. "I suppose she was right, and so is Vera. We do what we can. But your random-drunk theory doesn't strike me as a reasonable alternative to our present theorizing. In what way do you think we're overthinking this case?"

"I just think we are. I have weaknesses, as you well know, but overthinking is not generally one of them. Maybe I am over compensating."

"Point accepted. What does Vera suggest?" Arnold asked, almost seriously. It was Sunday morning, Inspector Sanders was coming, and he was open to new ideas.

"Vera says that most problems are simple. When you hit an object with a hammer, do so lightly but firmly. It solves a lot of problems."

"It does strike me as possible that we're focussing too much on Clayton's checkered past," Arnold offered, "which is interesting but possibly not relevant. As for using a hammer lightly, I was not aware we were using one at all."

"It was meant as a metaphor or something, Arnold." Billy laughed. "Never sure exactly what a metaphor is, but I agree with Vera that you can overcomplicate a case. I'm just saying, there might be simple explanation for the large footprint, and the difference in time of death, which we presume is the gunshot, and the cheese attack that broke his watch. For one thing, Dr. Morley cannot be precise about the time of death, or when the gunshot occurred. My goodness, he still isn't certain of the cause of death. Gunshot or poison."

"Dr. Morley is basing his time of death estimate on science. The body's temperature and the state of rigour mortis. It may not be as precise as we would like, but it is close. We need to be guided by his thinking."

"Sure. I'm not suggesting that Dr. Morley is wrong. I'm just saying that there could be other explanations. Remember when we found James Turner's body in the river? We were convinced it was murder. But it turned out to be a death by alcohol-induced misadventure. Clayton has a bad reputation in town. We know he has a checkered past, so we focus on that. But we could be taking our eye off what really happened."

"This is possible," Arnold said thoughtfully. "I've wondered about that as well. Is this where we return to your random-drunk theory?" Arnold fiddled with his top desk drawer for a minute, trying to open it to retrieve a pen that he liked using. He was not inclined to take Billy very seriously, but the man did have a way of sometimes hitting on helpful points seemingly by accident.

"It is, exactly," Billy said with building excitement. "My thinking is that Clayton drove himself to the meadow. He walks to the meadow from his car. He has a smoke, finishes his breakfast drink, puts it on the cotton-wood stump, takes off his coat, puts his glasses in his jacket, sits down, and shoots himself. About an hour later, a drunk wanders along and encounters Clayton. He happens to have a slingshot and some hard cheese. He shoots Clayton with the cheese and leaves. We know that the cheese incident happened after he was shot. Right? Drunks wander around all the time. It's what they do best. As to why, I have no idea. I'm not a psychologist. Drunken behaviour can be hard to understand. This guy obviously was open to shooting someone with a slingshot. Just saying, sometimes the explanation is simple. How confident are you about it being a slingshot?"

"Given the odd timing with the Medb play storyline, I'm fairly confident. But why would a random drunk have a high-powered slingshot and cheese?" Arnold asked, finally getting his desk drawer open and choosing between three of his favourite pens.

"Well, obviously, the drunk is interested in theatre. He has seen one of the rehearsals and is inclined to play acting."

"Does the man know that Clayton is dead in the woods?" Arnold asked, suddenly intrigued by the broader idea.

"Maybe he does. Maybe he's on a revenge mission and has followed Clayton into the woods. Drunks can be like that. Very obsessive."

"Your idea may not actually be as ridiculous as it sounds," Arnold said, looking out the window onto Mackenzie as the church bells started to ring.

"It might be ridiculous, Arnold, but a lot of ridiculous ideas turn out to be true. Landing a man on the moon was ridiculous for years. Then it happened. Proves my point, I think. Vera says that the Arts Centre probably has a high-powered slingshot in the prop room. All we have to do is find out who took it out on Saturday."

"I imagine a lot of people have access to the prop room," Arnold said. "It might not even be locked. I guess we should find out though. But a random drunk? I'm curious how you came up with the idea, Billy. I'm never really sure how you think."

"Vera gave me the idea. She said that being out in the rain makes her heart sing. It got me thinking that maybe someone was drinking in the rain on Friday night. Maybe this person happens upon Clayton's body the next morning. The person is a theatre fan and has stolen the cheese and slingshot from the prop room. Don't ask me why. Vera was confused about that too. She chalked it up to the known fact that theatre fans are weird. Vera says that only a weird person would choose to see a fictional drama in the first place. I rest my case."

"*Mannix* is fictional drama. Vera's favourite show."

"*Mannix* is a television police show. It's not fictional drama."

Arnold shook his head and tried to make a note, but his favourite pen did not work. Frustrated, he went back into his desk drawer and took out another. By the time he returned to his notepad, he had forgotten what he was going to write.

Billy sighed. "I guess your point is that a police television show is fictional drama. And I get that. And I do get easily confused about these technical matters, but still, my point is that the cheese and large footprints could have a simple explanation and be entirely separate from Clayton's actual death."

"There will be a connection of some kind," Arnold mused. "But you could be right that the two are separate."

"Vera would agree. She says that we're dealing with a random cheese shooter *and* Clayton shooting himself. Simple as that."

"Sometimes, Billy, I believe that Vera has some good points. But I continue to find it unbelievable that a man like Clayton, with rigid habits, would drive to the woods with his breakfast drink and shoot himself," Arnold said, getting up to ready himself for a visit to the pharmacy.

"Sometimes you just have to accept the facts, Arnold."

"I have no problem accepting facts when we have them. But the idea of a drunk with large boots, singing in the rain and sling-shooting hard cheese at Clayton's body is not a fact. Not yet. I suspect that it won't become one either. In the meantime, could you ask around about anyone seeing a large stranger lurking around town?"

"I'll ask around. Love doing that," Billy said, smiling. "Vera says that if a person loves their work, they never have to work a day in their life. Every day is a holiday to me."

"But isn't Vera a collection agent?" Arnold asked. "That must be hard to love."

"Not for Vera. She loves it. She loves human services. Very good at it, I might add. Instant connector, my Vera. She can get people to repay loans they didn't take out." He chuckled at the thought. "Just kidding. But Vera is stupid smart. Huge brain. If I had her brains, and she had my looks, we would be quite a team." Looking wistful, Billy tucked his shirt in quickly, as though he were getting ready to leave the station.

"You two *are* quite a team, Billy," Arnold said, rolling his eyes ever so gently towards the ceiling and noting the peeling white paint from the wet spot in the far corner. "Has that leak in the roof been fixed yet?"

"Don't believe so. Muscle John said he could do it. Cheap."

"But he hasn't."

"I imagine that he'll get around to it at some point."

"Maybe we should give him a deadline?"

"That's a great idea. Never thought of that."

"Always great to have an idea for the first time, Billy," Arnold grunted. "But I have to go. It's past noon, and the public can now go outside. I'll be filling my prescription and heading to the Dickey Dee for breakfast. Annie promised me a breakfast sandwich. Love her breakfast sandwiches. Mind you, with my heartburn, perhaps I'll have the chef salad instead."

"Too late for a breakfast sandwich, anyway, Arnold. Past noon."

"Fine, Billy. I'm off for a lunch sandwich, or maybe, a salad."

"By the way, Emily Little left you another message. She wants an appointment. I told her you were pretty busy, what with Clayton's death and all."

"That's true, but Emily might have information. I'll stop at the *Sentinel* after lunch," Arnold said, then left the office, whistling.

In the quiet of the station, Billy walked around Arnold's desk, and sat down in Arnold's chair. He swiveled around, hearing the squeak at the base, and looked at Arnold's cluttered desk. Leaning back in Arnold's chair then, he closed his eyes. For a moment, he considered having a nap ... and then he did.

Chapter 12

Sunday lunch at the Dickey Dee

Arnold had seriously considered a salad for lunch but then changed his mind. The medication had cleared his heartburn discomfort, and he felt that a delay in diet adjustment was in order. He ordered a toasted English biscuit, with a soft-poached egg and breakfast sausage, and had nearly finished it when Annie Russell came to his table with a steaming cup of coffee.

"Cool and rainy day for crime solving," Annie said cheerfully as she sat down.

"I wish," Arnold muttered. "Maybe when Dr. Morley is done with the autopsy, we'll have a more informed view of how exactly Clayton died. I'm not completely settled on the notion of death by gunshot. But at this point, I have no evidence to support an alternative notion."

"What do you suspect?"

"Maybe poison. We'll see."

"What do you make of the hard-cheese business?" Annie asked.

"Wish I knew. Billy and I were tossing around ideas. Mostly wacky ones. Brainstorming with Billy tends to drift far into strange territory. But the cheese is real enough. Why is it there? Billy thinks it might be a killer's trademark. Sending a message. But not much point in sending a message to a dead man, is there? Maybe it's a message to the rest of us, but we don't understand it, so if it *is* a message, it isn't very effective."

"Makes sense to me that it is though," Annie said, sipping her coffee and looking around the room. She fidgeted with her finger a bit, rotating her wedding ring, and then glanced out the window. Some kids were fooling around on the picnic tables, playing a game of some kind. "Clayton had the kind of life that encouraged resentments. Someone could be trying to trivialize his death."

"Yes, that's possible, except that it feels perhaps too random and ill considered," Arnold said, finishing his sandwich and wiping a bit of yolk from his mouth. "A note would have helped. Billy thinks a drunk with a slingshot discovered the body and shot him with hard cheese. Sounds crazy and can't possibly be right, though. Billy is never right."

"You're being unfair, Arnold. I'm sure Billy's right sometimes," Annie said softly. "You're quite hard on him."

"I am. It's true. Billy is a good guy, and he tries, but he is *never* right. When it comes to solving crime, the best Billy can do is avoid being far wrong. Occasionally he's close."

Annie leaned over and whispered in his ear. "Have you talked with Sheila yet? She was with Clayton on Saturday morning. Could have been the last person to see him alive."

"I called her at the hospital, but she was off sick. I'll catch up with her later. Don't see Sheila as being a person of interest. She was having sex with the man. Why give that up? Unless the sex was bad."

"I would think that bad sex is still better than no sex," Annie conceded. "Anyway, even bad sex shouldn't drive a person to kill."

"You wouldn't think so."

"And Clayton didn't leave a note?"

"No note has been found as of yet."

"I guess not everyone leaves a suicide note."

"Most of the time they do though."

"One other thing, Arnold. I have a confession to make," Annie whispered, looking around to ensure that no one could hear. "It's completely innocent, but still, I should tell you. Though of course, maybe Ken already did."

"If it's about the Medovik cake, I know about Ken bringing one to Clayton. Apparently, it was not well received."

"Clayton wasn't appreciative? Ah well, still ... one tries, right?"

"You do," Arnold said softly.

"If you see Natasha again, you might ask if Clayton liked it."

"I could do that. What about Natasha?" Arnold found himself wondering about the cake's possible relevance.

"Natasha doesn't eat desserts." She sighed. "Sad, really. Life is too short not to have guilty pleasures."

"Natasha is not without her guilty pleasures, I'm sure." Arnold pushed his plate away, contemplating briefly the guilty pleasures of Natasha Dalrymple ... and the list of Clayton haters.

CHAPTER 13

ARNOLD ENCOUNTERS AN INTOXICATED, DISGRUNTLED WILLIAM SAWATZKY

Rain descended in sporadically intense waves against the windshield of Arnold's cruiser as he drove to the *Northford Sentinel*. He slowly pulled into the loading zone on McKenzie Avenue, in front of the Capri, a half block from the *Sentinel*, and waited. All he could see was the vague red colouring of the traffic light ahead. It was a few minutes after one o'clock on Sunday afternoon. Beyond the millions of tiny bubbles bursting on the windshield's surface, Arnold noticed that the western sky was clearing. Outside of the immediate downpour, the sun shone, which it always does somewhere. But Arnold could see that the sun was about emerge overhead as well, signalling an end to the downpour.

Arnold sat quietly, carried away by Brahms Cello Sonata No. 2 (one of his favourites). There was something about the tone of the cello that carried Arnold far away from the cares of Northford and the investigation into Clayton's death. By the time the clouds had drifted to the west of town, taking the rain along with them, the sonata was nearing its conclusion. As Arnold turned the radio off, he contemplated the therapeutic value of cello music.

He did not understand exactly why the cello moved him the way it did. He wondered sometimes whether his mother's influence on him had been stronger than he realized. He had taken piano lessons as a child, on his mother's insistence, but he had lost interest. His mother had played guitar, sung in the church choir, and recited poetry in her idle time, but his father's opinion had carried more weight with Arnold. His father was a (somewhat) overly practical man and dismissed music as lacking social utility. At a critical decision-making stage in his life, Arnold had chosen to follow in his father's footsteps and become a police officer.

It had been a good decision in some respects. He liked the problem-solving aspect of his profession. But there was a cost to police work that he had not anticipated. Neglecting his artistic interests was one of them. As to the broader social utility of police work, he also had concerns. Policework was ideally a form of social service, maintaining order for the common good, but he was becoming increasingly aware that this ideal was difficult to achieve. Instruments like the cello, and music in general, worked wonders for taking the edge off life's disappointments.

Arnold stepped out of the vehicle, just missing a stream of water rushing towards the storm drain. As he moved to higher ground, he encountered a drenched William Sawatzky, who for some unclear reason, was standing in the middle of a puddle.

"Not a great idea to stand in the water, is it, William?" Arnold asked. "Dry sidewalk a few feet away."

"As if the police care where I stand," William snarled sarcastically, his words noticeably slurred. "The rain came on strong. Tried to step into the Capri, but Mayor Russell wouldn't let me in. Said I was drunk. I'm going to sue him."

"You are drunk, William. He has a right to refuse you."

"I might be drunk, but I am not a thief."

"Who said you were?" Arnold asked, regretting the question immediately. It both delayed his departure from William and gave the man an opportunity to express one of his many grievances.

"You did, Arnold," William snarled. "You told the judge that I was a thief."

Having inadvertently opened a sensitive topic, Arnold conceded that he needed to defend what he had (indeed) said about William. "The Belhaven commune, which you and Adele owned, stole from its devotees. You required them to sell their assets and give the money to Belhaven, which was you and your wife." Arnold felt that his summary was concise and accurate, a point that had been confirmed by the judge at the time, resulting in the Belhaven commune being forced to close. However, Arnold still regretted the statement, or having opened himself up for this conversation at all. It only promoted discussion with a man who was not part of his day's agenda.

"Belhaven was a church, a place of God, a religious community," William argued, as best he could while standing in a puddle of water, leaning against a parking metre. It was good for the devotees' soul to give to the church."

"Especially when you and Adele were the church."

"Hey! The only people who complained were the skeptical, money-obsessed families of our community members and our heathen daughter, Janet, who had a grudge against us, and after all we did for her! Belhaven was a loving oasis, free of material possessions yet rich in spirit. Then it was all taken from us. You'll have to answer to God for your part in our calamity, Arnold. After all the lawsuits, Adele and I had very few resources left. We bought the Capri Hotel, thinking we could contribute to providing housing for wayward youth, but that was stolen too. It makes me wonder how a poor man of God can stand such times and live."

"I believe that's a song, William," Arnold said, recognizing the lyrics from a classic Depression song. Arnold wondered whether William knew the song or had just stumbled upon the same phrasing.

"Song or not, it's true, Arnold. We live in desperate times. But not for long. Ken Russell will find that stealing the Capri out from under us was a bad idea. He'll pay for that sin. Mark my words."

"Ken didn't steal the Capri from you, William. You didn't pay your taxes for five years and refused to negotiate with the town. You gave them no choice but to auction off the hotel. All you had to do was pay your bill, or at least, say that you would."

"Taxes are just another form of theft," William spewed. "Government-sanctioned theft."

"Taxes pay for services," Arnold said, feeling somewhat strange defending taxes with an intoxicated man who was still standing in water.

"What services? Policing? That's a joke, Arnold, and not a funny one," William bellowed, attempting a laugh but not succeeding.

Arnold had had about enough. "What about the medical services at Northford Hospital, which saved the life of young Fyodor Rubenstein, who nearly died at Belhaven because you gave him herbs that he was allergic to and then refused to give him the medical attention he needed. The commune blew up on you because Doc complained, your daughter complained, and the families of your disciples complained. They *all* had cause to complain. You brought on your own demise, William. Now you are drunk, and on a Sunday. What would Jesus think?"

"That's blasphemous, Arnold. There's nothing funny about Jesus."

"Jesus didn't have a sense of humour; did he?"

"He didn't need humour. He had the answers, Arnold."

"To what?

"Everything. The signs of the end. The beginning of the time of troubles. Then shall appear the sign of the son of man in heaven."

"You think about the end times even when you're drinking?"

"I am a flawed vessel, Arnold. As are you. But today I am good spirits. I am celebrating the death of the atheist."

"You're referring to Clayton, I presume."

"Couldn't stand the man."

"Did you kill him?"

"Of course not. I leave the killing to God. But it's obvious that justice was done."

"How's that?"

"God works in mysterious ways, Arnold. We may not always understand how justice works, but let's face it, a man like Clayton took more than he gave. His death is addition by subtraction. Judgement comes for us all, but the day of reckoning for Clayton was overdue. I take it as a sign that we're closer to the end."

With that, William moved awkwardly out of the puddle, carefully placing one foot after the other as though the water were waist deep. Then, slowly navigating into a ray of sunshine that had just broken through a gap in the fast-moving clouds, he sat down in front of the hotel he once owned.

CHAPTER 14

ARNOLD MEETS WITH EMILY LITTLE

Emily Little was hammering away on a typewriter when Arnold walked in. "I've been trying to reach you, Sergeant," Emily said in a spritely tone. "I have information you may be interested in."

"You generally do, Emily," Arnold said as sat down in the badly weathered, brown leather couch in the *Sentinel* newsroom. "I have news as well. I just witnessed a drunken William Sawatzky get hit by a sunbeam. Quite spectacular, although possibly not enough for you to write an article about it. Not like the Belhaven story, which I might add, gave you some star billing. Much deserved too. What do you have for me?"

"I met with Natasha here on Saturday morning. Perhaps you already know that."

"Natasha told me. You're part of her alibi. What time?"

"We met between eight and eight-twenty or so and went over a promotional article for the upcoming Medb play. It will be in tomorrow's paper."

"That's the play the Arts Centre is putting on in a few weeks, right? Natasha's visit yesterday was about promoting it?"

"It certainly was. The play has a fascinating plot, especially given what I understand happened in the woods. I'm writing three article pieces on the play, including the original Irish myth."

"Which is what?" Arnold asked, casually lifting his feet a bit as a small mouse darted across the newsroom floor.

"The story focuses on Medb, a mythological Irish queen," Emily explained, rolling her chair away from her desk and curling her shoeless feet up under her body. "As a queen, she had to make difficult decisions to maintain power. One of them was ordering the murder of her pregnant sister. The mother was killed, but the baby was born by caesarean section and survived. The baby boy, Furbaide, resented Medb for killing his mother and plotted his revenge. Furbaide practised killing Medb with a slingshot, but then one day, he came across Medb bathing in a pool. He had not expected to run into her, so all he had with him was a piece of hard cheese, which he'd been planning on eating for lunch. He placed the cheese in his slingshot and shot Medb. Killing her."

"Not the first time that lunch killed a person. Was Furbaide a good shot or just lucky?" Arnold asked.

"Like I said, he had been practicing," Emily said. "He knew that Medb bathed in a particular pool, and he even measured out the correct distance. He'd practised for days, putting an apple on a tree stump at the right distance. But he had planned on using stones, not hard cheese."

"Poor planning."

"I suppose so. Unlucky for sure."

"Especially for Medb. What else do you have for me, Emily?" Arnold asked then, trying to sound casual but not succeeding.

"Right," Emily said quickly, moving her chair back towards her desk and digging around in a pile of papers for a particular sheet of paper. "I didn't have all day to talk about the Medb story. Neither did Natasha. She took her time here but seemed in a rush. I got the feeling that she was anxious to be somewhere else. Mind you, Natasha always seems like she wants to be somewhere else. Frankly, I think she does. But I don't know where. Not sure she does either."

"Natasha is outwardly composed, but inwardly unsettled. As a result, her comments tend to lack a synergy with her meaning. Any chance we can get back to your information, Emily?" Arnold asked, holding his notepad and pen ready. "I'm sorry, but Inspector Sanders is coming tomorrow. He will be late, but I can't be."

"Of course," she said, chuckling at the insinuation. "But Natasha's state of mind could be relevant. A state of mind can be critical. My ex-boyfriend, for example, would always say one thing and mean another, and you could tell that from his tone and the look of his eyes." Emily looked around the newsroom at the closed door of her boss, Ian O'Brien, and groaned slightly.

"Speaking of which," she said, "Matt, my ex, came by the *Sentinel* this morning. He apologized for not coming with me to Northford and said that he had changed his mind. He wanted to come and join me now, provided I give Northford a time limit. He figured he could be happy here for two or three years, but after that, we should move on to bigger and better things. Not sure what those were, and neither was he, but apparently, he didn't think they could be found in Northford. Even as he said this, he seemed in a hurry to get back to Saskatoon, and he kept looking around at the newsroom here as though it were the most disgusting place he had ever seen. Of course, it *is* quite disgusting, what with the mice problem we have, and now the cleaners refusing to come until we solve that problem, which is not going to happen in my lifetime, even though I am quite young and would like to think that eventually the mice will move on to other adventures, perhaps in Saskatoon, where according to Matt, prospects are bigger and better."

Arnold found himself taking a deep breath, both to calm his impatience and in sympathy for Emily's lungs after that mouthful of a sentence. He decided to just let her continue though, which she quickly did.

"That is all I have to say on that, except for one thing, and that is that I'm pleased Dan is moving into my building. Getting out of his marriage will do wonders for that man, and possibly, for me. I do find myself quite attracted to him. Never knew a man could love myths as much as he does. Quite inspiring. My love life has not been going well in Northford, Arnold, as you're probably aware. I've been a bit busy, snooping around and getting to know the Russians, and especially Clayton, who I understand has died under mysterious circumstance. Which brings me to the information that I've got for you, Arnold."

Arnold had so far not written any of this down. He'd thought about it but decided not to. Emily liked to talk, was skilled at it, and would certainly be happy to repeat everything, at any time, if needed. With a nod, he told her that he appreciated her thoughts on Matt, and Dan, and wished her well on her love life, and the mouse problem at the *Sentinel*, then politely asked, "So, what would this information be?"

Emily took a deep breath, smiled exceptionally broadly, and said, "I was out running on Friday, around six, when I saw Clayton peel out of the Arts Centre parking lot in an awful rush. Dan saw him too. He was having a smoke at the east doors of the Arts Centre and walked over to where the Clayton's Mustang had been and picked something up. I was some distance away, but it looked like a handgun. I left you a note about it."

"Did he take the gun with him?"

"I'm not sure about that. I think he did. But I'm sure that it was a handgun. Don't usually see them when I'm out for a run," Emily said, spinning her chair around a bit to look out the west window, past where Arnold was sitting.

"Anything else?"

"Not really. Weird question for you though: Can you tell me what Clayton was wearing in the aster meadow?"

Arnold did think that was a weird question, but then, he reminded himself that Emily was a writer and might want to visualize the scene. He felt there was no harm in sharing the details. "Clayton was wearing a disturbingly brown, tweed sports jacket, a mostly unbuttoned paisley satin shirt, saddled with a light scattering of randomly placed blood, and skin-tight bell-bottom blue jeans with brown leather cowboy boots."

"Eww!" Emily screwed up her face while raising her eyebrows (and somehow still managed to look attractive). "That must have been hard to look at."

"It didn't help that he was dead. Clayton was definitely not looking his best."

"Did he have an outdoor jacket? It was a cool morning."

"He had a black pea coat neatly folded and resting on a tree stump. I imagine he was wearing it when he arrived."

"He was from Siberia. Probably thought it was a balmy morning."

"Of course, if he was planning to shoot himself, he didn't need a warm jacket."

"Did he shoot himself?" Emily asked, curiously. "The public likes to know these things."

"We're investigating. There are some complications. But I can tell you that a gun was on the scene and a bullet wound was on Clayton's temple. His prints are on the gun. What more can I say?"

"Probably more than you're going to. Still, I get the point. Hard to get on with the day after that. Do you know how long he was lying there?"

"Since the early morning. Dan found him in the afternoon. Towards the end of a hopelessly long championship ballgame."

"Which we lost. That must have been difficult for Dan. He's such a sensitive man."

"He seemed fine with Northford losing."

"I mean he must have been traumatized by finding the body."

"Perhaps he was. He was running, and he had his shirt off. That was neither pretty nor normal for Dan. He did not look to be in great shape, though he did look considerably better than Clayton."

"It does seem odd that Dan would find the body of the man who was having an affair with his wife on the same day that his wife kicks him out," Emily quipped, hopping out of her chair to walk lightly to the *Sentinel* kitchen area and pour herself a coffee from a deeply stained-glass carafe. The smell and colour of the coffee suggested great age.

"Is it true that, at least half the time, the person who finds the body is the killer?" Emily asked.

"It is," Arnold said, wondering whether Emily had any more information, "although Dan has an alibi."

"Of course, he does. Dan would never hurt anyone, Arnold," Emily said, sitting down on the leather couch beside him. She took a sip of coffee, sighed, and leaned back into the soft confines of the couch. "Dan is a gentle, artistic soul. I do hope that he's not mixed up in this. I really think I could be quite happy with Dan."

"You might have to tell him that, Emily. Dan might be creative but sizing up reality is not his strength. Anything else?"

"There is," Emily said thoughtfully. "You should know that I actually got to know Clayton fairly well. I interviewed him a number of times and talked casually with him at the Community Partners drop-in. We actually got along well. He wasn't all bad. He actually said he felt bad about his affair with Sheila."

"Why?"

"Because of Dan. He hated Dan, but he didn't have any desire to wreck his marriage."

"He was happily trying to ruin his professional career," Arnold pointed out.

"That is true," Emily said sadly. "He was quite homophobic. He seemed to believe that Dan was gay. Sheila said that he was. Of course, he isn't. He's just artistic and broad-minded. Clayton was neither. But still, he felt bad about the affair."

"And yet he kept the affair going. Did he also feel bad about Janet Sawatzky?"

"He did. He actually liked her. Not like Sheila."

"He didn't like Sheila?"

"Not really. He liked the power he had over her though. With Janet too. Although with Janet, he actually wanted her as a friend. He said that she was a good listener, very understanding and insightful. He wanted to help her."

"Did he help her?"

"He was going to see to it that she achieved her career goals, whatever it cost. He was getting sex from Janet, but at least he was planning on sponsoring her medical-school ambitions. Still, I didn't approve of what he was doing. He was addicted to power, in my opinion. But I do think that he was really wanting to help Janet, even as he was taking advantage of her."

"What about Natasha?"

"They seemed to have power over each other. But he had guilt regarding Natasha too. He dealt with it by viewing her as his enemy. He was quite convinced that Natasha was oppressing him ... that he was a victim. He said that she was unappreciative of everything he had done for her. He had given her a career, and yet she gave him nothing but rejection. He conceded that she was pretty to look at but a dreadful lover. 'A frigid, cold fish,' he said."

"Natasha might be a cold fish, but she's been swimming in icy waters."

"True enough," she said. "Living with Clayton would not have been easy. How was the Natasha interview?"

"She was formal, cold perhaps, but I was wearing a jacket. And her policy on ashtrays needs review. Otherwise, some of what she said was believable. But she's definitely keeping some information to herself. A commitment to transparency was in no way evident."

"Why would she withhold anything if she has an alibi?"

"Could be protecting someone. Any other information, Emily?"

"Yes. On Saturday morning, after my meeting with Natasha, I went for a run around the fairgrounds track. I saw Clayton driving his Mustang from the east, down Main Street, and then turn onto the fairgrounds and enter the forest road. This was at around nine. A few laps later, I saw Madeline emerge from the forest road. This would have been 9:10 or so. She will have seen Clayton on the forest road as well, I expect."

"Interesting information, Emily. That does change some things. So, Clayton was still alive at nine on Saturday morning. He wasn't alive for long after."

"When did die?"

"His watch stopped at 9:30. But we think he died somewhat before that."

"You should definitely talk to Madeline," Emily said, getting up from the couch and returning to the kitchen for more coffee. "She would have seen Clayton on the forest road after I did."

"I have noticed that Madeline has taken to walking," Arnold said, getting up from the couch and putting his notepad in his breast pocket.

"She visits Oscar White at his cottage on Saturday mornings, before starting her reception gig at the Arts Centre," Emily said. "She's confronting that fine young man, who just managed to evade the Vietnam war, with a series of Bible study classes. Christian witnessing. It is a bit sad, really."

Arnold shook his head. "I have heard the rumours. Madeline should really leave Oscar alone. That young man is growing marijuana in the woods and smoking it, no doubt. I've chosen, wisely I think, to ignore his activities. It may be illegal, but sometimes, it's better to look the other way. I like him. He reads Carlos Castaneda books and is enthralled with the Buddhist middle path. I understand that Madeline is under instruction from her new partner, the devout and dour Gerald Schultz, but I think her time would be better spent gardening. She's an awesome gardener. Much more useful activity, in my view." He looked towards the door. "I'll stop in on her. Thanks, Emily."

"What was it like to find Clayton in the woods, anyway? Seems like a lonely place to die," Emily said, moving herself and her cold black coffee back to her desk.

"Death is a lonely experience," Arnold said, sitting back down in the couch almost without realizing he was doing so, and noting that his body needed another acid-reflex pill. "As a place to die, I think the woods are better than a care home …. but it's still just a place to die." He paused for a moment as a thought occurred to him. "On Friday evening, did anyone else see Clayton drive off in a rush?"

"William and Adele were at the ball-field entrance, getting their end-of-times placards set up for the tournament. They will have seen it. Also, Muscle John was standing in front of the pool hall. He likely will have noticed too, even though he was smoking. John tends to be quite focused and vigorous with his smoking, as you know. He must suck back half a cigarette per inhalation. It's a talent, I suppose," Emily said smiling.

"John has skills that he's not given credit for," Arnold observed, standing up once again from the couch and looking somewhat longingly at the door. He liked Emily very much. She was a treasure in Northford, and a pleasure to engage with. But it was time to take another pill. His inner discomfort was impacting his focus. "Tell me again what time you were out running on Saturday morning?"

"I started shortly after my meeting with Natasha, around eight-thirty. I ran down McKenzie to Main, onto the fairgrounds, and did some laps until nine-thirty. I saw Clayton driving by around nine and Madeline coming out of the forest road a little after nine. The baseball-tournament traffic was just picking up. William and Adele were at the entrance to the fairgrounds with the placards." She frowned. "Weird to think that I saw Clayton driving to his own death."

"That would feel strange, certainly. By the way, Emily, did you see a large stranger, lurking around the park entrance on Friday, when Clayton pulled out of the parking lot?

"No," Emily said firmly, digging around her desk to find a spot to put down her still-full coffee mug. "I did not. The park entrance was empty. I would have noticed if someone was there. I notice things."

CHAPTER 15

ARNOLD INTERVIEWS DAN MCCROSKEY AT THE ARTS CENTRE

Arnold entered the east-facing front door of the Arts Centre building, just after one on Sunday afternoon. He walked down the long hallway, with its posters of previous events lining the walls, past the men's bathroom and the staff kitchen, and turned into the office of "Dan McCroskey: Artistic Director." *Well, no question what Dan's job title is,* he thought. The nameplate was hard to miss. With its gold background and large-font black lettering, it stood out almost jarringly on an otherwise-bland, wood-grain office door.

Inside the room, Dan was seated, partially hidden from view by two towers: tower one, a pile of clothes, presumably destined for the wardrobe room; tower two, a stack of cardboard boxes that touched the ceiling. Packed bookshelves lined the east wall of the office, but there was no clear path to them. The floor was covered with theatrical props, so getting there would likely require considerable moving of materials. Dan's desk was completely hidden from view by boxes, costumes, and paper files, but Arnold presumed that one existed—as Dan was not a minimalist—somewhere in the vicinity of where Dan sat, with his back to the door, facing the north window, which looked out onto the lush lawn and flower gardens of the Arts Centre property along Main Street. The view from the window was seriously curtailed, though, by three large plants.

Philodendrons, Arnold noted. Madeline had kept similar light-obstructing plants in their living room.

There was a large west window that could have allowed in more light, and offered a clearer view, but a stack of boxes covered it. It was unfortunate. Even though it was daylight, the office was quite dark, making it difficult to make out the details of the photographs on the west wall. As far as Arnold could determine, they seemed to be photos of theatrical cast troupes.

Arnold cleared his throat and Dan turned his chair to face him, greeting him and offering him a (theoretical) seat. Considering for a moment, Arnold ended up removing a box of silver bells from a brown leather side chair and sat down.

"So, you like a healthy measure of disarray?" Arnold asked.

"In the theatre business, every object has potential," Dan said, briskly. "It may look chaotic, and perhaps some sorting would be good, but I don't have time for that. What matters is the product on the stage. No one cares what backstage looks like. I always have projects that are in some stage of development. It's a juggling act. Some of them will wither and die. Others will bloom and see the light of day in front of an audience."

"Makes sense. I get it. Must be tiring though. Stressful," Arnold said, looking around in amazement at the sheer number of boxes in the room.

"I suppose it is. But it's what I do. Wouldn't change a thing."

"Your marriage too?" Arnold asked.

"I was thinking of my work," Dan said lightly. "My marriage, well ... I suppose, in retrospect, it was a mistake. But you know about marital mistakes, Arnold. How many wives have you had? Still, even a bad marriage generates some good. You have two children. So do I. My two boys are easily worth the trouble of having lived with Sheila. And now I'm free. Who knows, I might have even learned something. Not sure yet."

"Staying at Emily's could be good for you."

"Hope so. But I'm not rushing anything. For now, I'm sleeping on her sofa. Not very comfortable. But good enough."

"In her bed would be better, I would think," Arnold said absentmindedly, taking out his notepad.

"I wouldn't push my luck if I were me."

"But you *are* you. You push your luck regularly on the stage. Why not in real life?"

"Because I understand theatre. Or at least I think I do. Real life is another language altogether. I'm not gifted with human relations in the real world."

"Don't you find this Medb play oddly similar to certain aspects of Clayton's death?"

"It is. I haven't been able to stop wondering about that."

"I imagine you have a slingshot in your prop room?" Arnold asked, not looking at him.

Dan paused, grabbing a cardboard box to the left of his desk, and started digging around for something. "Not in the prop room," Dan said. "But I have one at home. My boys love shooting with it. They don't shoot birds or anything. They just practise really. But my boys didn't shoot Clayton."

Arnold smiled crookedly. "No one's saying they did. Is their slingshot missing?"

"I looked for it yesterday," Dan said rather quicker than Arnold expected. "It was in my former bedroom closet."

"Why would you look for it?"

"I think you know," Dan said, swinging back around in his swivel chair to look out the window at the Arts Centre lawn through the spaces between the plants. "The yellow powder on Clayton was shocking. Someone is definitely trying to emulate a scene from the play. Obviously, part of me wondered whether our slingshot had been used."

"Was it?"

"Well," Dan said, looking away from Arnold, "if someone took it, they brought it back. Of course, slingshots aren't that difficult to find. Anyone could buy one."

"I suppose they could. Anyone other than your boys have access to your slingshot?"

"Sheila's brother shoots with it sometimes, but not by himself. He's mentally handicapped. Lives in a group home."

"I'm aware of that. I understand that Henry goes to your place a lot?"

"Oh yes."

"Has Henry seen any of the play's practices?"

"He's a regular. He's very devoted to Sheila, who plays Medb."

"Anybody else come to practice?"

"Muscle John comes occasionally. He's wary of theatre though. Doesn't approve of it generally. This morning he actually came to my office and told me that Clayton's death had been prophesied in the Bible. That young man is crazy. Bad enough when he was a petty-criminal nuisance, now he's a religious-zealot nuisance."

"Muscle John came specifically to tell you about Biblical prophecy?"

Dan shook his head and started looking through boxes again. "I need a system. Some kind of numbering system, so I know which box to look at. As for Muscle John, I can't say exactly what his problem is. He told me that Clayton's death was prophetic, and that it was a sign from God to repent. The Four-Square Gospel group has moved into lunatic mode and taken Muscle John with them. Sadly, your ex-wife as well. That must be annoying for you, Arnold."

"Not really. Madeline is looking. She is basically quite sane though. She'll return to the things of this world before long, I suspect. Mind you, I'm hardly an expert on what Madeline will do anymore."

"Well, in my view, Arnold, her choice of Gerald Schultz is not sane at all. You may be a policeman—we all have our problems—but at least you don't come into my office telling me that I need to repent, so that I can recover from my homosexuality. But that's what Gerald Schultz did. Said he was praying for me. It was very frustrating." Dan found a pair of leather sandals in the box he was scouring through and pulled them out.

"Not my area of expertise, Dan, but I suspect that you're safe from any such recovery requirements."

"I certainly am. But even if I were gay, why would I want to recover? It's not like it's a disease. I really don't understand why Gerald Schultz is so convinced I'm gay. Same as Clayton, who thought I was as well. Just because I work in theatre?"

"People have their ideas, Dan. Often very loosely considered ones."

"Well, I'll tell you that one of *my* ideas is that Gerald Schultz is an authentic snake-oil salesman. I wasn't big on Clayton either, as you well know, but since he's dead, I'll leave him alone."

"You should leave Gerald Schultz alone too," Arnold said. "He's not one to be messed with, I don't think. I mean—love him or hate him—look what he's managed to accomplish! He was burdened with debt and stuck in a dead-end job pricing farm implements for International Harvester. Depressed and beleaguered, one night in Saskatoon, he went to a revival meeting, 'felt the call,' began to preach, and found that he was good at it. Then he founded Four-Square Gospel Church, which took off. Now he's making more money than he ever could have imagined and has my wife cooking for him. It's impressive, if nothing else, and a happy story really ... for him if for no one else."

"Who told you that origin story of Four-Square Gospel?" Dan asked. "It's interesting. We could do a play of it."

"You could," Arnold said, nodding. "Madeline told me. We still talk."

"Madeline's a good person," Dan said, looking kindly at Arnold. "She works with us here."

"I'm well aware. What time did she start on Saturday?"

"She starts at nine-thirty and came to my office just shortly after, just to say hello. She spends early Saturday morning in a Bible study with Oscar White. His place is along the forest road. Madeline's convinced that he's a Muslim and understands the error of his thinking."

"I'm pretty sure that he's Buddhist," Arnold said, getting up and awkwardly maneuvering his way through the boxes and props to the west wall and stopping to study a photograph of Madeline and Clayton. "At least that's what Oscar's told me. But then, Madeline was never one to concern herself with those types of details. Speaking of which, give me another review of your activities on Saturday morning."

Dan paused, put down yet another box he had been rifling through, and sat back in his chair, swivelling around until he was facing the window again. "I left the house at seven, with the boys. We went birding in the woods until around eight-thirty. When we came back, Sheila was leaving for her hospital shift. She starts at nine. I ate some toast with the boys, and then I took them to soccer practice just before nine. After dropping them off, I drove to the office, arriving a little after nine."

"Did anyone see you arrive at the office yesterday?"

"No one was around when I came in, but William and Adele were at the ball-field entrance. They saw me. I waved at them, but they didn't wave back. Just stared. Madeline came in about fifteen minutes after I did. Natasha a little after that. She came into my office at nine-thirty, just after Madeline looked in. Natasha and I had a smoke together at the front entrance."

"And later in the afternoon, you went for a walk down the trail, and that's when you found Clayton?"

"That's right. I worked through lunch, and then grabbed my backpack in the mid-afternoon or so and headed to the woods. Thought I might have my sandwiches in the aster meadow. Turned out to be a bad day to do that. Encountering a dead body spoiled my appetite," Dan joked, and then cleared his throat, as if that would nullify his somewhat off-colour remark.

Arnold stepped away from the wall of photographs and towards the door, where he stopped and turned his head towards Dan. "When you saw Clayton speed away on Friday evening, you saw him drop the gun. You say that you picked it up, and walked with it, but then put it back?"

"Yes, that's right. I don't even know why I picked it up. It was a bad idea. When I saw the large man at the park-entrance arbour, I got scared and put it back."

"Did you see anyone else?"

"Emily was on the sidewalk nearby, walking."

"You didn't mention that last time I talked with you."

"I was a bit overwhelmed by all the events of the day. Wasn't thinking clearly, I guess."

"Are you thinking clearly now?"

"As far as I know. But I'm not a good witness. Never have been. I'm in my head too much. I often don't really see what's in front of me."

"Why did you put the gun back?"

"I'm not sure. Mostly because of the large man. Maybe because I saw Emily." He shrugged and shook his head. "Overall, I guess I panicked and realized that it wasn't a good look to be picking up a gun."

"And you're sure that you actually saw a large man at the entrance? What with being a poor witness and all?" Arnold said, his hand on the doorknob but still looking back at Dan.

"I am quite sure about that."

Arnold let go of the doorknob then and moved back into the interior of Dan's office, sliding a few boxes aside so that he could get closer to him. "After the gun-drop event, you went to talk with Natasha. What did you say to her?"

"I told her that I was worried for her. I felt that her life was in jeopardy. She needed to know that Clayton was carrying a gun. Or at least, that he had dropped a gun."

"Natasha was well aware that Clayton had a gun. Many guns. He was a collector. What did Natasha say to you? Did she give you cause to be concerned about her safety?"

"She was afraid for her life," Dan said. "She didn't confide deeply about her personal life, but that day, she admitted that she was afraid. She knew that Clayton was drunk and angry. The fact that he was running around the Arts Centre with a gun only added to her concern."

"If that's the case, she got lucky. The gun found another target," Arnold muttered, finally turning back towards the door and leaving the office. As Arnold turned towards his cruiser, he reflected on Dan's story. *There were some gaps—some withholding of details.*

CHAPTER 16

ARNOLD INTERVIEWS NATASHA AT HER OFFICE

Arnold climbed the wide flight of stairs to the second-floor office of Natasha Dalrymple, noting that she didn't have a nameplate on her office door. In fact, her door was made of decorative stained glass with a round, green doorknob. Light shone through the door but without the unsettling prospect of complete translucency. The door was slightly ajar and Arnold entered without knocking, ambling in and looking around the room. In due course, he sat down on the only available chair, which was hard, red, and plastic and placed close to the door, allowing ample distance from Natasha's desk.

"Save the hard chairs for the guests?" Arnold asked with a smile. "We do the same in my office. It's one of our more ineffective strategies. The thinking is that uncomfortable visitors are more forthcoming."

"Are they?" Natasha asked coldly.

"Not really. But we like working with an unproven theory until it embarrasses us."

"Sounds like a change in strategy is in order," Natasha advised with a superior tone.

"I'm sure that you're right, Natasha. But it's hard to change one's patterns; isn't it? Here you are, working in your office, the day after your husband dies."

"I take it you don't approve, Sergeant? Seems a little late in the day for judgements. That's a Sunday-morning activity," Natasha said, looking at him over her silver reading glasses.

"I judge early and often. Never too late in the day for that, Natasha."

She took off her glasses then and even laughed slightly. "Me too. I guess we have something in common."

"We do have something in common. I don't have my name on my office door either. What's the deal? Dan has a nameplate, but you don't?"

"I know my name and title. I suppose that you do as well."

"And Dan doesn't?"

"He used to think it would impress Sheila. It didn't. Now, it doesn't matter. But I think he likes seeing it."

"Is Dan a good worker?"

"He has insight and the right habits. Although he could write less. Is this a job-reference interview?"

Arnold ignored the snarky question. "He doesn't write well?"

Natasha pushed the stack of papers she had been reading away towards the centre of her otherwise spotless and object-free oak desk. "The document I am reading is a play that Dan wrote. It is not terrible. With some work, it could be good enough to put on stage but not good enough to intrigue an audience."

"A lot of plays are like that, in my opinion. What's it about?"

"It's a murder mystery of a kind. The kind where the reader does not care very much who did it or why. But it has a part for a police officer and a killer. The public might like it. What part would you prefer to play?" Her tone was genuine, and for the moment, soft.

"In real life, I prefer to play the police officer." Arnold glanced around the room again, paying attention to the few decorative items in the office.

"Isn't the line between the two quite thin? In the Soviet Union, those two professions are one. The difference is imperceptible. Perhaps it's different in Canada."

"Imperceptible is a fine word, but hard to rhyme."

"Rhyming is overrated. Are you a criminal or a police officer, Arnold?"

"I try to solve crimes, not commit them."

"How is that working?"

"One lives with a measure of failure. A good hitter only hits safely thirty percent of the time. Crime solving is no better, and sometimes worse."

"But you carry on, as long as they pay you."

"I do. If they didn't pay me, I would stop."

"So, you are doing it for the money."

"Certainly. I have to make a living."

"Is your work satisfying?"

"Occasionally. But one cannot always be satisfied."

"When Muscle John painted death slogans on my garage and was slapped on the wrist, sentenced to the same volunteer service that he was doing anyway ... was that satisfying?"

"Not really," Arnold said, wondering why Natasha had decided to interview him. He considered, however, that it was mildly enjoyable and might actually yield more information than interviewing her.

"In the Soviet Union, he would have been shot," Natasha said definitively.

"Stalin tended to be excessively firm."

"I would agree with you on that point. But Stalin was an equal-opportunity killer. He killed anyone he felt like. It was sometimes random, but always effective. Kept the country powerless with fear. He liked that."

"Not great for the Russian psyche."

"Quite damaging. But still, in Russia, being harsh is not frowned on. Personally, I find harshness to be useful, perhaps even a necessary survival skill."

"I have never been attracted to that approach," Arnold said carefully, crossing his legs and straightening the bottom of his pant leg over his ankle-high boots. "But I understand that a soft approach to law enforcement has its own problems. That tends to be the path I take, but then I have also been made to look the fool more than once."

"You would be an excellent Russian fool," Natasha said, squinting her eyes as if it gave her comment more substance.

"I am quite sure that I'm not Russian," Arnold said calmly, recrossing his legs. He was finding the conversation difficult but interesting.

"Given what we have been able to establish, Arnold, is there anything more that I can help you with?"

"You could explain your relationship with Dan."

Natasha put her reading glasses back on, preparing herself, it seemed, for a more formal turn in the conversation. "We are work friends. I owe him a great deal."

"For what?"

"For being my friend when I desperately needed one. He even volunteered to save my life. That was foolish, but honourable. Of course, the honorable is often foolish."

"How did he do that?"

"On Friday afternoon, I told him that Clayton was going to kill me on Saturday morning. He offered to intervene."

"Did he?"

"I told him that intervention was ridiculous and unnecessary."

"Why was it unnecessary?"

"It was unnecessary because I was prepared to die. To pay for my sins. I did not deserve or desire intervention."

"But he felt you deserved intervention?"

"Yes, I suppose that he did."

"Maybe you didn't need his help because you knew that you would not die. That someone would intervene on your behalf?"

"I am quite sure that you are wrong about that. As I said, Dan did offer to intervene, and I rejected the offer. I know of no one else who even knew of my situation."

"It's difficult to believe that a person would simply accept death and not try to protect themselves. I'm wondering if you found a way to kill Clayton before he could kill you."

"That might have been a good idea, but it did not happen. At least, not as far as I know. I thought that I would die, and I did not expect Clayton to die. I thought that it would be my body found in the woods, not Clayton's. But as we both know, that is not what happened. I was saved, and I don't know why. You don't appear to know either. It would be good if you could find out."

"That would be good. Did you believe that Clayton was serious in his threat to kill you.?"

"Yes. Clayton had a tendency to mention my upcoming death whenever vodka was imbibed. But on Friday, he seemed quite serious about it. I believed him. But I would never have imagined that he would kill himself. Even as stressed as he was."

"I don't think he did kill himself," Arnold said, looking around the office. "Of course, we're still investigating. I'm beginning to think that, perhaps, he intended to kill you, but something happened to change his plan."

"But you don't know that for certain?"

"Not yet."

"When will you?"

"In the course of time, I hope. On a lighter note, why do you have a handrail along your office wall?"

"It is not a handrail. It is a barre," Natasha explained in a flat but slightly condescending tone.

"It looks like a handrail."

"I suppose it does. I also suppose that it *is* effectively a handrail. But in dance circles, we call it a barre. It is used for balance during warm-up exercises. I guess you are not familiar with dance terms."

"You guess right. I'm also not familiar with dance. Should I be?"

"Not necessarily. But you have been to one of my performances," Natasha said. "Did you enjoy it?"

"I liked the music. I found the body movement beautiful but incomprehensible. My loss, I am sure."

A large southwest window behind Natasha's chair gave an expansive view of the Central Park walkway and water feature. The fall leaves were painting the park floor with dazzling red, green, and yellow.

"Anything else that I can help you with?"

"I would like to know the details of the conversation that you and Dan had on Friday afternoon or early evening."

Natasha leaned back slowly in her swivel chair. She slowly removed her reading glasses again, and looking out the window, spoke in an excessively calm voice, as though she'd been practicing. "Dan came to my office in a frantic state. He told me about Clayton dropping a gun, and some mysterious man lurking around the park entrance. We went out to look. The man and the gun were gone."

"You did not take the gun?"

"*Could* not. I am fairly certain I just said that it was gone."

"Dan admits to picking the gun up."

"He does? He told me that he left it lying in the parking lot. Why would he pick it up? He has no experience with guns."

"He does have some experience with guns actually. Despite his professed fear of them, it seems he does have a firearms license. Apparently got it to impress Sheila's father, though it didn't work."

"Really? I didn't know that. Still, he does not have the kind of life experience with guns that I have had. I have seen people shot with them. In fact, I may have been overly graphic with Dan about Clayton's aptitude for killing me with a gun."

"Did you tell Dan where and when Clayton was going to kill you?"

"More or less. I told him that Clayton said he was taking me to the woods after my Saturday morning run, and that we would perform a final theatrical event: a double suicide. And that I knew I would be the only person who would die."

"And how did you know that?"

"As I've told you, I had found his airline ticket for Saturday afternoon. He was planning to escape the country. Or try."

"Try?"

"Yes. I didn't think that was going to be successful, as I had notified the airport authorities that he would be arriving with a false passport."

"He had one under an alias?"

"Clayton had many contingency plans for himself. Not so many for me."

"When you returned home from your morning run, expecting to go to your death, he was gone and you have no idea what happened?"

"That is correct, Arnold. When I returned home, Clayton and his car were gone."

"What was your reaction to this development?"

"I didn't react. Not really. I assumed that he had changed his mind about shooting me and had taken off for the airport. It was not until later that day, when Dan called me, that I discovered Clayton was dead, leaving me to muddle along on my own."

"What do you mean? How are you left to 'muddle along?' You're alive, and your adversary, and also husband, is dead. Sounds like a reprieve to me."

"Of course, it is. But it is not quite that simple. I am used to having Clayton pave the way for me. Sadly, I might not know who I am without him. A girl from Irkutsk does not achieve training at the Bolshoi without a man like Clayton. A girl from Irkutsk does not immigrate to Canada without the aid of a person like Clayton. It is quite possible that I will be lost without him."

She has a point, but still.... "Being lost is better than being dead. Somehow, I have a feeling you'll manage. Tell me about that stranger who came to your house to talk with Clayton."

"He came by about a week ago. Clayton inferred that the man was demanding money for his life. Clayton might not have been in bed with me, but he was in bed with any number of corrupt KGB agents. He was vulnerable to blackmail."

Interesting, Arnold thought. She had previously claimed Clayton hadn't said anything about the man and that her negative impression had likely been inspired by paranoia. *So, was she lying yesterday or is she lying now?*

"Law enforcement should have been informed about this demand for money," Arnold said, frowning. "As you know, Clayton had Canadian governmental protection. They also should have been informed of this double-suicide threat."

"Should have been but weren't. Given that Clayton was being indicted by the RCMP, complaining to them about being blackmailed would likely have seemed rather trite. You know well enough that the RCMP had no intention of protecting Clayton from blackmailers when they'd already planned to hand him over to the Soviets. As for reporting his threat of double suicide, I considered it, but I wasn't confident that the police would or could help me, as I had no proof that he was going to kill me. Just my word. It wouldn't have been enough for you to arrest him. So, I ruled it out."

"But you called the authorities to prevent Clayton from leaving the country." Arnold walked over to Natasha's desk, intruding on her private space, watching to see her reaction. She remained perfectly calm.

"True," Natasha said, in a measured tone. "I didn't like the idea of Clayton hanging out at the Long Bar in Singapore with my body lying in the Northford woods."

"Makes sense to me, Natasha," Arnold commented, moving back to his chair to give her some space, standing behind it and glancing at his notes. "So, the name on the ticket was Raymond Drummond. Is that right? That was Clayton's alias?"

"He has a few. But yes, his Singapore airline ticket was for Raymond Drummond."

Arnold nodded and took a few steps towards the door, but instead of leaving, he turned back to Natasha and somewhat tentatively asked, "Can you tell me again what you did after you came home from your run and realized that Clayton was gone?"

"I had breakfast—yogurt and toast—and drove to the Arts Centre. I thought if Clayton wasn't going to take me to the woods and shoot me, I might as well get some work done."

"What time did you arrive at the office on Saturday?"

"At 9:25 or so."

"Drove your BMW?"

"Yes."

"Expensive car for a theatre director."

"It is. Clayton bought it for me. There was a price to his gifts, but he did provide."

"Did anyone see you arrive at the office?"

"William and Adele. When I got to the office, I walked over to them to complain about the doomsday placards. A little later, Dan and I had a smoke by the front doors. We both waved at them. Not to be friendly, of course. We meant to annoy them."

"And did you?"

"I believe we were successful, yes."

"Did you tell Dan about Clayton not coming home?"

"I did. I also told him that I didn't know what had happened to him and that it was possible that I might not get shot after all."

"How did Dan seem?"

"He seemed pleased about it."

"What would Clayton have had for breakfast on Saturday?"

"How is that possibly relevant?" she asked, sounding exasperated now. "You have a strange style, Arnold. You're standing at the door, getting ready to leave, but you keep asking irrelevant questions. Clayton had a vegetable and herbal drink every breakfast. What of it?"

"Just curious, I suppose," Arnold smiled. "What was in the juice?"

Natasha pushed her rolling chair back from her desk and stood up, walking over to the south window and looking out over the city park. Arnold waited for her to gather her thoughts, as she seemed to be deeply contemplative. Finally, she turned away from the window, towards Arnold—her eyelids fluttering for a moment, and her mouth opening as if to speak—but then she stopped, took a deep breath, and sat back down in her chair, as if she had answered his question, though she hadn't. Still, Arnold was hopeful. He wondered whether her self control was finally breaking down and if a torrent of confession was about to be released. Unfortunately, when she started speaking again, the information she gave (while potentially helpful) hardly warranted the dramatic delay.

"Various vegetable and natural plants," Natasha said with an even, sober tone, as if she were revealing some great inner truth. "He would put them in a juicer. He said it was good for his sex life. Could be. It didn't help ours, but then we had other issues. As I've told you, I poured us both a breakfast drink and then left for my run. I left the drinks on the counter precisely as Clayton insisted. Mine on the right, with the handle turned right. His was on the left, pressed against mine, with the handle turned left. I also left a piece of Medovik cake on the counter for him. I put it on a Depression-glass plate as per Clayton's specific instructions. He loves Depression glass. Also loves Medovik cake. Both have taste of a kind, I suppose. I don't love either."

"Did you know that Sheila was coming to your house on Saturday morning?" Arnold noticed that Natasha now seemed to be gaining some interest in the topic. It was evident that she did not like Sheila. *A reasonable position*, he thought.

"Of course, I did. I believe that I told you in our last visit. She has been doing so for over a year. Like clockwork. I even spoke with her. Briefly. Usually, she slips in the back door but not this Saturday. She boldly opened the front door when I was pouring the drinks. We exchanged cool pleas-antries, and she took off. I saw her having a smoke in the alley as I left the house a few minutes later. No doubt she was waiting for me to leave. I think that she was flaunting her access to Clayton. But I didn't care."

Interesting, he thought. *That's not what she said when I first questioned her. Could she have forgotten speaking to her and then remembered since?* It seemed unlikely.

"Perhaps she thought that you did care?"

"Perhaps. But Sheila has her elbows up her ass. Insight is not one of her strengths."

"Her elbows?" Arnold grinned in spite of himself. "Never heard that one before."

"Perhaps it's a translation issue," Natasha said, momentarily embarrassed at the coarseness of her phrasing. "But I think you get my point."

"I do, Natasha. It's fine. I often use words in places where they're not expected. Any sign of unusual activity in the house when you returned from your run?"

"The house was spotless. But my breakfast drink was gone from the kitchen counter. I generally drink it on my return. Sheila must have thrown it out, or perhaps Clayton. I don't know. Nothing else unusual that I recall. His bedroom was made up, but it always is. He was obsessed with cleanliness. He always took the sheets off and put them in the washer after their interludes. He liked to hide any evidence of sex with Sheila. Quite funny actually. He liked imagining that I didn't know about his sex life. Of course, to be fair, in the Soviet Union, I imagined that Clayton didn't know about me and Doc either. Imagination does serve some personal utility."

"I suppose it does. I imagine that the Yankees are once again a baseball powerhouse. They aren't, but that's another matter. It has helped me get through the fall season. Did you check the workshop when you came home?"

"I did. Nothing noteworthy to report."

"Was his breakfast drink in the workshop?"

"No, it wasn't."

"Did he typically bring his drink in from the workshop?"

"No, he didn't. And yes, I suppose, that was noteworthy." Impatience was becoming quite clear in her voice. "As I told you yesterday, he thought it was my job to clean up his dishes."

164

"Then you must have found it curious that the mug wasn't in the workshop. Was it in the kitchen?"

"No, it wasn't. But I didn't consider that odd at the time. Perhaps I found the fact that he was gone more curious. He was gone and that was good for me, so I didn't really think about the fact that his breakfast mug was also gone. The fact that it was found in the woods is peculiar, of course, and interesting, but I can't explain it."

With that, Arnold finally released his hand from the smooth contours of the glass doorknob and left her office.

Arnold walked down the main steps of the Arts Centre, admiring the beautiful building that had been the inspiration and creation of Doc and Sophia Rubenstein. It had been quite a gift for Northford, having the couple come to town. As for Natasha and Clayton, he was less certain of their benefits. Of course, Clayton was gone now, and apparently, wouldn't be missed. Especially by Natasha. Her story had some semblance of believability, but still, he felt that he wasn't getting the whole truth from her. She seemed to be handing out the truth in crumbly morsels of Medovik cake, like the fact that she had actually spoken to Sheila before her run yesterday morning. He wondered what else, if anything, she was hiding. *Of course, whatever it is might not be relevant,* he thought to himself. One thing that was relevant, however, was that Natasha had clearly been nowhere near the woods on Saturday morning.

CHAPTER 17

ARNOLD INTERVIEWS HIS
EX-WIFE MADELINE

Arnold parked on Boyd Avenue, across the street from Gerald Schultz's palatial river property. It had a wide expanse of green lawn with a winding sidewalk of paving stones, ending at the white, double front doors. A porch, overly stocked with rattan furniture, overlooked the front yard. Arnold wondered whether anyone ever sat there. The main action on the Schultz property appeared to be in the backyard along the river. Arnold followed the walkway around the east side of the house, where he was introduced to the micro-climate of the backyard.

The Schultz property was perched high on the north bank of the Saskatchewan River. The backyard was mostly cleared of trees, to enhance the south view, but a grove of cottonwoods, elm, and maples lined both the east and west sides of the long yard that gradually descended to the wild mint plants and willow trees growing along the edges of the muddy river-bank. Looking over this expanse was a concrete patio fully populated with still blooming black-eyed Susan and false sunflower, four perfectly match-ing bamboo lounge chairs, and a shining aluminum outdoor dining set.

Arnold paused for a moment to consider his options for sitting. The bamboo lounge chairs beckoned but also implied a friendlier visit then he was intending. He opted for one of the aluminum dining chairs. It was suitably uncomfortable, creating little chance of overstaying his welcome.

The temperature was warm enough for Madeline to be poking around in the backyard. She wore a white sleeveless top and blue pants, which hung loosely around her hips. Her feet were resting in a pair of brown sandals, and a white wide-brimmed hat adorned her head. Arnold was quite sure that Madeline looked younger than when they had been together. Madeline looked up from watering a trio of flowering potted plants and smiled at him.

"Would you like some coffee, Arnold? You always love a coffee in the afternoon."

"Not today, thanks. I'm in the middle of interviews. Not a social call."

"Of course. I've never been interviewed by the police. Should I be nervous?"

"No need to be nervous, Madeline. Just have a few questions that will be easy to answer."

"I don't believe I have anything to hide. That's exciting to say," Madeline blurted, considering the possibility that she might be on the wrong side of the law. "It's more interesting if you have something to hide, isn't it, Arnold? I mean from a policing standpoint."

"It would be. But you're not a suspect, so there's no need for hiding anything," Arnold said indifferently. "What were your hours at the Arts Centre on Saturday?"

"You could at least suspect me a little bit. You never know what a person is capable of, even at my age. Of course, I understand that I haven't lived a criminal life, and I suppose I have to accept that reality. Gerald either. Gerald is quite strict when it comes to living by a high moral code. My goodness, he refuses to be seen in public with another woman. It gives the wrong impression, he says."

"What impression is that?"

"Well, that something untoward might be going on. And he's only thinking of the women's reputations. Protecting them from gossip, I suppose. Gerald is quite an attractive man. He could easily be a philanderer if he so chose."

"I suppose that's reassuring to some. What time did you arrive at the Arts Centre yesterday morning?"

"I have a church assignment on Saturday mornings, so I come in a bit late. Natasha and Dan approved it. They said it was fine."

"Okay. So, what time did you arrive?"

"Nine-fifteen or so. I can't be precise."

"Who was at the office when you arrived?"

"Dan was there. Natasha arrived a bit later. Closer to nine-thirty."

"Did you see Dan?"

"Not right away, but his car was in the lot, and his office door was open, which it always is when he's in. If he's not in, the door is closed. He's quite fussy about it. He has a lot of theatrical valuables in his office. His office is basically a prop room, I think. Anyway, I went to Dan's office shortly after I arrived, closer to nine-thirty, and he was in his office then. So was Natasha. They went out for a smoke shortly after. A little after nine-thirty. It isn't unusual for them to have a smoke together in the morning."

"How did they seem?"

"Friendly enough. Neither of them is particularly fond of me. A bit skeptical, I believe, of my romantic choices, as I imagine you are, Arnold. I do understand that my leaving was a disappointment for you. But you, at least, tend to understand. That's one of your better qualities. You also have some flaws that we could discuss. But perhaps not today. Be that as it may, Dan and Natasha were both as friendly as can be, given the circumstances."

"What circumstances?" Arnold asked, watching as Madeline gathered her garden hose and began to water, seemingly at random, a variety of plants that were growing in her vicinity.

"Both of them with marital problems, you know," Madeline said in a confidential tone. "Please don't say anything about it, but I have told Dan many times that he should not be discouraged. His marriage may be over, but he'll find his soulmate. As for Natasha, well, that's another matter all together. I wouldn't think she's capable of finding a soulmate, or even desiring one. Not sure what Natasha wants. Maybe a scheduled arrangement of some kind, you know, to take the edge off one's needs, but nothing of a romantic nature. Natasha is not actively pursuing happiness. Still, that morning, she was quite pleasant. Not like Clayton. Clayton was quite rude; I can tell you that. Still, it's a shame what happened to him. I have to say that, while I did not like Clayton, I also did not wish him ill. Despite the coffee incident."

"What coffee incident?" Arnold asked, intrigued. He leaned forward to allow Madeline to express a possibly private confidence.

Madeline sat down on a brown beanbag chair on the edge of the patio. It did not match any of the other deliberately placed furniture pieces. She sighed happily as she settled into it. "Gerald loves the metal furniture," she said, more sadly than Arnold felt the topic warranted. "Personally, I prefer the bamboo and beanbag style. It's a point of disagreement between us. You may not be spiritual, Arnold, but you were easier to get along with than Gerald. He can be quite fussy. He has opinions, you know. Strong ones. About almost everything. But I can tell you that when it comes to furniture, I can hold my own. Even Jesus couldn't get me to give up this beanbag. It oddly reminds me of our life together, Arnold, though I'm not sure why. Gerald says that it doesn't fit in with the overall backyard look. He might be right, but you know what, Arnold? I don't care. There are only so many dramatic changes a person can handle in their life. The beanbag stays. What do you think?"

"Fitting in can be delicate. For furniture and for people," Arnold replied. "But tell me about the coffee incident."

"It was nothing really. One of my duties at the office is making fresh coffee," Madeline whispered. She had a way of speaking that gave an impression of strictest confidence. A secret, between her and the listener. "It sounds easy, but it isn't. Natasha, Clayton, and Dan drink coffee all day. Seriously, there is no stopping them. I've told them more than once that it's not healthy. But do they listen? No, they do not. None of them. Too busy and self important to accept my humble advice. Anyway, one day, I made an error. I confess to that. I failed to make the afternoon coffee. I do have other duties, you know. Well, perhaps you don't know, but still, I do. I take care of many matters at the centre. No one notices, but they would if I stopped doing them. It is frankly tiresome."

"The duties, or that no one notices?"

"Both, really. Offering a little recognition, a word of thanks, wouldn't kill the staff, not that I should use that word, given what's happened to

Clayton. Anyway, as you know, Arnold, I believe in being faithful to my duties. I carry on."

"Could you get back to the coffee incident, please?"

"Yes, I can. I will discuss the coffee incident simply in passing, though. It was nothing really. But still, it happened. I believe it was last summer. I'm not sure. I could look in my diary if you need me to be precise."

"That's fine, Madeline. The date may not matter."

"Well, you never know. If the case goes to court, and you get cross examined, you need to be precise with the dates. Anyway, the coffee incident happened. That is the important thing. It was really too much, even for me."

"What was too much?"

"Clayton, really. He marched into the reception area, holding an empty coffee cup. He stared at me for longer than was comfortable and then grunted disdainfully and shrugged his shoulders as if the meaning of his life had been stolen. Well, I can tell you that the meaning of his life was taken long ago. Anyway, eventually he tired of staring at me and marched off. I thought the incident was over, but it wasn't. He placed signs all over the kitchen declaring that administrative support staff, which is only me, are required by job description and board directive, to make coffee all day, every day."

"What happened after that?"

"What happened after that was that Clayton held a grudge. He never spoke to me again. That wasn't so bad, actually. Quite pleasant not to listen to him grunt. Mostly that's how he communicated with me. He never called me by my name. When I think back on it, I am pretty sure that he didn't know my name. Anyway, he's dead now, which is not good. At least not for him."

"I venture to guess that Clayton had had better days," he agreed, taking a deep breath, scanning the yard with his eyes. It was hard to even tell that he was in Northford. "A person could be quite happy with this view, Madeline. Nicer than the Reed Avenue backyard; that's certain. Especially now."

"What do you mean, 'especially now?' You aren't neglecting the yard; are you?"

"To be honest, Madeline, I am. The Reed Avenue yard has taken a substantial hit since you left. Sadly, a case of intentional neglect. It is not pretty."

Arnold looked at the massive barbeque sitting on the west side of the patio, perched under a large cottonwood, looking out over the backyard and the river. "Do you get cottonwood fluff in your food when you barbeque in the fall?"

"We would if we barbequed, but we don't. We're vegetarian."

"How's that going?"

"Not that well. I do miss the hamburgers. But it is healthier. More environmental. That's a good thing, right?"

"Certainly. You could barbeque vegetables, of course."

"We could, but we don't."

"You have a large, probably expensive barbeque."

"You have a lot of questions about the barbeque, Arnold. If it looks suspicious to you, it really isn't. Our eating tastes are not that interesting. To tell you the truth, Gerald got the barbeque as a gift from the church. It is essentially decorative. You could probably have it if you want it. I could ask Gerald. He's very generous with material things. He's focussed on spiritual concerns."

"I already have one that I don't use. But as you know, I am not vegetarian. I couldn't cope without hamburgers. But I go to the Dickey Dee."

There was a long pause. A hummingbird hovered nearby and a crowd of blackbirds descended on a maple tree next to the gazebo for a moment before collectively departing again. Arnold momentarily wished he had accepted the offer of a coffee. The view was so beautiful, coffee would have been enjoyable. He studied the glass top of the aluminum dining table beside him, noting that it had recently been wiped. The backyard of the Schultz residence was not casually maintained.

There was a six-foot-high cedar fence along the western boundary of the yard. "Don't like the west neighbours?" Arnold finally asked. "Even the Mongols would be held back by that fence."

"I don't know the Mongols. Our neighbours are the Clippertons. They just moved to Northford from Lloydminster. To be honest, I'm not sure that they work. They're at home a lot. They have a barking dog that does business whenever it feels like it, and based on their backyard, it feels like it a lot. Yellowed grass spots all over a yard is not my idea of a lawn. Doesn't seem to be theirs either. They complain about their dog constantly. Still, it's good to be kind to the neighbours. We smile and they smile, but I simply do not understand why."

"It's sometimes hard to know why we smile. Better than cursing the neighbours, I suppose."

"Of course, it is. We don't curse anyone, Arnold. We love the neighbours for who they are. Anyway, maybe they won't be staying long. I actually wonder whether they can afford to be on the river."

"While you contemplate that, Madeline, I was wondering whether you saw anything on the forest road on Saturday morning."

"What a rude question. Why would I be on the forest road?" Madeline demanded, her smile transforming into a frown. She had backed off her watering for a moment and sat down, but with Arnold's question, she got up again and began a vigorous watering of a flowerpot, creating a stream of overflow that splashed onto her sandals.

"Your reason for being on the forest road is not my concern, Madeline. But given that you were there, I was just wondering if you saw anything."

"But Arnold, I have no reason to be there."

"Madeline, I have a witness that saw you emerging from the forest road on Saturday morning. It is not illegal to be on the forest service road. It's fine. There's no problem. I hear that you are simply witnessing to Oscar White at his cottage. I don't know what he's done to deserve that, but so it is."

"He is a Muslim, Arnold."

"I thought he was a Buddhist."

"You might be right. I get those two religions mixed up. They are quite similar."

"No, they aren't, actually. I don't think they're similar at all."

"Well, they aren't Christian, are they?"

"I see what you mean. Back to the question. Did you see anything on the forest service road this Saturday morning?" He took out his notepad from his back pocket.

"Is this information confidential?"

"Madeline, we're dealing with a dead body. This is no time for petty secrets. Your reasons for being in the woods are not the concern of the police, and if possible, your information will not become public. Just tell me if you saw anything."

Madeline put down her watering can and sat down on the beanbag again, taking out a white handkerchief and dabbing her face to no avail. Thick beads of perspiration were emerging on her forehead. "I visit with Oscar on Saturday mornings. I'm trying to convince him as to the error of his thinking. There is nothing else going on. Gerald doesn't know, though, and he might misunderstand."

"Misunderstand what?"

"Of course, it's ridiculous. Oscar is at least ten years younger than me."

"More like twenty," Arnold said, smiling.

"You don't think it's possible that Oscar would find me attractive?"

"Of course, it's possible. But that's also not my concern. I just want to know if you saw anything?"

"Fine. I will do my duty. I saw Clayton Dalrymple. His blue Mustang was parked on the forest road as I walked south towards the fairground. It was little after nine on Saturday morning. Ten after or so. I thought it odd that Clayton would be there."

"Why would that be odd?"

"Clayton didn't approve of nature. He was quite against it as a general principle. Why would he be on the forest road? It made no sense to me."

"Are you sure it was Clayton?"

"Absolutely. That flat hat of his is nice on a man with his facial structure. Easy on the eyes. Or he was. Still, he was too beleaguered-looking in general if you ask me. Like a dog recently bit him in the private parts. Learning to smile wouldn't have killed him. I guess it's too late for that now."

"Did he see you?"

"I don't think he did. I went off the road into the woods pretty quick. I didn't want to be seen, due to the sensitive nature of my visits with Oscar. I glanced at the Mustang a few times, as I retreated, but Clayton stayed in the car. Looked like he was waiting for someone. People do sometimes park on the road, but usually just young people, doing who knows what in the privacy of nature. It's quite disturbing, Arnold, the kinds of immorality that go on nowadays. Including Clayton. A married man and yet he carries on. I don't know what to make of it all. Still, I don't think he was meeting with Sheila or Janet. He meets Sheila at his house and Janet in his car usually. Oh! That gives me an idea. Maybe Janet was in the car with him?"

"Was there anyone else in the car?"

"Not that I could see. He looked like he was alone. Just sitting there in his driver's seat, waiting. Maybe the person he was waiting for killed him? If that's the case, he would have been better off staying at home."

"Perhaps. Any other identifying features?"

"He had his black pea coat on along with his flat hat, like I said. It was a cool fall morning. It turned out to be warm later in the day, but in the morning, a person needed a coat. Even a person from Siberia. I had mine on. Do you think I'll have to testify?" she asked then, quite concerned. "I'm the pastor's wife, and Gerald is so sensitive. For a man of deep faith, he is quite insecure."

"Funny how that works," Arnold murmured, and he thanked Madeline for the information.

CHAPTER 18

ARNOLD INTERVIEWS
MUSCLE JOHN FRIESEN

The metal front door of Friesen's Pool Hall was excessively unattractive. Northford's aesthetic thinking, as far as it went, was unanimous on the subject. Even Muscle John, not a young man prone to deeply considered aesthetic views, conceded that the door replacement had failed to consider aspects of curb appeal. The old wooden door, while not attractive either, had at least had a window. Of course, that had been part of the problem.

The small window had been large enough to let light in but not large enough for thieves to get through. Still, a few years earlier, thieves had tried. The failure was disappointing to them, and as often happens when disappointment builds, they turned violent. Using crowbars, they destroyed the door and frame, including the small glass window, leaving thousands of glass shards, mixed with small pools of thief blood, on the recently finished hardwood floors of Friesen's Pool Hall.

By the time the police had arrived, the interior of the pool hall had been in shambles: tables smashed, the glass counter broken, pictures and artifacts removed, and soft drinks from the cooler gone. The incident had made the front page of the *Sentinel* the next day, with Emily Little giving a detailed background of Muscle John, his benefactor father, the wayward alcoholic mother, long deceased, why the thieves had not bothered with smashing the large plate glass beside the door, and the likelihood of Muscle John making a go of the pool business moving forward, given the fact that his insurance had lapsed. But Emily had also presented Muscle John as a courageous and committed business owner who cared deeply about his customers, and she'd acknowledged the value of his business contribution to Northford leisure. Muscle John had been quoted in the paper as declaring his determination to prevail, despite the town's criminal element. His larger view was that, on balance, it was better all around for a business like his to keep their insurance paid up.

Arnold entered the pool hall at mid-afternoon on Sunday. Muscle John was shooting a game of pool with a casually dressed young woman who appeared quite focussed on her game. Neither of them paid any attention to Arnold's entrance. Powell walked to the edge of the pool table where the young woman was lining up a six-ball side bank. She made the shot and scowled in the direction of Muscle John. "What's a cop doing here, John? I'm trying to knock down balls."

"She's on a run, Sergeant Powell," John said quietly and respectfully, setting the rubber end of his pool cue down on the sticky hardwood flooring. "Can I do something for you? Rachel doesn't like interruptions in the middle of a game."

"I don't like interruptions from the police at any time, John," Rachel snarled.

"I'll be quick, John," Arnold muttered. "I hear you were smoking in front of the pool hall on Friday, early evening. Did you happen to see anything unusual?"

"Why would I?"

"Just curious if you did," Arnold said softly. "Anything unusual?"

Muscle John picked up his cue as if he wanted to hit Arnold with it. But he didn't. Instead, he paused for a moment, appearing to contemplate the question as he watched Rachel, a lit cigarette dangling from her mouth, and a large tattoo of Jesus driving a tow truck on her right arm. Raichel tapped the four ball into the side pocket. It was a delicate shot. It was evident that she was skilled at the game.

"Define unusual," he said finally.

"Something that you don't usually see? Like Jesus driving a tow truck."

"Yep, that would be unusual. Actually, it would be ridiculous, Sergeant. They didn't even have tow trucks when Jesus was around," Muscle John said with an air of complete confidence. He walked over to the soft-drink cooler, pulled out a Pepsi, and snapped the cap off with such vigour that it fell to the hardwood floor and rolled towards a nearby pool table, where four rattily dressed teenagers were setting up a game. One of them, a long-haired boy with a scowl deeper than his years warranted, stepped on the cap in passing but didn't pick it up.

"You could pick the damn cap up, Sammy, or would that be too much work for Your Highness?" Muscle John muttered, wandering over and picking the cap up himself before returning, shaking his head. "Don't know why I even let these kids play here. Pool is a game of leisure. A person needs to work before you play. But Sammy doesn't know anything about work. I don't think he's even heard about it."

Muscle John tossed the cap into the wastebasket, adjusted the brim of his Chicago Cubs cap lower over his eyes, and stared at Arnold, seemingly in deep contemplation. "I did see something, but it was actually not that unusual. I've seen it before, just not as fast as that day."

"What had you seen before but not as fast as that day?" Arnold asked, moving closer to the pool table where Rachel was sizing up her next shot, another difficult side bank, which she pocketed with apparent ease. Rachel straightened up from the shot and gave Arnold a side glance, her mouth curling up a bit.

"She learns fast," Muscle John observed, poking Rachel lightly with his pool cue. "But not as fast Clayton's Mustang last Friday. He tore north along McKenzie Avenue like a bullet. Didn't stop for the red light. Didn't slow down either. He sped up as he approached the intersection, and then he was gone. It was something to see. I mean, my GTO *can* go that fast, but why? Now that I have Rachel and Jesus, I don't need to drive fast. Anyway, all I'm saying is that Clayton was lucky the cops weren't there. He would have been looking at a hefty fine."

"You're sure it was Clayton driving?" Arnold asked, as Rachel continued to run the table, looking up at Arnold with her curled front lip after each shot.

"Of course, Sergeant. No one touches Clayton's Mustang. It was him all right. The back end was weaving around, gravel was flying everywhere. Guess he wanted to get away from his icy bitch of a wife. Can't say as I blame him. But then I'm not a fan of either of them, especially Clayton. He can rot in hell, as far as I am concerned. He slashed my tires. Bad piece of work that man."

"When did this happen?"

"I don't know which day. Don't make notes about everything like a cop. But it was last summer, at the Capri when we had our big fight. Don't know a lot, Arnold, but I can tell you, Clayton won't be toasting to Janet again anytime soon."

"I was actually asking about when you saw Clayton driving through the red light on McKenzie?"

"Oh, that's an easier question. Don't know why you keep changing the topic, Arnold. I know that one even off the top of my head. This past Friday, just a few minutes before six, when the pool tournament was about to begin. It always starts at six every Friday. Rain or shine. I was steadying my nerves out front with a smoke."

Rachel finally missed a shot, cursing loud enough for the entourage of onlookers to be impressed. Muscle John walked around the table with his cue, looking over at Arnold and then smiling protectively at Rachel, who sat down by the soft-drink cooler, muttering to herself.

"Did you happen to see anyone at the park across the street, around the Arts Centre parking area?" Arnold asked. He found himself quite enjoying the pool-room scene. He wasn't sure that the interview was providing anything useful, but one never knew. "Maybe a large person. Like sumo-wrestler sized."

"What's a sumo wrestler?" Muscle John asked, as he missed his first shot. Frustrated with himself, he slammed the pool cue on the side of the table. "Too many distractions, Arnold. Are we done? No idea what a sumo wrestler is and not sure I care."

"A sumo wrestler is a very large person, John. Large enough that, if he fell on you, it would hurt and crush you."

"The person would have to be very large to crush me," Muscle John observed.

"Did you see such a large person in the park or in the area around the park?"

"Let me think...." Muscle John paused then, watching Rachel knock down a few balls while looking over at Arnold with a quizzical look. Finally, he shook his head. "No, I don't believe that I saw anyone large enough to crush me."

"Did you see anyone at all?"

"Now that you mention it, no, I didn't. The park was empty. Everyone was either at the ball game or inside the pool hall. I won the tournament by the way."

"Don't you always win?"

"Of course. Anything else? I do have work to do, Arnold. Not like the police. I actually have to earn a living."

"Almost done, Muscle John. Where you on Saturday morning, between seven and nine-thirty?"

"Well, I don't mind saying that I spent the night with Rachel here, my pool partner and new girlfriend. Pretty cool tattoo, eh? We were in bed when Doc called around ten. He needed me to pick him up at the Schoendienst farm and pull his car out of the ditch on 344. His car was in mud up to the axles. I thought Doc knew how to drive. Apparently not. He's pretty stupid for a smart guy. He did give me a bucket of blueberries though. The man might be a terrible driver, but he's a good blueberry picker. Have to give credit where it's due, I always say."

"Did you leave home right away when he called?"

"Not a chance. Had a bit of action to finish up before I left, maybe ten or fifteen minutes later. You don't leave a fine young woman like Rachel unsatisfied, if you know what I mean. But eventually, I went to pull him out. Got back around noon. Rachel was sleeping. Didn't want to have sex again. How does a person say no to sex? I never understood that."

"Me either. Did you kill him?"

"No, I just pulled him out of the ditch. I just said that. For a policeman, you don't listen very well."

"I was referring to Clayton Dalrymple."

"I didn't pull him out of the ditch. He wasn't stuck. Doc Rubenstein was stuck."

"Did you kill Clayton Dalrymple?"

"Oh, him! I didn't need to kill him. He was already dead. Divine judgement came for him."

"How do you know that Clayton was already dead?"

"At the time, I didn't know. But I do now. It's all over town. He died on Saturday morning. Right?"

"Can you confirm that John was with you on Saturday morning, before he got his call to tow Doc out?" Arnold asked Rachel, who momentarily stopped shooting and looked at him.

"One day is the same as the next to me," Rachel muttered, returning her focus to the table. "But yes, I was in bed with John yesterday morning and with him all day, once he got back, anyway. We hung out. We spent the day playing pool and having sex. That's what we do. You have a problem with that?"

"Not at all. More power to you," Arnold said. "Nice tattoo, by the way. You get that in town?"

"Muscle John did it. Next week, I'm getting one of Jesus playing pool."

"Didn't know he was a pool player."

"He was the best, Sergeant. Probably better than Muscle John. If Jesus was around now, there's no telling the kind of money he would make hustling pool. It's frankly scary to even think about it."

"I'll take your word for it. Please stay in town for a few days, Rachel," Arnold said. "We may need you to verify John's alibi."

"Sure thing. I'm sticking around until the going no longer goes, or something like that." Rachel smiled then, giving John a playful poke with her pool cue.

Arnold left them then, got back in his cruiser, and headed north along McKenzie Avenue, until (reluctantly) he arrived at the Sawatzky residence. A visit with William and Adele was like a dental filling. Unpleasant, but hopefully quick. Arnold was determined to be done in less than thirty minutes.

CHAPTER 19

ARNOLD PAYS WILLIAM
AND ADELE A VISIT

The front yard of William and Adele Sawatzky's residence, on the corner of Saskatchewan and Mackenzie, was uninspiring, featuring aggressive weed growth amongst mountains of end-times placards. The backyard, however, was quite interesting. It was home to the rusting carcass of a windmill. William had purchased it from a local farmer and dismantled it. His plan had been to set up the windmill in his backyard and generate his own electricity. Unfortunately, the plan required putting the windmill together again, and that did not appear to be something William had the desire to do.

Saskatchewan Street was not a throughway. Turning west off McKenzie Avenue, it had only five houses on each side, with a dead end to the west, along the border of the Northford Woodlands Forest Reserve. It was a quiet street, great for uninterrupted prayer. William and Adele had been quite happy there until Clayton and Natasha Dalrymple had immigrated to Northford and bought a house on the western end of the street.

The Dalrymples' presence was a problem for William and Adele. Clayton raced his Mustang Fastback down the street at least five times a day, and if that wasn't bad enough, Natasha flaunted her near-naked body every morning during her early morning run. To add to the problem, the Dalrymples were Jews, and to make matters even worse, self-avowed atheists as well. It was too much for William and Adele. They could not cope with so much evil living close to them. They began a letter-writing campaign to the *Northford Sentinel,* demanding that the sinners leave town. This failed to get public traction, as Northford had quite a few self-avowed sinners, including publisher and editor Ian O'Brien and his primary staff writer, Emily Little. The idea of singling out the Dalrymples did not have broad appeal in Northford. But all was not lost. William and Adele had convinced a recent Four-Square Gospel convert, Muscle John Friesen, to paint death slogans on the Dalrymples' garage wall. It seemed the very least they could do to help pave the way for the second coming.

William and Adele Sawatzky had initially moved to Northford in the mid-1950s, having left a small Mexican Mennonite community in a hurry. Rumour had it that they had invested time and energy into a burgeoning drug trade that had stopped burgeoning. The competition was stiff, and William and Adele had been forced to leave the area. They'd left, however, with ample cash reserves, which they were allowed to keep on the promise that they never return.

The Capri Hotel went up for sale shortly after they'd arrived. The property had been rundown, but the price was right. They'd bought the hotel and established it as emergency housing for Child and Family Services. While the merits of this strategy could be debated, the fact that they refused to pay property taxes couldn't. Given that they were providing a community service, their position had been that they were effectively a charity, and as such, property taxes should be waived. But no one agreed with them. After five years of them failing to pay their tax bills, the town had put the hotel up for sale. Ken Russell, the mayor, had bought it.

The loss of the hotel had been upsetting to William and Adele, but it had not curtailed their entrepreneurial spirit. They'd promptly bought forest property west of Northford and started the Belhaven Commune and Healing Centre. It was really more of a commune than a healing centre, with devotees living on site and building their own lodgings. The focus of the centre had been a trinity of healing through the use of prayer, physical labour, and natural herbal medicines, along with other drugs—peyote root and magic mushrooms in particular—that nurtured spiritual insight. It had been a clever business model. Devotees had been required to convert personal assets into cash and donate them to the Belhaven Commune and

Healing Centre. In return, devotees received an eternal-life certificate and easy access to Belhaven's range of inspiring drug options.

The good times at Belhaven had been short lived, however, due in good measure to Janet Sawatzky, the youngest and only daughter of William and Adele. Janet had informed the authorities that medical mistreatment and illegal drug use was happening at the commune, and an investigation had ensued.

It had all turned out to be true. Janet Sawatzky had been a key witness in the court case, giving evidence that Fyodor Rubenstein (Doc and Sophia's son) had been given St. John's Wort for a migraine, despite Fyodor telling them that he was taking a preventative, prescribed medication that could trigger an allergic reaction. The result had been Fyodor becoming very ill. He'd been saved only by Janet going against instructions from her father, who'd insisted that he had the matter in hand. Janet had hitchhiked into Northford to get Doc Rubenstein. Fyodor had been hospitalized and recovered, and charges had been pressed against the elder Sawatzkys. Janet's testimony had been particularly damning for William and Adele. They'd ended up losing both the case and their commune business.

It had also led to the Sawatzkys disowning their daughter, promising her eternal damnation, and kicking her out of the house. Janet had been fifteen at the time. Annie Russell had offered Janet a free apartment in Ken's apartment building, and organized a support team, including Sheila McCroskey and Doc Rubenstein, to pay for Janet's keep. The estrangement of Janet and her parents persisted to this day and was not helped by Janet's involvement in community theatre, or her relations with Clayton Dalrymple.

It was well into the afternoon when Arnold knocked on the front door of the Sawatzky home and waited. The doorbell was hanging by a single wire, and Arnold had decided not to use it. In due course, Adele appeared. "Ever try a doorbell?" she asked.

"I prefer the kind that are fully attached to the house," Arnold said. "May I come in? I won't be long. Just a few questions."

Adele wore a purple robe and a look of utter exasperation. Arnold wondered if her outfit was a nightdress or just relaxed Sunday wear. He didn't ask. Her long, greying hair was piled high on her head, topped by a small white cap with a circular pattern of rainbow colours. Adele was a frail-looking woman. She was only in her fifties, Arnold guessed, but she looked much older.

Adele shuffled to the kitchen table and sat down beside William. She did not look at Arnold or offer him a seat. Arnold thought it was just as well. He was hoping to keep the exchange short. William was sipping a hot beverage from a gourd-looking container through a large wooden straw. Arnold recognized the drink: yerba mate. He had tried it once but had not enjoyed it. Tasted like warm muddy water, he had thought. William had a pained look on his face.

"Not enjoying your yerba mate?" Arnold asked.

"The drink is fine. It has a soothing bitterness," William muttered. "But I do not like talking with the police. This is the second time today, Arnold. Didn't enjoy our talk on the street earlier, and I'm quite sure I won't enjoy this one. Surely you have other matters to attend to on a Sunday than harassing Christians."

"At least you're no longer standing in a puddle of water. That's at least improved the day for you, I imagine."

"Not really. I'm talking with you again. So, get on with whatever heathen questioning you have," William muttered angrily, as he moved his plate of two crackers and a slice of cheese towards himself. "We are fortifying our sinful bodies in preparation for afternoon prayer."

"I won't be long, William. At least I hope not," Arnold said, standing across the table from him. "Are you still in the herbal-medicine business?"

"Is that an official police question?" William asked, skeptically.

"I suppose that it is," Arnold said, surprised at the question.

"We have a garden shed full of natural remedies that can resolve most bodily ills, but not the sickness of this world," William answered, taking a small bite of a cracker but ignoring the slice of cheese. "We live in a wretched time, Arnold. But a better day will come soon. A day when no police will be needed, and the atheists and sinners will be crushed."

"Great. Just in time for my retirement."

"You joke at your own peril, Arnold," William said, leaning back in his chair and apparently savouring the chewing of his cracker. "But I suppose you might as well get your laughs while you can."

Like his wife, William was physically frail and emaciated-looking, with his grey shirt buttoned to his neck but still revealing the clear outline of his collarbones. Despite his slight physicality, he had a look of intense energy. The fingers on his left hand tapped the white laminate kitchen tabletop, with its chrome side strapping, as his eyes frantically searched the room. William was not a man who relaxed easily, if at all.

The kitchen smelled of some cleaning agent. A bottle of Ajax Blue sat on the faded-yellow laminate kitchen counter, which was otherwise clear of any appliances or dishes. Apart from the yerba mate, both William and Adele had a small plate with two crackers and a slice of cheese in front of them, and there was a small serving plate of Spam, with an oily layer of gelled fat around the edge, in the middle of the table.

"Can't offer you an afternoon snack," William said. "Not made of money like government workers. We barely have enough for ourselves."

"That's fine," Arnold said. "I don't need a snack."

"Soon, we won't either," Adele whispered. "For now, food is a necessary evil, but soon, we will be relieved of such obligations to our bodies."

Arnold glanced around the room. He noted a large black magnet with red lettering on the refrigerator: "The Lord giveth, and the Lord taketh away." He wondered if the message was comforting or disturbing to the Sawatzkys.

"I suppose you want to talk about the dead atheist," Adele said then. "Death comes to us all."

"It does," affirmed Arnold. "In Clayton's case, a tad early and perhaps helped along by someone else."

"Fiddles! He took his own life," Adele announced, over-chewing her cracker and then swallowing slowly, as if it were a demanding task. "That's obvious enough. A sinner like Clayton was well past expiry. The Lord gives, and the Lord takes away!"

"Yes, I read that somewhere," Arnold said, looking at the magnet sign on the refrigerator. "Is that actually in the Bible?"

"It most certainly is. Job 1:21," Adele announced proudly.

"I guess it's true then."

"It's not a guess, Arnold. It is in the Bible," Adele answered, cutting her cheese slice into four smaller pieces.

"I understand that you folks were not fond of Clayton Dalrymple."

"A detestable man," William Sawatzky said. "Good riddance to him. Still, our work is not done."

"What work are you referring to?" Arnold asked.

"Preparing for the end," William said calmly.

"And was Clayton in the way of this preparation?"

"He was an atheist. But he was not alone. There are other sinners. The homosexual Dan McCroskey for example."

"What makes you think Dan is gay?" Arnold asked. "He's married. Or was at least."

"His marriage was a smokescreen. His wife is a whore for the scoundrel Clayton. Mark my words, there is much cleansing to be done. Impurity is everywhere."

"Are you threatening anyone in particular?"

"I am not threatening anyone. I am simply conveying a biblical promise," William said. "Cleansing is the Lord's work. We are simply advising sinners that the time for judgement has arrived. Impurity will be crushed. Mark my words. It is all in the scripture."

"You seem very angry."

"Of course, I'm angry," William said. "Evil brings any righteous person to anger. There is a conspiracy of evil in the world. But hope lives in the hearts of the righteous. The judgement is coming."

"Before that happens, would it be possible for you to tell me where you both were on Saturday morning?"

"We were at home and in prayer until eight," William announced. "Then we had breakfast and left for the ballpark. Got there just before nine."

"Yes, I saw you both," Arnold said. "Did you leave the ballpark entrance at any time that morning?"

"We did not," answered William.

"Thank you. Just checking," Arnold said. He yearned for the fresh Northford air. He heard an ambulance siren in the distance and wondered who was ill. Then his attention returned to the room he was in, noting once more the smell of cleaner. He wondered if they might open a window. The room was stifling. But no move was made. William and Adele sat quietly, holding hands, occasionally closing their eyes in apparent prayer.

"While at your post yesterday morning, did you happen to see Dan or Natasha?"

"Of course," William said.

"When?"

"Lots of activity on Saturday morning," William reflected. "Brimming with sinners. But yes, Dan drove onto the Arts Centre parking lot with his old Falcon. Needs a muffler. Makes an awful racket."

"Are you sure it was Dan?"

"Of course. Impossible to miss the little pervert. That light, dancing step of his is unmistakable. He was wearing that same green Saskatchewan Roughrider ball cap and jacket he always wears. With the way he dresses, I have no idea how he lives with himself."

"What's wrong with how he dresses?"

"Dresses like a girl half the time," Adele said.

"At least it's only half the time. I take it both of you approve of the other half?" Arnold asked, teasingly.

"This is no time for humour, Sergeant Powell!" William said, slamming the table with his fist. "The Lord is very upset these days."

"Fine," Arnold said quietly. "What time did Dan arrive at the centre?"

"Just after we had set up our placard area. Must have been a little after nine. The first game had already started," William said.

"What about Natasha?"

"She pulled in maybe twenty-five minutes later," Adele said. "Drove in with her fancy BMW. Bought with stolen money is what I hear. She went inside, and shortly after, came out again. She walked across the street to complain to us. She disapproves of most people, but especially us. Very unlikeable woman. A few minutes later, Natasha and Dan came out again and had a smoke at the front doors of the centre. I don't approve of either of them. Most contemptable."

"Did you see Clayton?"

"Of course. Clayton drove his Mustang by the fairgrounds and disappeared down the forest road to his death."

"What time was that?"

"Shortly after we set up. About nine in the morning. Just after the first ball game started."

"You sure it was Clayton?"

"We are religious, Arnold, not crazy. Or blind. Of course, it was Clayton. Unmistakable. Driving fast too, like he does. In a rush going nowhere."

"What about Friday evening? You had placards up at the Arts Centre entrance on Friday. Did you see Clayton then?"

William nodded. "We did. Clayton came out of the building like a madman around supper time. We were getting ready to go home. That man was so full of evil, it's a wonder he managed to live as long as he did."

"Did you see him drop anything?" Arnold asked.

"That I couldn't say. My eyes were on the Lord," William answered. Adele shook her head, making it clear she hadn't seen anything either.

"Did you see anyone else?"

"Well, yes, I suppose I did," William said, pondering for a moment and scratching his head. "At one point, Dan came out of the building. I believe it was around the same time that Clayton left with his car. Dan was just standing by the McKenzie Avenue entrance. Looking for other homosexuals I would imagine."

"Did you see anyone else? Say, a large man standing at the park entrance, or in the parking-lot area?"

"No. As I said, Arnold, we had our eyes on the Lord."

"Thank you." Arnold moved to the door and opened it. "If you think of anything else, please call me."

"You know, Arnold," Adele said, "you may think that you're very smart, and that we believers aren't. But whatever trivial knowledge you have will soon evaporite into the air. It will come to nothing. You should put your faith in the Lord."

"Everything comes to nothing," Arnold said, stepping outside. "In the meantime, I'm here, trying to go about my business as best I can. Might not seem like much of a life, and perhaps it isn't, but it is the best I can do."

After closing the door behind him and as he walked back to his car, Arnold decided that Dan's sighting of a large man at the park entrance was definitely bogus. None of the other witnesses to Clayton's leaving the parking lot—including the critical eyes of William and Adele—had seen any large stranger at the park on Friday.

Chapter 20

Arnold visits with Janet Sawatzky

It was five o'clock on Sunday afternoon as Arnold waited in his police cruiser outside Mayor Ken Russell's apartment building. The warmth of the late afternoon sun was comforting. He took a moment to enjoy the sensation and prepare himself for his interview with Janet Sawatzky. He turned up the volume to Bach's Cello Suite No. 5. Then he took a deep breath. The melodic sounds of the cello took him to a pleasant place without dead bodies.

At his knock, Janet opened her apartment door with vigour. She was a slight young woman, with short brown hair, freckles on her nose, faded blue jeans with holes in the knees, a pair of seemingly new but grass-stained sneakers on her feet, and a general youthful look of confidence and vitality. "I was expecting you," she said. "Clayton's death was bound to bring a police visit."

Janet lived in a one-bedroom apartment on the first floor of the character brick building. As Arnold stepped in, he noted that the apartment was casually kept but still largely clean. The foyer featured a strewn sweatshirt in the corner, beside an open closet jammed full of jackets and cardboard boxes. In the open-concept living and dining-room space, there was an array of books littering both the coffee table and the kitchen table. There was a desk by the south window, piled high with books, and a thick pad of writing paper that looked to have been recently used.

He noted that she was holding a book: *Zen and the Art of Motorcycle Maintenance.* "Good book, Janet?" Arnold asked. "I've heard of it, of course, but do you think I would understand it? Or am I too old?"

"You're for sure not too old, Sergeant," Janet answered in spritely fashion. "It's just a book about life. We're all dealing with the same questions. Aren't we? I know nothing about motorcycles and I have not travelled, but still, I can relate to the author's journey. I imagine that you would as well. That's what I what I think, anyway. But then, I'm not that experienced. I may not really be understanding as much of it as I think I am. What about you, Sergeant? Do you understand as much as you think?"

"I am quite certain that I don't. I've been a police officer long enough to know that certainty is evasive. Still ... I try. Generally, I look at the possible paths of inquiry and choose the middle ground between extremes, minimizing assumptions. Helps in police work."

"You would make a good Buddhist."

"Then at least I would be good at something."

A small kitchen to the right of the front door looked out onto the open-concept living area. There were two south windows giving light to the space. The furniture was cheap but seemed well taken care of. The smell of fresh paint lingered.

"Clayton's death was a shock," Janet said, sitting down on the sofa. "I was expecting Clayton to leave the country, not die."

"You were expecting him to leave the country?"

"It struck me as a possibility, yes," Janet said nervously. "He did mention it. He didn't seem to think he had a future in Canada."

"Was his death difficult for you?" Arnold asked, noting Janet's observation and deciding that he might return to the topic of Clayton's potential departure later.

"How do mean?" Janet asked, innocently. "Because we were having a relationship?"

"Yes, I guess so. We have talked about this before."

"We have, Sergeant. I'm sorry that I was rude to you awhile back when you were asking me about it. I realise you were just trying to help. Just like Annie. At the time, I felt that it wasn't anyone else's business. I had as much control as I wanted. But I was naïve. I admit that. Still, Clayton wasn't bad to me. Not really. I'll miss him more than my parents."

"Your parents are still alive. You don't need to miss them."

"But they won't see me."

"Do you ever go to your parents' home?"

"No, I'm not allowed on the premises. Why do you ask?"

"Just checking details."

"My parents aren't right in the head. Madness takes on many forms."

"How would you describe your relationship with Clayton?" Arnold asked, still standing but considering having a seat.

"He was a friend, sort of. Although, the friendship took an expected turn."

"An expected turn?"

"Yes. I assumed that he would want to have sex with me, and he did. I guess that's why I called it an expected turn. We started as friends, just sharing problems, and then he asked if he could have sex with me. I haven't had a lot of experience, and to be honest I wanted to gain some. I admit that I was attracted to him. He had money and he was lonely. I need money and as a lonely person, I felt badly for him. So, I agreed."

"What did he offer?"

"Friendship. Sex. But most importantly, sponsorship. And yes, I know what that makes me, Arnold. I understand that. But I'm not in a good position in Northford. You know that. I needed help, more than Annie and the others could give. I needed a sponsor. Clayton offered that. Anyway, he was kind to me. He liked my 'naïve enthusiasm.' He was having an affair with Sheila, but he didn't like her. He found her crude and insensitive. Of course, that's probably why she was drawn to him. As for Natasha, they didn't sleep together and they barely tolerated each other. That's what he said anyway."

"What about this sponsorship you mentioned?"

"He offered to pay for medical school."

"Did he say why? His reputation in town wasn't exactly leaning in the direction of generosity."

"He didn't say." She shrugged. "Maybe he was looking for redemption? He's done bad things; he confessed to that. Maybe he was just looking to help someone. Thankfully, it was me."

"But you had to agree to sex?"

"Yes, but it was not quite the way you make it sound. The sponsorship was not tied to sex. Initially, I wanted to have sex with him. I liked the wickedness of it. It was thrilling, at least at first. But it soon became weird and awkward. It turns out that sex in a car is very unpleasant. I don't even think it was good for him, but probably better than it was for me. I soon came to regret agreeing to be with him. In fact, I went to his office at the Arts Centre on Friday and told him that it was over. Told him I didn't want to have sex with him anymore, and that I didn't want his money."

"How did he respond to that? Did he pull the sponsorship offer?"

"He fumed and fussed, but he did accept it. He didn't withdraw his offer to sponsor me or force himself on me or anything like that, even though he was quite drunk when I told him. I thought that he might get angry or violent. He is capable of that, but he didn't. Instead, he broke down and started confessing to all kinds of terrible things."

"What kinds of things?"

She grimaced a bit, not meeting Arnold's eyes as she got up from the sofa and started pacing a bit. "He shot his father in-law in the Soviet Union. He also confessed to killing Doc's wife, Sophia. Pushed her into Lake Baikal. Then he went on a bizarre rant of how he didn't deserve to live, but that he wasn't going to die alone. Natasha was going to die with him. He said couldn't escape because the police would be watching for him at the airport, and he knew that he would be handed over to the Soviets. He was panicked about his circumstances. It was all over for him, he said. Then he stormed out of his office."

"When did this happen?"

"Friday afternoon. Coming up to dinner time probably."

"What did you do?"

"I was too shocked to do anything at first and just sort of sat there in his office. No idea for how long. When I finally snapped out of it, I knew that I needed to tell Natasha, since he had just confessed to murdering her sister in Russia and then threatened to kill her too. So, I went up to her office. Her door was open, and she was talking to Dan. I could hear them. Natasha was telling Dan that Clayton was going to kill her on Saturday. Something about a double suicide. But that she didn't believe that Clayton would die too. Only her. Anyway, it sounded to me like she already knew more than I did. I took off then. Not sure why. Fear, I guess." Shrugging, she sat down at her kitchen table, grabbing a salt-shaker and studying it. Arnold noted that her hands were shaking a bit.

"You should have reported this, Janet," Arnold said, sitting down on a chair across the table from her. "That must have been traumatic for you."

After a long moment of pained silence, Arnold decided that she'd had enough questioning for one day, and he stood up, walking towards the door. When he turned back, he saw a teary-eyed Janet, now standing by her kitchen counter. He couldn't help but feel for her.

"You have a nice place, Janet. I haven't been in these apartments for some time and they're nicer than I remember. Dan is actually moving in officially next week."

"Yeah," she said, brightening a bit. "It'll be great to have him as a neighbour. Emily Little is down the hall as well. She's super nice, like so many people around here, like Annie, and of course, Natasha, who gave me a chance to be a part of her theatre program. I can't believe how lucky I got, having such an amazing teacher and mentor."

"Aren't Sheila and Natasha upset with you? For having a relationship with Clayton, I mean."

"Sheila is disappointed with me, for sure. She warned me about getting involved with Clayton. But for the record, I'm disappointed in her as well. She's been a great help to me, and I owe her, but her affair with Clayton was cruel. Dan deserves better. So does Natasha." She paused then and looked down. "They deserved better from both of us actually. How did I repay Natasha for all she's done for me? I had a thing with her husband." She shook her head, looking disgusted with herself. "Just for kicks and then to satisfy my ambitions.... I really regret that."

"Don't be too hard on yourself, Janet," he said softly. "You're still young and have a lot of learning yet to do."

Arnold wished he could leave their conversation at that, but he had one more question to ask. "Before I go, do you mind telling me where you were on Saturday morning, between seven and nine-thirty?"

She nodded. "I slept in till eight, hungover. I was out late at McKnight's on Friday with a few friends from Lloydminster, who were in town for the baseball tournament. Which reminds me, I have a confession to make. Another one, I suppose."

"Do tell. Please."

"One of the girls I was with at the disco made a wild promise to Hank Goertzen. Told him she'd have sex with him if Northford lost the game. She asked him to throw it. It was quite naughty. Not only that but she didn't even have any intention of fulfilling her promise. And she didn't either. She never showed up at the beach to meet Hank. Just skipped out of town. Hank must have been pretty pissed off, striking out for nothing."

"Interesting. And I'd thought that Hank just couldn't see the pitch."

"I was at the game too, Sergeant," she said skeptically. "He swung at a pitch that hit him."

"That he did. What was the rest of the morning like for you? Before the game I mean."

"After a quick breakfast, I walked to the library and was there all morning."

"Anybody see you?"

"Natasha waved at me when she was running down the river path by the library. That was shortly before the library opened at eight-thirty. I was the first person there, other than the librarian, Ms. Wilson. The library was quiet all morning. I left around noon."

"Thanks, Janet. That's all I've got." He put his notebook away, feeling rather impressed with her. She seemed mature beyond her years.

CHAPTER 21

ARNOLD MEETS WITH
ANNIE RUSSELL

Arnold Powell left Janet's apartment building and sat down on a sagging wooden bench outside that had been placed in front of a trio of robust blue spruce trees and a few well-aged oaks. He pulled out his notebook then, reviewing his interview notes. Janet's involvement with Clayton was troubling, but he was unsure what to make of it in terms of Clayton's death. That said, she had provided additional evidence that Clayton was a highly conflicted, troubled man. *He seems to have inflicted damage everywhere he went, but at least it seems like he felt bad about it.*

Clayton's response to his own actions appeared to have been guilt, or at least a measure of remorse, along with huge servings of self pity. Despite that, he did appear to have promised to kill Natasha and himself. He'd made plans to escape but hadn't followed up on these plans, perhaps knowing that the police would be waiting for him at the airport, just as Natasha had presumed. But whatever the reason, it was evident that Clayton had either adjusted the Saturday program or someone had adjusted it for him.

Arnold's thoughts were interrupted by the approach of Annie Russell, looking pleased with the day. She wore a full smile, along with a pair of high yellow boots, and a short, multicoloured, long-sleeved hippie dress in psychedelic patterns.

"Hi, Arnold. Just here to check if the new toilet was delivered to Dan's apartment." She looked up at a spectacular structure of clouds building in the eastern sky. "Not exactly elegant work, but Ken asked. Muscle John promised to do the install tomorrow, but he'll need the new toilet to be there. Property management is fun, but then again, not so much. You just interviewed Janet, I presume? She talked about her and Clayton?"

"She did," Arnold reported, as he watched a squirrel grab an acorn nearby and dash off to store it, or so he presumed. "Janet's relationship with Clayton was discussed in some surprising detail. She wasn't defensive or dismissive of my interest, as she was the last time I tried to broach the subject with her. Her self-reporting supports her position that she had felt a measure of agency at one point, but her self-awareness has grown on the matter. She still pushed away my concerns, but I believe that she was actually quite reflective and insightful about it."

"Janet's an independent girl," Annie said. "When I was her age, I pretended to be independent, but it was mostly just smoke and mirrors. I always had the backing of my parents, even though my mother was a drunk and my dad an irresponsible money waster. Not a good trait in a bank manager. Still, I wasn't alone in the world like Janet, so I'm not about to judge her."

"Good idea, Annie," Arnold agreed, unzipping his jacket as the sun shone through the blue spruce and oak. "Janet has layers of complex motivations. Her judgement could use some work, but then again ... join the club. On my way to see Leonard next. Then Sheila McCroskey."

"Sheila has judgement issues too," Annie said abruptly. "I wonder how good a nurse she is ... as loosely wrapped as she is. Leonard, on the other hand, has quality judgement, although he did arrive in town with a Ford Falcon." She grimaced. "Still, he saved himself by selling it to Dan. Now Ken has decided to donate his restored Impala to him. Leonard was underpaid, so the board decided we should offer him a bonus."

"Did he accept?"

"He did. Seemed quite pleased."

"Nice work, Annie. I imagine you advised Ken to make this donation?"

"Sometimes Ken needs encouragement."

"Don't we all." He sighed. "Alright, I'm off to talk to Leonard."

"When you get to Sheila, don't be surprised if she denies the affair with Clayton," Annie said. "Everyone in town knows about it, but she seems to have the idea that it's some big secret. A bit oblivious, she is. What are you going to ask her?"

"Maybe why she never goes to the Dickey Dee."

Anne grinned at that. "Sheila told me that she doesn't approve of fast-food burger joints. But Dan says Sheila often uses hamburger helper when she cooks. Not much of a health-food person. Her reasons for not coming to the Dickey Dee are different than Clayton's. Clayton was *actually* a vegetarian and a health-food fanatic."

"So, what *is* her issue with the Dickey Dee?"

"She's not fond of me. She told me that if she wore her blouse unbuttoned at the top like I do, she wouldn't be allowed on the church board. I thought that was interesting. I'm on the church board, and Sheila isn't."

"Does she want to be?" Arnold asked, quizzically.

"Maybe, but she doesn't even attend Four-Square Gospel. Anyway, her point was that I get away with dressing the way I do because of my connection to the mayor. She isn't entirely wrong. The church needs to keep Ken's support."

"They need Ken to approve the church-expansion building project," Arnold said, nodding knowingly. "When that's done, will you resign from the board?"

"Same day," Annie said quickly, getting up from the bench. "Can't stand that board. Gerald Schultz is a charlatan. And the other day at a church board meeting, James McCullum asked me whether I was having an affair with Schultz!"

"Schultz? That's ridiculous. Was he there?"

"He was. He formally disavowed it but seemed rather too pleased with the accusation. Kept staring at me to see if I might be interested. It was disturbing."

"Gerald Schultz is not your type," Arnold said, still sitting but taking his car keys out of his pocket and readying himself to stand up.

"He isn't. Ken is my type," Annie said defiantly. "I have zero interest in anyone else—no offense, Arnold. I appreciate our friendship, and I know you understand my views and position, but it confounds me how often I get asked why I cheat on Ken. It seems to confuse people when I tell them that I don't, and I won't. But I suppose, in Northford, if you wear a hippie dress above the knee, and yellow boots, and appear to be generally happy, you must be having an affair."

"Folks perhaps find the idea titillating. Northford is a great place to work and live, but sometimes I wonder if people have too much free time on their hands. Makes for too much idle chatter."

CHAPTER 22

ARNOLD MEETS WITH LEONARD
AT COMMUNITY PARTNERSHIPS

The Community Partnership drop-in centre had once been a Chinese restaurant but had been renovated to accommodate social-service offices, a large public space for music events and movies, and a coffee-shop drop-in, which had made use of the red vinyl booths from the old restaurant. The centre sold sandwiches, pastries, and coffee at a discounted price, donated by the nearby Princeton Bakery. But the primary revenue for the centre came from rent that local social-service offices paid for the space. The idea was to have a visible and accessible downtown public presence for service agencies.

The Community Partnerships board had brought in a summer director from Winnipeg to start up the centre. Leonard Heinrichs had arrived with his Ford Falcon in late April and was due to leave with Ken's Chevrolet Impala at the end of the week.

Leonard was a slender young man, mildly athletic, and good enough at baseball to secure a roster spot for the Northford Yankees but not good enough to improve the team. He was useful as a pitcher, first baseman, and occasional catcher. He was also useful as a sandlot basketball player in the local YMCA league.

As summer director at Community Partnerships, Leonard had demonstrated an ability to network with others. Together with Dan McCroskey, the partnerships program had started a Northford Film Group, bringing in old classic movies for weekly viewing. They'd also started a speaker bureau, so that locals with an interest in a particular topic could have the floor for half an hour every Thursday. That was how Leonard had met Clayton.

Clayton had presented on the topic of Russian identity as expressed in its literature. Clayton's view was that Russian literature was long-winded, overwrought, and obsessively dark. The fact that his speech was long-winded, overwrought, and obsessively dark ironically helped to make his point. After the speech, Leonard and Clayton had talked and discovered a mutual interest in both Russian literature and baseball.

■ ■ ■

Arnold Powell ordered a coffee and a carrot muffin with pink cream-cheese icing, and sat down in the southwest corner booth to wait, its red vinyl squeaking with every movement he made. Through the window, he studied the non-functioning water feature of Central Park. The feature had been built with considerable fanfare a few years earlier, but shortly after, the water had stopped flowing, an issue that had been one of the many municipal criticisms that Clayton had of Mayor Ken Russell.

While many of Clayton's criticisms of Ken were untrue and mean-spirited, there was no getting around the fact that the mayor had failed to resurrect the water feature. It looked forlorn, a tower of intricate engineering design that did nothing but accumulate pigeon droppings. As Arnold looked out the window, he noted Dr. Robert Morley walking along the park's footpath, his short quick steps presenting the story of a man in a rush. But apparently, he wasn't. Dr. Morley suddenly stopped, perched himself on the park bench by the water feature, and started tossing breadcrumbs. The pigeons seemed pleased. Dr. Morley, on the other hand, didn't.

Leonard brought Arnold's muffin and coffee over to him and sat down opposite him in the booth with a glass of ice water for himself. The young man was dressed in a plaid shirt with a grey vest, a fisher-man's hat, and black jeans. He looked at Arnold and smiled.

"So," Arnold said, "how did it feel to strike out Hank?"

"I didn't really," Leonard acknowledged. "Sun was in his eyes. Rumour is that he also wasn't that motivated to make the hit. Struck out on purpose. Could be. He usually hits me hard. Either way, I'll take it."

"Where did you hear that?"

"There were a few young women from Lloydminster in here after the game on Saturday. They were joking around about how one of them had promised Hank sex if he lost the game. They seemed to think it was quite funny." He shrugged. "Ah well, I got to feel pretty good about striking him out for a few hours at least."

"I can relate to the feeling. I've had moments when I thought a case was solved, only to find that it wasn't. But that doesn't apply to the Clayton situation. I'm not sure what happened there, other than that he's dead."

"Most unfortunate," Leonard said. "He was a regular at the centre. I talked to him a couple of times a week. Got to know him fairly well." Leonard took his cap off and looked around at the centre. "Clayton came in here to talk about himself, baseball and Russian literature. He told stories from his past. All of his stories were similar in theme."

"And what was the theme?" Arnold asked, pulling out his notebook.

"For example, Catfish Hunter signing with the Yankees as a free agent for pretty big dollars. Clayton was very annoyed about that. He predicted, and hoped, that Hunter would fail. He had a pattern of that kind of thinking. Generally, if someone was doing well, Clayton hoped that they would have a setback. I found Clayton complicated but interesting. The man lived with guilt about his past deeds. At the same time, he felt that he was a victim."

"Did he ever say anything about wanting to end his life?"

"Not specifically. But he was deeply unhappy with himself. Being in the world was hard for him. He told me once that, if he died, he was absolutely certain no one would care. He hated Western culture with some vigour, even though he'd defected. Still, he loved baseball. The statistical side of the game fascinated him. He isn't alone. It's intriguing for sure."

"Can you cast any additional light on his state of mind? This guilt you refer to?" Arnold asked, as he started on his coffee and carrot muffin.

"He admitted that he was guilty of murder, for one," Leonard said, quietly. "I got the sense it was back in Russia, though he never gave details. My feeling was that he was looking for forgiveness or some form of redemption, but he didn't know who could give that to him. He had long given up on the Church. He was on his own. Like, I guess, we all are."

Arnold took a bite of his muffin, considering its taste and texture for a moment. "Not great, but not bad. Been sitting for a few days but not months."

Leonard chuckled. "We pride ourselves on having week-old desserts. Keeps us from getting too busy." He took a sip of his water.

"Did Clayton ever talk about Natasha?"

"He was conflicted about Natasha," Leonard said sadly. "He felt betrayed by her, but at the same time, he was constantly betraying her. His description of their marriage sounded like it was held together by the threat of mutual destruction."

"They had information on each other that could be destructive?"

"I believe that they did, yes."

"He didn't give any details of that?"

"No, only inferences regarding past actions."

"Do you think he was suicidal?"

"Hard to be sure, but I will say that he seemed to be at the end of his rope. There was a kind of mellow but dramatic feel to conversations with him. He seemed to get some perverse pleasure from sharing self-deprecating information, and I suppose, I got perverse pleasure from listening to it."

"Good admission," Arnold observed, closing his notebook.

"Perhaps 'pleasure' isn't the right word, really. But I was drawn to listening to him. He demanded attention. My job here is to provide that. Still, it was sad, like watching a movie of despair and futility. Painful to watch, yet weirdly addictive."

"Did he ever share any fears about being killed? Having an enemy that he was concerned about?"

"He wasn't prepared to die at the hands of others, but that did seem to be what he felt was about to happen."

Arnold saw Ken's orange Chevrolet Impala in the back parking lot of the Arts Centre. "That's Ken's car. Is he around?"

"No. Ken was here this morning, but he left," Leonard said softly, looking out the window at the water feature. "He also left me his car. Told me to keep it. Apparently, Annie and Ken think I was underpaid this summer. They're not wrong, but still ... giving me a car? And one like that? Quite spectacular, really. Clayton would have been seriously annoyed."

CHAPTER 23

ARNOLD MEETS WITH
NURSE SHEILA MCCROSKEY

As Arnold pulled into Sheila McCroskey's driveway, hunger entered his consciousness. He looked at his watch. It was five-thirty, Sunday afternoon. The carrot muffin at Community Partners had teased him but wasn't enough. He told himself that he would drive by the Dickey Dee for a cheeseburger after his interview with Sheila. *I'll have to be efficient, though,* he thought. *I've got a debriefing with Ken at seven.*

Arnold had tried to meet with Sheila at the hospital earlier in the day and had been told that she had gone home sick. But when he called her at home, she had not picked up. He wondered if she was trying to avoid contact. He was about to find out. He knocked on the front door and waited.

The McCroskey house was on the west end of Douglas Street, just a block south of Clayton and Natasha Dalrymple's property. The house was decorated with fading-yellow stucco siding. Patches of stucco had fallen off in spots, revealing a growing enterprise in rotten wood. Evidently, neither Dan nor Sheila was vigilant about home maintenance. The house was in better shape than William and Adele's but not by much. It made Arnold's house look pristine.

It was a standard middle-class, 1960s split-level home, except for the fact that the living-room picture window had a crack running from the lower east corner to the upper west corner. The window was partially covered by a blue velvet curtain that hung precariously on a bent curtain rod. The thick material appeared to be too heavy for it.

The front yard was bordered on three sides by an old, white picket fence that leaned outwards from the property and was made up of a series of rotting white boards, many of which had come to rest on the grass. There were intermittent posts, but they had abandoned all pretence of holding the fence upright. The front yard itself was full of densely planted grasses and flowering plants. Arnold recognized some of the plants from the meadow where Clayton had died. Hundreds of purple asters were still in bloom.

The east side of the house sat up against the Northford Woodlands Reserve. The nature-trail entrance was just to the west of the McCroskey house. It was evident that the McCroskey front yard was emulating the Northford Woodlands Forest.

A young boy opened the door a few inches, somewhat hesitantly.

"Hello there. My name is Sergeant Arnold Powell. What's your name, young man?"

"I'm Nathan," the boy said tentatively.

"Is your mother at home?"

"I'm not supposed to say," Nathan said slowly. "Mom works at the hospital during the day."

"But is she at home today?"

"I guess she is. But I think she has a headache." The boy fidgeted with his hands, his eyes darting around the room. Arnold took initiative and stepped inside past him.

Nathan walked down the dark, narrow hallway to rouse his mother, skirting a basket full of folded laundry, and in due course, Sheila McCroskey emerged, wearing a deeply orange bathrobe. It was clear that she had been in bed. Her hair was seriously disturbed. Arnold made a mental note that Sheila really wasn't feeling well. She was only in her late thirties, but she looked tired and resigned. *But resigned to what?*

"If you're up to it, I have a few questions regarding Clayton's death," Arnold said, as politely and gently as he could.

"Sure," Sheila said, shrugging her shoulders. "Can't see what Clayton's death has to do with me, but you're the boss."

205

"I'm not the boss, but I do need to make inquiries," Arnold said carefully, looking at the disarray in the kitchen. It looked like a set from a disaster movie, one of those in which the residents had been called suddenly and mysteriously away, leaving everything precisely as it was. "I understand that you saw Clayton on Saturday morning. In fact, you might be the last person to have seen him alive."

"I resent the accusation, Arnold," Sheila said, looking momentarily energized by anger. "I don't need this. I came down with a migraine today, and it's defeated me." She shuffled into the kitchen and moved a few dirty pots around. Then perhaps feeling that the cleanup was hopeless, she sat down at the table. "Sorry for the mess. Housekeeping has never been one of my hobbies. I've also been under immense stress. What with my marriage falling apart and my migraines...." She sighed. "But sit down, Arnold. You can have a coffee if you want ... if we can find the coffee maker. Pretty sure it's here somewhere. But first, what is this foolish talk about me being the last person to see Clayton?"

"I'm sorry to intrude, Sheila," Arnold said softly. "One of my ex-wives had migraines, which lasted longer than our marriage. Can you confirm that you were with Clayton at his house on Saturday morning?"

"What would I be doing at Clayton's? I hardly knew the man," Sheila said, standing up, apparently to dig around on the counter for the coffee maker. She found it under a crumpled page of the *Northford Sentinel*. "I didn't know Clayton well. He was really just a neighbour," she said coolly. "Of course, I did sometimes borrow his chainsaw." Sheila wiped a strand of loose blonde hair from her eye. "Dan doesn't use power equipment, but I do. Clayton was well stocked with tools. But beyond that, we really had little to do with each other. What would I be doing at his house, anyways?"

Sheila was attractive with inquisitive eyes that probed the room. Arnold noted that she was observant and self possessed. He also noted that she was a good liar. Her face maintained a casually neutral expression as she spoke. She came across as perfectly genuine, even though she was having a great deal of difficulty finding the coffee filters.

"What you were doing at Clayton's is not my question, at least not at the moment," Arnold said softly, wondering if he should ask Sheila to forget about making coffee. It looked very much like she was not up to the challenge. He decided to soften his tone even further and try to put Sheila at ease ... except that he didn't.

"I know that you were with Clayton on Saturday morning. If I phrased it as a question, I am sorry. It wasn't meant to be. I am merely asking you to confirm that you were with him the morning of his death. I am interested in knowing how he was that morning."

"This line of questioning has gone far enough," Sheila said, giving up on finding a fresh coffee filter. She removed the used filter from her machine, tossed the old grinds into the sink, along with a myriad of dishes, and then put it back in, filling the rear of the coffee maker with water. Tired out, she sat down then. "I may actually be out of coffee. I'm not sure. Dan was in charge of buying coffee."

"There's a jar of Hills Bros coffee beside the coffee maker," Arnold pointed out. "But it's fine. Can you just please tell me how Clayton was on Saturday morning?"

"Arnold," Sheila said, sounding exasperated, "my marriage may be over, but I am still technically a married woman. In Northford, that stands for something. Not only am I married but I'm also a professional nurse."

"I am not disputing any of that," Arnold replied slowly, slouching a bit to appear less intimidating. "But you really need to come around to accepting your meeting with Clayton as a fact that we can agree on. Your affair with Clayton is not a secret, Sheila. Please ... let us move forward with this conversation. How was Clayton on Saturday?"

"Fine," Sheila said, getting up and grabbing the coffee jar with some energy, randomly tossing some fresh grounds into the used filter. "I was with Clayton. Why shouldn't I be? As to how he was.... Well, I can tell you that he was alive and well. Certainly wasn't dead. I would know. He was his typical brusque self. But now he's dead, which is not good."

"Not for him, anyway. Is his death good for you?" Arnold regretted the question almost immediately, quite sure that Sheila would be upset by it, but she wasn't.

"Not really," Sheila responded casually. "I wasn't in love with the man, but the sex was good. Even a married woman is allowed some pleasure."

"Was there any change in his mood on Saturday?"

"Same as always," Sheila said, shaking her head and trying unsuccessfully to turn on the coffee maker. "What is wrong with this machine? It worked yesterday."

"Probably will today too if you plug it in, Sheila," Arnold said softly, getting up and finding the cord and the outlet—behind a propped-up pizza pan—and plugging the machine in.

Sheila leaned back against the counter, crossing her arms. "Clayton was always the same," she said with resignation. "Other than sometimes being hornier than others. Things could get a little aggressive."

She had entered the room with flagging energy, and it was not improving. The conversation appeared to be utterly exhausting her. "He was quite aggressive yesterday. But who cares? Last time I checked, aggressive sex is not a crime. Even for a married nurse."

"Sex, aggressive or not, is *not* a crime," Arnold said quietly. "Even for a married nurse. What time did you arrive at Clayton's and when did you leave?"

"Got there just before seven in the morning. I was early. Deliberately. Wanted to annoy Natasha. She was quite unnerved when I poked my head in the front door. Usually, I go in the back. Clayton leaves the back door open for me." She shrugged. "But yesterday, I wanted to have some fun, so I looked in on Natasha. She was standing at the kitchen counter, decked out in her running gear, literally putting poison in Clayton's breakfast drink."

Arnold frowned. "Putting poison in Clayton's breakfast drink? How do you mean? What precisely did you see?"

"I literally saw Natasha pouring the breakfast juice into the mugs. Obviously, she poisoned Clayton's."

"I don't understand. How is that obvious?"

"I smelled fennel in the kitchen. I recognize the smell. Same as water hemlock."

"But Clayton was shot."

"That may be, but I know what I smelled. I say he was poisoned. Natasha did it, as sure as I'm speaking with you. She wanted to get rid of Clayton. I don't approve of murder. Too extreme in my view. Granted, I sympathize with her motive. I would kill my husband too if he had an affair. Of course, in my case, Dan lacks the required manliness for an affair. But Clayton didn't. Let me tell you, when it came to sex, Clayton was rough, greedy, and insatiable. That was to my benefit. Though, of course, he overdid it. Having an affair with Janet too was excessive in my view. But that was largely Janet's fault. A man like Clayton can't be expected to say no. Janet offered herself for money, basically. When you get down to it, Janet simply wanted Clayton's sponsorship, and he gave it. Well, good for her, I guess, but I still think the whole thing was in bad taste. Especially after everything I've done for Janet. I befriended her, helped her in her time of desperation, and she pays me back by horning in on my sex life? Not impressed, I can tell you. Prison isn't good enough for some people."

"Are you saying that Janet should go to prison for doing the same thing with Clayton that you did with Clayton?"

Sheila paused for a few moments to consider that. Finally, stroking her hair back, she managed to recover her composure, and then poured Arnold a coffee. "I overstepped with that comment. No, I am not suggesting that Janet should go to prison. I don't approve of her actions, but a girl without parents and support sometimes has to step outside the rules to get ahead. I am, however, suggesting that Natasha should go to prison. She murdered her husband. I'm sure of it. What am I supposed to do now? I already kicked Dan out. Am I destined to be a single mother of two boys? Good boys, mind you, but still.... What about my social life? Clayton's death impacts me. This whole business is very bad for me."

"All good questions, Sheila," Arnold said. "But to be clear, your accusation against Natasha is based solely on you smelling fennel in the kitchen?"

"I know my poison smells, Arnold. Studied all about poisonous native plants in my nurse training. Most of the nurses didn't find the study of poisons interesting, but I did. In fact, I found it interesting that they *weren't* interested. But trust me, you're talking to someone in the know on poisonous native plants."

"Okay, so there was a fennel smell. But people do cook with fennel."

"They shouldn't. Too strong a flavour. Quite pungent."

"But perhaps Natasha and Clayton didn't mind the smell. I eat fennel sausages. Quite good."

"Fine. Disregard my observations. If you don't care about solving the case, just say so, and I'll stop helping you."

"I appreciate the help, Sheila. But I prefer to be more tentative about conclusions. What did you do after looking in on Natasha?"

"I walked to the back alley connecting our streets, lit a cigarette, and then smoked and watched. From where I stood, I could see the front door. Natasha left the house shortly after, but I stayed in the alley to finish my smoke. Then I went back inside through the front door. Clayton was in his bedroom as usual, waiting for me. We had sex. It wasn't as good as usual, but not as bad as sometimes."

"What happened after you had sex?" Arnold said, taking a sip of coffee. The used filter gave the coffee a taste similar, in some ways, to the day-old coffee he often drank. He was beginning to feel at home in Sheila's mess of a kitchen.

"Nothing much. We don't cuddle or anything. That's not our thing. Clayton got dressed and went to the workshop to meditate. I went to the bathroom, then doodled on the kitchen table for a few minutes, just unwinding, then had a drink of water. Sex makes me thirsty. Finally, I joined Clayton in the workshop with his breakfast drink and Medovik cake. He'd asked me to bring it to him."

"Did he seem stressed? You mentioned that he was aggressive."

"You keep asking that. There was *nothing* different about Clayton on Saturday. He was the same as he *always* is. Yes, he was aggressive. That is true. He did me again on the hood of his Mustang. That was better than in the bedroom, although the metal hood was cold. Didn't seem to bother him. A bit rough can be good. But then our relationship was primarily physical. He wasn't interested in my feelings, and frankly, I wasn't interested in his."

"Did he mention any commitments that morning?"

"He mentioned that he was going out to meet with 'an associate in the woods.' That was after our second bout of sex, when he told me to leave because he had stuff to do. I didn't ask for more details. I just left."

"When did you leave his house?"

"When he told me to go. About eight. Never stay more than an hour, anyway, sometimes less."

"What happened when you came home?"

"Nothing much. Had a shower and prepared for work. The house was empty. My boys had gone birding with Dan, leaving before seven. They got back at around eight-thirty, just as I was leaving for work."

"What was Clayton wearing?"

"Nothing when I first arrived. He was in bed. When I left, he was wearing his disco outfit. Dreadful fashion sense, that man."

"Cowboy boots?"

"Probably. I'm not very observant about stuff like that. But he loves cowboy boots and paisley shirts. Does it matter?"

"I'm not sure if it does. Can you describe the workshop scene? Did he drink his mug of juice or eat the piece of cake while you were there?"

"As I say, I'm not very observant. Not like Dan. He notices everything. A very annoying characteristic. But I am quite sure that Clayton's breakfast mug of juice was still in the workshop, untouched, as was the cake that I brought him. I went back into the house to have a glass of water before I left. As I said before, sex makes me thirty."

"Was Natasha's breakfast drink on the kitchen counter?"

"No. The counter was clean."

"But you said that Natasha was pouring two mugs of breakfast drink. You brought one to Clayton. There should have been one left on the counter."

"True. There were two mugs on the counter when I first looked in on Natasha. But when Natasha left, and I returned to the house, one of the mugs was gone."

"So, when you went back to the house, only Clayton's mug was there?"

"That's correct. When I picked up Clayton's drink, there was only one mug on the counter. Maybe Natasha drank hers before she left. Or maybe Clayton dumped hers out. What do I know? I'm not in charge of their kitchen counter. I have my own kitchen to deal with. Quite enough if you ask me. Although you didn't."

"Do you recall the handle position of Clayton's mug?"

She thought for a long moment, rubbing her temple. Finally, she nodded. "It was pointed away from the front door. To the right."

"You are sure? You did say that you're not observant."

"Clayton likes his mug handle pointing to the left, towards the door. Lord knows why. Anyway, the mug was pointed wrong. I noticed it when

I was doodling in the kitchen. I turned the handle the way he liked. Didn't want to upset him if he came in and noticed it. He was bothered by those types of details. Seriously anal."

"That's why your fingerprints were found on Clayton's breakfast-drink mug?"

"Oh, my goodness," Sheila gasped. "I never thought of that. I guess they would be."

"What about the cake?"

"What about it? The cake slice was on a small plate. Clayton loved the cake. He said it was a Russian dessert."

"Did Clayton drink from the mug or eat any of the cake that you brought him?"

"You already asked that. As I said, we were having sex on the hood of his car. He didn't touch the mug or the cake while I was there. He had other things to touch."

"Did Clayton go into the kitchen while you were there?"

"No. He went directly into the workshop from the bedroom. He was still in the workshop when I left."

"Did his mood change at all as he told you to leave?"

"He was rude, telling me to go, but then ... that was Clayton. His rudeness was highly developed. But then I wasn't there for friendship. We both got what we wanted. It was time for me to go."

"You left when he asked you to?"

"When Clayton tells you to leave, it's best to leave. It wasn't a big deal. I just live two minutes away."

"Do you have a slingshot in the house? Any hard Parmesan Reggiano?"

She raised a confused eyebrow. "What a ridiculous question. Not to get personal, but is being stupid required for joining the police force?"

"I'm not aware of any such requirement. Would you please answer the question?"

"The boys have a slingshot. And yes, we do use Parmesan Reggiano. It's the best cheese for pasta, although it's ridiculously expensive and hard. You have to grate it. Quite annoying. But what of it?"

Sheila poured herself a coffee, took a sip, and sighed pleasantly. "This coffee is almost as good as from the vending machine at the hospital," she said, as she set it down too close to the edge of the table. It fell to the floor, breaking into many small pieces and staining a pile of *Life* magazines on the kitchen floor. She just stood and looked at it in numb silence.

Sighing with sympathy, Arnold bent to pick up the broken ceramic shards. "Do you have any of that cheese at the moment? Here in the house?"

Sounding and looking frustrated at everything, she moved towards the refrigerator, slipping on a sheet of notepaper lying blamelessly on the linoleum floor and hitting the ground with a thud, her back taking the brunt of the impact. "Damn it!"

Arnold helped her up. "Are you okay? Good thing you missed the broken glass."

"I'm going to have to get the boys to clean up. My brother Henry can help. He doesn't mind housework." She tried to take a deep breath and winced, muttering, "Might have cracked a rib. And all for the sake of showing you where I keep the cheese. I do hope the interview is over soon. I need to go back to bed." Sheila managed to hobble over to refrigerator, open it, and study the interior, moving various items around. The effort didn't appear to satisfy her. Finally, she slumped her shoulders and looked sadly back at Arnold. "Guess we used the last of it. I can't find it. Strange though."

"Why strange?"

"We had a large block of it. We don't use that much. It's expensive, and nurses are hugely underpaid."

He nodded. "Alright. Thanks, Sheila. That's all for now. Good luck with ... all of it," he said, gesturing vaguely around. *The ribs, the broken mug, the headache....*

As Arnold left the house, he encountered young Henry, Sheila's brother, who was moving around awkwardly in the front yard of the house. "How are you doing, Henry?"

"Great. When I dance, I feel good all over. I might be big and getting bigger," Henry said, patting his stomach, "but I love to dance. I am very good at it, and I'm quick on my feet, like when we play Robin Hood. My grandfather didn't think I was like Robin Hood, but I am. My grandfather didn't like me. It made Sheila sad. He is dead now. But she is still sad. I think she doesn't want me to be like Robin Hood either. I don't know why. It is very confusing."

Henry was not well coordinated. His dance moves were awkward and somewhat spastic, but he was certainly moving, although it was to music that Arnold couldn't hear. Henry wore a pair of loose yoga pants, a white shirt featuring the Beatles over his fleshy upper body, and a pair of white Foster running shoes that looked brand new. They didn't have a mark on them.

"What do you do when you play Robin Hood, Henry?" Arnold asked.

"I make the bad guys pay."

"How do you know who the bad guys are?"

"I listen and watch. That is how I know," Henry said, turning a pirouette but tripping on a gopher hole just beside the sidewalk. He fell but picked himself up, still smiling.

"Have you had those shoes for a long time?" Arnold asked.

"Sheila just bought them for me. I had work boots, but Sheila said that they were not good for dancing. She was right. They were heavy. Sheila said that all the boys are wearing running shoes. Sheila is right. Sheila is always right."

"Do you still have your work boots?" Arnold asked.

"Gone," Henry said.

"Gone where?"

"Sheila got rid of them. They are out of style."

"Were you wearing those work boots in the woods yesterday, Henry?"

"I was," Henry said. "The bad man was dead."

"What bad man?" Arnold asked, working hard to keep his voice steady.

"The man who hits Sheila," Henry replied, starting to swing his arms around nervously.

"Did you have a slingshot with you?"

"It didn't hurt him. Dead people don't feel things."

"What did you put in the slingshot?" Arnold asked.

"Cheese."

"Like in the play? Have you seen the play?"

"Yes. Sheila is a good actor. She is my sister," Henry said proudly.

"I know, Henry. How did you know that Clayton would be in the woods?"

"He told Sheila."

"What did he tell her?"

"He told her that he was meeting someone in the meadow."

"You know where that is? You can go there by yourself?"

"Yes, all by myself," Henry said. "Robin Hood knows the woods."

At that point, Sheila came out to the backyard. "Hey! Get away from my brother! It's not fair interviewing him. You know better than that. He doesn't understand."

"I think he does understand," Arnold said. "Henry says that Clayton was a bad man. Why would he say that?"

"Maybe he was," Sheila said. "But you have no business interviewing Henry without permission. He needs an adult advisor with him."

"Henry's not in trouble, Sheila. What happened to the work boots that he had on yesterday?"

"I burned them," she said defiantly. "Anything wrong with that?"

"Yes, there is. Those were evidence, Sheila, which I think you know. Thankfully, Henry has been very helpful. He has just solved a major question in this case. No thanks to you."

With that, Arnold left the yard, feeling confident that he at least had the large footprint and hard-cheese mystery solved.

Is it possible that Natasha and Dan's story of a large stranger was contrived to protect Henry?

CHAPTER 24

COUNCIL CHAMBERS MEETING

Ken Russell loved the way the massive, black-leather mayoral chair enveloped his expanding body. The chair gave him a feeling of belonging that was hard to come by. The exceptionally reinforced chair had once belonged to Judge Jerry Clipperton, a man so large that on his death McCullum Funeral Home had needed to build a custom-made casket. Ken was a lightweight compared to Clipperton. He looked positively slight in the chair. Still, to be fair to Ken, he was still a relatively young man, only in his third mayoral term, and in the early stages of a promising weight-gain trajectory.

Ken sat back, puffing on a Cuban cigar, blowing smoke circles into the stale air of the poorly ventilated council chamber. Framed photographs of past mayors lined the west wall. The south wall had a full-length window. Council members could look out on Boyd Avenue, to the southeast, and had an unobstructed view of both the Saskatchewan River and Northford River Park. It was seven o'clock on Sunday evening, with the next sunrise not slated until Monday morning, but given a clear sky, the morning sun would fully illuminate the mayor's chair, while council members would sit in the dark. It was a phenomenon that was not lost on Ken.

The meeting started with Ken clearing his throat and introducing the agenda to a largely empty council chamber. Only Arnold Powell was present, sitting comfortably in the council chair that was reserved for Clayton Dalrymple. "Firstly," Ken stated firmly, "I want to acknowledge rumours that I was somehow involved in Clayton's death. Even though we all know that Clayton was not a supporter of mine, he was a valued council member and a member of the Northford community, and we are grieving his loss. Just to get ahead of the Northford rumour mill, I want to be totally transparent about my activities yesterday, Saturday, the day of Clayton's death. I was golfing in the morning and was at the ball-field the rest of the day, umpiring our championship-game defeat at the hands of an inferior Lloydminster team. Quite upsetting. Lost a hundred dollars. Not only that but there are also rumours that Hank Goertzen, one of our grader operators, may have conspired to fix the game. We are investigating."

He shook his head briskly to bring himself back on track. "Alright. Just wanted to put those rumours out on the table, where hopefully they will die a sudden death. Next, I want to thank Sergeant Arnold Powell for his diligent police work. He has determined that the large footprints at the scene belong to Sheila's handicapped brother, Henry. Henry is also responsible for shooting Clayton with hard cheese. Clayton was dead when Henry did this, and given his situation, being in the care of a group home and all, Arnold advises me that no legal action will be taken against Henry. It also allows us to say with some confidence that there are no KGB agents presently in Northford. Arnold assures me that Dan and Natasha made up the story of a large stranger to protect Henry. This is quite a relief to me, as I am doing a national-news interview tomorrow and was desperately hoping to assure listeners that Northford is a safe city in which to do business."

"Do you have evidence that KGB agents discourage business, Ken?" Arnold asked with a slight smile.

"I do not. I have no experience whatsoever with the KGB and would like to keep it that way. But I can read. Business is not exactly booming in the Soviet Union, whereas we're on the cusp of big things in Northford. We certainly don't want to emulate Soviet failings, or for that matter, the failings of Lloydminster. That is all I have to say on that subject. I will now pass the floor to Arnold, who will proceed with the briefing."

"Thanks for addressing the matter of the hard cheese, Ken," Arnold said quietly. "Sheila was quite upset with me for interviewing Henry, but she has settled down. Seems to have accepted that it's for the best. Our favourite *Sentinel* reporter, Emily Little, assures me that Henry will be kept out of the newspaper. That will be hard for her, as we know how she loves to dig up scandal, but in this case, I have convinced her that there will still be a broader story for her. As for other matters, Dr. Morley will be with us soon, providing a report of the more detailed autopsy I requested."

"Excellent," Ken responded. "Dr. Morley probably overlooked something. He's somewhat prone to doing that. Still, regardless of what he comes up with, I would suggest that we have a strategy for dealing with the fact of Inspector Dick Sanders' arrival from Saskatoon tomorrow. We need to be on the same page, so that we can ensure local control of the message."

"What message, Ken?" Arnold asked quizzically.

"That we have the matter in hand," he said confidently.

"Do we?"

"We do not," Ken replied. "That is precisely why we need to be on message. Optics are everything. We can't let Sanders dictate how we handle a local-death investigation. I realize that Clayton's past puts the case into sensitive territory; however, we need to set boundaries. That is my view, from a political-optics standpoint. Are you okay with that, Arnold?"

"I suppose so, although frankly, I'm not sure what you mean by setting boundaries. I'm just trying to find out the truth of what happened, and if Inspector Sanders can be helpful in that regard, I'm all for it. I don't believe there's any need to be territorial."

"We just don't want to be embarrassed by the national news," Ken said. "News services are already calling me and asking me to comment on the death of a man who was, as we all know, a former KGB agent, a defector, and a man who was about to be indicted for local and international criminal activity. It doesn't reflect well on Northford if we don't have the matter well in hand. My position is that we need to be very clear on that point: We have the matter in hand."

"I suppose there's no harm in saying that," Arnold said, smiling and closing his notebook. "We don't owe the media transparency. As far as I can determine, we definitely do not have the matter in hand, but for the moment, I have no problem pretending that we do."

"Sorry I'm late," Dr. Morley said, rushing into the chambers and plunking himself down in the soft leather chair beside Arnold. His shirt was wet with perspiration. Massive sweat stains extended from his armpits to his chest and around to the back of his white shirt. "Clayton had enough hemlock root in his system to kill him a few times over!" Dr. Morley said as he struggled to catch his breath. "He died from poisoning, not a gunshot."

"But you said the breakfast drink was clean!" Ken said, sitting suddenly upright in his mayoral chair. It wasn't easy. The chair seemed to inspire leaning back.

"On first testing, it was," Dr. Morley said, sitting down beside Arnold. "But we only had a small trace of the dried liquid. Still, given that his body was riddled with poison, we will obviously retest the breakfast drink."

Dr. Morley looked around the room, gathered some of his documents together from his well-used, brown briefcase, and arranged them in front of himself on the council desk, just as the breeze from an oscillating fan turned in his direction, scattering his papers off the desk and onto the council chamber floor.

Dr. Morley got up with a grunt, slowly gathered up them up, and returned to his seat. Clearing his throat, he then explained that some of the Medovik cake had also been tested. "Crumbs were found on the driver's seat of Clayton's car. Toxicology reports indicate that the crumbs were soaked with hemlock poison. At first, we thought that Clayton must have ingested poisoned cake, but that wasn't the case. There was no evidence of any cake in Clayton's stomach contents. All Clayton had for breakfast on Saturday morning was a mug of juice. Therefore, it's reasonable to conclude that Clayton died from drinking poisoned breakfast drink. The gunshot was just extra, and frankly, from a death standpoint, somewhat irrelevant. As for the toxic cake crumbs, I have no idea. That's a police matter. But as far as I can tell, the cake crumbs have nothing to do with his death."

"So, the initial testing of the breakfast-drink residue was wrong?" Arnold asked.

"I don't know that as of yet," Dr. Morley said, "but it would seem likely. Clayton's stomach contained ample poison to kill. Given that all he had that morning was his breakfast drink, that must have been where the poison came from."

"But why would there be poisoned cake crumbs in the car?" Ken asked. "What relevance do they have if he didn't eat cake?"

"No relevance," Dr. Morley said. "Arnold thinks the crumbs were planted to distract. My guess is that he's right."

"It's a puzzle," Arnold mused, standing up and ambling around the exterior of the circular council chamber. "We examined the cake that Ken delivered to Clayton on Friday morning. One piece had been removed, but the rest of the cake was in the Dalrymple refrigerator and a sample of it tested clean. We also found the single piece of Medovik cake in Clayton's garbage bin, missing just a few morsels. It was also clean of toxin. I am guessing those morsels were dipped in poison and dropped on Clayton's driver's seat."

"But why? By whom?" Ken asked.

"We don't know," Arnold said. "My theory, at this point, is that the crumbs were dipped in poison to make it look like Clayton had ingested the poison in the car while he was driving to the woods."

"But he didn't eat cake," Ken said, looking confused.

"No, he didn't. But someone wanted us to think that he did."

"Maybe the same person who placed non-toxic cake in the garbage?" Ken suggested.

Arnold shrugged. "Natasha acknowledges that she cut a piece for Clayton and left it on the counter, along with a mug of breakfast juice. She claims that both were still on the counter when she left for her run. When Sheila arrived at Clayton's, they had sex in the bedroom, and then Clayton retreated to the workshop, asking Sheila to bring him the cake and the breakfast drink. She did. Sheila says that the cake was still in the workshop, uneaten, along with the breakfast drink that had not been touched, when she left. Sheila could be lying. She could have placed poison in Clayton's mug. She knows about hemlock poison and eagerly told me as much. She is also quite strident in her accusations that Natasha placed poison in Clayton's drink. Either women could have theoretically poisoned his drink, but Natasha wasn't around the house to place crumbs in his car, and why would Sheila kill the man she was willingly having sex with?" He shrugged again." Still, perhaps we are making progress. Not sure, though."

"But the fact remains that Clayton was poisoned," Dr. Morley said.

Arnold nodded. "Someone put poison in his drink, we assume. But why would they tamper with evidence like they apparently did? Would they not assume that Clayton would drink the poison in the workshop, where he typically drank his disgusting morning health drink? There was no need to place poison crumbs on the car seat, since they wouldn't be thinking Clayton would be capable of driving anywhere. Still, someone wanted us to think that Clayton was eating cake in the car while parked on the forest road. I think it's like the fake sumo-wrestler stranger, though. Just a bogus detail meant to baffle and confuse. Still, as painful as it is to admit it, Sheila was right about Clayton being poisoned. Does hemlock smell like fennel, by chance?"

"It does," Dr. Morley said, nodding.

"Anything else on the autopsy?"

"Clayton did have a cardiac event, but either the poison or the bullet to the head could have caused that that. There was also some vomit on his pea coat, which we didn't notice at the scene as it had been folded neatly and put aside. Cardiac events and vomit can both happen as a result of trauma. I would certainly consider hemlock poisoning and a gunshot blast to the temple as traumatic. Overall, it would be fair to say that Clayton's body experienced considerable trauma resulting in death on Saturday morning. My best guess is that he died around eight-thirty. But ... I must be wrong, because according to Madeline, he was still alive as late as 9:10, sitting in his car on the forest road."

"Or was he?"

"Madeline says he was," Ken said.

"True," Arnold said. "She places him there at that time, but she didn't walk right past the car. She took a detour around the car, into the woods. She didn't want to be seen; it appears. Still, she wasn't the only person to identify Clayton as driving the Mustang after nine a.m. A number of reliable sources saw him. It makes a person wonder."

"About what?" Ken asked.

"About what we see," Arnold said, stopping his tour around the chamber and making a quick note in his pad.

"If you can't trust witnesses, pretty hard to make a case, Arnold," Ken said. "Maybe review with us where all your possible suspects were on Saturday."

"Dan McCroskey was with his boys till just before nine," Arnold said, finally sitting down again beside a heavily perspiring Dr. Morley. "Dan was out birding and then at soccer practice with his boys. The whole soccer team saw him drop them off. He was seen driving his Falcon to the office a little after nine. He was smoking with Natasha at a little after nine-thirty."

"What about Natasha?" Ken asked.

"Natasha left her house at seven, ran her route, and stopped at the *Sentinel* to meet with Emily somewhere between eight and eight-thirty. Emily has confirmed that appointment and time frame. Natasha also went to Lieberman's Pharmacy, confirmed by Bernie Lieberman, and then ran home. Lots of witnesses saw her. She got home around nine, dressed for work, and drove to the office in her BMW for about nine-twenty."

Double-checking his facts from his notebook, he went on. "Sheila arrived at Clayton's at seven and left at eight. Then she went home, got ready for work, and walked to the hospital at eight-thirty, arriving shortly after.

"Doc left Northford around seven in the morning, was at Lake McCaskill picking berries from eight to nine, got stuck on his way back, and waited at the Schoendienst farm until Muscle John came to tow him out at around ten-thirty.

"Muscle John was in bed with Rachel, his new girlfriend, until nine or so, and then he left to tow Doc out of the ditch.

"Janet was sleeping in, hungover from a night on the town. She walked to the school library, was seen entering it at eight, and has witnesses confirming that she stayed in the library till noon.

"William and Adele were at the ball-field entrance in full view of the crowd from nine through the rest of the day. Prior to nine, they claim to have been home praying."

"What about the witnesses seeing Clayton?" Ken asked. "Are you confident in those reports?"

"Increasingly less so," Arnold said. "Emily, William, and Adele all saw Clayton driving to the forest road around nine. Then at about 9:10, Madeline saw Clayton in his Mustang on the forest road. Henry discovered a dead Clayton at nine-thirty and shot him with his slingshot, breaking his watch. In a sense, the witnesses' story fits."

"Except that you're skeptical," Ken said. "How reliable is Madeline?"

"Not particularly, since she left me for Gerald Schultz," Arnold joked. "But seriously, I have no issue with the quality of our witnesses. Emily is absolutely reliable, and frankly, so is Madeline. William and Adele are crazy, but they can see, and they have no reason to lie about seeing Clayton drive by the fairgrounds."

Ken considered this. "They all know Clayton well, or at least know what he looks like. Hard to imagine any of them could be wrong about seeing him. Anyway, we know that Clayton was dead in the woods at nine-thirty, so they must be correct in what they saw."

Noticing the lingering scepticism on Arnold's face, Ken leaned back a bit in his chair, folding his hands on his lap, and asked, "Do you have additional thoughts on the matter or are you just thinking?"

"Just thinking, really," Arnold mused. "I was at the Dickey Dee on Saturday evening, when Dan pulled in with his Falcon. Got me thinking how easy it would be to mistakenly identify a car's driver. We see a car, or perhaps a distinctive hat, and you assume it is the person who belongs to the car. Did they just assume it was Clayton upon seeing the car, or maybe, that silly flat hat of his? Could someone else have actually been driving the Mustang?"

"But if Clayton wasn't driving," Ken said, picking up his pen and fiddling with it as he worked to understand, "how did he get to the woods?"

"Believe me, that's a line of inquiry I'm contemplating. But enough of that for now. Inspector Sanders is arriving tomorrow," Arnold said, "and he will likely bring some political directives with him."

"What do you mean by that?" Ken asked, turning his chair a bit to look out at the darkening sky and flipping his pen in the air. Ken had a momentary concern that Inspector Sanders might be a public-relations nightmare. He had interviews to do soon, and questions would be asked. The last thing he wanted was to be hamstrung by political directives. He knew well enough how annoying that could be.

"Inspector Sanders has already indicated to me that he has a directive from the Ottawa RCMP that could influence how we proceed with the investigation," Arnold said, swiveling back and forth in his chair absentmindedly. "As you know, Ken, the Canada Cup is being negotiated. External Affairs does not want anything to disturb Soviet relations at such a sensitive time. Everybody wants the hockey series to proceed."

"Enough so that a police investigation can't proceed without political interference?" Ken asked.

"Sometimes there are political considerations," Arnold said casually. "I'm not saying that I like it any more than I like heartburn. I'm just saying that I feel the breeze of political considerations. Inspector Sanders is a good man, but he has his quirks. Still, this case has quirks too, so maybe he's the right man to assist. We shall soon see."

CHAPTER 25

KEN AND ANNIE

Ken Russell returned home from the debriefing session in a reflective mood. He had been to Ottawa any number of times for political meetings, but he had never been connected to a case with an element of international intrigue. He was feeling mildly self-important when he entered the bedroom. He'd heard things that evening that were highly confidential. It was not often that he had information that Annie didn't have. But as he saw her undressing for the night, he reflected that he should approach the situation humbly. If he played the moment correctly, he might get lucky. Even after over twenty years of marriage, he continued to view sex as an act of occasional good fortune. Ken approached the situation gently, looking Annie in the eye and smiling slightly, placing his left hand gently on her shoulder. He anticipated that Annie would draw herself into him and invite him to a period of love making, frenetic or otherwise, but she didn't.

In human relations, it is difficult at times to know precisely what the problem is, even while being certain that there is one. Had Ken told Annie that she was beautiful, and that he loved her more than ever, the lovemaking might have happened. But he didn't. All Ken did was smile and touch her gently. From some folks—Cary Grant for example—this might have been a clear enough signal, but from Ken, it wasn't. Ken had a fine smile, excellent for formal political apologies, but he didn't have a smile that invited lovemaking. It was somewhat smarmy, inviting sympathy perhaps but not passion.

"It must have been a very difficult meeting," Annie said, "and you have so much on your plate. Perhaps we should simply go to sleep?"

Sympathy can at times be much appreciated, but it was not the response that Ken had been hoping for. He did not want to go to sleep, and frankly, it had not been a difficult meeting. It had been quite stimulating. But Ken didn't say this. Instead, even though he regretted it immediately, he began to complain in a distinctly recriminating tone.

"Who can sleep with all that flirting you do with Arnold?" Ken asked. "It is not a good look."

"Why is it not a good look?" Annie asked. "You know that Arnold and I are just friends. I confess that flirting is my style. Always has been. You know that. I flirt with you too. You don't seem to mind that. I love flashing a sexy smile. Especially at you, of course. It helps our performances when we sing, connecting us to the audience. You don't want me to dress and act conservatively, do you?"

"No, I don't. I love the way you dress," Ken added, momentarily dropping the negative tone.

"It's settled then," Annie said, laughing lightly and crawling into bed. "Let's not create a problem where none exists. You had a tough day, and you have a busy day tomorrow, what with the big-shot detective coming. Hopefully the new guy will respect Arnold's efforts. I think he's been doing a fine job. Anything new come up in the meeting this evening? Did the cake come up?"

"Sort of," Ken said quietly, sitting on the edge of the bed.

"How do you mean?"

"Arnold knows about me bringing Clayton the Medovik cake. There was no need to talk about that. But they found cake crumbs in Clayton's car. Poisoned with water hemlock."

"My goodness! That's terrible!"

"It is. Makes me wonder if Arnold suspects me of some involvement," he said with a concerned tone as he started rubbing his feet with cream from his nightstand. He had a rash that simply would not go away. His feet itched and the cream helped, just not enough.

"I'm sure that he doesn't. Your only involvement was bringing a cake to Clayton," Annie said, surprised at her husband's suggestion. "You didn't poison the cake. You have nothing to worry about." Annie looked at Ken reassuringly and then pulled the sheets up over her shoulders and shut off her lamp.

"It just doesn't look good," Ken whined, still rubbing his feet. "What with Clayton and I being enemies and all."

"Yes, you were enemies. Everyone knows that. That's why I made the cake. You just delivered it. You were trying to make peace. It was a kind, thoughtful gesture," Annie said with a tone that suggested she would prefer to be sleeping rather than still talking.

"Self-serving too," Ken reminded her.

"Of course, it was. Kindness often is," she mumbled. "Still better than not doing it." After a long moment, sensing the tension coming from the other side of the bed, which clearly wasn't going to lessen any time soon, she turned her light back on and sat up in bed, propping a few pillows up behind her and sighing. "Okay, so what else was discussed?"

"Arnold did a summary of the evidence at the council chambers. He has done his homework; I'll give him that. But starting tomorrow, Inspector Dick Sanders will be in charge. Arnold will be making the coffee. He's probably more comfortable with that anyway. I just hope that we can avoid any bad publicity for Northford."

"Constable Stafford says that Arnold makes terrible coffee."

"He does," Ken said, screwing the lid back on his jar of foot cream and lying back on the bed to dry his feet. "But Inspector Sanders may not have anything else for him to do."

"Arnold says the RCMP handles these matters as a team," Annie said then. "I'm sure that they'll work together."

"He would say that, wouldn't he?" Ken said gently. "He has his pride, after all."

"Like you. Right, Ken? What are the implications for you? For Northford's reputation?"

"Could actually be good for Northford, strangely enough. Advertising is like that. Initially, the Belhaven fiasco looked bad for us but ended up putting us on the map. Some tourism was even generated by the court case. It wasn't good for William and Adele, of course, but they brought it on themselves. In this case, there's potential for some international intrigue.

We could be in the news a fair bit. Hate to think of any advantages to a dead body in the woods, but there could be some."

"Even apart from getting rid of your nasty mayoral opponent?"

"You shouldn't even say that, Annie," Ken said. "Yes, Clayton caused me grief. He was a political enemy. But I did not wish him harm. At least, not this kind of harm."

"You think it *is* murder?"

"Well, his body was poisoned, and he was shot. Maybe he shot himself, but the combination is a weird way to commit suicide."

"So, Clayton *was* poisoned? They've confirmed this?"

"He was. But not from the cake. The cake crumbs in the car had hemlock, but Arnold thinks that they were planted. Dr. Morley said that the breakfast drink at the scene was clean, but that he's going to retest it because his body was loaded with poison. Dr. Morley figures he must have missed it in the drink left at the meadow."

"Is there possibly KGB involvement?"

"Arnold thinks the idea of a stranger is bogus, and that's what really started that line of thought. The large footprints and slingshot cheese belonged to Henry, Sheila's brother, as you know. As a result, the KGB idea is pretty much dead." Ken got up then, walked to the window, and looked out at the stars. He liked to imagine life on distant planets, orbiting distant stars, even though he thought the notion quite unlikely.

"But didn't Natasha and Dan see a large stranger?" Annie asked.

"They did. But now that we know the large footprints belong to Henry, Arnold thinks the whole large-stranger business was just smoke and mirrors."

"But both Natasha and Dan have alibis. Why would they lie about seeing a stranger?"

"To protect Henry is the assumption. Though maybe they have some-thing else to hide." He shrugged and made his way back to bed.

"Who would have thought we could have this kind of crime in Northford?" Annie said wistfully. "My guess is that Clayton just killed himself. Took poison and then shot himself for good measure. But what do I know? By the way, Ken," she whispered, sliding back down under the sheets, "Gerald Schultz called me today. He wants us to perform three songs at the mega service on Monday. Gospel tunes. I told him we can do that. Let's open with 'Amazing Grace.' Fitting with Clayton's death."

"Sounds good to me," Ken whispered. "Carter Family style."

They kissed lightly and then both turned out their lamps at the same time.

Ken turned on his left side, cradling his right arm on a small pillow. It helped to ease the discomfort of a chronic rotator-cuff injury. For a short while, his mind wandered around in the debris of his childhood memories: his alcoholic father's anger, his mother's self-pitying behaviour, and his sister's chronic illness. He was thankful Annie had agreed to marry him. He felt fortunate. Then his mind drifted off to self criticism for seeing the bright side of Clayton's death.

Annie Russell, meanwhile, lay on her back, listening to the ascending notes of the prairie warbler outside her bedroom window. As she listened, she reviewed a list of supplies she needed to order from the wholesaler in Saskatoon and reflected on what other two songs she and Ken could perform the next day at the mega service.

CHAPTER 26

BREAKFAST AT KEN AND ANNIE'S

The sun did not flood Annie and Ken Russell's breakfast alcove during the night, of course, but Annie and Ken did not sit in the breakfast alcove at night. They did so in the morning though, and on a sunny day, especially in the fall when the angle of the sun allowed for full intrusion into the kitchen, the glare was a problem. They had installed blinds on the floor-to-ceiling windows on the east wall, which helped with the morning solar assault, but not enough to eliminate the need for both of them to wear sunglasses at breakfast. Their boys, Steve and Michael, generally chose to have breakfast in the basement instead. Not that they didn't have sunglasses. They did. But eating with the parents could not compete with their GI Joe action figures. So, Ken and Annie were on their own on Monday morning, sipping coffee wearing sunglasses, and eating a breakfast of eggs (easy over) on rye toast.

The Russell family lived on the west end of Boyd Avenue, at a bend in the Saskatchewan River. Their house sat on a hill, so that from the breakfast alcove, they had a pedestal view in three directions. Some people said that they had the finest home in Northford. Perhaps they did, but it never stopped them from looking at other properties.

Ken had a ministerial meeting to attend after breakfast. The planned open-air joint ministerial service had been rescheduled for Monday evening, postponed from Sunday due to Clayton's death. But this morning, the pastors needed assurance that the town was ready for traffic control, and of course, security. It promised to be a massive event, and with Clayton's death still not solved, there were concerns that a killer was on the loose.

"What kind of security has the town set up?" Annie asked. "Volunteers, I imagine."

"Arnold and the constables will be out, but yes, it will mostly be volunteers," Ken griped, sipping his black coffee. "The whole thing is ridiculous. If Clayton was killed, it was for some specific grievance with him, not with the random public. But the ministers want a security plan, and so they'll get one. Oh, I had a call from the CBC in Saskatoon. They want an interview. I'm likely to be on the evening news tonight, Annie. No idea what I'll say though."

"Remember to be concise, Ken. Just answer the question, or if you need to, use diversion tactics, but don't ramble. Did they give you the questions?"

"They want to know about security for the big service too, given Clayton's death. It's a big news story locally."

"Are you doing it with Arnold?"

"They'll talk to Arnold as well. Inspector Sanders too. He arrives later today. None of us can say much, and we won't. It would be a lot easier if they just cancelled the damn service," Ken grunted. "Suggested that to Pastor Schultz. He refused. Said that he was not going to let the Russians shut down worship."

"Why does he blame the Russians?" Annie asked. "It was a Russian who died."

"Schultz blames the Russians for many things. He said that before the Russians came, as in Clayton and Natasha, Northford didn't have dead bodies in the woods." Ken took a bite of his breakfast. "Perfectly done egg, Annie. Don't know how you do it."

"Thanks. Has Schultz forgotten that Doc and Sophia Rubenstein moved here before Clayton and Natasha, and put us on the map with the arts? And that before *their* arrival, James Turner's body was found in the woods by the river? Turner was not a Russian. Schultz needs to rethink his complaints."

"True enough, but Schultz conveniently forgets any information that doesn't fit his storyline."

"I guess we all do some of that."

"For sure. Don't want to give Schultz credit for his thinking on the matter, but I do agree that having a Soviet defector in town was always a potential problem for us. The police kept his background a secret, or tried to, but now we find that the man was not only ex-KGB but also involved in criminal activity back in Russia, and with a possibility at least of him continuing that here. What did Northford do to deserve that? The whole thing smells to high heaven." Ken gulped down the rest of his breakfast, and then, grumbling about the sun, closed his eyes to calm himself.

"Does heaven smell?" Annie joked.

"If Gerald Schultz is headed there, it does," Ken said, grumpily. "The man is so difficult to deal with, although ... still not as bad as Clayton."

"Now you do sound like a suspect."

"Maybe I am." He chuckled humourlessly. "Arnold has been friendly enough, even confiding in me, but he could be trying to catch me off guard. Police do that. Everyone knows that I didn't like Clayton."

"I know, Ken. You have a motive, but so do lots of folks. You have an alibi for Saturday morning. Although ... it sounds like everyone with a motive has an alibi. Inspector Sanders sure has his work cut out for him."

"So do I. I have to dress for the media," Ken said, adjusting his red tie, upon which a printed diamonds floated. *It's a good look,* Ken thought to himself. With his blue suit jacket, he liked the colour combination. He thought it looked quite mayoral.

"Wear your solid blue tie, Ken. It gives a nice look of stability. The floating diamonds make you look unsettled," Annie said. "Very uncertain."

Ken sighed deeply but relented. He charged up the stairs to their bedroom, giving the appearance of annoyance, though not too much, and promptly changed his tie. He had come to understand that following Annie's guidance was in his best interest.

"Much better, Ken," she said gently when he returned. "The ministerial folks might not notice, but the public will. If you do go on television, you'll be thankful you changed."

"Fine," Ken responded. "Anyway, all I have to do is look better than Arnold. That's the nice thing about an overweight sergeant."

"Arnold is well fortified with Dickey Dee cheeseburgers." Annie laughed and then seemed to get a random thought. "By the way, thanks again for agreeing to give Leonard the Impala. It was good of you. Very generous."

He smiled at his wife. "It was quite generous, wasn't it? But you were right; it's time for a new restoration project. Still, I love that car. I sure hope that he takes good care of it."

They slowly finished their breakfast and sat sipping their coffees for a while, with Annie proposing planting some aspen trees in the back of the Dickey Dee and adding more picnic tables, and Ken agreeing. Finally, they cleaned up together, made sure the boys got off to school, and then left the house and parted ways.

Annie drove to the Dickey Dee to get the place ready for the ministerial pastors, who would undoubtedly descend on the place after their meeting. And Ken got into his Dodge pickup and headed for the Four-Square Gospel church meeting hall, reminding himself that the church's members accounted for a lot of potential votes. As Ken drove, he wondered what the town would think if they knew that he wasn't really a believer. He was fairly sure that he was indifferent to the idea of belief. He was pretty sure that the planet, and all life forms, were basically on their own. He didn't want that to be true, and he found the idea troubling, but still ... he felt that it was probably the case. For the sake of voter support, though, it was in his best interest to play the role of a man of faith. It was easy enough to do. He suspected that was what most of Northford did as well.

CHAPTER 27

INSPECTOR DICK SANDERS ARRIVES

Ken had expected the senior inspector from the General Investigation Unit of the RCMP to be tall, perhaps even handsome, with a raspy, baritone voice. But Inspector Dick Sanders had none of these characteristics. He was short, balding, somewhat paunchy around the middle, and had a wandering eye with a mind of its own. He also had an unnerving habit of sneezing frequently, followed by series of astoundingly raucous, full-body coughing fits.

Ken was disappointed. He had a high level of confidence in tall people. Being over six feet himself, and pleased about it, he held a weakly considered view that short people were to blame for their predicament and as a result were not to be trusted. In Ken's view, being short reflected an essential inadequacy that warranted his sympathy but not his confidence. Annie had instructed him that this view was incorrect, as many powerful politicians and businesspeople were short. Ken recognized that Annie was right. In his dealings over the years, he had met many highly trusted and successful personalities who had been short. Still, he chose to view his experience as anecdotal (which of course, it was) and Annie's opinions as simply her opinions (which of course, they were), all of which allowed him to continue his diminished confidence in short people.

After the ministerial meeting, Ken stopped at the Capri's cafe for an open-face, hot-beef sandwich. An hour later, he was back in his office, wishing that he had backed off on the sandwich. He was still actively regretting his culinary choice when Inspector Sanders walked into his office. Indigestion was never enjoyable, but when it came with gas, it significantly detracted from his mayoral dignity. As Ken stood to shake Sander's hand, he sadly could not hold back a gas-passing event. The embarrassment of the moment was not lost on Ken, even though Sanders was short and somewhat dishevelled. Ken noted that his initial feeling of superiority over Sanders faded quickly. Sanders may well have had his physical limitations—and in fact, he did—but at least he wasn't passing gas.

"General Investigation Unit, Inspector Sanders," the inspector announced in a high-pitched tentative voice, as though his introduction were a question.

Sanders wore a well-used, beige overcoat that fell all the way to his scuffed black shoes. Ken felt strongly that the coat was too long. The job of an overcoat, according to Ken, was to warm the upper half of the body but leave the legs free to directly experience the world. Sanders did not appear to share that fashion opinion.

Sanders' overcoat itself—at least at first glance—was decidedly unimpressive, tattered at the cuffs and collar, and covered with a generous array of stains, some of which had been neutralized by time while others were disturbingly fresh. Ken wondered whether Sanders had any recollection of how these sundry stains had come about.

"Welcome to Northford, Inspector. I'm Ken Russell, the mayor. Sergeant Arnold Powell will be with us shortly to brief you. Coffee?" he asked, still standing beside his desk. "I hope you're comfortable in your rooms at the Capri?"

"They are intrinsically inadequate," Sanders said firmly. "My bed provided a restless night, and I expect, will continue to do so. However, I do not plan on being uncomfortable at the Capri for long. This case will be wrapped up quickly. As for coffee, I don't drink the stuff." Apologetically, he added, "Bothers my prostate, and a bothered prostate is something you want to avoid."

With a quick side-step, Sanders moved past Ken, around the desk, and settled his slight body into the inner recesses of the mayor's leather chair. "Nice chair, Ken!" Sanders exclaimed. "Superbly comfortable. Think I would like to be a mayor, sitting in a chair like this. We only have hard plastic chairs at the Saskatoon detachment. Still, I'm always thankful to sit down, no matter what the chair is. I tire quickly these days. No more running down back alleys, chasing criminals for me. I like to sit."

Ken was taken aback. He had not expected such an aggressive move by this diminutive, high-pitched inspector. Ken had little choice but to sit on one of his guest chairs, a cloth fabric affair that needed a thorough cleaning. Ken looked up as Arnold and Constable Billy Stafford walked in, but he didn't stand up. Neither did Inspector Sanders. Arnold and Billy stood for a moment and then pulled fading-yellow, hard-plastic chairs from the corner of the office and sat down, just as Doc Alexei Rubenstein walked in and handed Arnold a file. "Clayton's medical history," he mumbled.

"I do not believe that we'll need that file, Arnold," Sanders said. "My understanding is that Clayton Dalrymple is dead, and as such, his medical status has been determined." Sanders laughed at his own comment, finding it more comical than did anyone else in the room. "I may look like the person least likely to solve a crime, but as Arnold can tell you, I am known for a certain expertise in file closure. That is our goal."

"Is closing the file the same as solving the crime?" Ken asked.

"Not necessarily," Sanders replied. "But that is not the point. We have an implied directive from above, not from God precisely but from Ottawa. In this business, that's the same thing. We should investigate, check all the boxes, but not be overly zealous about it." Sanders was looking mostly at Arnold. "It will be good to work with you again, Arnold. I have always appreciated your diligence. In this case, however, your diligence is somewhat wasted. I am aware that you have already uncovered certain evidence and developed some theories. That is fine, as far as it goes. But at the same time, it's also good to remember that the Canada Cup series is just around the corner. Hockey brings us all together; doesn't it? Beautiful thing. Hate the game myself. Hockey may well be a magnet for coaching perverts and deviant players, but it is our game, as Canadians, and I am only echoing the public mood when I say that the Canada Cup series needs to happen. Hockey is tape that holds us together, or so they say, and who am I to disagree? Therefore, while I understand that making inquiries, uncovering evidence, and generating theories is our job, it is also our job to arrive at a satisfactory outcome. When you get right down to it, we all want the same thing, right?"

"And ... what is it that we want?" Ken asked, somewhat confused.

"We want the Canada Cup to carry on without distraction or interruption," Sanders said in an even tone.

"What are you getting at?" Arnold asked.

"As you know, Arnold, Clayton was a corrupt KGB agent. He wasn't alone. He was involved with a network of corrupt agents, all working out of Soviet Embassies around the world. They sold confiscated art on the black market. The Soviets feel that if the story came out, it would reflect poorly on the image of the KGB. They seem to prefer the image of a firm but fair organization, opposed to any form of corruption both in principle and practice. Their position is that the Canada Cup can only proceed if this death is ruled a standard suicide. A case of a Soviet defector who understandably missed his home country and regretted moving over to the capitalist chaos of the West. External Affairs has agreed."

"So, what are we supposed to do?" Arnold asked.

"We have to proceed with our file work, making inquiries and turning over rocks, but if necessary, replacing some of them. At the end of the day, the outcome of our inquiries needs to be that Ivan Kalik, or Clayton Dalrymple, however you wish to refer to him, committed suicide in the Northford aster meadow on Saturday morning. Tragic, but then again, not overly so. Any questions?"

"But the evidence is clear that he was poisoned as well as shot," Arnold said. "Did he give himself poison and then shoot himself?"

"Perhaps he did. Who are we to judge a distressed former KGB agent's choice? It may not be your preferred story, Arnold, or one that fits with the evidence to date; however, it remains the story that we need to end up with. The KGB are quite sensitive about poison. They feel that they have been badly tarnished with a reputation for poisoning."

Sanders leaned forward a bit in Ken's chair, which looked like it might swallow him whole. "They don't mind one of their agents poisoning themselves or shooting themselves, but they are troubled by any suggestion of murder by poison, or for that matter, a gunshot ... unless it was self-inflicted. We will have to see how we can solve the problems that we have encountered in this case. I understand that having discovered certain evidence; we have to deal it. The question of poison *has* come up. It's a shame, really. Finding poison in Clayton's stomach could easily have been missed with a less exhaustive examination. I thought that was one of Dr. Morley's specialties. Still, the examination was done, and he discovered that Clayton's body took on poison. That is, simply, what it is. I believe, however, that with some broad and flexible thinking, we can overcome it."

"What kind of broad and flexible thinking do you have in mind?" Arnold asked.

Sanders leaned back once more, ignoring Arnold's question. "In this chair, I would run for re-election," Sanders said confidently. "I cannot remember the last time I felt this relaxed or comfortable." He smiled then, revealing a significant gap in his front teeth. Noting that Ken was staring at the gap from his missing tooth, he shrugged. "A dentistry matter that remains unresolved."

Sander's left eye wandered aimlessly around the room, while his right focused on the ceiling before moving rather aggressively back to Arnold. "The initial autopsy did not indicate poison. Neither did the mug at the scene. We had a Soviet defector who was about to be deported, with a bullet in his head. Without poison in Clayton's system, suicide was the obvious explanation. We could have closed the file and gone home happy. But we did not do that."

"The problem of the cheese and the large footprints had to be considered," Arnold said.

"Of course," Sanders replied. "And it was. Good work. You discovered that both the cheese and the footprints were a random, happenstance event. You could have returned to the suicide conclusion without any fuss. But instead, you ordered a second autopsy. I am not sure what you were thinking, Arnold."

"I requested a second autopsy because I was not satisfied with the first," Arnold said simply.

"Understandable, Arnold. I wouldn't have been satisfied either. Still, it's a shame that the broader view was not considered."

"What broader view?" Arnold asked. "The Canada Cup hockey series?"

"Precisely!" Sanders cried suddenly, slamming his fist on the mayor's desk. "But this is not only about hockey! Wheat needs to be sold! It doesn't sell itself! The Soviet farming practices, being what they are, allows them to be a major customer for our wheat. But now, the Soviets are saying that if the Clayton story is not silenced, they will buy wheat from Brazil! How will the prairie farmers feel about that? Just a question, of course, but have you any idea what happens to people who disrupt the sale of prairie wheat? They lose the next election. That's what happens. That's all I am saying."

"But why does his death have to be a suicide?" Ken asked.

The room was a quiet for a time, seemingly in consideration, and then Sander's high-pitched voice started up again. "Absolutely fair question, Ken, although I thought I'd already explained that. Perhaps I was being obscure. I can be sometimes. Let me speak in a simpler vein. It is not just the Soviets who are weighing in on this matter. Clayton's various criminal involvements were becoming an embarrassment to both Soviet *and* Canadian authorities. The Soviets had come to understand that corruption existed within the KGB and that Clayton was part of it. They were taking steps, together with our agency, to resolve the problem quietly, without public notice. External affairs were on board with this too, embarrassed that they had offered protection to a corrupt Soviet agent. Both countries agreed that a finding of suicide would be the best approach. A murder would have to go to court, the media would go into a frenzy, and the corruption story would spread like grasshoppers in a hot prairie summer. I have looked over your report, Arnold. Good investigative work. I have nothing but respect for you, as you know, but we need a suicide conclusion, and this report takes us in another direction."

"But we were already investigating Clayton before he died," Arnold insisted. "We were about to charge him. The story would have come out anyway."

"True, but only in part," Sanders reported. "The story would not actually have come out. We threatened to charge him, yes, but we had no plans to do so. We had no intention of proceeding with a court case. We had already made a deal to hand Clayton over to the Soviets. The whole matter would have been quietly resolved. Clayton would be returned to his home country, where his life would run its course. But then Clayton died. Now we have to deal with your investigation and what it has revealed. The simplest way of doing that is to determine that he died by suicide. Suicide shuts down the truth seekers. That is why your report requires some adjustment."

"What kind of adjustment do you have in mind?" Arnold asked.

"The answer to that question will unfold over the next few days," Sanders said. "We may be stuck with the story that Clayton was poisoned. The evidence is irrefutable. But it is not irrefutable that he was murdered. Clayton, being a Russian experienced in the functional use of poison, could have taken it deliberately or even accidentally. Does it matter? He was into native herbal plants. It was a health thing for him. As so often happens in life, a person is bitten by his own obsession. Clayton was stressed and distracted. He had reason to be. He knew what was about to happen to him. There were hemlock plants in the area where his body was found. Maybe he added some to his drink not knowing what it was. Or maybe he knew and did it anyway. It doesn't really matter. He was going to shoot himself in any case. My very cursory thinking on the matter is that he put hemlock leaves in his drink, drank it, and then shot himself."

"But the drink was clean," Arnold said.

"That *is* a problem," Sanders conceded. "But a solvable one. I am confident that when toxicology retests the mug's residue, evidence of hemlock poison will be revealed. Dr. Morley makes mistakes. We all know that. But I am confident that he will be able to correct this one."

"You've talked to Dr. Morley?" Arnold asked.

"I have, but it was not necessary. He already understood the problem," Sanders said soberly. "Let's face it. We have four witnesses who saw Clayton driving to the forest road a little after nine. We have a witness who saw him on the road in his car shortly after. It seems to me that we need to accept that Clayton drove himself to the woods and committed suicide there. You were understandably thrown off track by the large footprints and the cheese. But you solved that problem, uncovering the bizarre but apparently true tale of Sheila's handicapped brother, who acted out a revenge idea that bizarrely involved shooting a dead man with hard cheese. But now, we can, and should, return to the suicide explanation."

"But there are other problems," Arnold said. "Like Natasha and Dan lying to us about seeing a large stranger."

"Good point, Arnold," Sanders said. "We need to convince Natasha and Dan to drop that story. They don't need it. Protecting Henry is not necessary. I suspect that, by now, they realize this. No one wants to easily admit they have lied to the police. But I am confident that you can convince them."

"I'll chat with Natasha and Dan," Arnold said. "I'm still not convinced that protecting Henry was their only reason for lying though."

"Could be, Arnold, and you're right to be suspicious. Something is certainly wrong with their stories. But we need to ask ourselves whether we care. We cannot care about everything, can we? Sometimes, we just have to let things go," Sanders mused. "Perhaps, on top of protecting Henry, they have some secrets they would like to keep to themselves. Secrets can often be like that. Most people, including in the lovely town of Northford, have an array of secrets they hold dear. Sometimes the secrets are interesting and relevant, but just as often, they are not. They're just secrets, like skeletons in the closet, best left to fend for themselves and be forgotten in death. Whatever the case, Natasha and Dan need to be allowed an opportunity to drop the story without undue embarrassment or legal complication."

"How do you mean?" Ken asked.

"We can forgive them the lie," Sanders said. "Let them know that we will not pursue legal action against them for their pathetic efforts at deceiving us."

"So, do you have an explanation for why a man would poison *and* shoot himself?" Arnold asked, skeptically.

"He wanted to ensure death but minimize his suffering," Sanders replied simply. "I gather death by poison is painful and slow. A gunshot speeds things up."

"But even if the breakfast drink *is* toxic, why did he take his mug to the woods? This would be well outside of his regimented routine," Arnold pointed out. "And if the juice *is* found to be poisoned, why were the cake crumbs poisoned as well? Who tampered with the cake crumbs? Who put the clean Medovik cake in the garbage?"

"Those are problems," Sanders conceded. "On the face of it, we can't have a man who is about to kill himself sitting idly in a car eating sweet honey cake. Dreadful choice on an empty stomach. Why take on such sweets at the end of life? Of course, on the other hand, why not? But I concede that the cake was tampered with. That is a problem we need to fix. Which is why we will soon find that the cake crumbs will disappear," Sanders said, sounding almost amused. "As for the cake in the garbage, I imagine that Clayton had a last-minute insight regarding the deficits of Russian honey cake. Pure sugar. He dumped the cake in the garbage himself. Wanted to die healthy. As for breaking his routine, I think it's obvious that Clayton was under immense stress. Routine breaking is not inevitable but certainly understandable."

"But if we are not interested in the truth, what's the point of even investigating?" Ken asked.

"Good question," Sanders said. "We are police officers. We investigate. That is what we do. Sometimes we turn over a stone and do not like what we find. Then decisions need to be made. Sometimes, the right decision is to put the stone back where you found it and move on."

"Okay, fine." Arnold sighed. "According to Dr. Morley, Clayton did have cardiac arrest, likely as a result of the poison. Dr. Morley says that the poison could have been taken and then been followed shortly by a gunshot."

"I like that kind of thinking," Sanders said. "We know he drove to the woods, as we have ample witnesses, and we know that his body took on hemlock poison. So, he had to poison himself in the woods. We will see what the updated toxicology report from the breakfast juice has to tell us. I remain confident that I will be checking out of the Capri shortly."

Sanders stood up and started to move back around the table when he sneezed three times, each one a little stronger than the previous, finishing off the performance with a series of resounding coughs. As he gathered his composure and walked out of Ken's office, he called back, "It's nothing. Just an asthmatic reaction. I'm fine."

Back in the office, the men watched as Sanders ignored the "No Exit, Stairs Under Construction" sign on the back door of the council building, opening the door and stepping out into the autumn air before they could even shout out a warning. The small man then disappeared from sight, having fallen six feet straight down onto a heap of concrete rubble that had previously been the back steps.

It struck Arnold that something was deeply wrong with Inspector Sanders. Leaving a public building requires minimal concentration. Generally, it is casually managed without injury. But not with Sanders, whom they could now hear moaning and coughing from the pile of rubble they all knew was beneath the doorway, leaving little doubt that he was moving even further away from wellness.

CHAPTER 28

MEETING AT THE NORTHFORD POLICE STATION

Tuesday morning was bitterly cold, windy, and rainy. The temperature had apparently checked a calendar and decided to accept the fact that winter was approaching. A brisk northwesterly breeze would blow rain sideways through the streets of Northford until noon. Then the sun would come out and the wind and rain would move west to trouble the fine folks of Saskatoon, though the cold would only intensify, emptying the streets of Northford except for a few wandering souls with yellow plastic raingear over winter parkas.

The break in the rain was still almost two hours off though when Sergeant Arnold Powell, Inspector Sanders, and Mayor Ken Russell met at the Northford RCMP detachment at ten that morning. The meeting had been scheduled for nine sharp, but punctuality was not part of Sanders' character. When he arrived, he looked in distress. "Goddam beds in the Capri are criminal," Sanders announced as he entered and plunked himself down in Arnold's chair without asking. "You can't possibly have any repeat business, Ken."

"Never have heard of anyone admitting to a return visit, now that you mention it," Arnold said, stroking his chin thoughtfully.

"People come back for the bar," Ken said, defensively. "Including you, Arnold."

Inspector Dick Sanders chaired the meeting as best he could. He had spent a few hours at the Northford Hospital the day before, being checked for injuries from his fall, but it was determined that nothing had been broken. They did a series of tests, however, and by the time Sanders was released to return to the Capri for the night, he had been in a bad mood. He had chosen to drink heavily to compensate for both his emotional and physical distress, and so he had not slept well. While he denied any problem, other than his Capri bed, it was evident that he wasn't well. His coughing was getting progressively worse.

"Filtered cigarettes would be something to consider, perhaps?" Arnold said.

"Just a tickle," Sanders replied, shaking his head in denial. "I've had a cough all my life. It's nothing."

"It is a most irritating nothing," Ken said. "Had a complaint from your floor last night. People wondering whether an ambulance was needed. You really should get yourself checked out."

"Let me be clear about this, Ken," Sanders responded, staring intently at him. "If you have customers who think that my coughing is worse than their bed, I *should* get myself checked out. I will promise you this: If I am still at the Capri on Thursday, I will shoot myself. I am under duress here. Maybe that is the answer to the Clayton question. Perhaps he spent a night at the Capri and determined that poison and a gunshot blast to the head would be welcome relief."

"Quit exaggerating, Sanders," Ken responded angrily.

"Fine, let's get real then," Sanders said slowly, pausing to cough again before continuing. "Clayton had a serious problem. He was about to be handed over to the Soviets. He understood this. His could have tried to escape. Frankly, we were expecting that he would try. We already had people at the airport in Saskatoon when, on Friday morning, we got an anonymous call saying that Clayton was going to escape the country under the name of Raymond Drummond. We checked with the airport, and sure enough, Raymond Drummond had a ticket for Saturday afternoon. Destination, Singapore. We have no extradition deal with Singapore, but we know Clayton has contacts there. He also has a nephew there. As we all know, he did not make the flight. Rather than checking in, he checked out. It is pretty obvious what happened. He knew he was done and took the only reasonable course of action. Killed himself. Just like I will if I have to sleep at the Capri one more night. I don't like it, and frankly, I don't like Northford. I can't emphasize that enough. Too much crime. And you don't even have goddam steps leaving your town office!"

"New back steps were installed today," Ken said.

"A lot of good that does my back," Sanders griped. "Falling on a pile of concrete and rebar puts a person in a foul mood. Don't recommend it. I could sue, you know."

"You could also have obeyed the sign that said those stairs were closed for construction," Ken said.

"Who reads those signs?" Sanders asked rhetorically. "Probably been there for years. The font was faded!" He gritted his teeth, seemingly choosing to stop himself from proceeding with his rant, and forcefully dragged himself back on topic. "In any case, on a more positive note, you will be pleased to know that the retest results on the breakfast drink came in, and just as I suspected, the residue is toxic. Dr. Morley makes mistakes. What can I say?"

"No one would argue with that," Arnold smiled. "Fits your narrative like a glove, Dick. How did you do it?"

"What do you mean, Arnold?" Sanders asked innocently. "I don't make the rules. I just follow the science. Questioning toxicology results could lead to chaos. Who wants that?"

"Never been supportive of chaos," Arnold said. "And Dr. Morley is error prone, I get that, but this feels overly convenient. Or are we in the business of just making up stories, ignoring some facts and exploiting others? I don't imagine that we actually believe the fantasy of Clayton poisoning *and* shooting himself?"

"Nothing wrong with fantasy, Arnold, with all due respect," Sanders muttered. "The more often you tell a story, the more people come to accept it as true. I gather you are bothered by fantasy?"

"Not generally, but in this instance, somewhat," Arnold said calmly. "It leaves some considerable loose ends. Natasha says that Clayton was going to kill her and then himself. But that did not happen. Why? I don't think

Clayton just changed his mind. Why would he decide to let Natasha live? He was not an exemplary character, but he kept his promises."

"Those are good questions, Arnold," Sanders said. "I wish I knew the answers to them, but at the moment, I don't. It's fine to be skeptical of my preferred story, but we don't have a better theory."

"You make a good point, Inspector Sanders," Ken said hurriedly, as if he needed to leave for a church ministerial meeting that he was not prepared for. "All of our suspects have alibis. If Clayton didn't choose to take poison himself, who did it for him? We don't know. Natasha and Sheila both had opportunity; we have been through that, but their stories make me think that neither of them did it. The mugs would not have been moved if they had done it. It appears that Clayton took poison in the woods, and then took a bullet to the head. None of our persons of interest were in the woods with him. They all have alibis that place them elsewhere. Unless we get new evidence, we may need to go with Sanders' preferred tale. Don't you think, Arnold?"

"Perhaps," Arnold muttered. "But perhaps we should pursue further evidence first."

"Pursue evidence all you want, Arnold," Sanders said. "I will play along. In due course, you will all accept my version of events. But in the meantime, please proceed with the case as you see fit. Tying up the loose ends is always a good idea. I am well aware that my story has problems. What story doesn't? But you will come to see that returning to my story is the best way to proceed."

"I have a suggestion," Arnold said, softly. "Let's shake things up a bit. I would suggest that we ask Emily to write a vaguely worded article in the *Sentinel*, inferring that a reliable witness has come forward with credible information about Clayton's death, and that the case is close to being resolved as one of murder by both poison and gunshot."

"Do we have such a witness?" Ken asked.

"We don't. But maybe a witness will come forward," Arnold said. "Maybe someone will get concerned and talk to us, or else two or more people of interest will challenge each other. We'll watch the key players and see what kind of action, if any, is stirred up. If nothing happens, we move forward with the theory that Clayton poisoned and shot himself."

"Go ahead." Sanders sighed. "Emily likes to write stories. She's a damn good reporter too. Love her stuff. But my guess is that you'll uncover secrets that you don't like and wonder why you tried so hard. Then you'll have to work to cover your tracks on your way back to the conclusion that both External Affairs and the Soviets wanted you to draw in the first place. That's how investigations can sometimes be. This one, I think, is like that."

Chapter 29

Reliable Witness

At seven on Wednesday morning, shortly after perusing the morning edition of the *Sentinel*, Natasha left her house as usual, wearing her running gear, though she did not go for a run right away. Instead, she walked across the street to the McCroskey residence and knocked on the door. "It's open, Natasha," Sheila called out. "I was actually expecting you."

Sheila was sitting in her kitchen, surrounded by dirty dishes and other assorted clutter and mess, calmly sipping her morning coffee. "Have a seat if you can find one. Be careful where you step though. There's a broken coffee mug on the floor somewhere. I couldn't find all the pieces. My house is decorated differently than yours, as you might have noticed. I'm not exactly a clean freak."

"That is clear," Natasha said, surveying the scene with distaste. "How can you live like this? And why were you expecting me?" she asked, raising her eyebrows and reluctantly sitting down on a wobbly chair a few feet from Sheila.

"You know perfectly well why I was expecting you. I saw you pouring poison into Clayton's mug. And you know that I did. Now that the police are close to solving Clayton's death, according to the morning paper, you're getting nervous. You think that I told the police what I saw."

"No, I don't know," Natasha said coldly. "What could you have seen?"

"I saw you putting poison in Clayton's drink. You know I did."

"You saw me pouring the breakfast drinks, Sheila. That is all. Where does this idea of poison come from?" Natasha was nervously tapping her feet on the floor, angry but trying to compose herself.

"It comes from me. I could smell the fennel," Sheila said, puffing up her chest as if she had achieved a considerable victory.

"Is that what you told the police?"

"Yes, I did. Arnold interviewed me, and I told him clearly what you did."

"That will prove to be embarrassing for you, Sheila. I already told Arnold that I poured the drinks. It was what I always did. Nothing more."

"The word is that Clayton was poisoned," Sheila said defiantly. "I just put two and two together. Not that hard. Obviously, you did your husband in. Can't say as I blame you, but still, murder is murder, and last time I checked, murder is against the law."

"Well, that's most interesting, Sheila," Natasha said, shaking her head. "I am truly not sure how you qualified to become a nurse. I came here today because I also read the *Sentinel* and assumed that the police were on to *you*. If Clayton was poisoned, you had the opportunity."

"You know that I didn't poison him. You know that because *you* did it. You and your accomplice. You placed poison in his drink, and then arranged for someone to meet him in the woods and shoot him. I have no idea how you knew that he would take his drink to the woods, but obviously you had an inside scoop."

"Where do you come up with these ridiculous notions, Sheila? I did not put poison in Clayton's drink! I also did not have an accomplice. I did not need one. I don't know who is responsible for Clayton's death, but I know that it was not me. I was thinking that it was more likely to be you, Sheila. Jealous of Clayton's affair with Janet, or so I had imagined. Though, now I am not so sure."

"How dare you accuse me of murder!" Sheila said, staring intensely at her. "I am a professional nurse, not a cold-blooded killer like you."

"Who have I killed?" Natasha asked calmly, looking directly at Sheila.

"You know perfectly well who you killed. Clayton is only the latest. You also killed your sister, Sophia. She goes to the Soviet Union for your mother's funeral, spends a weekend with you, and dies, her body pulled from Lake Baikal. Pretty convenient death, I figure. You were shagging Sophia's husband. I know all about your despicable past life, Natasha. Sophia won't make the mistake of being alone with you again. But then ... she can't, can she? You pretend to be so cultured and artistic, but you're just a common criminal. You and I both know it."

"I am guilty of many things, but I am not a common criminal," Natasha said, anger clear in her voice now. "I would *never* hurt Sophia. It is true that I had an affair with Doc. We were in love. That did hurt Sophia, and I am sorry about that. But where do you get the idea that I killed her?"

"I have sources." Sheila sighed. "It doesn't matter. I saw you at the kitchen counter. I smelled the fennel. I wasn't born yesterday. I know what hemlock smells like. Would you like me to make you a coffee? The coffee in prison is quite bad, I hear."

"Coffee is poison, wherever you drink it," Natasha said. "I like to start the day with vodka and a breakfast juice of natural vegetable and herbs. I know what you saw. You poked your head in to annoy me. But I didn't put poison in Clayton's drink. I don't even know what hemlock looks like. Not my area of expertise, though it seems to be yours. Does hemlock smell like fennel?"

"Yes, it smells like fennel. Not being a qualified nurse, you wouldn't know that. It's a very sharp smell."

"Well, I can't speak to that," Natasha said dismissively. "But why are you trying to pin poisoning on me? The reason I came over was to challenge you! I can also assure you that, if your 'source' was Clayton, he likely didn't share actual facts with you. He manipulates to his advantage, Sheila. That is his special gift. And you could not have smelled fennel in our kitchen. I never cook with fennel."

"I did smell it," Sheila said. "No doubt of it."

"Well ... I can't explain that," Natasha said, shaking her head and looking at her quizzically. "Did you really poke your head in the door just to annoy me?"

I did," Sheila said defiantly.

"Why? I knew about your affair with Clayton. It was not a big deal to me."

"I wanted you to know that I wasn't afraid of you. That I could do as I pleased. If I wanted to have sex with your husband I would, and I did."

"I understand that, Sheila, but nobody cares. Certainly not me. Where did you go after you closed the door? You didn't go home, did you?"

"I went for a smoke in the alley. I saw you leave. Then I went back inside. I felt that I had made my point."

"Not much of a point, if you ask me," Natasha said crossly, looking around the room. "You seem weirdly upset with me, considering that you were the person having an affair with my husband. I really don't understand it."

"You just refuse to face the truth, don't you, Natasha," Sheila challenged, getting up to walk to the kitchen window. "You should be nice to me. I could tell the police everything I know. I have information that would be damaging to you. Clayton told me things about you. Bad things. Clayton told me that you killed Sophia."

"He told you that!" Natasha yelled, losing her composure completely now. "You want to share? Fine! I'll start! *Clayton* killed Sophia! I have the evidence written in Clayton's own hand! I do have guilt over Sophia's death, but *not* because I killed her! It is because I should have stayed to protect her! I have to live with that mistake! But Clayton killed Sophia! I have always suspected it, but on Thursday night, I discovered proof of it in his journal. I saw his confession in his own handwriting, and when I challenged him about it, he admitted it to me."

"I don't believe you, Natasha," Sheila said confidently. "You know perfectly well that Sophia stood in the way of you and your lover, Doc Rubenstein. You wanted to have Doc and Fyodor to yourself—"

"Because he's my son!" Natasha blurted out then, before dropping her head down into her hands, clearly distraught. After a moment, she explained. "Fyodor is my son, and Doc is the father." Her voice was quieter now. "But I did not harm my sister. I could never have killed her. I loved her."

Sheila took a moment to absorb that before speaking again. "So, how did Fyodor come to be with Doc and Sophia in Northford then?"

"It wasn't easy. Sophia and Doc were already living in Toronto when our mother became quite ill. Sophia came to visit from Canada, and I told her that I was pregnant with Alexei's child. Sophia was a practical person. She is the one who suggested that we switch passports. We are identical twins.

I went to Toronto to have Fyodor, and Sophia stayed in Irkutsk, pretending to be me. After the birth, I travelled back to the Soviet Union, and Sophia returned to be with Doc. It was arranged in this way because both of us wanted the child to grow up in Canada."

"That can't be true. Surely Clayton would have noticed."

"He was away most of the time, so he did not realize at first that we had switched places, but when he did and I explained our reasoning, he agreed with the plan, assuming the child to be his own and accepting that it would be better raised in Canada. I told him only this week that he was not the father of Fyodor. He was devastated. He had longed to be a part of his son's life from the time he was born. You've seen that sculpture he'd been working on for months? With the man and child?"

"I have," Sheila said. "I told him that it was beautiful and poignant. He said that it was about suffering. He cried." She sighed and shook her head in disbelief. "Now I understand why."

"He tears up easily. Should have gone into acting," Natasha said. "I have to accept that my having an affair and a child with Doc, never mind withholding that fact from Clayton, does not look good for me. It was cruel in some respects, I suppose, but the circumstances were such that I could not tell Clayton. The costs were too high. And in any case, it is nothing compared to killing Sophia, and that is what he did. All by himself."

"Why?"

"Sophia was going to expose his art-theft scheme in the Soviet Union. He was on the verge of the assignment with the Soviet Embassy in Ottawa, which he needed in order to defect. He pushed her into Lake Baikal to prevent her from ruining his promotion and defection plans."

"But you wanted to defect as well, right?"

"I did. I benefited from all of it, and he held that fact over me, though he smartly kept the murder of my sister to himself. I had to discover that on my own."

Sheila was stunned. None of this had been expected. "Why are you telling me this?"

"If you are thinking that I poisoned Clayton, you should at least know the truth. I have no idea how he died, or what happened to him. Truly. Did you know that Clayton was planning on leaving the country on Saturday afternoon? Of course, he wasn't going to get away. I saw to that with a phone call to the authorities. He would have been travelling on a false passport."

Sheila clearly couldn't believe what she was hearing. Shocked, she said, "He promised me that he would leave you. We were planning on starting a life together. That's why I kicked Dan out."

Sheila and Natasha sat together in the kitchen for a few quiet minutes, processing everything that had been said. Natasha's feet now rested on a spread copy of the *Northford Sentinel*, with Emily's cover story, which rested on the floor, covering parts of a strawberry-jam puddle that had congealed on the linoleum. Finally, Sheila stood up and started busying herself with moving dirty dishes from the counter to the already overly full sink. It wasn't a quiet activity, but the dominant sound in the room was their breathing.

"Kicking Dan out for a life with Clayton was a mistake," Natasha said finally. "Clayton's life was about to implode. He was in deep trouble. Getting to have sex with you was probably one of the few things that was going his way."

"What kind of trouble was he in?"

"The kind of trouble that causes a person to kill themselves. He told me that I had to join him in the woods on Saturday morning, and that there we would commit a double suicide, but something happened. I just don't know what. Maybe he just changed his mind."

"So, you really didn't poison Clayton?"

"I really did not," Natasha said, her voice calm now. "Did you?"

"Of course not. I thought we had a future together."

"Sadly, you are not the first person to bet on the wrong horse."

With that, Natasha left and headed out on her morning run. She thought to herself that she would stop in at the Arts Centre, before going home, to chat with Dan. She wondered if he had any new information to share.

CHAPTER 30

NATASHA'S HOME GETS A COMPLETE INSPECTION

Late Wednesday afternoon, Sergeant Arnold Powell, together with a team of officers from the Northford RCMP detachment, invaded Natasha's house on Saskatchewan Street. Sheila's accusation of Natasha had prompted a second search of the residence.

Having arrived with a warrant, the police combed through the house, with Natasha (cooperative in her fashion) sitting calmly on the white sofa while they searched. "Tell me what you are looking for, Arnold," Natasha said. "Objects are often hard to find. I am happy to help."

"Well, Natasha," he said, "we're looking for hemlock. Sheila claims you have some."

"Sheila is quite unreliable." She sighed. "I met with her this morning to discuss our shared suspicions. As for hemlock, I have no idea what it looks like. But feel free to carry on the search. I will sit here and wait. I have no place to go."

"It is not just the hemlock we're looking for," he said. "We're also looking for straight answers to new questions. Like why you and Clayton changed your wills last week, giving everything to Fyodor? Fyodor is only a nephew."

"What's wrong with nephews?" she said calmly. "Though in any case, he is more than a nephew. He is my son."

Arnold paused, his eyebrows shooting upwards. "Can I assume that Clayton is the father?"

"You could, but you would be wrong," Natasha said, picking up her favourite distraction magazine, *Chatelaine*, and flipping through it. "Clayton assumed he was the father as well, but he was also wrong. He was quite upset when he discovered the truth. Doc Rubenstein is the father."

"But when Clayton made the change in his will, he must have thought that he was the father," Arnold said, mostly to himself.

"That is correct," Natasha said, looking at a photo of a woman dressed quite similarly to herself. "We changed our wills early last week, on Clayton's insistence."

"When did he find out that he wasn't the father?" Arnold asked.

"On Thursday evening. We had quite a heart to heart, as you know. Many things were said. Details discovered. Emily should have been there. It would make for a riveting story."

"I guess Clayton didn't have time to change it again after you told him the truth? What other details were discovered in that conversation?"

"Clayton admitted to killing Sophia."

"He admitted it?" Arnold asked. "How did you manage that?"

"I found a note in his papers, confessing to the murder of Sophia. Clayton loves to document his life. Bad deeds and all. I confronted him with his own journal and he confessed. He had little choice."

"How did he handle this event?"

"Not well," Natasha said, shaking her head, and putting her magazine down for a second. "It was a sad evening. We broke each other's hearts. It was, in some sense, quite pathetic."

"How did you break his heart? About Fyodor not being his son?" Arnold asked. "Surely he knew about the affair you had with Doc?"

"He knew about the affair and my pregnancy, but he assumed he was the father. He also knew that I had switched passports with Sophia and flown to Canada to have Fyodor. He had said that he was okay with that. He wanted the child to grow up outside the Soviet Union. He was planning to defect so that he could be with his son. But on Friday, when I told him that Fyodor was not his child, it hurt him deeply."

"I noticed the sculpture of the man and child in his workshop," Arnold said. "It was very touching."

"It was," she said, nodding slowly. "He came to Northford in good measure because he wanted to be close to Fyodor. Clayton felt a deep desire for a son and had made his decision to defect, in part at least, around this desire. But it was all based on a flawed assumption. When I told him the truth, he said that if he did not have a son, then he had nothing. He had no reason to live."

"Did you believe him?" Arnold asked, pulling a chair up close to her.

"In part. His sadness was genuine, I think, but Clayton has a strong survival instinct. I didn't think that he was surrendering to death."

"But he was still going to kill you?"

"Oh yes, that is what he said. He seemed clear about it. He was not about to let me carry on with my son."

"That is when he threatened the double suicide for Saturday morning?"

"Yes. He told me that after my run, we would drive to the woods and he would shoot me and then himself. I still thought, however, that he would only shoot me. I assumed that he would try and escape, even after my call to the authorities, perhaps buying another ticket under another alias. He has various passports and could have used a disguise. He was not without skills." Natasha's voice was still calm but more full of doubt now than Arnold had ever noticed before. She seemed to be letting her cool, professional veneer slip a bit. Arnold wondered what kind of persona Natasha might take up next.

"Did he give you any options?" Arnold asked.

"Of course not. Clayton isn't in the habit of providing his victims with options."

"But when you met with Emily at eight-thirty at the *Sentinel*, you were reported to be calm and forward looking. Doesn't sound like someone who was about to die."

"I am a Russian. I am always ready to die."

"What happened to the suicide plan?"

"I wish I knew, but I don't. As I have told you before, when I got home, Clayton and his car were gone. Perhaps God is having mercy on my soul."

"Pretty sure that isn't the case," Arnold mused. "When Dan called you on Saturday afternoon, before I came to meet with you, did you think he was involved in some way?"

"I thought it was possible. But I didn't know. He said nothing about being involved."

"But he did call you ahead of the police coming to see you. It was curious that he would do that. So why did he? Perhaps the full truth this time, Natasha. It would save time and cut down on these police visits."

"Dan was very concerned about the evidence of cheese and large footprints. He was concerned that Henry or his boys might be involved. So, we agreed to come up with a story about a stranger with large feet. I am sorry. I know that you no longer believe that story, and you are quite right. We should not have done that."

"You shouldn't have. No. Did you lie about anything else?"

"What are you getting at?" Natasha asked, seeming almost startled. Once again, Arnold noticed that her composure was developing cracks. The sound of officers scouring her home likely didn't help, although she did not seem overly concerned about the police finding anything. Arnold began to doubt they'd find any hemlock in the house. In fact, he was beginning to doubt that they would find anything incriminating at all. But that didn't mean that Natasha had not been up to something. Arnold firmly believed that she was. He decided to check out his thinking on the matter.

"I am wondering about the plan that you and Dan came up with on Friday evening."

Natasha was silent for a moment before responding carefully. "There was no plan, Arnold. You are fishing in the wrong pool."

"I have done that before, Natasha. We'll see. That will do for now, though. Thank you." Arnold stood up and moved his chair back up against the wall where he had found it, right beneath Natasha's dancing certificates and the award from the Saskatchewan government.

"Is there any cash stashed anywhere in the house?" Arnold asked, as he started to move towards the outside door. "Clayton withdrew all of his money last week and closed his bank account. But there is no sign of where he put it or what he did with it."

"No idea," Natasha said. "I know nothing about Clayton's money. Perhaps he sent money out of the country. That would be possible, would it not?"

"Or perhaps you did?" Arnold suggested.

"Or perhaps I didn't. Is there money missing? I would not put it past Clayton to have sent money out of the country. But he had his money, and I have a little bit of my own. I don't know where he left his."

"Do you have any idea how a piece of Medovik cake ended up in your garbage bin?" Arnold asked then, seemingly losing interest in the money topic.

"No, I don't." She seemed genuinely surprised by the question.

"Do you think it possible that Clayton would have put the cake in the garbage himself?"

"I can't imagine him doing that. That would be very out of character. He did not like to put anything in the garbage if he could help it. He liked to reuse things or compost them. I'd assumed that he ate the cake. The plate was empty and on the workshop table when I came back."

Arnold again reached the front door looking back at Natasha, still sitting poised and upright, facing both the front door and a few of the police officers bustling about. "Alright. Well, do you have any idea why we found one of Clayton's hairs in the trunk of his car?"

"I do not. Perhaps he changed a tire recently?" She seemed to think for a moment, then shrugged slightly. "He stored his duffel bag in his trunk. Other than that, I have no other idea."

"Right," he said, then abruptly changed the subject. "So, do you have any idea why we found your hair on Dan's Saskatchewan Roughrider cap?"

"Probably because I occasionally wear Dan's cap for running," Natasha responded coolly.

"Why?"

"Because I don't have a Saskatchewan Roughrider cap, and he does. I could buy one, but Dan already has one. He likes the idea of me using his cap. Kind of like we are in high school and dating or something." Natasha smiled then. "Dan is cute that way. I like the idea too, though oddly perhaps. I never had that kind of experience growing up in the Soviet Union."

"I would be happy to get you a cap, Natasha. They are available for sale at Lieberman's Pharmacy. You will be staying in town until we have finished our inquiries, right?" Arnold added, turning to grip the doorknob. Then pausing, he released it and returned to where Natasha was sitting. "By the way, the postmaster says that you mailed a large parcel on Saturday at noon. What was in this parcel?"

"I sent Fyodor a Peter Goodhand painting," Natasha promptly responded, not appearing bothered at all by the question. "I bought it from Peter Goodhand directly. Nothing to do with Clayton. I have very little cash to send Fyodor. All I had was a painting." She sighed. "Fyodor does not accept me as his mother. I wasn't there for him. Sophia was. He hates me. That is hard for me, but I do understand. He hated Clayton too. He is a smart boy. I have tried to explain my circumstances to Fyodor, but he does not appear to care for my explanations. I don't blame him. I am not loveable. I know that. I am removed, a cold fish, as they say, and certainly not a mother by almost any definition ... except that I did give birth to him. I have to live with that assessment, I suppose. Although everything is temporary. Including a son's disappointment with his mother."

With that, Arnold finally called off his staff, leaving Natasha to leaf through her *Chatelaine* magazine, admiring photographs of women who dressed the same way she did.

CHAPTER 31

ARNOLD CONSULTS WITH CONSTABLE BILLY SOUTH

On Thursday morning, Arnold sat in his office and reflected on suffering. Everyone suffers. He thought about how people respond to it. In particular, he wondered about Natasha. She had suffered in a viscerally unique manner. She had been given a death notice. He wondered what action that notice had prompted her to take.

He put his feet up on his desk and looked over his notes, sipping what even he considered to be exceptionally strong, day-old coffee. He thought about the young, blindfolded Dostoyevsky, waiting for the firing squad to shoot him. Dostoyevsky wasn't shot, but he thought he would be. Natasha didn't get shot either. But she thought she would be."

Arnold reviewed his notes from the day. A not-so-startling development had emerged that morning when Sanders had announced that a retest of Clayton's mug had revealed traces of hemlock. Bizarrely, on the same day, the cake-crumb evidence had disappeared from the toxicology lab. Arnold smiled, but it was not a happy smile. It was beginning to look like Sanders was moving quickly towards file closure.

Sanders reported that Doc Rubenstein and Dr. Morley had jointly visited the lab to supervise testing results. By the time they'd left, the cake evidence was gone and the breakfast-mug residue was toxic. Arnold shook his head. *Guess Sanders is getting some help with problem solving,* Arnold thought to himself. *Impressively convenient.*

Arnold was reflecting on his notes when Constable Billy South walked in.

"Any action from the article, Arnold?" Billy asked, plunking his body down on the visitor's chair.

"A little," Arnold said. "Sounds like Natasha and Sheila had a heart to heart. Good for both of them, no doubt. We have spoken to them but remain unclear on exactly how Clayton died. We do feel confident, however, that Clayton killed Sophia. But that is not the case we are working on."

"It does give Natasha motive," Billy said.

"It does. But she already had motive. Protecting yourself from death is a powerful one," Arnold reflected out loud. "But I have no evidence implicating Natasha in poisoning Clayton."

"Natasha is experienced in deception and she's smart. Exceptionally cold perhaps, but smart. But what about Sheila?" Billy asked. "She's apparently a qualified nurse, as she loves to point out, but I personally wouldn't count on her judgement in the hospital. She's a loosely wrapped package that's coming undone."

"I tend to agree with that assessment," Arnold said, "but that does not make her a killer. Sheila thought that she had a future with Clayton. Her judgement can be questioned, but her motive for killing Clayton is weak. Overall, Emily's article helped to eliminate both Natasha and Sheila as suspects. I don't believe that either of them poisoned Clayton."

"That's something, anyway," Billy said, seemingly quite relieved. "Although Vera told me that from the beginning. You really should talk to my wife, Arnold. So where does that leave us? With the person who poisoned the cake crumbs in Clayton's car?"

"The person who placed the cake crumbs in the car is involved. That is certain. Except, that the cake crumbs no longer exist as evidence. They have magically disappeared from the police lab."

"Stolen?"

"That would be one way to describe it. I suspect they found their way into Clayton's mug residue, which is now magically toxic. The whole business is confounding, but you know, I have begun to seriously consider that my approach to the case needs a reset."

"How do you mean?"

"I believe that Clayton was poisoned with toxic breakfast juice," Arnold said, as a file that had been precariously balanced on the edge of his desk dropped to the floor. "Sanders may well be messing with the evidence to suit the official story line, but it's also helping to clarify what happened. It's caused me to review. I think that, initially, the mug did hold poisoned drink but was later cleaned. Now, thanks to Sander's footwork, the mug has been restored to an earlier toxic state."

"Should we put that file together again, like Humpty Dumpty and all the king's men?" Billy asked, smiling and watching intently as various documents lay silently on the floor.

"In a minute, Billy," Arnold said thoughtfully, his mind clearly on another matter entirely. "I am busy contemplating the possibilities that the breakfast mug in the woods was actually toxic."

"Are you saying that Clayton really was poisoned with toxic juice?" Billy asked. "That is a new one for me. Vera never mentioned that possibility."

"But I am."

"But the mug residue was clean."

"It was. But I suspect that the mug was cleaned at the Dalrymple home," Arnold mused.

"But then Clayton was poisoned at home?" Billy said, putting his feet up on Arnold's desk right. "Pardon the familiarity, Arnold, but I have had it with formality. Natasha's constant composure makes me feel like slapping her. Whether she's guilty of killing Clayton or not, she's guilty of being insufferable. That needs to be in the criminal code, Arnold. But back to the case. What is your thinking on how Clayton managed to drive to the woods, if he was poisoned at home?"

"I believe I actually know how that happened," Arnold said, pushing his Stetson back on his head far enough that it fell behind his chair, among the file documents that still lay there. He didn't bother to pick it up. "I think you killed Clayton, Billy, and now the whole business has unfolded. He insulted you, and you couldn't take it." He grinned at Billy to let him know he was only joking. "Just kidding, Billy. I know you were in the gym that morning."

"What happened? I am all ears," Billy said, "except for my waistline, which only listens to the sound of an open refrigerator."

"I need to check some details first," Arnold said softly, "but I feel a sense of progress in this case."

"Do you think the thefts are connected?" Billy asked, smiling at him.

"Thefts?" he asked, momentarily distracted by a car horn outside.

"From the Arts Centre and Four-Square Gospel?"

"Ah, right," he said, putting his coffee down on his desk. "The Arts Centre's discovery that over a hundred thousand dollars is missing from their account, and Four-Square Gospel discovering a hundred thousand missing from the construction-project account. Clayton was financial administrator for both. So, yes, I assume it's all related."

"Two hundred thousand dollars in cash would be hard to hide. I know I don't have it. My hunch is that Natasha has it," Billy said. "Pretty sure that is what Vera would say."

"Maybe she does, or did, but there is no cash in Natasha's house. We have looked," Arnold said. "There was nothing in her home safe, or in either of their safety deposit boxes at the bank. His bank account is cleaned out, and nothing has been added to Natasha's account."

"Maybe Clayton or Natasha sent it away?"

"Maybe. Natasha sent a Peter Goodhand painting to Fyodor on Saturday afternoon. Maybe she stored cash in the frame. Still, I don't see Natasha stealing from the Arts Centre. From her husband, sure, but not the Arts Centre."

"How do you feel about Inspector Sanders' approach to this business, Arnold?" Billy asked, expecting Arnold to be annoyed, which he was, but only somewhat.

"Sanders has always been a peculiar man with a unique approach to police work," Arnold said. "He can be unethical, but he is usually careful to pick his spots. We may not be as far apart in this matter as it seems. We'll see. Sanders told me once that he had no confidence in eye-witness accounts. On that point, I agree with him."

"Generally?" Billy asked, smiling and still slouching in the visitor's chair with his feet resting on Arnold's desk.

"Yes, generally. But also, specifically, in this case."

"What does that mean? I don't understand."

"Do you trust your eyes, Billy?"

"Sometimes."

"But not always?"

"No, not always. I can be fooled. I can make inferences that are incorrect."

"Exactly. People make assumptions based on expectations. It happens," Arnold said, as he bent down to the floor, to pick up his Stetson, and return the paper file to a safer location on his desk.

CHAPTER 32

ARNOLD MEETS WITH DAN
AT THE ARTS CENTRE

It was two o'clock on Thursday afternoon, and Arnold was walking down the hall of the Arts Centre to visit with Dan. He found the man busily screwing a decorative sign on the theatre door when Arnold walked in. He was wearing his Saskatchewan Roughrider cap, as per usual.

"Sun in your eyes, Dan?" Arnold asked as he entered. He lifted a few boxes of clothes from a large, vintage chair and sat down. Arnold felt his body sink deeply into its fabric. "You are surprisingly handy, Dan, especially for an artist."

"Don't be knocking the artist class, Arnold. We have our priorities. Everyone does. Just different ones. But to be honest, I had no choice. Oscar was busy." Dan smiled at him. "Do you like that chair? It's a beauty. People don't appreciate the value of old objects. I found that chair at a thrift store in Saskatoon. Hard to believe. A lot of junk in that thrift store, but that chair stood out like a Senet boardgame in an Egyptian tomb excavation. I grabbed it."

"Did you also grab a dead body?" Arnold asked.

Dan dropped his screwdriver. When he tried to pick it up, his hand failed to grasp it. He missed it entirely. He finally gave up, staring at Arnold for a moment, before gesturing that he should follow him.

"How do you mean?" Dan said, his voice likely not as steady as he hoped, as he led Arnold through the door and into the theatre. "What dead body?"

"Clayton Dalrymple's, for example?"

In silence, they made their way down the main aisle and through another door, which led backstage. Arnold noticed that the area was almost as crowded with boxes and props as the man's office.

"Where is this coming from?" Dan lowered himself into a nearby chair. "You know perfectly well where I was on Saturday." His tone was rather loud but came across as weak just the same.

"I know what you told me, Dan. But you are a man of the theatre. Theatre involves deception, right?" Arnold asked. "Tricking the eye. An image is presented, within a context that is familiar, like a hat, a jacket, and a vehicle. The objects and the context encourage the eye to see what it expects to see. Is that not how mystery theatre works?"

"I would agree with that," Dan said. "But Clayton's death was not theatre. It was real."

"Very much so. But covering up the reality of events involved theatre. We are left with a dead body, real enough, but efforts have been made to deceive people, the police specifically, as to how the death occurred, and how the body got to where we—or I should say you—found it."

"I have no idea what you mean. What kind of efforts? By whom?"

"You for one, Dan. But you didn't do this alone. I am thinking that you and Natasha came up with a plan on Friday. You couldn't stand by without helping her. She was in crisis. And I understand that. I even think I know how you did it."

"Did what? You are going down a wrong path, Arnold. Natasha and I made no plan. I thought about having a plan, I admit. But I didn't come up with one. But you're right that I was not alone. I was with my boys until nearly nine that morning. Then I drove to the arts centre. You know my schedule. Witnesses abound."

"I accept that you were with your boys until nearly nine. Not to put too fine a point on it, but I suspect that it was actually more like quarter to nine or so. The soccer folks suggest that you came to practice early. Still, that is a minor point. It is where you were and what you did *after* nine, that is of interest to me."

"Why is that of interest? I was just at my office. Quite a tedious morning really."

"I think that you had quite an efficient, action-packed morning, Dan. I think that you were driving Clayton's Mustang to the forest road. You were impersonating Clayton, driving to the woods in his car, dressed in his hat and coat."

"That is quite an accusation, Arnold. If I was impersonating Clayton, where was Clayton?"

"In the trunk of his car. That's where we found one of his hairs."

"But how could I do that and still be at my office? I have witnesses who saw me there! Anyway, Clayton was obviously driving his car."

"Why is that obvious?"

"For one thing, he was seen. Witnesses. There were also poisoned cake crumbs on his car seat."

"How do you know that?"

Dan stopped for a moment, readjusting his body position and glancing at the ceiling fan. "I heard about it. A rumour. Is it true?"

"You're lying, Dan. This town is full of rumours, but the cake-crumb story has been kept under wraps. The only reason you know about it is because you put them there. You also lied about the stranger at the park. Why did you make up that story? We know that it was Henry who shot cheese at an already dead body."

Dan paused for some time. He cleared his throat then and lowered his voice for some unclear reason, "I admit that I thought it might be Henry who shot the cheese. I admit I made up a story to keep him out of this mess."

"So did Natasha. You both tried to deceive me. You gave false evidence."

"I admit that the stranger story is not true. It's just that Henry is so vulnerable. I didn't want him involved. Natasha was just trying to deflect attention away from Henry. Protect him. She was doing me a favour. Anyway, if Clayton was already dead, what Henry did is not that serious." He pulled a box of props onto his lap and started rummaging through it.

"Let me be the judge of that. But I will tell you clearly that lying to a police officer in an investigation is serious."

"Okay, fine. Natasha and I accept guilt for that. Well, I shouldn't speak for Natasha, but I know that she regrets lying to you, Arnold," Dan said sadly. "We were wrong to do that. But your theory about us having a plan is wrong. Also, Clayton being in the trunk is ridiculous. Only Clayton's tracks are going from the car to the meadow."

"Clayton's cowboy boots took that trip," Arnold said. "But Clayton wasn't wearing them. You were."

"If I was wearing his cowboy boots, how did Clayton get to the meadow?" Dan asked, quite exasperated, lighting up a cigarette from a Rothmans package he pulled out from yet another box of props. "You haven't thought this through, Arnold."

"I didn't know you smoked, Dan. You are a man full of surprises."

"I'm just a little bit stressed, Arnold, what with you accusing me of murder," Dan said, taking a long drag and blowing smoke out into the room.

"No one has accused you of murder, Dan," Arnold said. "Where do you get that idea?"

"Well, you're telling me that I wore a dead man's cowboy boots. Sounds suspiciously like an accusation to me."

"It is suspicious, Dan. Your behaviour I mean, though it doesn't necessarily mean you killed him. But yes, I am telling you that you wore the dead man's cowboy boots. Why did you do that if you didn't kill him?"

"Maybe I didn't wear them," Dan retorted, taking another drag. Smoking made Dan feel like a tough guy, but a heroic one, not a killer.

Arnold decided to back off and travel a different path with Dan. "You told me that you were on the Saskatoon volunteer fire brigade some years back, right?"

"That's true," Dan answered. "But what does that have to do with anything?"

"So, you learned how to do manage a fireman's carry, right, Dan?"

"Yes, I suppose so," he said cautiously.

"Carrying Clayton from the forest road to the meadow could have been done with a fireman's carry technique, right, Dan?" Arnold asked, confidently.

Dan's forehead was running with perspiration. "Technically, it might be possible, Arnold."

"You also told me that you had a firearms license. You know how to discharge a handgun, Dan, despite your earlier claim that you're afraid of guns."

"I *am* afraid of guns. I only got the license because I wanted to hunt with my father-in-law. Also, I thought it might come in handy for a theatrical production. But I never got around to hunting. Never used it for the theatre either. Guess that was a waste. Funny to think I did that to impress my father-in-law. Didn't even like the man."

"You didn't like Clayton either."

"That's true, but no one did," Dan said defensively. "I don't understand this questioning, Arnold. I'm an innocent man. All I did was find Clayton's body in the woods. I panicked on seeing the cheese and big footprints and thought that Henry might have come across the body. I told Natasha about it, and she agreed to make up a story about a stranger. I admit that and that it was wrong. But that is *all* that I did wrong."

"But that's not all, Dan," Arnold said. "You found Clayton's gun in the parking lot on Friday afternoon. You didn't put it back. You kept it."

"You have no proof of that."

"I don't. I just have a theory. I think that you attended the Dalrymple residence on Saturday morning to intervene on Natasha's behalf. Either she was in on this plan, or she wasn't, but it still happened. You were going to save Natasha by shooting Clayton, right? But you were saved. You did not need to shoot him. When you got to Natasha's house, Clayton was already dead on the workshop floor. Poisoned. Perhaps you didn't know how he died, but you assumed that Natasha had decided to save herself. Your theatre passions took over, and you went right into production mode, creating a diversion."

"But I was with my boys till nearly nine, and at the Arts Centre shortly after nine!"

"Your Falcon was, but you weren't. I think that Natasha drove your Falcon to the office. She had your ball cap on. I noticed a strand of straight, dirty-blonde hair on your ball cap's sweat band when we were having a burger the evening of Clayton's death. I thought that was odd, so I picked off one of the hairs. We tested it, and sure enough, it belongs to Natasha."

"She wears my cap sometimes."

"Exactly. Including Saturday morning."

"And what was I doing?"

"Placing poisoned cake crumbs on Clayton's car seat, for one. You were busy that morning. You had a lot of work to do and not much time."

"If you found poisoned cake on the driver's seat, he must have eaten poisoned cake."

"But he didn't eat cake," Arnold said.

"How do you know?"

"We examined his stomach contents. We found a nearly full piece of Medovik cake in Clayton's garbage bin. The cake in the garbage is not toxic. Which is why it is curious that the cake crumbs in the car were full of hemlock. What do you make of that?" Arnold asked.

"I guess the cake was too sweet for him," Dan said, sounding defensive.

"You know that it wasn't, Dan. Clayton liked the cake. I imagine that, despite his worries that morning, he had every intention to eat it. But he didn't. I propose that Clayton did not throw it away, but rather you did. I propose that you placed a small piece of the cake into the poisoned breakfast juice and spread the crumbs on the car seat. Your plan worked quite well, although there were complications. Like getting some of Clayton's vomit on your t-shirt as you transferred him from the car trunk to the meadow and shot him. Your shirt was quite stained and unpleasant. If you remember, I even commented on it at the ballfield. When I met with Sheila, your house did not appear to have been cleaned in quite a while, but I noticed that the laundry had been done."

"I did the laundry. I was moving out. My t-shirt was sweaty and gross, just like my other dirty clothes that needed cleaning before I could pack it. Anyway, I had been running on Saturday, and stressed out at what I'd seen. That's why it was so dirty. You know how hot it was on Saturday." He shook his head dismissively. "No way. It's an imaginative story, Arnold, full of speculation but empty of actual evidence. It doesn't even explain how the mug got to be poisoned in first place! Who did that? Natasha? Sheila?"

With his outburst, Dan seemed to feel a surge of energy, dropping the box of props on the floor with a resounding bang and raising his head and tilting it back a bit, as if somehow, a more erect posture might exonerate him from Arnold's accusations.

"I don't think either of them poisoned him. Neither did you. But I'll share my views on that at the right time. For now, I admit that proof is presently in short supply. But you could help with that. If you confessed, which is what you should do, it would go better for you. Confess, and I can see what I can do for you. Otherwise, you're on your own."

As Arnold left, he made a note to himself to radio Constable Billy Stafford as soon as he got back to his cruiser and have Billy put a tail on Dan. Given how their visit had just gone, it seemed prudent to consider that Dan might decide to leave town. There was no question the man was feeling the squeeze and could easily panic and try to run.

CHAPTER 33

ARNOLD PAYS SHEILA ANOTHER VISIT

It had been six days since Clayton's body had been found. The weather had turned from unseasonably warm to unseasonably cold, but as Arnold left the detachment office, he reflected that the changing weather was of no consequence to Clayton. Arnold reflected that death had stabilized Clayton's situation. There had been much danger and intrigue in his life, but no longer. Clayton's physical makeup, his atoms, everything he had needed in life, had moved on to other projects.

As Arnold stepped outside, he zipped up his jacket. The autumn air was brisk, with a bite that demanded winter garments. The haze of harvest dust had settled, and now the air was clear but tinged with a hint of the coming prairie winter.

Arnold decided that he would drive to Sheila's, but first, he needed to eat. He had been making phone calls all day, interviewing witnesses, and looking into the theft allegations at the church and arts centre. He was exhausted. He walked past the park bench outside the detachment with a trio of giant elm trees growing beside it, giving the bench shade. Although the bench was mostly used in the summer months, when the shade of the elms was comforting, there were times in the winter when Arnold would spend a few minutes sitting there, marvelling at the silent beauty of the frozen snow. But not today.

He went straight to his cruiser and drove to the Dickey Dee, marveling as always at the miles of undulating grainfields broken up by the woods along the Saskatchewan River and surrounding valleys. It was a great land-scape for imaginative thinking.

As Arnold walked through the front doors of the Dickey Dee, he con-sidered changing his order. He wondered whether a fish burger would be satisfying. Or perhaps a BLT with fries. Then again, he loved Cobb salads, even though he rarely ordered one. Annie's Cobb salads were a delight. By the time Annie came to take his order, he had changed his mind. He ordered the cheeseburger and fries. With all the uncertainty in Northford, he figured it was a bad time to mess with the tried and true.

To add to Arnold's feeling of uncertainty, his Oakland A's had been trounced 7–1 by the Red Sox in the first game of the baseball playoffs. He had felt confident that Holtzman would prevail over Tiant, but the opposite had occurred. Arnold had gone to bed feeling a deep sense of disappointed malaise. Baseball could do that to him.

■ ■ ■

An hour later, Arnold pulled into the McCroskey residence. It was just after seven in the evening when he knocked on the front door and waited, listening to the sounds of general mayhem inside. Arnold looked around, seeing that the blue velvet curtain had made good progress on its journey to the living-room floor. The curtain now lay on the shag carpet, leaving the curtain rod to fend for itself. The front yard had been mowed, and a straightened basketball hoop with netting had been attached to the driveway backboard. Arnold wondered whether Sheila had done the work herself or had found herself a new man.

When Sheila opened the door, a paper airplane flew out and hit Arnold on the forehead. Arnold caught it as it fell, and handed it to the young Nathan McCroskey, who was standing beside his mother. "Never have chil-dren, Sergeant," Sheila said, shaking her head. "I was pretty sure we were finished with our meetings. I believe that I've shared everything relevant."

"Years too late on the child advice, Sheila. But there can still be chal-lenges, even when they're grown. I regularly get calls from my son asking for advice he has no intention of following. As for police visits, if your sharing had been more helpful the first time, I might not have needed to return. But so be it. Do you mind if I come in? A few things to clarify."

Arnold walked past her into the kitchen and was immediately struck with how clean the room was. He was startled but pleased. He sat down on a chair by the kitchen table, without having to remove any objects. The table was also clear and wiped, as was the kitchen counter. Arnold noted that the countertop was badly worn around the sink, but overall, the kitchen felt enticing and comfortable. He looked gently at Sheila as she stood by the counter. Sheila did not appear to anticipate any need to sit. "In your initial statement to us," Arnold started, "you said that you saw Natasha place poison into Clayton's mug. Do you hold to that statement, given that all you really saw was her pouring a breakfast drink?"

"I might have been overzealous in my accusations," Sheila said defensively, looking out the kitchen window, rather than directly at Arnold. "But I did smell fennel."

"When you first looked in the front door or after you came back from your smoke?"

She frowned and looked back at Arnold, as though she hadn't considered that before. "I'm not sure. Probably after my smoke. It is quite an unpleasant smell, as I have said. I likely would have said something to Natasha if I had smelled it when she was there. So, I guess it must have been after she left."

"Did you say anything to Clayton about the smell?"

"I did. I always say what's on my mind. I told him that his kitchen stank of fennel."

"What did he say?"

"He was dismissive. He said that Natasha was not skilled in the kitchen."

"Is that all he said?"

"Pretty much. We didn't get together to chat. I believe I have explained that."

"You have mentioned that before."

"Because it's true. The truth is worth repeating," Sheila said, sighing and finally sitting down across the table from Arnold. She seemed resigned to a longer visit.

"Perhaps it is. What precisely did Natasha come to see you about the day after the article appeared in the *Sentinel* about how the investigation was going?"

"She wanted to know if I had killed Clayton. Ridiculous. She also thought that I was the witness the article referred to. Which, as you know, I was," Sheila said rather indifferently. "Do I need to offer you coffee?"

"No, you don't. But you could tell me if you poisoned Clayton."

"Of course not. Why would a professional nurse do such a thing? Anyway, where else would I get that kind of sex in this town?"

"I have no idea. Clayton was that good?"

"Best sex I have ever had; I will say that much. Hank Goertzen has moved in and tries his best, but he's no Clayton."

"Did you tell Natasha about the fennel smell?"

"I did. She claims to know nothing about fennel. Says she doesn't cook with fennel. Irrelevant, if you ask me, because all I'm saying is that the kitchen smelled of it. She obviously has hemlock."

"Why is it obvious?"

"Because I smelled it."

"Okay, let's move on from fennel and hemlock. Tell me again ... and think carefully ... what was the position of the mugs on the counter when you first poked your head in the front door and saw Natasha pouring the drinks?"

She rolled her eyes. "This is unbelievably stupid. I don't have time for this!"

"If you answer the question, you will have more time."

"Fine. The mugs were positioned like a two-handled trophy," Sheila said. "The same way they always are. Clayton liked precision."

"What was the position of the mugs when you returned? After Natasha had left," Arnold asked.

"Irrelevant, but easy," she said. "One mug was gone. Obviously, Natasha drank hers before she left for her run."

"Natasha says she always has her drink after her run. She was expecting it to be there when she returned. But the mug was gone."

"Then she lied. It was gone because she drank it, cleaned the mug, and put it away."

"That's speculation, Sheila. Try to stay with the facts. We can finish quicker that way."

"Fine. But it's obvious. I know I did not take the mug, and so clearly, she did. There was no one else around. I thought the police were at least capable of logical deduction."

"What position was Clayton's mug when you returned? Was the handle turned different than usual?"

"Clayton's handle was wrong when I returned. I told you that. The handle should have been turned to the left, but it wasn't. It was turned away from the door. Clayton wouldn't have approved. Natasha must have moved it before she left."

"Why would she have moved Clayton's mug? If she poisoned him, that would be suspicious."

"I can't answer that question," Sheila said, seeming inordinately tired of the whole thing. Sighing, she looked around her clean kitchen. "But I can tell you, Arnold, that if you are looking for cleaners, call Martha Clapperton. She came in here, and without a single recriminating word, which frankly I was expecting, she cleaned this house so well that I hardly recognize it. It was an impulse decision, frankly. I thought if Clayton wasn't going to take me away from all this, I might as well get someone to clean the place. Granted, it cost me, and now that I'm a single mother, I'm not made of money. What they pay nurses is a crime, I tell you. If you want to investigate something, you should investigate social injustice. I haven't had a raise in two years, and my duties keep expanding. I work my fingers to the bone, but I don't get ahead. That's my life, Arnold. It is not pretty, let me tell you, and now all I have is Hank to fuck, and he is just not that skilled. Not like Clayton. Those days of pleasure I enjoyed are gone, but I have to let it go. What choice do I have? Dead men don't fuck."

If she had been hoping to distract him with this rant, it failed. "How many minutes did you wait before returning to Clayton's house?" he asked then. "You simply walked to the alley and had a smoke?"

"That's right. I don't know how many minutes though. Whatever time it took to walk to the alley, have a Rothmans, and return to the house." Sheila's facial muscles were so tense, it looked as though her head would explode.

"Could you see the front door of the house from the alley?"

"Yes, I could see the front door. I was standing near the footpath entrance to the woodland trail. Maybe halfway between Clayton's house and mine."

"How soon did Natasha leave after you had poked your head in and seen her at the counter?"

"Just a few minutes. It wasn't long. She was already wearing her running clothes, so she was ready to go."

"Did anyone come into the house or leave while you waited?"

"No. I had my smoke in the alley and walked in the front door."

"Could you see the back door?"

"No, I couldn't. Obviously. How could I see both the front and back door at the same time?"

"You usually go into the house from the back door, right?"

"That's true. Clayton leaves it open for me."

"You can see the alley quite well from there?"

"Oh, yes. Once, when I was entering the house through the back door, I saw a group of teenagers in the alley, smoking weed. It smelled like weed anyway, and it must have been. They were laughing. Teenagers don't laugh in Northford unless they're on something."

"After seeing Natasha at the counter, did you have any reason to be concerned for Clayton's well-being?"

"Not at the time. They've always had their weird nutritional habits. It was only later, when I heard that Clayton had been poisoned, that I remembered the musty smell and all that. If I had suspected at the time that the mug was poisoned, I would have warned him."

"What did you do after handing Clayton his drink?"

"He was in the workshop. We talked for a minute or so. Not much to say, really. He wanted to have sex again, and so we did. But I already told you that."

"Did he drink at all from his breakfast mug?"

"Oh no, he was too busy for that. Generally, he drinks his mug after sex. The mug was still full when I left. It was still sitting on the workshop table, along with the cake. We fucked on the car hood. A bit rough, which he liked. But I told you that already too, didn't I?"

"You did. Rather than move the drink and the cake, you had sex on the car hood."

"Correct. Why shouldn't I? I like sex, okay?"

Sheila was growing quite agitated by this point. She went to the refrigerator and started unloading items, seemingly at random. "I have lunches to prepare, Sergeant, if it's all the same to you. I don't have all day to blather on about the death of one man, who was, to be honest, not all that nice to me. What can I say? I do miss the sex, but I will get over it. I have Hank in my life now. He's more helpful than Clayton anyway, although rather ignorant. Funny how that is. Clayton was smart but not helpful. He refused to participate in trivial conversation. Hank is not the brightest person, but he loves to help. He's also quite good at trivial conversation. I don't mind that, since neither of us has anything interesting to say anyway, but at least we say something. Thankfully, the conversations are never long."

Just then, Hank Goertzen trudged into the kitchen from the hallway. He was wearing striped pajamas, with the top shirt open, his muscular chest in full view of the refrigerator's light. "Anything I can do to help?" Hank offered. "Fix that curtain rod maybe?"

Sheila thanked him but said she was all good and that he should wait for her in the other room. Once he was gone, she looked at Arnold. "See what I mean? I am so over Clayton. He never offered to fix a thing. But still, I didn't kill him or anything. Neither did Hank. Hank is very principled that way."

"Good to hear, Sheila," Arnold said. "I hear that he has flexible views on throwing a ball game though. Still, it's good to see your grieving process has gone well. So, just to confirm your story, Sheila, as far as you remember, the mug placement on the counter changed between the first time you looked in on Natasha and when you returned after she left."

"Yes, it was changed."

"Alright. One final thing, Sheila. Has Dan done laundry since Saturday? Or did you?"

"Dan did his whites on Sunday. Getting ready to move out."

"Does he generally do his own laundry?"

She shook her head, looking at him like he was crazy or stupid. "Why on earth would you care about his laundry?" Then she held her hand up as if to stop him from answering, which he'd had no intentions of doing. "Doesn't matter. I have never done Dan's laundry. I don't have time for that. I'm too busy as it is. Run off my feet what with being a nurse and a mother."

"I am beginning to understand that, Sheila."

Arnold got up to leave, but before he did, he bent down to pick up a small shard of broken coffee mug from beneath the table, which the wonderful Martha Clapperton had apparently missed, and he placed it in the wastebasket.

CHAPTER 34

ARNOLD PREPARES FOR THE DAY

Arnold padded down the hall to his kitchen and turned on the coffee percolator at the counter, beside a stack of *Sport* magazines that he had been perusing the night before. The cheeseburger and fries from the previous night weren't sitting well. The food had tasted great at the time, but now, combined with a restless night's sleep, his body was feeling a distaste for any kind of food, including burgers. Arnold considered that his fascination with cheeseburgers could use some review. A few days of Cobb salad would be good for his health, he decided.

The percolator beeped, and Arnold poured himself a coffee. He took his coffee cup to the sunroom and sat down, looking over his notes. Sipping his coffee, he mused about possibly visiting Natasha again. *Necessary or not?* He decided that it was and hoped that, after his chat with Dan, she might be more forthcoming. He finished his coffee and then wandered back into the kitchen for some breakfast. He looked in the fridge and decided that nothing desirable lived there. It didn't take long to decide that driving to the Dickey Dee for a breakfast sandwich was the answer.

In less than ten minutes, Arnold was sitting in a protected corner of the Dickey Dee patio. He ordered a breakfast sandwich, a soft egg with sausage and cheese, and another coffee, and sat back to ponder why his upper body was sweating profusely. He often felt that he was coming down with something, bronchitis being a family trait he had inherited from his father. His fresh undershirt was soaking wet and starting to seep through into his RCMP-issue shirt. He decided that after his sandwich, he would go home and change before visiting Natasha. She would notice. He did not want to give her any more reason to feel superior.

It was late morning, and the sun beat down directly on Arnold's table. He took his jacket off and rolled up his shirt sleeves. It didn't help. He considered moving out of the sun, to an empty table on the north side of the restaurant, but he didn't feel up to moving. A housefly was flitting around his head, landing for short moments only to take off again, seemingly in a desperate search for the perfect perch.

Arnold did not like flies. He wondered whether they had any significant purpose. He knew, of course, that they were (at minimum) a food source for other insects and animals, and as such, they played a role in the ecosystem, just as he did. (He still disliked them though.) He felt quite certain that his own life served no significant purpose either, and that in due course, he would also become nothing but a food source. Just like Clayton Dalrymple, he would only exist for a short time within an infinity of not existing. Arnold reflected on this truth for a while, and then his breakfast sandwich arrived, and he ate, savouring each bite and thinking about what he would do with the truth of Clayton's death when it finally solidified.

Arnold thought about Natasha and her son. He thought about the metal sculpture he'd seen in Clayton's workshop: an adult man with his arms wrapped around a child. It was a beautiful and loving art piece from a man who had been unable to demonstrate love in his actual life. It made the statue touching, but at the same time, undeniably tragic.

CHAPTER 35

ARNOLD VISITS WITH NATASHA AGAIN

Natasha did not offer Arnold a seat as he sauntered into her office without notice. The south window revealed that the Central Park water feature was working again. Water was spraying thirty feet into the air in an intermittent pattern. The lights on the fountain presented the water with an array of rainbow colours. It was a beautiful fountain when it worked, and Natasha had an exceptionally bountiful view of it, along with the walkways and greenery of Central Park, and the golden brown of autumn leaves.

There was silence initially, though Natasha had smiled warmly at his arrival, surprising him. He had not been expecting that. Her face was softer than on previous encounters. She even looked vulnerable. Still guarded, but somewhat less so.

"Was it disappointing not to find anything in my house, Arnold?" she asked finally. "All those police working overtime, with so little results. I almost felt for you, though not really. Anyway, I hear that Dan has been sharing. I also hear that you have a theory I should be concerned about, but that it lacks evidence. Is this true?"

"It is," he said, sitting down on the only available chair. "I am developing a theory that has merit but lacks evidence. But this is not a permanent state of affairs. Sadly, you and Dan both have an alibi. That is also, I might add, not a permanent state of affairs."

"You feel that our alibis are not strong?"

"They are based on some assumptions that will not ultimately hold up."

"I disagree, Arnold. I feel good about mine. Of course, it helps to be innocent."

"Innocence is the best defense. But someone poisoned and shot Clayton."

"Really?" Natasha asked, putting down her pen and squinting inquisitively at Arnold. "I heard a rumour that Clayton had poisoned himself at the scene and then shot himself. Odd way to commit suicide, but the world is full of odd occurrences."

"Do you believe that?"

"What difference does it make what I believe? Anyway, I am sure that you will find the answer to all of your questions in due course," Natasha said calmly.

"Clayton ordered you to attend the aster meadow with him on Saturday morning for the purpose of double suicide?"

"You know that he did."

"You believed that Clayton was going to kill you?"

"Of course. He promised."

"You are asking us to believe that you were prepared to accept death and not take action to protect yourself."

"That is correct."

"I find that hard to believe."

Natasha scoffed, her walls going up again. Now she sat behind her desk as though it were bulletproof, seeming to feel entirely safe. It annoyed Arnold. If she did have anything to hide, she was able to repress it remarkably, pushing it into some deep recess of her mind, confident that Northford police would never be able to access it.

"Many things are hard to believe, Arnold, but I cannot help you with that."

"Generally, when something is hard to believe, it is because it's not true."

"That is sometimes the case. Perhaps often. But not this time."

"You say that you were surprised when, coming home after your run, you discovered that Clayton had left without you."

"I said that because it is true. I was surprised, confused, and cautiously optimistic."

"You say that you did not call the police because you felt that Dan might be involved."

"It occurred to me as a possibility. I had perhaps overshared with him."

"You did more than that."

"What else did I do? I would love to know."

"You know what you did. But I will play along. You and Dan set up false alibis."

"That is ridiculous, Sergeant. You know where Dan was that morning. You also know where I was."

He noticed that she was back to calling him Sergeant, instead of Arnold. "I do know where you were before nine. That part of the alibi is fine. But after nine, your alibi is false. So is Dan's. You both tried to trick me."

"Trick you how?"

"I don't believe I need to answer that question, Natasha. You know how."

Natasha paused for a long moment, looking out the window, with the water fountain spewing high into the cool autumn air. Taking a deep breath, she said, "I don't want to trick anyone."

"Then why did you?"

After another long moment of silence, her shoulders dropped a bit. "Because Dan asked me to. He wanted me drive his Falcon to the office at nine. To wear his jacket and hat. To appear to be him. I did as he asked. That was deception, for sure. But I didn't kill Clayton. Neither did Dan."

"I actually believe that. So why the elaborate deception?"

"You understand that I didn't kill Clayton?"

"I do."

"Do you understand that Dan didn't either?"

"Yes. Technically, Dan did not kill Clayton."

"So, what did he do?"

"I suspect that you know much of what he did. Perhaps not all of it, though. I'm not sure. But let me leave that explanation for later. Right now, I want to know where the money is."

"What money?"

"Clayton embezzled money from the Arts Centre and the Mega-Church project. He cashed out at the bank last week, but he had nothing on his person in the woods. There is nothing in your home safe and nothing in his safety deposit box. Where is the cash? Perhaps you hid it in the Goodhand picture frame?"

"You are a man of deep suspicion, Arnold. It was simply a painting," Natasha said.

"The postmaster said that the painting was quite heavy. Must have had a large frame."

"It did. I got it framed at Clapperton's art supply. It was a good frame for the picture."

He nodded. "I have a strong feeling that, for your purposes, it was a perfect frame."

CHAPTER 36

ARNOLD MEETS WITH INSPECTOR DICK SANDERS

At two o'clock on Saturday afternoon, a week after Clayton's death, Inspector Sanders was still in Northford and not pleased about it. A meeting had been called at Arnold Powell's office, and Sanders arrived late as usual, coughing and looking like the apocalypse had arrived, still buttoning up his shirt, revealing a concave but hairy chest. It was not a pretty scene by any standard. Sanders said that he had been napping. "Goddam Capri will be the death of me," he muttered. "The noise from the bar builds all evening. Hits a crescendo peak around one in the morning, gradually resolving into the quiet of a drunken stupor by two, by which time all I can do is pray that death will come and take me. Which, incidentally, is a prayer that has been answered."

Arnold frowned from where he was standing by the window. taking a sip from a cup of steaming coffee that (amazingly) had been made that day. "Answered in what way?"

"The incident at Ken's office, falling out the back door, and then my cough, encouraged the doctors to dig around in my body. They have discovered that I am dying. Not to be too obscure about it. I appear to have cancer. Beyond treatable, they say. If I was brave, I might be inclined to shoot myself. But I am not brave. Anyway, enough about me. Let us review what we know about this case," Sanders said, settling himself into Arnold Powell's chair. He clearly had a thing about sitting in other people's chairs.

The room was silent for a moment, as Inspector Sanders took out a cigarette, lit it, and blew a perfectly oval smoke ring that collapsed against Arnold Powell's notebook.

"I am sorry to hear that," Arnold said. "The cough was a symptom of the cancer?"

"It was, and it is," Sanders said. "Not much time left, thankfully. But let us not belabour my problems. They are short lived. I am not an advocate of unnecessary ceremony. I was about to retire anyway. What does a retired policeman do? Review old cases. I will not have to do that. But speaking of reviewing a case, are we at a place where we can finally put this Clayton business to bed? I know you're busy trying to uncover the truth of his death, and I'm sure it will make for fascinating reading, which I imagine Emily Little is working on as we speak. But first, remind me what we actually know."

"We know that Henry McCroskey is a highly motivated hard-cheese sling-shooter," Arnold said, inhaling the lovely aroma of his coffee. "Today's coffee isn't bad. But it'll be better tomorrow."

"Yes, indeed." Sanders sighed, enjoying the view of unsolved files surrounding the desk as he swivelled back and forth in Arnold's chair. "Love it when the expectations of tomorrow are like that. Yes indeed, Henry McCroskey is a damn good shot. Remarkable young man. Good listener too. We should hire him. He would probably have this case wrapped up by now. What else?"

"Clayton died of poison, not a gunshot. But of course, he was also shot with a gun. Leaving out the slingshot incident for now, the gunshot occurred about an hour after he was poisoned. Dr. Morley has definitively determined this. All of which makes it difficult to argue that he poisoned himself and then shot himself at the meadow. A person who takes hemlock would not wait an hour to shoot himself. He would have been incapacitated within thirty minutes."

"Dr. Morley tends to be wrong a fair bit," Sanders muttered. "He is certainly capable of being off by an hour or so. Based on past performance, I don't think we can describe anything Dr. Morley determines as definitive. Let's stay with what we actually know. Personally, I prefer the idea of

Clayton taking poison at the meadow and shooting himself. I think we should go with that. But I digress. What else do we know?"

"We know that the breakfast juice at the woods tested positive for hemlock. Of course, we also believe that it was tampered with."

"Possibly, Arnold, but we do not know that for sure."

"We have reasonable suspicion of tampering," Arnold surmised. "Dr. Morley and Doc went to the lab, and suddenly, the cake evidence disappears and the juice residue goes from negative to positive. If it wasn't tampered with, it was a miracle."

"Miracles happen, Arnold," Sanders warned.

"Well, I do hope, for your sake, that they do."

"I don't," Sanders mumbled. "I am ready to walk through the final door. Let me go, Arnold. It's fine. It's my turn. Bring on the facts, Arnold. Do we have any more?"

"The poisoned cake crumbs in the Mustang were not put there by Clayton. He didn't eat cake. The cake we found in Clayton's garbage bin was clean of toxins. That means that someone was at the Dalrymples, putting the cake in the garbage, poisoning a small piece, and placing it in the car. It also means that poison was being used in the Dalrymple workshop. Hard to believe that Clayton would throw out clean cake, poison some crumbs, drop them in his car, and then drive to the woods, drink poison, wait an hour, and in his dying moments, shoot himself. Completely derails your theory that he poisoned himself in the woods, Sanders. Sorry."

"No need to be sorry, Arnold. Your points are well taken. Something we will need to deal with, I suppose. But my theory continues to be a better fit with the general mood."

"Fine," Arnold said. "I'll play along. We also know that Clayton's prints are on his gun, and the bullet is from his gun."

"Wonderful," Sanders said, leaning Arnold's chair back as far as it would go. Sanders studied the ceiling for a moment, noting that a stain in the corner of the ceiling was spoiling the view. He wondered whether Arnold was aware. "Sometimes, you jump to conclusions, Arnold. We have witnesses who saw Clayton drive to the woods a little after nine on Saturday morning and parked at the forest road by 9:10. We have his boot prints leading from his car to the meadow, and none returning. Clearly, he walked to the meadow with his poisoned drink and drank it. Then he waited for a while to reflect on how badly he felt, and in due course, when the reflection was more than even the Russian in him could handle, he shot himself."

"That does appear to be an explanation that is supported by the witnesses," Arnold said hesitantly.

"You seem disappointed by this explanation, Arnold," Sanders said. "You don't agree?"

"I do not. Too much tampering with evidence. There would have been no need for tampering if Clayton simply killed himself."

"As usual, Arnold, I'm sure that you're right. However, we have no proof of tampering, do we? We think the cake crumbs were planted, but it would be hard to prove that, considering that we have no cake crumbs. They have disappeared."

"Suspiciously," Arnold said.

"You are a very skeptical man, Arnold," Sanders observed.

"In this instance, there's good cause for skepticism."

"Of course, there is. There is always good cause for skepticism. But it's a hell of way to live. I prefer to look at the big picture and size up the demands of the moment. If I can speak off the record for a moment, I confess that I am not satisfied with the poison/gunshot suicide story myself, but it is the explanation that we need. It solves a lot of grief for quite a few people. We all know that testing errors were made, but through police diligence and a willingness on our part to take a second look at our own work, we finally arrived at a satisfying conclusion. External Affairs will like it. Ottawa head office will like it. I cannot speak for the Soviets, but I think it is reasonable to believe that they'll like it as well. Saves them the bother of executing Clayton or sending him to some recovery camp deep in the Siberian outback. Of course, we have some details to massage, but I think the story can be made to work. You may find my approach to this matter difficult, troublesome even, but I tell you, Arnold, you can go ahead and pursue your alternative theory, and maybe you will even manage a confession or two, but at the end of the day, I predict that you'll agree with me that the best story, all things considered, is that he did himself in."

"Even though you know perfectly well that he didn't."

"Arnold, that's a major reason we need the story I am proposing," Sanders said. "I think you will find that the truth will hurt a lot of people, while helping no one. There are times for truth, but this isn't one of them. But please, feel free to tell me what you think happened."

CHAPTER 37

ARNOLD HAS A BEER WITH ANNIE

Saturday evening, Arnold Powell went for beers with Annie. He had gone home to watch the end of the Oakland A's playoff game against the Boston Red Sox. Boston had prevailed again, taking a two-game lead. Arnold had been confident that Vida Blue would dominant the Boston hitters, but he hadn't.

Arnold and Annie sat at a corner of the Capri Hotel bar, trying to stay removed from the young people who were hanging around the pool table. Arnold sipped his Extra Old Stock and sighed. "Been a long day," he confessed. "Had interesting sessions with Dan, Natasha, and then, Inspector Sanders."

"Anything new?" Annie asked.

"Sanders is dying. Terminal cancer. He also thinks the truth of this case will hurt a lot of people. He isn't planning on pursuing it."

"But you still want to know the truth?"

"Yes, I do."

"Do you know what you'll do with it?"

"Not sure. But I still want to know. Then choices can be made."

"I understand that. But I also think that you might regret it," Annie said. "I think Sanders might be right."

"What are you saying, Annie? Do you know something?"

"All I know is that Ken and I make a good singing duo," she said with a smirk.

"You two are awesome," he said with a grin. "Is Ken joining us? He's welcome to. It's not like we're having an affair or anything," He took a deep swig from his beer.

"That's more or less what he said."

"More or less?"

"Both more and less, I guess. He said that he realized that he was welcome to join us, and confident that we weren't having an affair. He also said that he had more interesting things to do, which I suspect means that he's aware that he's putting on weight, and even though he loves beer (probably more than life itself), he's desperately afraid of his expanding waistline. He didn't say that, but I'm confident that's what he meant."

"I had no idea that Ken was concerned about his physicality."

"We all are, Arnold. Vanity is one of the last things we lose with age. At our age, maybe no one else cares what we look like, but we do. I can tell you, though, that Ken is also concerned about investment in Northford and wishes this nasty Clayton business hadn't happened—even though it means he no longer has to deal with the man. Ken says we need business investment to pay for the new water-treatment plant. Infrastructure is expensive. We can't pay for it with residential property taxes alone. It takes business taxes to support the kind of infrastructure we need."

"I am sure that Ken's right," Arnold said. "Not that it helps me with this case. What are you hearing about Clayton's death anyway? People are always talking trash at the Dickey Dee."

"That they are. Rumour has it that the case is wrapping up. Suicide seems to be the word. Any truth to that?"

"That's what Sanders says," Arnold said.

"It might be best," Annie said, taking a long drink from her glass. "Good beer. Not the bottom of the keg like usual."

"People like talking to you, Annie. You should open a burger place. You could be quite successful."

"Very funny. Oh, by the way, Emily Little is going to join us," she said rather glibly. "She says she has something you'll be interested in."

"Sanders will be pleased." Arnold ordered another beer, while a sober Emily Little strode into the bar, carrying a manila envelope, and slipped into a seat beside them.

CHAPTER 38

EMILY HAS AN ANNOUNCEMENT

Emily Little was wearing a loose-fitting tie-dye t-shirt with red hip-hugger jeans and black boots. She was holding a manila envelope and she placed it gently in front of Arnold.

"Today is the day that I bring *you* news," she said. Despite her colourful attire, she was more subdued then usual. "It seems Ivan Kalik, more commonly known as Clayton Dalrymple, sent the newspaper a confession, which we apparently received yesterday but I only discovered this morning. The envelope was addressed to me. I have read it, and though I'm not sure that it solves your case, it might. At least, it might if you can look past the fact that his confession doesn't reflect what actually happened."

Arnold could hardly believe this, but eagerly opened the envelope, pulled out its contents, and started reading:

By the time anyone reads this, I will be dead. I will have shot myself in the aster meadow. This will come as a pleasant surprise for some, especially Natasha, as I had promised her that we would drive to the meadow together on Saturday morning, and that both our lives would end. I told her that I would shoot her, and then myself. But this will not happen. I have not advised her of my change in plan because I choose not to. This is, I think, my prerogative. The fear of death is considerable punishment in itself. Natasha will feel this angst on Saturday. She believes that she is going to die because I told her she would. Generally, I am a man of my word when it comes to threats of violence. But this time, I have changed my mind. Natasha will not die. She will have a better day than she was expecting, given a reprieve from death. She will also be free of me. She will like that.

Initially, when I first informed Natasha of my double suicide plan, it was a trick. My intention was to shoot her and escape the country. But Natasha ruined that for me. She found my airline ticket and called the authorities to warn them of my escape plans. Escape became much more difficult, dauntingly tiresome, and in the end, of no interest to me. Still, I realize that if I do not escape, I will be handed over to the Soviets. That is not going to happen. I will kill myself.

I will die in the aster meadow. My body will be found in a pleasant place. The gunshot will make a mess. But microbes will take care of that and leave behind some fertile Ivan Kalik compost.

I presume that I have been found by now, but if not, you can advise the authorities of my location. My guess is that Dan will find me. He walks the nature path on Saturdays and can be counted on to linger at the meadow. He regularly mentions his love of it in the Arts Centre staff room. He insists that the flowers and shrubs attract a varied selection of birds. I will take his word for it. I am quite confident that, regardless of the bird activity at the meadow, if Dan discovers me, he will find the experience quite satisfying. But he will not be the only one satisfied by my departure. I leave behind a crowd of locals who will smile at my demise.

I believe that my death will be apology enough to all my local enemies. But there are a few people for whom special mention is warranted.

Dr. Robert Morley will enjoy performing an autopsy on me. The cutting of my dead flesh will, I believe, please him. He may even whistle one of his incessant Broadway tunes. My death provides a considerable upside for Robert. Perhaps, most importantly, it allows him to return to being the king of Northford chess. I was, of course, a vastly superior player to Dr. Morley, but I did unnecessarily humiliate him. Dr. Morley can also return to being an amateur scholar, free to present his limited knowledge without my critical interjections and dismissiveness. Dr. Morley is not as knowledgeable as he thinks, but he is also not as ignorant as I have tried to portray him. Being competitive has always been a love of mine. There is nothing wrong with demonstrating knowledge, but admittedly, as Dr.

Morley will attest, I could have learned to do so more gracefully. Too late for that.

Ken Russell can return to being the mayor without my spreading misinformation about him. I have been loose with the truth. I admit that. I have unduly harmed his reputation. He is a good mayor, committed to the city. He is also a good singer, and he and Annie have entertained Northford with their harmonies for years. And myself as well. I have disrupted his life here, damaged his reputation, and even caused him to consider leaving politics. That would be a shame. It is not easy for people to take on civic duties, and they should be respected for the service they give. I did not do that.

Still, I think it should be said that Ken Russell is not as innocent in all of his doings as he presents. In particular, the city seizure of the Capri Hotel was self serving. I have no love for William Sawatzky. He is deluded. So is his wife. The city sale of the Capri was not wrong, but the fact that the mayor benefitted from the sale always struck me as questionable. Nevertheless, Ken brought me some Medovik cake that Annie made, and while I was cool to his peace offering, I concede that he tried. It is more than I did.

Sheila McCroskey may or may not be happy for my demise. She did appear to enjoy our affair, although I was never entirely sure why. I did not treat her well, was physically aggressive and rude to her, but she kept coming back. Perhaps I benefitted from her obsessive desire to punish her husband for his limited traditional masculinity. Dan has objectionable qualities to be sure. I avoided conversation with him for good reason. He is tedious, consistently overrating the value of ancient knowledge. But he is also creatively gifted, curious, and passionate. Sheila married the wrong man for her, but she will not find another man as gifted, and decent, as he is. Sheila will find another man, but he will be like me. Hopefully, for her sake, somewhat less so.

I need to also mention the young Janet Sawatzky. She agreed to have sex with me, encouraged no doubt, at least in some measure, by my offer to sponsor her medical-school training. But then, she impressively informed me that she wanted to stop. She held her position and forced me, by way of her determination, to accept it. I acknowledge that I took advantage of her desire to rebel against her parents and experience the adult world. Janet is a good listener, and a sharp, insightful young woman. Despite her parents being certifiable, Janet is remarkably astute, principled, after a fashion, and skilled at sizing up her circumstances. She will likely be indifferent regarding my demise. She will have a good life, I hope, despite her involvement with me. She will continue to be sponsored. I have left money for her in a trust.

A word to my brother-in-law, Alexei Rubenstein. We were marginally friends at one point, but circumstances changed. It did not help our friendship that I had his father was arrested and sent to his death at a labour camp. For me, it was the beginning of a KGB career path. For Alexei, it was the beginning of a deep distrust and distaste for me.

Granted, Alexei also benefitted from my KGB position. I was able to facilitate the request that Alexei and Sophia immigrate to Canada. I might add that it was not an altruistic move on my part. I wanted to get rid of Alexei. He was having an affair with Natasha, and I preferred that he leave the country.

Finally, a note to Natasha, the person who will likely benefit the most from my demise.

Natasha never liked me. But she married me to advance her situation. She understood that there would be a cost to that decision, and there was. I facilitated her entrance to the Bolshoi, among other favours, including helping Sophia and Alexei emigrate, securing both a quality apartment for her mother in the Soviet Union and a research position for Sophia in Canada. I have been useful, but I do not work for free.

This week, Natasha and I had a truth-telling conversation. She discovered that I was responsible for Sophia's death. She is right. I did kill Sophia. Sophia had come to Irkutsk for her mother's dying days, and the night before she was to return to Canada, we got into an argument at a Lake Baikal resort restaurant. Sophia knew about my criminal activities within the KGB and threatened to expose me. I was, at the time, positioned to be sent to the Russian Embassy in Ottawa, where I planned to defect. I had a lot on the line. As we walked back to the hotel along the banks of Lake Baikal, a high cliff presented an opportunity, and I took it. I pushed Sophia into the lake and watched as she slowly slid under the ice. I was placed in charge of investigating, and naturally, determined that Sophia had fallen in and drowned. Of course, she did.

Natasha also advised me that I am not the father of Fyodor. I had always thought that I was. One of the reasons I wanted to defect was to be close to Fyodor. It was heartbreaking to learn this truth. I knew that Natasha had been pregnant, and had switched identities with Sophia, so that Fyodor could be born in Canada. I did not have a problem with this. I wanted Fyodor to have Western opportunities. But finding out that I was not the father was a devastation. This information explained why I had not been allowed access to Fyodor in Northford, but it also led to my already growing despondency. I realized the degree to which my efforts at manipulation had proven to be unsuccessful.

I had always understood that Sophia and Alexei would raise Fyodor, and that it was in the boy's interest that Natasha and I be treated as an aunt and uncle. I had imagined, though, that when Fyodor came of age, we would collectively inform him who his true parents were. That is what my mother did. As a teenager, living near Chita, near Lake Baikal, she informed me that my true father had been found dead in the woods on the day that I was born. He had been hiking into Chita for help in my delivery but was shot by the man who took his place. This man was only my stepfather, rather than my true father, as I had believed until my mother's confession. My mother lived in difficult times and made questionable choices that she was not proud of. I am in no position to judge her, as I have also made such choices. So, it is.

I am quite certain that there is no more to say about my short time on this planet. It is done.

Clayton Dalrymple (Ivan Kalik)

Arnold finished reading the confession and replaced the document in its envelope. Swigging down the last of his Old Stock, he shook his head.

"Sounds like your case is solved," Emily said. "He admits to shooting himself."

"He does. But he didn't shoot himself. He was poisoned."

"He could have decided to add poison to the program," Emily said. "To make sure. To add some suffering to the event. He could have done both. He does admit to changing his plans. He was in a state of despondency, as he says. Maybe he felt he deserved to suffer the poison's effects for a while before ending things quickly with a bullet."

"He could have, but he didn't," Arnold said. "I accept that the confessional describes what Clayton intended for Saturday morning, but it's not what happened. Somebody interfered with his plan. We might end up using the confession. Sanders will certainly like it. I might come to like it as well. But at present, I don't. In any case, my department is checking out a promising theory as we speak. Hopefully the answers it turns up will be more satisfying than the questions."

CHAPTER 39

ARNOLD GETS A SURPRISE VISITOR

Janet Sawatzky arrived at Arnold's office, pausing at the door for a long moment (looking in at him) before entering. Then she walked directly to the visitor's chair and sat down, smiling nervously all the while. She wore a New York Yankees ball cap low over her eyes, as if the sun were glaring, which no doubt it was somewhere, though not in Arnold's office. As she settled into the uncomfortable chair, she zipped her blue fleece jacket right up to her neck, as though it were cold in the office, which it wasn't.

"Thanks for coming to the station, Janet," Arnold said, still standing, as he had risen to welcome her to his office and gesture for her to take a seat. "Could I get you something to drink? A coffee perhaps? Do you drink coffee?"

"That's a lot of questions, Sergeant," Janet remarked, still smiling. "I don't drink coffee, but if I did, I believe I'd still decline. The coffee here at the station is not highly recommended."

Arnold sat back down and looked kindly at her. He tried his best to pose as a friendly adult, not an interrogating police officer. This was a challenge, considering that he was an interrogating police officer. "I need to clarify a few things with you, Janet. You told me in our last visit that you do not go to your parents' home. Is that correct?"

"Yes, that's right. They banned me from the property when they disowned me," Janet said, pushing her hands into her jacket pockets, her

300

smile finally disappearing even as her posture softened a bit, as though in resignation.

"In that case, why did we find your fingerprints on your parents' garden-shed door?"

Janet paused. "Perhaps I'm wrong, but it's not a crime to go there just because they banned me. Sadly, they're still my parents."

"They are. But I would have thought you'd try to go to the house, not the shed."

"The advantage of the garden shed is that my parents are not there. They tend to be in the house."

"The other advantage of the garden shed is that it held water hemlock plants."

She nodded. "For people who like water hemlock, I suppose that *is* an advantage."

"And what is *your* position on water hemlock?" Arnold asked, trying to appear as casual as possible on the subject.

"I think it can be a useful plant."

"Useful for killing people?"

"I suppose. But it's also useful for saving lives. They keep all sorts of herbal remedies in there. Always have. Why are you asking?"

"Because water hemlock was the cause of Clayton's death."

She was silent for a moment, thinking deeply, before finally seeming to come to a decision of some sort. "It was also what saved Natasha from certain death."

"Did it?" Arnold asked innocently, looking at Janet and then outside the west window of his office.

"That's the way I prefer to look at it."

"I suppose that you would. On another matter, you told me that you heard Dan and Natasha talking in her office on Friday evening. Did you hear what they said?"

"Not clearly," Janet responded. "But Natasha was concerned about being killed by Clayton. I told you that. I decided not to interrupt. It was clear to me that Natasha knew about Clayton's plans."

"His plans to kill Natasha on Saturday morning?"

"That's right."

301

"But you did not inform the police."

"I didn't think anyone would believe me."

"So, you took action," Arnold said softly.

"I did. I had no choice," Janet said, seemingly resigned to the truth. "I had the capacity to save Natasha, and so I did. I took water hemlock from my parents' shed on Friday night. I had a plan. Worked perfectly too."

"You waited for Natasha to leave on Saturday morning. You saw Sheila light up a smoke in the alley. You knew you had time to slip in the back door, deposit some hemlock in Clayton's drink, and leave. And that's what you did. Your fingerprints are on the back door."

Janet paused a long while before forming her answer. "It's true. That's all the time I needed." She frowned. "I have to ask how you know this, Arnold. As soon as I got here, I could tell you'd figured it out. I could see it on your face, but ... I was pretty sure my plan was perfect."

"It was very near perfect, Janet. But you removed Natasha's mug and moved Clayton's. That was a mistake. What was your thinking there?"

"I wanted to make sure that Clayton drank the mug with poison. I couldn't take a chance of a mix up. So, I dumped Natasha's mug and put it away. I might have moved Clayton's mug a bit. But how was that suspicious?"

"Because Clayton was fussy about his mug placement. You didn't know that."

"But I had an alibi for Saturday morning."

"Your alibi was soft. You said you slept late before going to the library. But I noticed you had grass stains on your new sneakers. You didn't get that from going to the library along the sidewalk. But Doc saw a backpacker crossing the fairgrounds around seven o'clock that morning, even though the hostel was closed, which was odd. I checked the backpack in the prop room, and sure enough, it had a few hairs on the back straps that probably belonged to you, Janet. We can test them if we need to, although I've pressed pause on doing so for now.

"In any case, finding them prompted a search of your parents' garden shed, where your father recently told me they kept a variety of natural remedies. We found both water hemlock and your fingerprints on the door, just as we found them on the back door of Clayton's house. There was about a ten-minute window of opportunity between Natasha leaving for her run, and Sheila's return. Clayton was in his bedroom, waiting for her. All you had to do was wait for Natasha to leave and get in and out before Sheila finished her cigarette."

"But how did you know it was me? Natasha or Sheila could have poisoned Clayton. They both had opportunity and motive."

"That is certainly true. But you were the only one who didn't know about Clayton's fussy mug-placement fetish."

She shrugged and shook her head, seeming worn out and tired by the whole thing. "You got me, Arnold. I poisoned him. It was wrong, obviously, but in my view, it was still the right thing to do. I'm willing to pay the price for that. I had to save Natasha. She didn't deserve to die. But I didn't shoot Clayton. Or hit him on the head with cheese. From what I hear, that's how you found him?"

"I know, Janet. You also didn't move his body to the woods."

CHAPTER 40

ARNOLD DROPS IN ON NATASHA

Natasha was in the front yard when Arnold pulled up, raking fall leaves, and looking more relaxed than he had yet seen her. She was wearing a pair of white Foster sneakers, blue jeans that had a high, tight waist, and a loose peasant top with embroidery trim. Her jeans were a perfect match for the circle of blue Adirondack chairs on the paving-stone patio, with small side tables between them. A small fire burned in the metal firepit. The patio was surrounded by four well-developed Japanese Lilac trees. She smiled brightly as Arnold emerged from his cruiser. "Fine fall day, Arnold. Could be my last chance to rake leaves. You come by often enough I don't need to offer her a seat, do I? A drink? I make a very nice Arnold Palmer."

"I'm on the job, Natasha," Arnold said, rather more stiffly than he intended. He didn't sit down, though he wanted to.

"It is non-alcoholic," Natasha said in a pleasantly engaging tone. "Three parts iced tea, one part lemonade. Quite tasty. Clayton sometimes complimented me on the drink. He didn't think that I was much good at anything, really. Maybe dancing. Not that he cared about dancing, or me, for that matter."

"In that case, Natasha, it would be my pleasure," Arnold said, finally deciding to give in and sitting down in one of the Adirondack chairs. It was quite low, and he felt awkwardly unprofessional in it.

Natasha went inside to make the drinks, and in a few minutes, came back out with a tray carrying two large glasses filled with ice, a pitcher of cold tea and lemonade, a few cloth napkins, and a pink depression-glass plate, on which sat what remained of the Medovik cake, sliced into quite small portions. Slices of lemon floated in the pitcher. Putting the tray down on the small table beside Arnold, Natasha filled both glasses and handed him one before settling down in the Adirondack chair next to him. "Help yourself to the Medovik cake, Arnold. Still surprisingly moist. Please, have it or take it with you. I don't eat sweets. Not much of a Russian, I suppose. Would be a shame to have it go to waste."

"You could give it back to Ken Russell," Arnold said jokingly. "A peace offering is no longer needed. I have to ask; will you miss Clayton at all?"

"I will actually, but I'll get over it. Having smoke breaks with him could be pleasant enough. But I can smoke with Dan. We like smoking together. Or I can hang out with Doc if he is willing. So, what is on your mind, other than the draw of my warm personality?"

"There is that," Arnold said slowly, sipping his drink. "Though you are capable of holding back your charm, we have talked quite a lot recently. More than you seem to like." Arnold leaned to the side and took a piece of the Medovik cake, cradling it in one of the napkins. "We have a confession from Clayton, Natasha. It is quite interesting. Are you aware of its contents?"

Natasha was surprised. She put her drink down and stared for a moment at Arnold. "A confession? Whatever do you mean? I know he had a lot of confessing to do, and he did love to record his life. But I can't imagine him sharing this with the police. To what does he confess?"

"He confessed to killing himself," Arnold said empathetically.

"Did he?" Natasha asked. "And are you accepting that?"

"Sanders is. I'm not."

"Maybe you should."

"I've never been good at following direction. What do you think about Clayton killing himself?"

"Well, I really don't know. I am genuinely confused. But I assume that, when a person confesses to suicide, it is likely what happened."

"Generally, yes, but in this case, there has been much misdirection, tampering, and even lying."

She nodded slowly. "I have lied and deceived, but I did not kill Clayton."

"I know."

"You do? Then why are you continuing to visit with me? Is my alibi that bad?"

Arnold took a sip of Arnold Palmer, which he had to admit was quite good, and leaned back gently into the confines of the chair. A chickadee flew into the faux-gingerbread birdhouse hanging on one of the lower lilac limbs as a light breeze blew across the yard. Arnold could hear the slight fluttering sounds of the trembling aspen in the Northfield woodlands just west of where he and Natasha quietly sat.

"You lied about part of your alibi. That's a crime, Natasha," Arnold said softly.

"What part? Did I not go for a run?"

"You went for a run. But you lied about what time you drove to the Arts Centre."

"I have witnesses that confirm the time of my arrival."

"They were deceived. You drove to the Arts Centre shortly after nine, pretending to be Dan, dressed in his jacket and ball cap, and driving his Falcon. Apparently, you even walked like him. That is what witnesses saw. Then at around 9:20 or so, witnesses saw a person dressed in your jacket and one of your hats, driving your BMW to the Arts Centre. But that wasn't you. It was Dan."

Natasha was clearly shaken by Arnold's comments. Generally, poised and calm, she spoke abruptly and defensively. "You don't have proof of that."

"Dan's confession should be proof enough."

"Dan also confessed? To what?"

"What do you think he confessed to?"

"I would genuinely like to know. I don't know what Dan is up to, or was up to, but I suppose it's time to stop the pretence. Dan and I did switch identities. You are right about that. Dan left a note at my house, as well his car keys and cap, advising me that we needed to impersonate each other." Natasha got up from her chair, looking around the yard as if the conversation was over, though she had the sense to know that it wasn't. "I was unclear as to why we needed to do this, but I cooperated. He told me that it was imperative that I cover for him. So, I did."

"Why did you think that he needed you to cover for him?"

Natasha sat back down and took a sip of her drink, and then a deep breath, letting it out slowly. "What do you want me to say?"

"Try the truth?"

"I do not know the truth. I never have. Truly. And when I've tried to broach the subject since, Dan has been quick to change the subject. At the time, though, I suppose I thought it was possible that he had come by the workshop to intervene on my behalf and shoot Clayton. He had asked me to impersonate his arrival at the office, so it seemed reasonable that he had needed to be somewhere else at the time when he normally would have arrived there. I played along. But when I heard that Clayton had also been poisoned, I was confused. I simply could not see Dan doing that."

"He didn't."

"Then what did he do exactly?" she asked, in a tone rich with confused frustration.

"He picked up Clayton's gun on Friday, when he saw it on the ground in the parking lot, and he kept it. He came here to your house on Saturday morning, shortly before nine, after dropping his boys off early at soccer practice. He brought with him both the gun and an intention to intervene. To save you from being killed. But when he arrived, Clayton was already dead. Lying on the workshop floor."

Her eyes were wide now, as she shook her head slowly. "He had planned to confront Clayton.... He is a very brave man."

He nodded. "Brave, yes. He was also surprised. Shocked probably."

"Shocked that Clayton was dead?"

"I think so. He was expecting Clayton to be alive and ready to take you to the woods. But instead, he found Clayton dead. Dan guessed that Clayton had been poisoned and assumed that you were responsible. Knowing that you would need a strong alibi, he began what was essentially a cover-up on your behalf. He dunked a bit of the uneaten Medovik cake into what he assumed was the poisoned drink and dropped it on the car seat. He dumped the remaining clean cake in your garbage bin. Then Dan poured out the poisoned drink and replaced the mug with clean drink from the fridge."

Natasha was leaning fully forward in her chair, her elbows resting on her knees as he laid it all out for her.

"Thinking fast, he left you his Falcon keys, his jacket, and his hat, as well as a note, explaining what he wanted you to do and asking that you leave him your BMW keys, one of your hats, and your jacket, and saying that he would return for them shortly. Dan then put on a pair of tight gloves, took off Clayton's cowboy boots and put them on, and also apparently cleaned up any lingering signs of Clayton's death."

Arnold paused to take a small bite of cake, carefully catching his crumbs in his napkin. "Regardless of the timing of those actions, though, without doubt, at some point he placed Clayton in the trunk of the Mustang, put on Clayton's hat and pea coat, and then drove to the forest road and parked. This would have been at about ten after nine, or just before, as Madeline spotted him and the parked Mustang at that time. He waited for her to pass, hoping she would not look too closely at him in the driver's seat."

Arnold paused to take a sip of his drink and noticed that Natasha seemed riveted by his narration. He carried on. "Once the coast was clear, he took Clayton out of the trunk, and with a fireman's carry, walked with him to the aster meadow. He set Clayton down, removed the pea coat, and folded it neatly on the cottonwood stump. He took off Clayton's glasses and put them in the jacket pocket. Then he placed the mug containing a trace of clean juice, on the stump as well. He'd even thought to take a cigarette butt from Clayton's workshop and tuck it into a crack in the stump. Apparently, his theatrical experience really came in handy for setting the stage. In any case, he then shot Clayton in the right temple using Clayton's own hand."

Arnold paused to take another bite of the cake, which really was surprisingly moist considering it was more than a week old. Natasha waited (as patiently as she could manage) for him to continue, certain that he had far more to say.

"Once that was done, he ran back to your house through the woodlands trail, leaving a deeper, running footprint behind, which he later claimed he'd left upon 'discovering' Clayton's body. When he got to your place, he saw that you had done just as he'd asked in the note—driving the Falcon to the office shortly after nine, pretending to be him—and so he put on your coat and hat and drove the BMW to the office, pretending to be you, at around nine-thirty. The two of you showed up outside together for a smoke shortly after."

`His story complete, Arnold took another bite. "Good cake. It is a bit too sweet though."

Natasha leaned back in her chair and digested this new information for a long moment before finally speaking. "That is an impressive cover-up, and it explains a lot, which Dan has failed to do since that day. I suppose he didn't want to ask me exactly what I had done, just as I didn't want to ask him. Except that I didn't poison Clayton. So, everything Dan did was entirely unnecessary. Someone might have poisoned Clayton, but it was not me. Frankly, I don't think it was Sheila either."

"I agree," Arnold said. "Dan went to a lot of trouble to distract us from something you didn't even do."

"But he didn't poison himself, correct? Someone else did?"

"That's right."

She nodded. "This whole business has been incredibly confusing to me, I confess, because frankly, there is no way that Clayton would ever take his breakfast drink with him to the woods. Yet the mug was there. It was all very strange."

"But you knew that Dan was involved."

"Yes. Or at least, I assumed as much, because he seemed to think we needed alibis. If he had done it, though, why would he think I needed an alibi as well?" she asked, seemingly to explain her lingering uncertainty and confusion. She shook her head again. "In any case, when I read in the paper that Clayton had been poisoned, I thought that maybe Sheila had poisoned him and had perhaps gotten Dan to help. I didn't know. But after talking with Sheila, I dropped that idea. I imagined that Dan must have shot Clayton and poisoned him as well, though how Clayton could have managed to get poison into his system was still confusing. Frankly, I soon stopped thinking about it. I am good at not thinking about unpleasant things, having had far too much practice. Thinking about such things seldom gets me anywhere."

"Thinking can result in some wheel spinning for sure."

"Do you know who poisoned Clayton?"

"He was poisoned, at your house, by Janet Sawatzky."

"Janet? How did she manage that? And why?"

"You left for your run, Sheila went for a smoke, and Janet slipped in the back door to drop ground hemlock leaves into his drink."

"How do you know this?"

"Janet confessed, although there were a number of factors that had already led me to the conclusion, which I had forensics confirm through testing. Fingerprints and whatnot."

"There seems to be a tsunami of confessions as of late." She took a sip of her drink and another deep breath, clearly nervous at what might be revealed next. "So, what happens now? Janet goes to prison for killing the man who was about to kill me? Dan and I go to prison for covering up the murder of a man who was about to kill me? Even though, the dead man has confessed to killing himself? So many confessions.... Too many, really."

"There has certainly been a plethora of confessions," he said, nodding and taking another bite of cake.

"Perhaps..." she said, hesitantly, "it is time to stop the inquiry?"

"Perhaps it is."

CHAPTER 41

SUMMATION MEETING AT THE ARTS CENTRE

"Let me be perfectly clear, crimes have been committed," Arnold Powell said firmly, addressing the small group of specially invited guests at the Northford Arts Centre boardroom. "There has been a murder, the moving and shooting of a dead body, tampering with evidence, withholding information, and deceiving the police in an investigation. No matter how devoted a person is to viewing the big picture, it's hard not be deeply bothered. I am bothered. Inspector Sanders is bothered. I suspect that all of you here are bothered. The question is ... what do we do about it?"

The boardroom was not large, just large enough to comfortably house a massive oak table that had been carefully restored by Ken Russell. The room had south and west walls made up almost entirely of glass, and because of the leather swivel chairs around the table, everyone present had a lovely view of the Northford Central Park.

Sitting around the table were Natasha Dalrymple, Dan McCroskey, Sheila McCroskey, Janet Sawatzky, Doc Alexei Rubenstein, and Dr. Robert Morley. There was a mood of sadness in the space—the kind of sadness that comes from inexperienced wrongdoing. It was a sadness that went well beyond the fact that the Central Park water feature, clearly visible from the Arts Centre boardroom, had stopped functioning again.

"I imagine that we're done," Dan said solemnly. "All we can hope for is that the folks we love will wait for us to get out of prison. Emily says that she'll wait for me, but I wonder if that's a reasonable hope." Dan looked lost, his body squirming in his chair as he searched, in vain, for a comforting position. His hair stuck out from his head as though he had touched a live light socket. He looked to be both a physical and emotional trainwreck.

"How do you manage to have hair like that at this time of day?" Arnold asked Dan. "You would think that gravity alone would have settled it by now. You should be wearing your ball cap."

"You make a fair point, Arnold," Natasha said, rather tersely. "A person should always look their best when their fate is being decided by the police. I have tried to look at the bright side. It is presently dark, perhaps, but the morning sun will rise. Perhaps in time, when I am sitting in prison reflecting on my life, I will see matters more positively."

"Well, Natasha, you may be pleased to know that I have no proof of your wrongdoing," Arnold announced. "Frankly, I have no proof of any of your wrongdoing."

"But I confessed to poisoning Clayton," Janet said. "Pretty sure that I did. And you have evidence implicating me. I had no choice but to own up to what I did."

"It's good that your actions are clear to you, Janet," Arnold said. "But given the broader picture to which I referred, your clarity does not need to be generally known. You confessed in a private conversation with me. We did not take a formal statement from you."

"But my prints are on the back door of Clayton's home."

"They are, but then, you were having an affair with Clayton," Arnold said. "You did have cause to enter the house from time to time."

"That's true," Janet countered. "But Doc saw me crossing the fairgrounds. My hair was on the backpack in the prop room. My fingerprints were all over the place."

"Doc saw a backpacker crossing the fairgrounds. It could have been some straggling hiker. Granted, a few strands of your hair were on the backpack, but then ... Dan says that you used the backpack during rehearsal. Your prints on the garden shed are clear enough, but prints last a long time, even in the outdoors, and it was your parents' shed. In any case, it is all circumstantial. No one saw you put poison in Clayton's mug. The bottom line is that we don't seem to have sufficient evidence to successfully take it to court."

"Or the desire to do so?" Natasha asked.

"There is limited enthusiasm to press charges," Arnold conceded.

Natasha looked very confused. Her normally poised posture was coming undone. She leaned forward in her chair, squinting her eyes as if to see more clearly. "But Dan and I did the identity switch."

Dan nodded. "And I also confessed to moving and shooting Clayton's body, Arnold. Didn't I? I am fairly sure that I did, but then, I suppose may have lost track of what I said and what I didn't. Although I just said it again and—"

Arnold held up his hand to stop him and restrict any further outbursts. "Granted, it's hard to keep track of all the lies and deception. That is why I keep notes. But then, Sanders tells me that my notes are woefully inadequate. He may be right. Sometimes I write what a person has said and sometimes I don't. Sometimes I think that I will remember. But then, sometimes I don't. Sometimes I remember, but my memory is incorrect. Memory in general can be a shit show. I have checked my notes, and I do not seem to have a record of Dan confessing to moving or shooting Clayton's body. Based on the witnesses we have, you were birding with your boys and driving your Falcon to the office during the timeframe in which Clayton died."

"So ... are you saying that crimes were not committed?" Sheila looked very confused, not only by the odd direction the conversation seemed to be taking but why she was even there at all. "You just started this meeting by saying clearly that we were guilty of crimes."

"Of course, crimes were committed! Dan moved a dead body to the woods and shot it. He tampered with evidence. He falsified his alibi, and enticed Natasha to do so as well. But that's not all, Sheila. You destroyed evidence by burning Henry's boots, and withheld information. You also gave false evidence, claiming to *see* Natasha poison Clayton."

Arnold turned to the medical professionals then: Dr. Morley and Doc. "And you two tampered with evidence at the forensics lab, placing the cake-crumb evidence into Clayton's mug, so that it magically returned to the toxic state it had been in before Dan tampered with it. And last, but certainly not least...."

He turned towards Janet, who seemed to have shrunk a bit in her chair. "You took it upon yourself to slip into Clayton's house and poison the man's breakfast drink. What a thing to do to a person first thing in the morning! Granted, I understand that your intentions were to save a life by taking one. But that's generally not considered best practice. Whatever happened to letting the police in on a threatened crime so we can do our job?"

Janet had no answer for him, but Dan had a question. "So, where does that leave us?" he asked, running his hand through his messy hair. "You know what we all did."

"That's right, but thankfully for you, and a range of other folks—including, perhaps, myself—you are all left free to move on with your lives, though with the burden of truth in your hearts. Hopefully, you feel its weight. The Northford Police, the RCMP, and the head office in Ottawa, not to mention a number of interested overseas parties, have decided that, given the confessional statement we have from Clayton, we will be satisfied to consider this case closed, ruling his death a suicide. He poisoned himself ... and then shot himself."

He shrugged. "We see no long-term value in disagreeing with the central theme of Clayton's confession, except for one point."

"Which is?" Natasha asked.

"His confession did not mention poison," Arnold said. "Regardless, we have decided to overlook the man's omission. He was under stress after all and likely wanted to ensure his death by taking poison as well as shooting himself."

"So ... I'm not being charged with anything?" Dan asked, hardly able to believe what he was hearing.

"What should we charge you with, Dan?" Arnold asked. "Harbouring Henry, a known slingshot criminal? Stocking hard Parmesan Reggiano in your fridge? Given that we have accepted Clayton's suicide confession, we cannot prosecute anyone."

Natasha frowned. "Surely, I must have done something illegal."

"Of course, you did!" Arnold said, his frustration with the whole situation overflowing briefly. "You all did!" He took a deep breath then to settle his nerves and let it out slowly before continuing. "But nothing we are choosing to pursue. I do, however, want to know what happened to the cash that Clayton took out of his account on Friday." He stared intently at her.

"I gave it to Doc, Alexei," Natasha said. "Clayton left the home safe full of cash. I have no idea how much it was, but I knew it would be more than enough to return all of the money Clayton had embezzled from local agencies, plus pay off what he owed the CRA. Alexei, or 'Doc,' as you call him, will also be expanding on the trust that Clayton had asked him to set up for Janet—although he hadn't told him why—which will now endow scholarships for a number of worthy students, though the first to receive support will, indeed, be Janet."

"But not for medical school," Arnold said, looking knowingly at Janet, who wouldn't meet his gaze. "Janet and I have had a little chat, in which I convinced her that healthcare might not be a good field for her. Not sure society is ready for a doctor who's trigger happy with water hemlock."

"Even for a good cause?" Natasha asked.

"Especially for a good cause," Arnold replied. "But I do have a question, Natasha: *Is* Fyodor going to receive any cash with the Goodhand picture?"

"I do believe that he might," Natasha responded with a matter-of-fact tone. "As I said, the picture has value."

CHAPTER 42

ARNOLD SAYS GOODBYE TO INSPECTOR DICK SANDERS

Dick Sanders was awake but groggy when Arnold arrived. His hospital room had a west window, so the late-afternoon sun was sending rays of light throughout the room. It did not improve the look on Dick Sanders' face. He was pale, his eyes glassy and defeated. Arnold noted lines on his face that he had not seen before. Sanders looked like he was finished.

He was sitting up in his bed on the third floor, a G. K. Chesterton mystery on his lap, along with a scattering of the weekend edition of the *Northford Sentinel*. The Saskatchewan River was in clear view from his window, but Sanders wasn't looking. He also wasn't reading the paper ... or his book. He was just staring into space.

"Good to see you, Arnold," Sanders said, with a slight cough. "Did you meet with the suspects?"

"I did," Arnold said, taking a deep breath and settling into a chair near the bed. "They're all off the hook, thanks to you, Dick. I don't always agree with your ways, but in this matter, your path may have been the right one. You have a strange style, but I'm going to miss you."

"I'll miss you too, Arnold. You plugged away on this case in an admirable manner. I respect that. You eventually figured the whole thing out, but I have to tell you, I'm not sure what took you so long. It was always quite obvious that Janet was the killer."

"It was?" Arnold asked, removing his Stetson. "You gave the impression that you didn't care about the truth."

"Maybe I didn't. Doesn't mean that I didn't know what it is."

"Why didn't you talk to me? Share your thoughts."

"My last police job was not going to involve ruining the life of a young woman who—though wildly misguided on some matters—basically performed an act of courage. Anyway, I didn't know for sure. Just fairly sure. Sure enough that I didn't want to give you any big ideas. You're bloody persistent with ideas. I was more focussed on resolving the evidence we had. As I've told you on a few occasions, the Canada Cup series needs to be played, and Janet needs to achieve her goals, though not in the medical field, as we agreed. She has much to offer if she can channel her capacities within a legal framework."

A nurse came in then, bustling around, checking Sanders feeding tube, and then suddenly, as though she'd just became aware of some emergency, rushed out of the room in a seeming panic.

"She's in a rush," Arnold observed, watching the departing nurse as Sanders was overcome with another bout of coughing. "Have you had Sheila as a nurse yet?"

"Sadly, yes. She's not the gentlest of care providers."

Arnold nodded, unsurprised, and picked up a glass of water from the bedstand, handing it to Sanders. "When my son was born, we had a nurse like Sheila. Very determined to make a lasting impression. So, how did you know about Janet?"

"You noted that Janet had grass stains on her new sneakers and no real alibi for Saturday morning, claiming that she'd slept in. Seriously? On the same morning that her sponsor and likely exploiter died in the woods? Truthfully, it never occurred to me that she wasn't involved. Initially, I wasn't sure how she'd managed it, but then Doc said he saw a backpacker on the fairgrounds at around seven on Saturday morning. I thought to myself, 'Well, self, was that Janet?' Then when you said that Sheila had been outside having a smoke and didn't go back inside for a few minutes after Natasha left for her run, it was pretty clear that Janet would have had time to pop in the back door and do what she had to do."

"If you thought Janet had poisoned him, how did you explain the witnesses who saw Clayton drive to the woods?"

"Arnold, as you know, I've always been skeptical of eye-witness accounts. Most of us see what we want to see. Frankly, I didn't take the story of Clayton driving to the woods very seriously."

"So, you considered that Natasha and Dan might have done an identity switch all along?"

"Of course. How else is a dead man going to get to the woods? Someone has to take him there. If he was dead, which I assumed that he was, someone had to have impersonated him driving the car. That had to be Dan. He had a firearms license. He had been trained in the fireman's carry. And just the day before, he had spotted a dropped gun in the parking lot that just happened to have disappeared when he brought Natasha back to see it. Simple logic. In any case, since he and Natasha are about the same height, both with slim builds, it was clear that they'd acted as each other's alibis. Remember, when Madeline arrived at the office, she said that she didn't actually see Dan, just his car and his open office door. Never mind the fact that Dan and Natasha were clearly just making up some story about a large stranger. I'm with Billy's Vera on the unlikelihood of the KGB ever visiting Northford. Dreadful little town. Where would they even stay? Northford doesn't have a decent hotel."

"I agree with you on all of those points. I guess it just took me longer to figure it out." Arnold smiled, moving his chair closer to Sander's bedside.

"Sure, it did," Sanders said. "That's understandable. You're not terminal, Arnold. I am. You had time to probe matters. I didn't. I was eager to get out of town even before I found out this would be my last case. I had to be efficient with my thinking, even more so once I learned I was dying. This is why I also had to be quick about resolving evidence that would lead us to the dark consequences of truth. It wasn't that difficult. Doc and Dr. Morley were immediately on board with the idea of ridding us of the poisoned cake crumbs and resolving the question of the mug's toxicity. Sometimes, when you know what you want, you have to roll the dice a few extra times to get the desired combination."

"Was that satisfying?"

"Not really, but I don't ask for much. I'm satisfied with a state of dissatisfaction."

"I can relate to that."

Sanders sighed then, even though it triggered another coughing fit. Finally, he said, "I've had a good life, Arnold, for the most part. True, my ex-wife hates me. My children barely tolerate me. And my friends like to talk trash about me behind my back. But they will all likely have at least a *moment* when they think of me and miss me ... and say something nice about me at the funeral. That's something I will settle for."

"I really will miss you, Dick. I hope you know that."

"Sure, you will, Arnold. Or at least, you'll miss my file-closing skills."

"I will. As well as your advice about not striving too hard. Sometimes, the answers to a problem really will just emerge like a friend you didn't even know you had. Just like with this case. We didn't anticipate getting a confession from Clayton, but we have one just the same."

"So I heard. What does he confess to? Being a shit? That it was time for him to get off the stage in the best interests of all concerned, including him?"

"That's more or less right. He reviewed his options and decided to proceed with suicide, but to leave Natasha out of the event. Except that Janet beat him to it."

"Hell of a story," Sanders said in a voice that sounded more tired with practically every word he spoke. "A windy road with lots of ups and downs."

Arnold nodded. "Emily tells me she's working on a novel based on the case. Says it will give her more flexibility to tell the story the way she wants to. As a journalist, she's been remarkably cooperative and understanding about the sensitivity of certain questionable aspects of this investigation, as well as its conclusions. Perhaps the idea of a novelisation is helping her live with it.

With that, Arnold pulled out a manila envelope with a copy of Clayton's confession. "We actually thought you might like a bit of reading material."

Sanders grimaced, his face showing signing of discomfort. "Never been much of a non-fiction reader, Arnold. But I will read Clayton's confession. Won't last long enough to read Emily's book though. How do you think it will end?"

"Emily is understandably cagey about that," Arnold said, chuckling quietly. "My guess is that the book will take liberties with what actually happened with the case, and that, at its conclusion, she and Dan will be together as a couple, Doc and Natasha will become lovers again, and Fyodor will learn to accept Natasha as his mother."

"Fairly likely is my guess," Sanders said, coughing on and off as he perused the confession. "Other than Fyodor and Natasha, anyway. Can't see Natasha evolving into a nurturing mother. Mind you, I guess that's different than accepting her *as* a mother. My mother wasn't nurturing either, but I did manage to concede that she was, in fact, my mother."

"Emily is drawn to romance and familial resolution," Arnold observed, taking the empty water glass back from Sanders. "I understand that she didn't have much of that growing up, and not much in her work at the paper either. With fiction, she can change that. That's the nice thing about the genre."

"It is." Sanders sighed, not coughing afterwards this time. "In fiction, Emily could have me recover to the point where I can check out of the Capri and go home. Dreadful hotel, Arnold. Perhaps I have mentioned that before." Sanders winced a bit then and looked over at his luggage in the corner of the room. "I actually did check out of the hotel, of course. Didn't want to die with my luggage in that place, but I suspect I won't make it out of this town again."

An awkward silence fell, as Arnold was unsure how to respond to that.

"So, tell me," Sanders said finally, "how is Natasha feeling about all of your adjustments to standard legal precedent. Pleased, I hope?"

"She is," Arnold said softly. "Or as pleased as she's able to be. I imagine that our superiors in Ottawa will pleased as well."

"I suppose so. Not that I care. The dreadful debacle of the Canada Cup will proceed, and our ships will continue loading wheat for Soviet shores." Sanders put the confession back in the envelope and looked out the window at the passing cars. "You will have to submit a final report, of course. Maybe you should get Emily to send Ottawa her novel. Would make for a more interesting read."

"It would," Arnold said quietly as he looked at former colleague, and as it turned out, friend.

"Think it's time for my nap, Arnold," Sanders said, holding out his hand. Arnold shook it carefully. "You need to get on with your day, and I need to get on with mine. Just one favour?"

"You name it."

"I want to be buried in my overcoat, but please ... have the damn thing dry cleaned first. I don't know if you have noticed, but the coat has stains. Disgusting stains, to be frank. As the song says, I don't mind the dying, but I don't want to be lying in the ground wearing a dirty overcoat."

CPSIA information can be obtained
at www.ICGtesting.com
Printed in the USA
LVHW090326240723
753218LV00002B/186

9 781039 166332